RONALD R. LEEDY

ISBN
978-1-961250-83-3 (Paperback)
978-1-961250-84-0 (eBook)
978-1-961250-82-6 (Hardcover)

TABLE OF CONTENTS

PROLOGUE

The young male lion lay panting in the sparse shade of a lone tree on a broad and arid African plain a few kilometers north of Lake Chad. Not far away, downwind, a small pack of hyenas furtively roamed through the scattered dry tufts of savannah grass. Overhead the metallic blue sky rippled with waves of heat rising from the sun-baked soil.

Suddenly the hyenas caught the scent of the lion and stopped in their tracks, their noses gesturing toward the sky, intently sniffing to further explore the story in the breeze. Their olfactory glands, remarkably sensitive for such smelly beasts, informed them that it was a lone male lion. It had been several days since their last meal and they were, collectively, almost hungry enough to try to bring him down. Almost.

The young lion was also famished. If he had known the Hyenas were nearby, he might have taken desperate initiative and tried to isolate and kill one. A hyena carcass would feed him for days if he could protect it from thieving scavengers.

But the hyenas, as cunning as they were hideous, carefully stayed downwind. They could smell the lion, but he couldn't smell them. It gave them a critical advantage.

Then the lion and hyenas all detected the powerful scent of a very sweaty human. By his scent alone the wild predators tracked his approach and remained aware of his exact location, soon helped by the scuffling sounds of his shoes in the dirt. The man panted as he hurried along a nearly overgrown track across the silent savannah.

It was the hottest part of the afternoon, when most animals sought shade and rest. He was the only thing in motion. His fast pace made it impossible to travel quietly. He was fleeing from something that frightened him more than his certainty that numerous predators lurked hidden around him.

The young lion rose to his feet in one lithe motion, stretched studiously as he tested the scent, then moved soundlessly toward the sound and smell of the man. He slunk along; the ridge of his spine just lower than the height of the savannah grass. His tawny coat blended perfectly with the golden yellow of the grass so that he was nearly invisible.

The man passed within eleven meters of the starving young lion's poised form. The lion burst up from the grass in a gigantic silent leap. A second such leap and he was upon the oblivious man, easily knocking him to the ground. Huge jaws gaped and the lion let out a brief roar before he enclosed the man's neck in his deadly teeth for a quick kill.

As the victorious young lion crouched over his dying prey, he released the man's throat with a roar of pain and anger as the hyena pack swarmed him from behind, their crushing jaw muscles driving large canine teeth slashing deep into the young lion's flesh. Wounded and bleeding, the lion whirled and lashed out with disease-inflicting claws, ripping a swath of hide from the ribcage of the nearest hyena.

The pack's grunting and chortling suddenly rose to a frantic crescendo as that wounded hyena spun away. Two others sank their teeth deeper into the muscular frame of the frantic young jungle prince, while others fell maniacally upon their wounded pack mate. After all, for the ultimately pragmatic hyena pack, meat was meat.

The man's limp body beneath the vicious struggle was like a lump of inconvenient carpet atop the deep dust. Scrabbling claws ripped and thrusting paws pummeled his dead flesh, tearing at his thin clothing as the wild beasts fought for the bountiful meal.

With a desperate roar the lion made a last attempt to leap away from the melee and escape. His huge hind claws dug for traction on the dead man's torso, crushing a small plastic vial the man had carefully buttoned inside his shirt pocket, next to his heart where he felt sure it would be secure. The deadly toxin in the vial was released into the air.

The shirt that slid loosely across the human corpse's chest did not provide the traction needed by the weakening young lion, and so he finally fell beneath the snarling pack of hyenas. They made quick work of him, further trampling the dead man's remains.

The hyenas feasted on all three carcasses—their pack mate, the young lion, and the man--yelping and whimpering in a famished frenzy. They had mostly consumed the man, snuffling aside the foul-tasting crushed vial, and were shifting their attention to the young lion when they were themselves suddenly beset by a much larger pack of hyenas. The larger pack drove the smaller pack away and leisurely finished off the kill. Opportunistic African vultures and ravens gathered nearby to await their turn, along with some jackals and other small scavengers.

The meat from the three carcasses fed more than thirty hyenas that day, dozens of vultures and many smaller carrion eaters. On a broad scale it seemed to be a minor event in the natural order of life and death on a vast earth.

The spilled contents of the broken vial in the man's pocket, however, was a major event that would forever change the entire history of the earth. The lion's talon that had punctured and scattered the glass vial would produce a consequence that would soon impact the entire world because when the sealed container was broken a deadly plague was released into the air.

The weaponized plague had been conceived and developed in a secret research laboratory hidden in the jungles of northern Chad. It was extremely biologically precise, designed to attack and destroy all water molecules in a human body. It was aimed only at humans--animals were not affected.

The deceased man whose body had contributed to the survival of the large hyena pack had been attempting to sneak out a sample of the militarized plague to sell to NATO agents in a nearby city. He desperately hoped to obtain enough ransom money to purchase his wife and daughters out of slavery to a local radical Muslim terrorist group. His mission had failed.

Now the vial's contents drifted in the air, fanning out from the site of the desperately impoverished man's scattered remains. It lingered in the fur and feathers of the predators and scavengers who took part in the fatal skirmish and subsequent cleanup.

The hyenas had no knowledge of the plague they had helped the lion to unwittingly set free in the world. They would never experience it, since it had been diabolically engineered to infect only humans. Now, as the last tidbits of the carcasses were consumed, the hyenas drifted away one by one. Each carried the airborne toxins away from the kill, microscopically entangled in, and wafted along by, their filthy fur.

Two days later a passing safari discovered the human remains and picked up the few identifying articles left on the ground, including the now broken vial. Microscopic residue of the plague, lingering in the vial and in the stale air that palled over the site of the man's demise, made clandestine contact with the members of the wealthy hunting safari.

When the hunters returned to camp that afternoon, they all, without exception, had raging headaches. An hour later they all felt increasingly nauseous. Within a few hours the entire hunting safari was dead. Within a few more hours their bodies had decomposed to small piles of ash-like debris.

Afterwards, a subsequent safari came through, following the same popular trek route. They discovered the puzzling remains, or lack thereof, and dutifully collected the scattered personal effects and carried it all back to civilization. All sickened enroute and died shortly after arriving back to the safari staging village. Within two days the entire village was dead. Their bodies, like all who had contracted the plague before them, rapidly decomposed to an ash-like residue, leaving a growing number of clothing outfits lying on the ground in the exact last position of the deceased.

The plague that would come to be known as The Cremation Virus was now loose in an unsuspecting and unprepared world.

PART ONE

CHAPTER ONE

BARRA-BURRA

In the deepening dusk a breeze shooshed secretively through the dry needles of majestic evergreen trees forming a verdant perimeter around the lush alpine meadow like a green friar's fringe. Slanting rays of the late afternoon sun cast a soft glow on the pale blond hair of the tall young woman wearing a faded red plaid flannel shirt, worn denims and dusty work boots.

She stood motionless, hands on her hips, straight backed and square shouldered, facing the sunset across a small stream. Her nearly white hair hung in a long pony tail, but loose strands or shorter locks formed a soft halo around her face. She had sun-rouged cheeks and vivid blue eyes, with brows and lashes as pale as her hair.

Despite her humble backwoods clothing her appearance was angelically beautiful. The stillness of her graceful form complimented the beauty of her countenance, so that to an observer she might have seemed ethereal in the same sense as the Venus De Milo, or the Elven queen in Lord of the Rings.

The woman turned and smiled with deep contentment as her gaze slowly swept her modest homestead. It may never be finished, she thought to herself. But I've accomplished a lot. She really liked the fact that she could hear no traffic sounds, and there were no electronic gadgets chirping for her attention.

Working from first daylight and not stopping all through the long day, she had built almost a hundred yards of fence line today, adding to the perimeter of her pasture. Another two hundred fifty yards and it would be completely fenced, enclosing nearly twenty acres of meadow grass in strong livestock fencing. She had set steel posts every eight feet with well braced corner posts. The wire was heavy mesh up to four feet, then three strands of barbed wire—a proper livestock fence.

For the moment she simply stood still, resting. Her muscles ached—she was good and tired, which was a good tired, as Uncle Cliff would have said.

Here in her homestead valley, fence building all by herself was very labor-intensive. Throughout the day she had tromped up and down steep slopes, repeatedly jammed her post driver down on steel posts to imbed them into the hard ground. Then she had wrestled heavy rolls of wire along the line of posts and stretched it into place. No part of the task was easy or convenient. It was bone-jarring and muscle straining work.

No part of her body, it seemed, was free from hurting. Even the skin on her face and arms hurt because of her mild chronic sunburn--typical for fair skinned people. Her occasional "breaks" throughout the day were not breaks from work, but only from fence building. She used those times to carry and stack firewood, slowly adding to her winter woodpile as she continued the ongoing task of clearing the ground inside her perimeter fence.

So now, at the end of the hard day, though she hurt, she felt fulfilled and satisfied. She breathed deeply of the familiar evergreen scent, turned away from the sunset and eased her weary frame down onto the smooth sitting log which she had previously wrestled into a strategically planned spot near her fire pit. Right now, the log felt better than an easy chair.

The gentle warmth of her evening fire felt good as she loosened her hair band and shook out her long tresses. The pale autumn sun setting over the ridge behind her cast a discernible warmth against her tired back. With the warmth of the fire against her front side it felt like a gentle embrace. In her smug opinion, it beat central air conditioning any day.

After resting a few minutes, she picked up the old journal from the log beside her. Its cover was ragged and dirty, swollen with oft-dampened dog-eared pages. She held it gently, almost reverently, in her work-roughened hands as her muscles slowly relaxed to the lullaby of the nearby stream. She bent to review the little she had penned in the journal thus far. So much had changed in the years since she was only eighteen and wrote those few paragraphs. Now it was almost like reading them for the first time.

I don't know when I first got the idea to become a hermit. The notion just showed up in my mind one day—and felt like it had always been there. I never used to think about it, then one day I thought about it and it seemed like an old familiar thought. It started sometime after my thirteenth birthday when I first met my Uncle Cliff. By my fourteenth birthday a year later it seemed I had known for a long time that I someday would be one--a hermit, I mean.

The problem wasn't my family. Well, at least not at first. I'd have to say I was sort of neutral about them right up until just before I left. I was used to Dad regarding me as "a daughter instead of a son." I heard that a lot. Once was more than enough. It always added salt to my wounded psyche (I know that's a mixed metaphor but Hey, this is MY journal.).

When I was five my little brother Bobby was born and Dad mostly paid attention to him after that. He would occasionally include me, of course, and he was always polite, same as he was with Mom. But he overtly favored Bobby, and I just had to deal with it.

Bobs and I always knew of course that Mom loved Dad. She talked about him all the time when he was away at work, which was a lot. He would typically be gone all week and only home on weekends. His jobs sometimes lasted months. With Mom it was always "Your Dad said…" or "Let's show your dad when he gets home," or "Your Dad thinks…"

We also knew that Mom loved us. Her love language was words of encouragement. She never had anything bad to say about anyone, ever. Mom's love, or at least our certainty about her love, was sort of the glue that held our family together through the various crises that I assume are probably normal to all families. I never felt very confident of Dads love. Bobby did.

Bobby was eight when I turned thirteen and my personal problems suddenly began to escalate. Now don't get me wrong; as far as little brothers go, Bobby wasn't actually all that bad. But he was, after all, just a boy. Any girl who grew up with a little brother will understand what I mean. By my fourteenth birthday a year later I had figured out that I had no real use for him. He was more negative than positive. He had become superfluous.

Before I get too far into my journal let me introduce myself. My name is Barbara Sinead Odell. I like my actual name, but not the nicknames derived from it.

The ones I heard most at school were BO, and BS Odell. BO as in body ordor, of course, and BS as in, you know, manure from a bull. At home I was mostly called Babs by my family, which wasn't all that bad. At first it was sort of cute--Babs and Bobs. Then my bratty brother Bobby played with the nickname Babs and came up with the very annoying and slightly embarrassing nickname 'Boobs'. He got in trouble for it, but it got around at school and I was mortified whenever I overheard it.

Bobby was actually Robert Ian Odell. Not surprisingly, Bobs didn't mind his one nickname, but I began to mind mine a lot. More about that later. Maybe.

Uncle Cliff always called me by my full first name, and I loved hearing it in his strong Irish accent, rolling the 'r's and making it sound like four syllables--'Barra-burra'. He almost always said it with a smile, as if he enjoyed my name. That was my dear old Uncle Cliff.

Uncle Cliff was Mom's older brother. She could never really figure him out. Neither could Dad. When he showed up on my thirteenth birthday I didn't even know who he was. I had been an infant last time he'd been around. He had never even met bratty Bobs.

I'll never forget his first words, smiling, "You must be Barra-burra!"

Honestly, my innocent adolescent heart melted!

Now that I'm older (eighteen) I realize I was no doubt ripe for the proverbial crush on an older man. Uncle Cliff fit the bill nicely. Even better, he loved me back! From the moment he arrived until the day he died I always knew Uncle Cliff loved me--and of course I mean that in the nicest, most proper way! (Do NOT even go there, reader!)

He always took me seriously. He looked me in the eye and listened when I spoke. He gave me his attention. No one else in my family seemed to care what I thought. And it soon got so that no one else ever looked me straight in the eye, which I'll explain shortly, but Uncle Cliff always honored me by looking me in the eye and listening to what I said.

I admit it--I began to follow him around like a puppy. Most people would have become annoyed, I'm sure, but Uncle Cliff never seemed to mind. In fact he would seek me out when he got home from anywhere. I always felt safe and confident about his affection for me.

Uncle Cliff helped me figure out how to actually become a hermit someday. He didn't physically help, but in a general way he encouraged me to make real plans instead of just dream about things. When I got a little older he helped me figure out exactly how to do it—become a hermit, I mean--at just the right time when a huge crisis was looming over my life.

I guess I better go back to when I was just thirteen and tell it all. It's way too complicated for a short storytelling."

The journal ended there. Though it was tattered and worn on the outside, between the covers all the rest of the pages were as blank and pristine as when it was new. She had started it with good intentions when she had just turned eighteen, just one day before the two horrible incidents that precipitated her running away from home to become a hermit.

The little bit that she had written in the journal back then now seemed immature to her; very childishly self-absorbed. She had been so confident back then that life would continue the same forever. But alas, it had not.

More than four years had passed--almost five years--since she wrote those words. Her life had taken a sudden cataclysmic turn just after starting the journal. Things had gotten so crazy that she had never picked up the journal again, until today.

Today she would observe her twenty-third birthday--alone. The journal was beat up now, but she resolved to resume writing her story. She hoped it would someday help someone. In any case, her story was important to her, so she wanted it written.

Barbara picked up a freshly sharpened pencil stub and absent-mindedly chewed on it while she pondered what to write. Though she had only written a little, she had already discovered two things about journaling. First, it didn't really have to be grammatically correct. She preferred to write correctly, in general, but she also liked having the freedom to write however she chose. Second, after so much time had passed, many of the events of her early life that had seemed major at the time now seemed less gigantic; not quite so intense. It almost felt as if she would be writing about someone else. That was a good thing.

After a few moments she began to write.

Everything changed when I turned thirteen. Until then I had been very feminine. I liked to play inside with my girlfriends. We would play with our dolls, or play dress-up, and chatter endlessly.

When Bobs was very young I liked to play with him like an alive toy. But then, of course, he developed personality (got bratty) and it became more like baby-sitting. Baby-sitting was even sort of fun at first, pretending I was a mommy and Bobs was my little boy. But it was only fun if Bobs cooperated, which happened less and less as he grew up.

In any case, when I was little I definitely was not a tomboy, and had no idea why some girls were. Mom always told her friends I was naturally feminine, and I liked hearing her say it so I made choices to cultivate it.

On my thirteenth birthday an amazing thing happened. I was having a tea party on the front lawn with my four best girlfriends. I still remember their names--Carlene, Leslie, Kimberly and Samantha. We were all wearing frilly grownup type dresses (and our moms' high heels for the first time, which didn't work very well in the grass, but it felt grown up so we liked it). The sun was shining brightly, and it was a perfect day.

I was carefully raising my full cup of tea to my lips when I suddenly froze to watch a big bright red convertible with a loud motor come driving up the street. We all paused to admire it as it went by.

Only, it didn't go by! To my amazement it slowed down and pulled into my driveway! The driver revved the motor with a roar of pipes and we all jumped when he shut the motor down with a loud backfire.

The man who climbed out, Uncle Cliff, was soooo handsome! Of course, the red convertible with its brilliant white leather interior really, really helped! I had only ever seen a car like that once, in a TV commercial. A bright red convertible with loud pipes was just about as exotic a car as I could even imagine.

I remember exactly how Uncle Cliff looked that day. His white-blond hair (just like mine) glistened in the sun like a halo. His fair skin (also like mine) was so sunburned that his face flamed red beneath his thick mane. His blue eyes (also just like mine) were well protected under thick white eyelashes (long, like mine). Bobs told me once when I was sunburned that my face was patriotic--red, white and blue!

Uncle Cliff was tall, slim and broad shouldered in a pale green Hawaiian shirt and loose khaki trousers over really cool hiking boots. I immediately knew we were related, of course, and many times since his impressive arrival I secretly wished he was my dad.

He got our relationship off to a really great start when he smiled directly at me, as if I was the only person in the whole world, and he had all the time in the world, and addressed me by my real first name.

And in front of my best girlfriends! Somehow, at that moment and in that act I read love in his eyes and I knew it was genuine, and my young girl's heart melted.

Now that I'm a little older I realize how sappy and childish that sounds, but that's exactly how I remember feeling back then. There was something about Uncle Cliff's smile that communicated a love I didn't feel I was getting from anyone else. I've thought about it a lot, and I think I've figured out the difference—unlike everyone else who loved me, he loved me unconditionally. He had no agenda or expectations for me.

Everyone else seemed to want something from me. My parents wanted good manners, good grades and behavior, completed chores, a daughter they could brag about to their friends, yada yada yada. Bobs wanted at various times a victim, a confederate, a confidante, or even an advisor--and usually in that priority. My girlfriends wanted me to be not quite as pretty as they all thought they were (What…ever!).

I honestly believe that Uncle Cliff, in contrast, cared more about me than about himself. I can tell you, that kind of selfless love is truly awesome. Every girl should have a father figure who loves her like that. I think it's the very best kind of love. It's probably even better than the love between a husband and wife, though I haven't experienced that kind yet. And, at this moment, it appears I may never.

CHAPTER TWO

MY IDOL

By my fourteenth birthday a year later it seemed Uncle Cliff had always lived with us. I didn't know why, or even wonder about it at the time, but he had apparently come to stay. In hindsight I realize that he had discovered that he was dying and had come to spend his remaining time with his only family.

I had reached a tender age when I needed a hero. My girlfriends had all begun to idolize their fathers that year as if it was the latest fad. I used to hear all about "My dad this and that." I simply didn't have that connection with my dad. With me it was "Uncle Cliff this and that…"

It was easy to idolize Uncle Cliff. He had been all over the world and done many fascinating things. He had been a merchant seaman in every major ocean of the world and an oil derrick rigger in the Gulf of Mexico. In the States he had been a longshoreman in Galveston, a forklift driver in Miami, a crane operator in Seattle, and in other places a truck driver, a pastor, a cowboy, a veterinarian's assistant, a zookeeper, a beekeeper, a corporate executive, and he was even a published author! He had written lots of short stories and magazine articles and even a full-length book, but the only thing he ever actually got published was a book of poems.

He used to laugh, "My novel took hundreds of hours to write and was repeatedly rejected! My poems only took a few hours to write, but the book was accepted the first time and sells out every time it's reprinted!"

He lived quite comfortably on royalties while he lived with us.

Uncle Cliff and I enjoyed each other's company, and I spent lots of time with him. We became what Bobs snidely called "joined at the hip." Whenever I wasn't in school or asleep I was handing out with my Uncle Cliff. We both liked it when people mistook us for father and daughter. He was like the Dad I'd always wanted, and I was the daughter he'd always wanted.

Uncle Cliff had never married or had kids. He was straight and all, of course, but I thought he had probably been deeply wounded emotionally or something. That might have been just my girlish romanticism. What...ever! But he loved me like a dad, and I loved him back like a daughter. It was what we both needed at the time.

Because of Uncle Cliff's influence I quit playing with dolls and doing other girlie things and instead became an athlete and a tomboy. He simply loved sports, and in our conversations he naturally encouraged me to go out for some school teams.

I couldn't have cared less about athletics, myself, but I was really happy to have a way to please my new hero, so I went out for the swim team and girls' volleyball. We were both surprised when I turned out to be good in both sports. I wasn't exactly the best at either one, but I was good to enjoy many opportunities to compete.

My advantage was that I was tall. My disadvantage was that I was tall! After my thirteenth birthday, when all my girlfriends had stopped growing taller, I grew another five inches! To make matters worse, I suddenly developed a big bust! It happened so fast I skipped training bras and went straight to regular ones!

Lots of people don't realize what a problem extreme height (and the other) can be for an adolescent girl--most especially in things athletic or social--which (go figure!) were my only two significant spheres of existence! Okay--this is my journal and I want everything in it to be the truth, the whole truth, and nothing but the truth-- otherwise what's the point? Right? So I'll put it this way: it wasn't my height that was the main problem. It was the other--my bust.

Being tall was actually helpful in volleyball, and being slender was actually helpful in swimming. But my "excess upper body mass" was and continued to be a handicap in both sports which I never could figure out a way to overcome.

On the swim team I competed against girls who could slice through the water with hardly a wake, while I, on the other hand, plowed along like a tugboat. I only stayed competitive by sheer determination and brute strength. On the volleyball court my height gave me an advantage, but it was intuitive for me to NOT leap at the net for a spike. I was paranoid about the alarming way I bounced. It drew very unwanted attention to a part of me that had nothing at all to do with my personality or athletic ability! So anyway, I played volleyball to the best of my athletic ability without actually doing any more leaping than I felt was absolutely necessary.

And all that's merely the aerodynamics of my situation. The socio-dynamics were "a whole 'nuther story," as Uncle Cliff used to say! I began to subconsciously slouch and choose nondescript clothing, thinking maybe I wouldn't be so noticeable. I earned a reputation for being a bit of a slob--and figured it was a small price to pay. But I worked very hard in both sports and competed well for three whole years.

At the start of my senior year I gave up and quit team sports. I never said why. I never even discussed my reasons with anyone. Even now, after several years, it's still awkward to write about it. But here goes: the reason I gave up team sports was because during the summer before my senior year I grew even bigger!

I was "lean and mean" in Uncle Cliff's words, but by the start of my senior year I had grown to a height of six feet three in my stocking feet! And of course there was the other problem! Imagine the cruel irony of such narrow-hipped but top-heavy dimensions on a socially awkward former princess turned tomboy! It was all just so unfair!

But, as Uncle Cliff would say, no use crying over spilt milk. The day I told him, with disgust, about quitting the teams, he calmly suggested, with his characteristic sensitivity, that I might want to try martial arts instead. I was shocked and confused at first, but as he continued I became intrigued.

He explained that, first of all, my aerodynamics would not be a factor, and secondly, learning how to really hurt someone might even help with some of my social concerns. He was carefully tactful and didn't tell me what he thought about why I had quit. But I knew he was very smart, so I sort of figured he knew. I wondered what he thought of it, but I didn't want to ask.

I was glad to realize I had other options though, and as it turned out I did really well in Karate. I was already used to doing chin-ups, push-ups and sit-ups, jogging, and all the other things my "feminine" former girlfriends either could not or would not do. And I was agile and motivated enough to endure and learn to manage the pain of the gut kick issued to each student by the Sensei (teacher) at the end of each training session. I readily learned how to manage the other "graduated" assaults to my face and body which were part of the training for every pupil.

I'm proud to say that I progressed through the belts so rapidly that the sensei was impressed. I was his first student to ever advance to brown belt in just one year. It was very hard work. But, know what? Hooray for me! I did it!

To celebrate, Uncle Cliff treated me to dinner at The Olive Garden, which immediately became my favorite restaurant in my hometown of Redding, California. Uncle Cliff couldn't be there with me (a whole nuther story), so I had to eat alone, but the dinner was on him. He was my mentor, role model and idol all rolled into one.

CHAPTER THREE

MY LOSS

I guess I could say in retrospect that, in general, during my teenage years I did pretty well. But Uncle Cliff wasn't doing so well. Soon after he settled in at our house he started seeing a doctor. By the time I turned fourteen he was going to the doctor every month. I didn't realize where he was going, or what was happening, for a long time. Eventually I did, however.

I came to understand that he was dying. I'm not sure when he told Dad and Mom, but they knew before I did. After more than a year of him visiting the doctor with increasing frequency, and visibly weakening, I figured it out. I'm a natural blond, but not naturally dumb!

Near the end of my senior year Uncle Cliff moved out of our house and into a nursing home. His health was failing to the point that he needed 24-hour care. I went to see him every day on my way home from school and we had long wonderful talks.

That was when I confided to him that for a long time I had secretly wanted to be a hermit. At first he tried to talk me out of it, probably thinking it was just a phase I was going through because I didn't have a social life. He knew that my former girlfriends all avoided me because the boys wouldn't look at them when I was around.

He also knew that the boys I had grown up with, even Bobs, now treated me like a headless wonder—never looking above my bosom. Of course, since they only came up to my shoulders, my "problem" was *right there at their eye level. I felt very much like a non-person. No one ever looked me in the eye any more—except Uncle Cliff, of course.*

When he realized I was totally serious about going off to live by myself, he offered to help me "think it through a bit." He had lots of great ideas, too, having lived on his own for so many years. By the time he passed away a few months later, I had pretty much finalized my plans, with his many helpful ideas factored in.

During those final months I tried to always make sure he knew that I appreciated his concern and his help. I would hug him and kiss him on the cheek whenever I arrived to visit him at the nursing home, and again when I left.

While I was there I would often fuss over him, fluff his pillow, and even feed him when he felt listless and weak. Anybody who didn't know we were related might have thought we were some kind of weird cross-generational married couple because of the way I sweet talked him.

His face would light up when I arrived. Toward the end, when I would say sweet things to him his eyes would glisten with tears. Sweet-talking my Uncle Cliff was one of my favorite things to do. And I even enjoyed the harmless opportunity to make people's eyebrows go up!

On one of our long visits while he was in the nursing home he said he had "become a Christian" as a young adult. He explained that the words meant something very special--much more than simply not being atheist, Jewish or Muslim, as I had thought. It meant to become an actual follower of Jesus Christ on His terms, not my own terms.

That day he showed me in the Bible (it's really in there), that everyone is a sinner and deserves God's wrath because we have rejected His standards and the salvation He offered through His Son Jesus. That's a mouthful, and a brain full, and I pondered the idea for several days. I didn't like the thought that I was not a Christian, after thinking I was all my life. Uncle Cliff didn't push.

As I "pondered it" (Uncle Cliff's words) it seemed like such a hopeless dilemma for the human race--and for me! Those were dark and heavy days for me, dealing with the fact of MY sin problem, as well as my ongoing social problems (which perfectly exemplified how sinful we all are), and worst of all also dealing with the impending death of my beloved Uncle Cliff!

I became increasingly aware of the way my body shape affected the actions of the people around me. I overheard some of the wicked innuendos the boys at school muttered to each other about me and I seethed with inward rage. What the Bible said about sin really rang true.

Then one day, to my intense relief, Uncle Cliff showed me in the Bible that God loved all of us sinners so much that He provided a way out of our dilemma that was just and right, that was consistent with His divine nature. God allowed Jesus, His only Son who had never sinned, to receive the punishment for all our sins so that any of us who might choose to receive his sacrifice on our own behalf is fully and justly pardoned. Jesus got our punishment, and we get the blessings and reward that are due to Him.

That's another huge mind full. I was totally blown away by the whole concept of what Uncle Cliff called the "substitute atonement" of Christ for our sins. Uncle Cliff showed me all this in the Bible, and it's a good thing he did because it's really hard to believe.

How could someone besides me pay for my sin? How was it fair to Jesus, who never sinned himself, for me to get off free, and Him be punished in my place? It seemed impossible.

The days passed by, and Uncle Cliff continued to weaken, and I continued to process all this in my mind, and it slowly began to make sense. In reality, Jesus dying in our place was the only way God could be absolutely perfectly right in every way, yet still provide a way out for all of us humans, who didn't really deserve a way out. Only an all-powerful sovereign God could accomplish that impossible mission.

By this time, now that we'd known each other for several years, Uncle Cliff had learned to read me very well. When I reached the point of being ready to personally trust Jesus Christ as my Savior, Uncle Cliff came right out and asked me if I wanted to do so.

Initially I panicked, for some reason, but then I calmed down and said yes. He led me, phrase by phrase, in a simple prayer—my very first. I remember the exact words, "God, I deserve to die for my sins, but Jesus died in my place. Please forgive my sins in the name of Jesus. I receive Jesus as my Savior and Lord. Thank you, God, for saving me. I pray this in Jesus' name. Amen."

I'll never forget that prayer. It seemed then, and still seems now, far too simple for such a huge, magnificent, life-changing decision! But I believed Uncle Cliff, and I believed the Bible. After I had prayed that prayer I suddenly felt different! It was amazing! I literally felt completely clean inside for the first time! I don't know how else to describe it! No guilt! I was forgiven!

After I prayed that prayer (called "the sinner's prayer") Uncle Cliff showed me more stuff in the Bible to describe and explain what I had just done. For example, it says that if we confess with our mouth that Jesus is Lord, and believe in our heart that God raised Him from the dead, we shall be saved. It says whoever calls on the name of the Lord shall be saved, and that whoever has the Son has life, but whoever has not the Son shall not see life, but the wrath of God dwells on him. These amazing statements, and many more, really are in the Bible. I knew now that they were true, and that they applied to me personally, and I really was "saved."

Uncle Cliff also explained that being saved means the same as being a Christian, that the Holy Spirit lives inside every Christian, and that sometimes unsaved people say they are Christians because they mistakenly think it only means they're not atheist, Jewish or Muslim--like I used to.

Sometimes Uncle Cliff's idioms were funny. Whenever he'd explain something complicated he'd finish by saying, "Capisce?" He had to explain the word to me the first time he said it. It's basically Italian for "Do you get it?"

We studied the Bible together and I learned more about being a Christian. Then the day came when Uncle Cliff went to heaven. But, because we are both Christians I know I'll see him again someday whenever I get there. He is waiting for me. But I feel very alone right now.

So. Uncle Cliff went to heaven on September 11th during my first week of college. I think he might have been glad he died on Nine Eleven, because he was patriotic to the point of sappiness. Nine Eleven was an infamous day because on that date way back in 2001 several thousand Americans were senselessly slaughtered in a terrorist attack at the twin towers of the World Trade Center in New York City. That date has great significance for patriotic Americans.

Uncle Cliff had been too weak to attend my high school graduation a few months earlier, but he learned that I had earned honors and was Valedictorian. He was so proud. At my commencement speech I gave full credit to my Uncle Cliff, and I broke down and wept. His death at the end of that summer was the worst loss of my life and I doubt I'll ever finish grieving.

CHAPTER FOUR

MY JOB

After high school graduation, during the summer that would turn out to be the last few months of Uncle Cliff's life, my own life entered a new stage--employment. Dad was owner and foreman at his job and he hired me that summer. My first (and only) paying job turned out to be physically demanding. Dad called me his personal assistant, but his crew called me The Gofer.

Dad's company did brush clearing and tree replanting—with occasional fire-break construction--for the government. It was a contract service unique to the western states where seasonal wildfires pose an annual threat. Dad's crew almost always worked in the mountains where the high elevation made it hard work just to breathe. As the "Gofer" I had to walk many miles every day up and down steep terrain at high altitudes.

I was in good shape, athletically, but Dad's crew made it uncomfortably obvious that they admired my shape! They were, without exception, dirty-minded men. And some were felons! Did I mention the crew was from a local Department of Corrections minimum security camp? Prisoners who behaved themselves in the prison could opt to train and serve as firefighters and fire prevention labor. They were "doing time for doing a crime" but were allowed to work for minimum wage (which went toward restitution for their crimes and fines).

If Dad hadn't been the foreman I'd never have taken that job, but I trusted Dad to keep the men in line. However, he didn't seem concerned about the way they ogled me and made crude comments. When I mentioned it he said that I had to learn how to deal with it in the real world.

I felt that my virtue was being threatened and I was disappointed in Dad's passivity about it, but at the same time I was confident that I could protect myself because of my martial arts training. I was pretty sure I wasn't being naïve about my skill level. But even so, Dad's crew made me nervous and Dad's passivity disappointed me.

My job duties did not allow me to avoid contact with the men, but I always dressed modestly and avoided eye contact as much as possible. Two of the guys in particular were really creepy. A big beefy guy named Brian was more obnoxious than the others. He would make kissing or smacking sounds with his lips. His sidekick was a skinny retard named (yep) Bubba. Brian and Bubba were extremely gross. I doubt they ever showered or did their laundry. They always stunk with rancid body odor and foul breath.

All the men in the crew would 'check me out' all the time, but Brian and Bubba would literally stop working and just stare at me as long as I was in sight. I dreaded the moment when there would be a confrontation. It loomed inevitable in my mind. I was just out of high school and they were grown men. Each and every day was an endless ordeal, and I really felt the strain.

Each day at quitting time I would head for the nursing home to see Uncle Cliff. Those visits helped me stay sane. He would let me unload my frustration, listening patiently till I was finished. Then he would deftly change the subject and I would find myself emptied of my rage and hatred toward those aggravating men. Still, I was hugely relieved when that summer ended without an incident and I went off to my first (and, it turned out, only) year of college.

Uncle Cliff went away to heaven at the end of my first week of college. (Did I already write that? Hmmmm. I guess it's still big in my mind, even after all this time!) The intellectual challenge of my classes helped me stay focused during my initial grief, but in some sense *my heart was already in the woods by then. I constantly yearned to escape the stares of men, which was a ceaseless aggravation in my life.*

College guys were worse than high school boys! They didn't seem as dangerous as Dad's crew, but all day I was constantly annoyed to see them doing what I called "eyebrow calisthenics" as they tried to monitor both my neckline and my hemline. Oh yes, my hemline!

Did I tell you that Mom insisted I wear skirts to college? Mom had wanted me to stay a girly girl all my life and didn't like it that I had become an athlete. There were very few things Mom ever took a stand on. Strangely, me wearing a skirt to college was one of them. She declared "a young lady should always wear a skirt or dress."

She was clueless about what my life was really like. I don't mean to be unkind, but seriously, Mom herself was as flat as a board and short to boot! I doubt that she had a single clue about the problems I had to deal with every single day because of my size and shape.

So, anyway, wearing a dress or skirt and blouse at college every day, I could never have a basic, normal conversation with any guy ever. Every single 'face to face' with a guy became a social crisis! I even sat in the back during all my classes because my male professors turned out to be as bad as the boys! Ironically, the only relief I ever experienced from guys checking out my bosom was when they checked out my hemline!

It pretty much came down to this: including Dad and Bobs, of all the men I had ever known in my entire life, Uncle Cliff was the only one who genuinely, consistently saw me as a real person, not just a female. Now he was gone. In my mind, it was about as bad as it could get.

Then, that year, just after Christmas, even Dad and Bobs became a problem. You see, by the time my brother turned twelve and started noticing girls I had turned eighteen and had 'maxed out' physically. To my great chagrin, Bobs sort of fixated on me.

It was decidedly awkward, and Dad and Mom seemed blissfully unaware. It came to a head one day when Bobs pretended to be trying to tickle me but was actually copping a feel (his words). I deflected his arms out to the side and, without thinking, planted a chest kick on him. He darted a wide-eyed glance up at my eyes just before he slammed against the kitchen counter and slid to the floor with a loud "Ooomph!"

I snarled "Knock it off, Bratty Bobs!"

I knew I had hurt him, but I didn't care. I intended to make him regret bothering me and I succeeded!

But then...of all things! Dad butted in and took Bratty Bob's side, passing off the sexual assault with a comment about my brother "just being a guy, for crying out loud!" Then, to add insult to injury, he made me apologize to Bobs for kicking him! I was furious!

Bobs' pain and bruising probably went away in a couple days, but my rage simmered inside me for a long time. I began to notice then that Bob seemed to sort of "hover" whenever I was home. It was a real nuisance having to be on my guard in my own home. I more or less had to avoid Bobs as much as possible, all the time. It was like the threat of another sexual assault loomed over my head. I didn't trust Bobs anymore, or even Dad, for that matter.

I understand now, looking back, that the emotional trauma went way deeper than I realized at the time. Reader, whoever you are, I can't even begin to describe how much I hate remembering all this, and I hate having to write it down. I only tell it because I want you to understand that I was very, very frustrated. A reason is not always an excuse though, and this reason didn't excuse what I did later, but it was part of the reason I became a hermit.

CHAPTER FIVE

RAGE AND REPENTANCE

A couple of months later when I went back to work for Dad after my year of college I had a very negative and destructive attitude. I missed Uncle Cliff. I no longer had him to talk to so it felt like no one 'had my back.' Life seemed so unfair.

My resentment and bitterness (and overconfidence in my martial arts training) soon got me into trouble. I'm chagrined, looking back from a distance, that my Christian faith didn't guide me as it should have. I was spiritually weak. God would have been there for me if I had stronger faith during the horrible events that followed, but I tried to tackle it on my own and I really messed it up.

It started falling apart one morning at home before work when I caught Bobs maneuvering around me so he could look down the front of my shirt as I was tying my workboot laces. I made sure I was covered and ignored him. But then, in my mind's eye I registered a particularly vapid look on his face. It's hard to describe, specifically, but basically he was practicing how to leer! I know how weird that sounds, that I would suddenly figure out what his expression indicated, but somehow I just knew. I had, after all, seen the look on many faces by this time.

I was instantly furious. It didn't seem appropriate to knock Bobs down again, so I just gritted my teeth and walked away. It didn't lead to a crisis at the moment, outwardly, but inwardly I really seethed. My anger was a slow boil just beneath the surface and didn't die down. It set an ugly tone to the whole rest of my day. A few minutes later my inner rage caused me to do something very stupid. I've seen that same thing happen in other people and despised them for it. This time it was me.

The weather forecast for that day predicted a typical high temperature--over a hundred. In the hot upper Sacramento Valley it was blithely called 'another triple digit day.' As I loaded up to go to work I raged inwardly at the unfairness of me having to wear the extra overshirt for the sake of modesty, when all the guys (who caused the issue) were free to go shirtless!! It just wasn't fair that I had to always be on my guard because of them, just like I always had to be on my guard because of Bratty Bobs in my own home!

So in anger and self-pity I defiantly took a dumb stand against the unfairness and refused to wear my overshirt! I purposely left it at home and headed off to work feeling like a noble martyr wearing only my olive drab sleeveless tee-shirt tucked into my khaki work pants! It felt daring and bold. It was thrilling, like a scary carnival ride.

Yeah, I know, it even sounds stupid to me, now, as I write this. Of course I always wore my bra, but even so. It was a totally idiotic moment in my life, but it seemed like a way to sort of even things out somehow. And how bad could it be, anyway, with dad there and all?

Dad didn't seem to even notice the difference in my attire as we rode in his pickup together to the jobsite. But when we got there, the crew sure noticed! This time it wasn't just Brian and Bubba--they all stopped whatever they were doing and stared as I got out of dad's pickup. I literally felt their eyes on me as I lifted the heavy water jug off the truck and onto my shoulder and carried it over to set it down on a stump in a shady spot.

I felt like a raw steak in a kennel full of voracious hounds. I hardened my heart and raged inwardly at Dad for not being my hero and protector. In my heart I even raged at God. I remember thinking, 'If anything happens Dad will have to protect me this time.'

I felt my face flame red many times as I worked around the jobsite that morning., nursing my bitter spirit. It was unfair! At one point I pushed the envelope and exaggerated my movements so that I jiggled under my shirt. For the first time and only time in my life I didn't do my usual ballerina walk to keep from bouncing. Instead, I stomped around. The men's usual background murmuring quickly rose to overt catcalls and whistles.

It was so loud and raucous that it caught Dad's attention. He actually looked. But he just laughed and went on with whatever he was doing. I glared daggers at the men, of course, but as usual they didn't seem to notice my face.

And so that horrible day went—excruciatingly slowly, and not at all like I had planned. At the afternoon break I held the water jug up off the ground on my shoulder for the guys to fill their cups, as usual. It was the only time during the day that the crew ever got to get near me, usually. This time my sweaty tee shirt was plastered against me so that every seam of my bra probably showed through. When Brian stepped up he stared right at my chest and said loudly, "Hey! Boobs!" He had the exact same leer on his face that Bobs had practiced that morning at home. My secret inner rage flared hotter.

The other crewmembers guffawed at Brian's jibe. I was deeply offended, which was illogical because I'd heard the nickname many times during my high school years. It had been introduced by Rotten Robs when he called me that in front of some of his buddies. As a school girl I had hated it even worse than being called by my initials--BS! Those schoolgirl times seemed distant now, and far less offensive than this.

At this moment it all just suddenly seemed absolutely intolerable! I set the jug down, turned toward him, put my hands on my hips, threw my shoulders back and tried to think of a really cutting reply. All the men stared at me in the sudden silence, waiting.

Bubba, standing next to him, eyes also aimed at my chest, chimed in, "Yummy, yummy!"

That was when I finally lost it. I saw red, literally. I took a deep breath to snarl back and every man's eyes got big. I was, at that moment, out of control. Even if I had realized it I probably wouldn't have cared! I wanted a stinging rejoinder, but all I came up with was ...

"*Eat your heart out, you jerks—you'll never taste this!*"

It was totally inane, completely stupid, absolutely ridiculous! But it was what came out of my mouth at that crisis moment. I was shocked at my own words. Why would I even express such an awful idea? What was wrong with me? Why didn't Dad stop these wicked men from harassing me? Why was God letting this happen to me?

Anger flared up in Brian's eyes and I knew I had scored. I felt good about it--briefly. Ominously, however, no one replied. Satisfied for the moment with my hollow victory, however, I flipped back my hair and sauntered off, exaggerating my swagger the way I always hated when other girls did it.

I already regretted my idiotic impulse. I felt hugely relieved when I realized it would soon be quitting time. I finished up my last tasks and went and sat in dad's pickup where no one could see me for the last half hour. It was unbelievable how much like a total nitwit I had sounded! And acted! I was so miserable.

That night at home during my devotions before going to bed I tearfully confessed my sin to God. I asked the Lord to help me control my temper and not let Satan use me to tempt those men. I intentionally chose to believe what the Bible says in First John chapter one, verse nine, and I felt peace settle softly into my soul like gentle music.

I hated that I had once again found it so easy to sin. Of course I had been philosophically convinced of my "sinfulness" when Uncle Cliff led me to faith in Jesus Christ, but somehow I still thought of myself as basically a good person. How could I do something so bad, now, as a Christian? Before I trusted Christ I had never even thought of doing anything like this!

For the first time in my life I glimpsed the hard reality of the wickedness inside myself. I was forced to agree with God's assessment of my own immorality. I found myself amazed afresh, and deeply grateful, that God loved me. God's love truly is a miracle. Uncle Cliff had shown me that same kind of love but I hadn't fully understood where it came from.

I wondered to myself, 'If even I, as a follower of Christ, find it so easy to sin, what about all the unsaved people like Brian and Bubba who don't really care what God thinks of them? How can they not be like they are?'

I knew there were deep doctrinal truths involved in this issue, but at the moment it was too much for my human mind to comprehend. I felt sorry for myself and cried for a while, then fell into an exhausted sleep.

CHAPTER SIX

TRINITY HOUSE

I woke up the next morning in unresolved spiritual distress. My old hermit plan suddenly welled up in my mind as I lay there. It felt like sort of an emotional refuge. It soothed me once again to contemplate living alone. It helped me to sort of mentally turn a page, and I never went back. It helped me calm down, emotionally.

In my heart I bowed down before my God and sincerely re-surrendered my will to be in complete submission to His will for my life. As God had promised, I received the blessing of another chance for yet another new beginning. I got up and started my day once again.

I can honestly say I never again intentionally tempted any man. I put that ugly part of my life behind me from that moment on. I trusted God to protect me from the men at work, who had no doubt lost whatever mote of respect they might have ever had for me. I also trusted God to protect me from my own thoughtless impulses based on anger and pride that had led me to sin against Him.

From that day forward I studiously ignored their gibes and innuendos. I acted as if I was deaf and didn't hear them. I resumed maintaining a modest appearance and demeanor at all times. I began to faithfully pray for all of them (and Dad and Bobs) in my daily devotions.

It wasn't easy. I had to renew my resolve many times. My anger kept trying to flare up, and my pride suggested I shouldn't have to live this way, but I kept on anyway. I was sure it was what God wanted from me.

29

I also began using every penny I earned to stockpile things I would need to have in order to someday became a hermit. I purchased my first vehicle—a used Jeep Wrangler. My evenings were free now that Uncle Cliff was gone so I spent many tired evenings after work studying the owner's manual and learning how to maintain the Jeep. I bought an old army surplus utility trailer to tow behind it. I got my hands dirtier at home after work than I did during the day at my job. I fell into bed late almost every night and slept like a log.

Dad didn't object when I took over a corner of his garage for my growing collection of "camping stuff." He had always been jealous of anything that took up space in "his" garage, but I think he must have figured that I was going a little overboard on religion and he could divert me by encouraging my interest in what he thought was auto mechanics and camping.

I had never discussed my plan with anyone but Uncle Cliff, so I'm sure Dad and Mom must have wondered at the odd things I collected for "camping." I acquired all the normal things, of course, such as a huge ice chest and water jug, a propane lantern, a top quality 12x14 cabin tent, a sturdy folding cot and mattress pad, and a sturdy camp chair.

But I also picked up four weeks worth of dehydrated campfire meals, a top-quality rope hammock, a 100 foot nylon rope, extra tarps, a complete set of good (expensive) mechanic's tools and carpenter's tools, a bow saw, a pick and shovel, an axe, a mattock, a post-hole digger, a chainsaw, and a splitting maul and wedges. I began to wonder if I would be able to fit it all in my Jeep and trailer!

Every Saturday after I did my martial arts and physical fitness workout I studied maps and went exploring in my Jeep. It took weeks, but I finally found what seemed like an ideal spot to "homestead" as a hermit.

From where we lived in Redding, about thirty miles west along Highway 299 there was a turnoff to the village of Lewiston in the Trinity Alps. Between the highway and Lewiston there was a turnoff called Browns Mountain Road. The pavement ended after about a mile. Several miles of dirt road later a small dirt road branched off up a steep gully alongside a stream.

"Trinity House" was spray painted on a tree trunk, so I guess it was either Trinity House Road, or maybe Trinity House Creek, or both. I called it "my road" and "my creek." There was a stout iron gate bar, with flaking yellow paint, installed across the road entrance. It was intimidating at first, but I discovered (don't ask me how) that the padlock was defective and could be jimmied open. I always made sure to put it back into place so it looked secure whenever I left for the day.

My road was narrow and rutted. It climbed steeply for about two miles and then dipped down into an alpine meadow just below the peak of Browns Mountain. There the road crossed a little twelve-inch culvert over the trickling headwaters of the stream (Trinity House Creek?) that originated at a spring higher up the slope. After my road crossed the culvert it wound around as it climbed back up over a ridge and dropped down through another iron gate (with a good padlock) back onto Browns Mountain Road. Eventually Browns Mountain Road reconnected with Highway 299 near the town of Weaverville.

The whole stretch of "my" road from iron gate to iron gate was a rough five miles that had no houses, no ranches, no fences, no fishing holes, no camp sites or anything else that would attract visitors. Browns Mountain Road, I learned, might have originally been part of an old stagecoach road providing access from Redding to Weaverville, way back before Highway 299 was built in the early 1900's.

I decided that if I ever acted upon my hermitage dream I would make my camp right there at the twelve inch headwaters culvert. The place had a certain ambiance that appealed to me. Above the little culvert the stream was very small, discreet. It was covered by brush upstream in the steeper, narrower part of the gully. I couldn't even see the spring emerging from the ground somewhere beneath the dense gorse.

The peak of the ridge circled around me from left to right as I stood at the culvert facing north. As I stood with north at my 12:00 o'clock, the ridge started on my left at about 8:00 o'clock, circled in *front of me all the way around to about 5:00 o'clock where it ended at the highest peak of Browns Mountain overlooking the Trinity River and Lewiston several miles away and probably a thousand feet below.*

On my near right, at about 3:00 o'clock, a forested slope reached from the ridge top all the way down to the creek so that my road cut through the bottom of it. My road was a little steep coming up from Browns Mountain Road, but after it crested the cutout it dropped gently down the last hundred yards to the culvert.

The timbered slope with the road cutout curved back toward the southeast as it climbed steeply to the peak of Browns Mountain, which was over my right shoulder as I faced north. Another steep brush-choked gully came down between that slope and the ridge that encircled the meadow.

The culvert was centered in the middle of the fan shaped headwaters meadow, which was protected by the encircling ridge with its dense evergreen forest. Capricious winds often blew fiercely among the mountain peaks, but down in the sheltered meadow there was never more than a gentle breeze. In my meadow there was, in fact, always a breeze ruffling the treetops, even when there was no wind higher up.

In every direction for many miles there was only wilderness. My high meadow was cut off from the public by the iron gate bars at either entrance to my road. My meadow had a year-round stream, plenty of firewood, it was protected from the fiercest weather, and it had that strangely appealing pastoral ambiance. It was exactly what I wanted.

It felt like a reward from God for my sincere repentance. I often drove up there just to spend a few quiet hours renewing my spirit.

CHAPTER SEVEN

TWO "IT"S

I hadn't decided when I would go, or even IF I actually would ever go. Even after all my preparation, and all my growing frustration, the idea of becoming a hermit was still just more of a mental refuge than a firm plan.

It was almost the end of summer. I had turned eighteen and Mom gave me this journal for my birthday. Not knowing all that would follow, I made my first brief entries with optimistic hopes of keeping my journal light and upbeat. I meant well.

But then it happened. "It" was actually two events. One "it" happened to the whole world and I didn't even know about it at the time. The other "it" happened only to me, and almost nobody else in the world knew about it besides me. I know... ironic.

The event that happened to the whole world was a catastrophic plague. I'm sure that anyone reading this journal already knows as much as I do about it. I learned later that the whole population of the world was almost totally wiped out. Humanity, from what I pieced together, instantly became an endangered species—not quite extinct, but almost.

The plague was new and unknown, violently contagious, with death typically occurring within mere hours of exposure. The person's dead body, without exception, decomposed rapidly—within a few hours—until nothing was left but a small pile of ash-like debris, hence the nickname "cremation plague." The human race essentially, and *quietly, disappeared in about a week. There was no time to find out where the plague came from or how to cure it.*

I survived. I don't know why, or how. I assume that since I survived others did too, but I don't know for sure. I unexpectedly became a true hermit--more alone than I imagined I would ever be. For all I know I may be the last human being alive on earth. The whole fact of the plague and its extent and the finality of its result is inconceivable--a possibility I have not yet been able to comprehend.

On the very same day that the Cremation Plague struck, before I had even learned about the plague, by coincidence (or, as I've come to understand, by divine design), the other "it" happened. I knew all about this other event.

The other "it" was what drove me to begin what I thought would be a relatively short-term hermitage. Not knowing about the Cremation Plague, I more or less assumed that in a year or two I might be able to return to society, healed and whole.

The other event is what I'll write about next. It'll be hard to mentally process it again, but I will make myself get through it--finally, after all this time. It feels almost as if there must be some sort of emotional statute of limitations. Last year I could not have told this story, but now I finally can, and I am determined that I will.

Barbara reread what she had just written then heaved a deep sigh as she once again laid the journal aside. She hated writing so much detail, but the story seemed to demand it. She wished she had thought to simply summarize the crisis with Brian and Bubba as she had the incident with Bobs. But she didn't want to tear out pages and rewrite them. She would leave it as written, but she resolved to write the next part differently--with less detail.

Right now she felt drained. Writing by hand with a pencil took much more time than reading. She had been writing all day. Now it was getting dark and the lantern light wasn't bright enough to keep her eyes from straining. She needed to take a break, get some rest, ponder things before deciding how to commit her personal tragedy to print.

Tomorrow, if it comes, I'll write some more during the daylight.

But, before she could sleep she had chores to do. She got up, stretched her sore muscles, drank a dipper of water from the fifty-five-gallon barrel she had made into a cistern, grabbed her flashlight and headed away from the fire pit.

First she made the circuit of her livestock pens, making sure the chickens, rabbits, goats and cows were all safely penned for protection against night time predators. When all was secure she went down her road and checked the gate, then went up onto the ridge and checked the other gate. Back at her homestead she carried in several armloads of firewood so it would be protected from the night time dew, dry for her morning fire. Lastly, she topped off the half-empty generator fuel tank so her reefer motor would run for the next twenty-four hours and keep her food supplies from spoiling. The generator was well muffled behind a good sound barrier, so if it ever did happen to run out of fuel she'd never hear it stop.

My chores, she mused, are both a nuisance and a comfort. I'm always tired by the time I finish the chores, but I get a sense of safety and continuity by doing the same routine every morning and every night. My animals do too. If I get off my normal schedule they certainly complain! Nanny gives less milk, the cow moos pitifully as if she's dying, and the hens pretend to be deeply offended. They make sure I know it by laying fewer eggs.

An hour or so later when her head finally hit the pillow she fell into a deep healthy sleep and knew no more until daybreak.

The next morning Barbara set aside her mental list of projects that needed doing so she could devote another day to writing in her journal. She had anticipated that getting the journal caught up would be a laborious process, and it was, but she felt it would prove to be well worth it. She got right back to it after her morning chores.

Dad's crew was planting evergreen seedlings along Interstate 5 north of Yreka. The highway went through steep high mountains and deep gullies. Some of the gullies had small streams of runoff during the rainy season that would dry up by mid-summer. By mid-August the heat and humidity seemed almost unbearable. During my lunch break one stereotypical scorcher of a day I stumbled upon a tiny private oasis.

About fifty yards up hill from our equipment staging area a trickle of water dropped down the front of a huge granite boulder that completely blocked the mouth of a sharp gully that climbed the steep slope we were clearing. Below the huge boulder was a small pool--about the size of a kitchen table--well shaded by a huge old gnarly willow tree. There was no outflow, with just enough trickle coming in to offset each day's evaporation. Above the house-sized granite boulder a dense willow thicket choked the gully on up the steep slope. I claimed the tiny, shaded pool as my lunch spot and the guys left me alone each day while I sat in the shade and ate.

I was pleased that the crew gave me some privacy. Before finding that shady pool I had always sat by myself in the cab of Dad's pickup, and later in my Jeep, listening to Christian radio while I ate lunch. It was a welcome daily reprieve from the innuendos and leers of the work gang. Now I could enjoy the cool shade and the soothing sound of water softly tinkling down the face of the boulder while I rested and ate my lunch.

During lunch break one hot day, while I sat near the huge boulder in "my" shade, I began to wonder what might be on up the gully above the boulder. As I considered the face of that huge granite boulder I noticed that at the northern edge, on my left, where it merged into the hillside, there were regularly spaced indentations going up from the ground. It looked almost like crude steps chipped out of the granite.

I looked closer. It looked like there could have been a pathway up the little gorge at one time, with steps chipped out of the granite for access. I remembered that California had been settled during the gold rush. It was probably just an old Native American trail for access to the spring, but wouldn't it be something if there was an old, abandoned gold mine up there? On impulse I decided to check it out. First, I looked down the hill to the equipment staging area and both ways along the slope to be sure none of the men were watching.

I quietly got up, moving slowly to avoid drawing attention, and brushed the leaves and dirt from each of the steps as I carefully climbed. I made it all the way up the nearly vertical rock face to the top, where I found a faint trail entering the willow thicket. The trail was a very narrow corridor almost invisible beneath the dense foliage.

I turned and visually swept the area, noting that everyone within sight had their eyes down toward their lunches, then I carefully moved forward, gently pushing the willows back with my hands so they wouldn't brush my clothing. I'd learned the hard way that ticks lurk on willow branches, waiting for a warm body to pass so they can leap onto it.

About twenty-five feet upward into the thicket I found a small level clearing with another, larger, pool of water. This oval pool hidden among the shrubbery was about fifteen feet across and the water was a good sixteen inches deep in the middle. It was really just a deep depression on the upper surface of the huge boulder, but with the trickle of water keeping it full it formed a perfect bath of cool, fresh water. Completely hidden! To me this was even better than a gold mine!

The spot was completely private and I saw possibilities right away. My lunch break was nearly over, but I quickly sat down, took off my shoes and socks and dipped my feet into the pool. Ah, it felt so good! It was extra delicious just knowing that nobody else knew about it!

For the rest of that week I discreetly climbed the boulder every day, ate my lunch while soaking my feet in the cool water, and returned to work refreshed. The next Monday, after I had thought about it all weekend, I "took it to the next level" as Uncle Cliff used to say.

I quickly ate my lunch. Then…. I stripped and lay naked in the pool! The water covered almost all of me, and that's all I'll say about that. And it felt oh so good! But I immediately climbed out, shocked at myself! (Had I really just done that?)

I fidgeted for a minute while my skin air-dried, then hurriedly got back into my clothes. I couldn't believe I had been so bold! But that day I returned to work feeling clean and refreshed, and it was without a doubt the best day I'd had on the job so far!

The next day, Tuesday, was another scorcher. I agonized briefly over the idea, and again treated myself to a soothing session in my own private pool during the lunch break. I was less fearful than before and soaked a bit longer. Wednesday I relaxed a bit more and gave myself a whole fifteen minute tanning session! Thursday was perfect. The areas on my body that were perpetually white were actually getting slightly sunburned!

Then that fateful Friday came. As I lay in the cool water that day, tanning naked under the hot noonday sun and thinking how great it was, I suddenly heard Brian's voice—very close, and gruff with tension, "Hey Boobs, want yer clothes back!"

So, reader, here we are. This is the moment of the other "it."

I've thought about this a lot and decided I am not going to relive the awful details of that moment on paper. I remember it vividly, but no one else needs to know exactly what happened, or how. Only the outcome matters anyway, so this is only a summary.

The short version: Brian and Bubba had been watching me more closely than I realized. They had tracked me into the clearing. They attempted to rape me that day, and I instinctively fought them off. I recalled and executed by muscle memory the perfect Karate moves that were called for at that moment. Brian and Bubba failed and I succeeded.

Ultimately, of course, nobody really won. We all lost. The final outcome was that I became a murderer, and they became dead. That is all.

When I finished dealing with them I was in a complete daze. I dressed, woodenly, and went back to work. I left the bodies there, hoping nobody would miss them.

I was in a stupor all afternoon, inwardly, but outwardly I was calm. At the end of the day when I got into my Jeep and headed home their bodies were still hidden in the clearing in the thicket atop the huge boulder. That afternoon nobody seemed to even miss them. To my knowledge, no one ever found them. I knew that I would never go into that thicket again. Ever.

When I got home from work the house was empty. Mom had left a note that she had gone out shopping with a friend and they planned to have dinner and catch a movie. Bratty Bobs had gone away for a weekend basketball camp and I knew that Dad planned to go straight there from work. I had the house to myself all evening.

I took a long hot shower, trying to wash away the overwhelming sense of filthiness on my body and in my soul. The soap and water only cleansed my outer body. Inside I still felt contaminated. I put on clean clothes, but that didn't help my inner turmoil either. After grabbing a bite of supper I hooked up my utility trailer and started loading my stuff. All of it.

I was thinking: 'This is it. I over-reacted and killed two men. I can't possibly get away with it. I don't even know how to begin to get away with it. I don't even think I want to get away with it. Therefore, my whole life has become a disaster. I'm ruined. They will lock me up when they catch me. It isn't even a matter of if, it's simply a matter of when.'

But then I thought, 'Hmmm. Maybe it is IF. I could run away to my secret place and stay hidden a long time.' Not only was it possible, but it also suddenly seemed absolutely necessary! Not as if I had a choice, right? My secret location was really my only option. Strangely, that realization at that moment was a huge relief because I had been preparing for this departure for years. Now I had a valid reason to go ahead with the plan I had enjoyed toying with all these years.

Before I drove away from the only home I'd ever known, I remembered to leave a vaguely worded note that said I was going camping, I'd get in touch, not to worry.

So, that was the other "it" that happened that day; the event that made me a hermit.

I never saw my parents again. Or, so far, anyone else.

God's timing is weird. Apparently that very same day all over the world people started dying in massive droves. Dad and Mom and Bobs all died. All of our neighbors died. All of my friends at church. As far as I can tell everyone in Redding and maybe all of California died. They all died except me.

I read a little about the plague in a newspaper I found a few weeks later when I finally had to make a trip to town for supplies. The newspaper article, hastily prepared and distributed by journalists who knew they would die, predicted that maybe about one out of every five hundred thousand people might survive. I tried to do the mind-boggling math in my head and calculated that there may be as few as only one or two thousand people left in the whole United States. Or there could be as many as a million. But the article said they weren't sure. I wonder, if anyone survived, where are they?

Barbara put the journal down, exhausted once again. It had taken another whole day to accomplish the worst of the telling. She hadn't expected writing it to be as bad as living it, but she felt dirty all over again, just like when she had stepped into the hot shower at home before packing and leaving. She wondered if writing it out was really worth it.

But she was not a quitter! Life was hard, that's all! All of life! If she was a quitter she'd be dead by now. She had restarted the journal and she would not quit! Even so, a tiny sob caught in her throat as she rose from her sitting log and stepped away from her evening fire into the dusk of evening.

People had been the source of all her deepest heartaches, but they weren't any more. Right now, at this moment, she would give a lot just to see another human being. But she was completely alone. Possibly forever.

She again felt the need to take a bath. The animals would warn her, in their various ways, if any human survivor or even an animal predator came around. She could bathe in her own private creek in complete safety and privacy as she had become accustomed to doing.

Later, after the sun was down and she was dry and dressed again, she did her evening chores, late for the second evening in a row, but enjoying each step of the familiar routine. Finally, late at night, she lay down on her cot and let herself relax, body part by body part. She had forgotten to eat supper, but it didn't matter.

The only sounds were the familiar chirrup of crickets in the grass, the occasional garumph of a bull frog near the creek, and the occasional soft whoooo of a nearby owl. She sighed, snuggled deeper into her sleeping bag, and let her mind idle down until she slid into the blessed oblivion of slumber.

CHAPTER EIGHT

HOMESTEAD

Okay. I got through it. This journal now includes, I'm pretty sure, every significant aspect of my life up until the day I became a hermit. I'm writing the rest of this by memory after having lived alone here at my homestead over four years now.

I have not been writing faithfully in my journal as I had planned but I assure you, reader, that all these events I'm now going to write about are still very fresh in my mind. I have no one to talk to and lots of time to ponder. There really aren't that many distractions here at my homestead. So, anyway, I'll get back to it…

When I fled from my parents' home with all my gear loaded into the utility trailer behind my Wrangler, I drove straight to my hidden alpine meadow near the peak of Browns Mountain. I arrived after dark, of course. I was so exhausted by the trauma of the day that I shut off the motor, reclined the driver's seat of my Jeep, and just went to sleep.

When I awoke the first light of dawn was just beginning to intrude over the darkness of night in my mountain meadow without streetlights. I sat in my Jeep looking out the little circle where I had wiped the fog off the inside of my windshield. My meadow was hazy with morning mist and I was stiff and cold. I was sure that down in Redding it was probably near seventy degrees already, but up here it felt more like fifty. My coat was packed in the trailer somewhere. I was wearing my long sleeved over shirt, so it could have been worse. I warmed myself up by getting busy.

First, I spread a tarp and unloaded everything onto it. Everything! The item I needed most urgently, of course, was at the very bottom of the load--my camp shovel, so I could dig a latrine! I did not want to begin my homesteading experience by squatting to pee on the ground.

I picked a small clearing in some dense shoulder-high gorse and dug a hole about a shovel blade wide and two blades deep. Then I set up an arrangement of large stones and short thick branches so it would be comfortable and practical for me to use. In other words, it had a seat!

There was enough room in the small clearing so I would be able to move the hole back and forth among four different spots. It would be adequate for now and by the time it was ready I was grateful for the opportunity to finally use it!

When I finished doing my business I carefully covered my "sign" with a thin layer of soil. I realized I would need to build a proper outhouse as soon as possible. I did NOT want to use an outdoor latrine in winter! And winter was not very far off.

Next I set up my tent. It was made of durable waterproof canvas--not plastic or vinyl like most modern tents. Canvas is heavy. Did I say it was large? Ten by fourteen to be exact! Did I mention that it was heavy? Ugh!

I erected the frame by myself with no one to hold up the other ends of the cross members. I took my time and figured out ways to use straight limbs as temporary jacks and as pry levers. The latrine had taken me several hours and it was almost dark by the time I gave up on the tent. Yep, I gave up for the day. I was exhausted and famished. I had been so busy that I forgot to eat all day.

It took me awhile to get a fire going because I hadn't collected any firewood. I scrounged a few pieces of wood that looked dry, but it took a lot of newspaper to get it to catch. It was damp, I guess. After I got the fire going I realized I should have made a fire pit first. The breeze was whipping the little flames around, so I reluctantly doused it.

I was too tired, and it was too dark to do anything more, so I made my supper from a cold MRE and lots of water. Slept the second night in the Jeep again, determined to get that cabin tent and a proper fire pit finished tomorrow!

I worked all the next morning dragging the heavy canvas up and over the framework, piece by piece. I was frustrated and exhausted by the time I finished, but I got it done.

That afternoon I got everything stowed where it belonged. I didn't get a fire pit built, but that night I slept in MY sleeping bag, on MY sleeping pad, on MY cot, in MY wonderful cabin tent. It was most satisfying, even though MY body odor reminded me that I needed to address MY personal hygiene very soon.

The next morning after using the latrine I scraped out a twelve-foot circle of bare dirt for a small campfire and made myself a pot of coffee. Then, to celebrate, I ate my very first HOT MRE campfire meal at my homestead. I had hoped that heating it would make it taste better. It didn't. But it nourished me enough to get back to work.

My next project was to build a proper fire pit. Took all the rest of the morning to find, haul, and place just the right stones in just the right way by size and shape. It was hard work.

After lunch I napped all afternoon. Hard physical labor is different than working out with weights. My body let me know. As it turned out I hauled twice as many stones as I needed, so in the evening I lined up the extras to mark the paths to my latrine and the creek.

By the morning of my fourth day I had a great looking camp with a proper fire pit with a nice sitting log on the west side of it facing east toward my tent and the sunrise. My tent faced west toward my fire pit and the sunset. The creek gurgled a dozen feet away behind the sitting log. The peak of Browns Mountain rose up behind my tent. It felt like home. I rested all day and it was very good.

The next morning I put on cutoffs instead of long pants. After coffee, breakfast and morning devotions I waded into the chilly waters of my little spring fed creek. All day I dug and pried out large stones and shoveled out dirt and sand. I used the stones to build a low dam below the hole I was digging and managed to end up with a waist-deep bathing hole. I spread the sand along the shore. My "bath" is only twenty-five feet from my fire pit.

After the water had cleared up again I ended my day with a refreshing bath. It was chilly so I finished in a hurry and got back to my campfire. It felt good to be clean.

Didn't start any major projects for a couple of days. I was worn out and feeling disorganized. Everything seemed to take lots more time than I expected it to. Day and a half just to erect my tent. Most of a day to make a good fire pit. Most of a day to make a bathing hole.

I needed to somehow make better use of my time. I had to start by establishing daily morning and evening routines for meals and cleanup. My morning and evening routines would provide the framework for planning my project workdays.

It was autumn so the days were getting cooler and shorter. I discovered that after breakfast and cleanup, personal hygiene needs and morning devotions, I only had about three hours until lunch. After lunch I only had about four hours to work before my evening routine so I could be finished before dark. Only seven hours a day to do all I needed to do before winter. Whew! It motivated me to work hard and fast, every day.

I would need lots of firewood. Also a rain fly over the tent and a drainage trench around it. If I wanted a companion dog, I'd need a dog house and dog food. I needed to do all these things before the first snow. I wasn't sure my steep muddy road would be passable, even in a Jeep, with snow on top of mud.

I'm not afraid of hard work. And once I start a project I like to work hard until it's done. So I fixed my list in my mind and got to it.

I discovered there were things I needed but didn't have--such as, for starters, gas for my chain saw! I had the foresight to bring a chainsaw but forgot about gas for it! I also needed a pick for digging and prying, and definitely a better shovel. The camp shovel I had packed, feeling so smug that I even thought of it, was only good enough for simple camping but was frustratingly inadequate for any more serious digging projects such as the bathing hole and a rain drain trench around the cabin. I had begun to actually hate that little fold-up camp shovel.

At this point I started thinking I would make an occasional very discreet trip into Weaverville for supplies and stay hid out at my homestead as long as I could until I was finally caught and arrested. But I didn't dwell on getting caught. I had read a story about a fictional character named Jack Reacher whose motto was "Hope for the best and plan for the worst." That's what I tried to do. I planned for long term, as if I'd never get caught.

I started a list of things I would need soon. My "soon" list rapidly expanded to include a dairy goat and milk bucket, a half dozen hens and an egg basket. I also needed to get enough feed to keep the goat and chickens through the winter, and of course I'd need a good dog to keep me company and warn me of predators or visitors. I would also need a cast iron skillet and a cast iron pot to hang over the fire pit (a Dutch oven) for all my cooking, along with salt, sugar, spices, flour, sugar, corn meal, more oatmeal, and of course sugar! Just kidding about the sugar, but I had already learned that it definitely boosted my short-term energy to use sugar.

My list was actually much longer than that, but I had to prioritize. I definitely wanted to get the hang of campfire cooking very quickly so I could save the dehydrated campfire meals for emergencies. I did NOT want to eat MRE's every day! My list included what I figured I'd need to supplement any meat I could hunt and kill.

CHAPTER NINE

NEW PLANS

The moment finally came when I knew I had to leave my homestead and get supplies right NOW! After several weeks I had reached the point where I was heartily disgusted with MREs. I had also used the last of the gas siphoned from my Jeep for my chain saw. And, lastly, I felt a strong desire to never ever pick up that hated little camp shovel ever again.

I was also becoming curious about what might be going on out in the world. Had charges been filed against me? And, if so, what were the charges? Was I a murderer, or had Brian and Bubba only been unconscious when I left them? I was pretty sure they were dead, but there was always a possibility that in my distress and my adrenalin explosion my judgement might have been off.

In any case, I resolved that I would plan the excursion with the goal of being able to return to my camp and continue my hermitage, but I really needed those supplies and I really wanted those answers, so I had to make a trip back to civilization.

After my morning chores I skipped breakfast, had a cup of coffee while I did my Bible reading, then hooked up the trailer while I was having my "out loud" prayer time. I headed out my road by mid-morning. Not knowing the exact time reminded me that I also wanted to buy a good windup clock for my camp.

At the gate I jimmied the lock, let myself out and rehung the padlock so it looked locked again. I drove away and made it all the way through Lewiston to Highway 299 without seeing any other *traffic. Unusual, but so far, so good. The fewer people who saw me the less likely that I might be identified and arrested.*

I had planned to go to the smaller town of Weaverville, where I was less likely to encounter any acquaintances, but on a sudden impulse I decided to go to Redding instead. I rationalized that I would be more likely to find what I needed and also less noticeable in a larger population. So, at Highway 299 I headed left instead of right.

From there I drove all the way to the top of Buckhorn Summit before I finally saw another vehicle, and then it was only a parked car in the turnout at the summit. No one was in it or near it, so I was still "unseen" and safe.

As I drove past the car I noticed a pair of blue jeans, a long sleeve flannel shirt and a pair of shoes laid out on the pavement in front of the hood of the car as if arranged on a flat invisible body. Sort of strange. There was even a baseball cap.

Nine miles further down the highway, as I approached the shoreline of Whiskeytown Lake, I still had not yet met another car. I mentally noted that it was unusual for traffic to be so light during the daytime. As I entered the first long straight stretch of the characteristically winding highway I could see no one for at least a mile out in front of me, and when I reached the far end of that straight stretch no one had appeared in my rear view mirror.

It was a little spooky--almost as if I was the only one on the road. Since Highway 299 is a major arterial between the central part of northern California and the coastline towns it's always busy with traffic during the daytime. This lack of vehicles was very unusual.

Was this a holiday? I wasn't sure of the exact date but the only holiday this time of year might be Halloween or Thanksgiving, but I thought it was probably not yet that late in the year. They were both all commercialized anyway, so if it was one of those holidays there would be more traffic, not less, with vacationers and shoppers out in force. But there were no shoppers or vacationers. No travelers except me, it seemed.

After I drove through the silent town of Old Shasta, where no one was out and about so that it seemed like a ghost town, I arrived at the first traffic light in the outskirts of Redding. It was green, so without stopping I turned right onto Buenaventura. At the next traffic light I pulled into the large upscale market where it was unlikely any of my family would see me. But when I pulled into the parking lot everything appeared to be closed. It was only late morning, but there were very few cars in the parking lot and no people walking around. No lights on in the stores.

Now I was spooked for sure. All my life I had lived in Redding and I'd never seen the Holiday Market and it's satellite shops totally deserted, even on a weekend or holiday. Something unusual was definitely going on. No billows of smoke rose into the sky anywhere, so it wasn't a major wildfire that had caused an evacuation. I was almost certain it wasn't Sunday. But even on Sunday there was always SOME traffic at the fast-food restaurant in the parking lot.

Not one car. Not one pedestrian. Even as I had driven through Old Shasta there had been no one. No one was out and about here on the edge of Redding either.

I parked my Jeep near the market entrance door and got out. The quietness was eerie. I looked around warily, my senses on high alert, and noticed a newspaper kiosk next to the door right in front of me. It had one paper left in it. I could see the headline through the glass as I hastily put in fifty cents and lifted out the paper.

NO CURE FOR CREMATION VIRUS!

I had no clue what a cremation virus was. I quickly scanned the article, which took up the entire front page. There weren't even any pictures to break up the text. It was like a giant, takes-two-hands-to-hold-it book page. You already know what it said, reader. The gist was this:

A phenomenally potent man-made plague had broken out somewhere in Africa and swept across the world. It had no known medical name but had simply been called the Cremation Virus because of its symptoms. It was completely contagious, spreading by every known way. It was incurable and it was one hundred percent fatal.

It was called the Cremation Virus because it seemed to attack all the water molecules in human (only) bodies. The victim developed a high fever and within hours of contagion lost consciousness due to extreme dehydration, which was a mercy. After going unconscious the dehydration process continued and a victim's vital signs began to cease within an hour. After death the dehydration process continued unabated. The corpse immediately began to dry up and decompose, very rapidly. The flesh would completely wither to a dry husk within a few more hours and finally completely disintegrate to an ashy powder.

From first contagion to final dust was only about eight hours. People had little time to do anything other than land their plane, lock their doors or prepare for their last breath. No time to write a will, or even to have a nice last meal. Once you contracted the plague, you very quickly passed out and soon died and turned to ashes.

Reader, since you are alive and reading this you obviously already know all about the Cremation Virus that swept the planet. Every nation on the whole earth was decimated to, essentially, near-zero population. The newspaper's final issue said it had been roughly optimistically estimated that only about one in a hundred thousand people might possibly be immune, but nobody knew why or how. That was it. End of story for Americans, Chinese, Mexicans, Canadians, Africans, and every other nationality.

Presumably the whole nation of America now has a population of from about ten thousand up to possibly as many as a couple hundred thousand people. That's it for the whole United States. I'm one of those lonely few survivors.

I had no idea why that was so.

When I finished reading that one page newspaper it felt like my face and my whole body had gone numb! My eyes had blurred and I realized I was crying. Whew! Talk about being in shock! I don't remember how long I just stood there crying, struggling to get my mind around the idea that I was really and truly all alone. It felt like I cried for an hour. I eventually ran out of tears, so I finally stopped crying.

Suddenly my brain started working again and I took a fresh look around me with a whole new perspective, coming to some immediate mind-blowing conclusions. The reason why I hadn't seen any traffic was obviously because there wasn't any! Duh!

Most likely, even if I found other survivors and we managed to keep the human race alive and viable, in my lifetime there never would be any "traffic" again. It was even possible, and maybe even likely, that I might never ever see another human being the rest of my life!

Amazing implications! My hermitage and homestead suddenly now had a whole new significance. I really was on my own. Whatever comforts and conveniences and supplies I might ever have at the homestead, from now on and for the rest of my life, would be entirely up to me to either scavenge, grow or make. There was no longer any Plan B.

I must reprogram my brain to always think in terms of "forever" instead of "for now." Oh sure, I could scavenge for some while, possibly years, but certainly not for the rest of my life. I had access to everything right now, but it would be entirely up to me to figure out ways to make it work for the rest of my life. And I needed to start right now. There was no reason to wait or hesitate, no obstacle would ever be imposed by laws, ordinances, or regulations.

On the upside of that truth, if any store was closed I could simply break in and take whatever I needed. There was no one to stop me, or even care. I didn't need to worry about leaving stuff for anyone else--whatever I find is mine for the taking. That would help a lot.

Even better, no cop would ever come after me for the murder of Brian and Bubba. If I ever met any other survivors someday they need never know I had killed two people. Or that I had been molested by my brother while my dad watched, or that two men had tried to rape me. All those things were suddenly ancient history, known to no one alive but me.

My mind raced as I considered this new paradigm. Obviously all the old rules were now subject to change. Everything was now up to me. Whatever I decided would have to be right the first time. Every time. If I ever blew it there was no one to call. No backup. For at least a whole hour I sat there like a zombie, thoughts whirling in my mind about what all this would mean.

Finally I breathed in deeply, breathed out deeply, and mentally shook myself. Then I got busy. Before I could second guess myself I stooped down, picked up a landscaping brick and broke out the glass of the market's front door. I ducked under the grab bar and stood up inside, then turned and unlocked the double doors. The electricity was off so I forced the doors apart and blocked them open, the glass shards crunching under my boots.

I habitually do everything quickly anyway, so it only took about an hour to pack my trailer with all kinds of long-shelf-life foods that I liked. I only grabbed stuff that didn't need refrigeration, such as boxes of Mac N Cheese, all kinds of "helpers" like Tuna Helper, Hamburger Helper, etc., and whole cases of prepared canned foods like pork and beans and spaghetti-O's. I loaded all I could fit into the trailer, then on top of all the cans I piled large quantities of the staples--sugar, flour, salt, rice, beans, peanut butter, miracle whip, catsup, and of course ramen noodles.

When my trailer wouldn't hold another single thing I loaded the back seat of my Jeep with eight brand new plastic gas cans then drove on into Redding to find a working gas supply. I was able to top off my Jeep and fill my new gas cans from a 5,000 gallon above-ground fuel tank at the Redding Police Department vehicle yard, which was not locked. Then, emotionally drained and physically exhausted, I headed back to my safe little homestead in the Trinity Alps.

I felt strangely empty. It hadn't been a physically difficult day, but somehow it seemed like one of the longest, most exhausting days of my life. I was actually no more alone today than I had been yesterday, but now a heavy sense of loneliness overwhelmed me.

I felt sorry for myself. My feelings of self-pity threatened to overwhelm me too. How could God allow this to happen? What if I got sick? What if I broke my arm? Why did God do this to me? I was so wrapped up in my own sorrow that the audacity of my taking offense against God completely escaped my thinking.

I drove through the little town of Old Shasta, quiet enough before, but now absolutely silent, and headed on up the steep grade toward Whiskeytown Lake. As I made my way along the shoreline of the lake toward where Buckhorn Grade began to climb I started crying again.

By the time I got up to Buckhorn Summit I was crying so hard I could hardly see. Apparently my tear glands had already replenished. I braked to a stop right in the middle of the empty highway, straddling the centerline, and shut off the motor. I climbed out, catching my right foot on the lip under the driver's door and almost falling down. It wouldn't have mattered if I'd fallen flat out. There was no one to see me anyway.

I had no worry that anybody might witness my moment of weakness, so I let it all out. When my fright and grief began to ebb I forced myself to continue. I pushed. I sobbed as loud as I could. I shook my fist at the sky. I stomped my feet. I kicked the dirt. I shouted at God, demanding an answer, and getting none.

Finally I cried myself out. I wiped away my tears and got back in my Jeep. I noticed, again, the clothes laid out in front of the parked car. This time I understood that it was the last remains of a person who had come to this scenic turnout to die. He or she had sat back against the front bumper of their car and looked down into the Sacramento Valley as they died. So sad.

My own personal way of handling grief had always been to get busy. This time it had overwhelmed me. But only briefly. Now I had lots to do so I wiped my eyes and drove onward.

Back at my homestead I unloaded and stored everything, got my chores done before dark, then ate what I hoped would be my last cold campfire meal ever and wrote some in my journal. I fell into bed late, and more weary than if I'd carried heavy logs all day.

In the morning after chores and devotions I headed back down the mountain again in just my Jeep, without the trailer. I went to south Redding and broke into a big rental yard. I broke into the locked office, surprised at how many people took the time to lock up before they died (who were they worried about?). There were no leftover clothes laying around, so apparently the employees had all managed to go home before they succumbed.

I searched until I found their assortment of equipment ignition keys. I chose a large tilt bed flatbed truck, experimented with it until I figured out how to work it, and then loaded my Jeep onto it. I chained my Jeep down the same way I saw a car secured on an identical flatbed parked nearby. I managed to get hooked up to a 1,000-gallon fuel tank trailer, got it filled with gas, and very carefully drove the rig back up to my homestead.

I arrived in the early afternoon, parked the fuel trailer out of the way, offloaded my Wrangler and headed right back down to Redding in the flatbed. It drove a lot easier with no load on the bed or heavy trailer hooked to it.

On my second trip that day I brought home a six-wheel drive ATV called a Gator. It had bucket seats, a steering wheel instead of handlebars, a little tilt dump bed, wide soft tires, a rifle rack built on, and a very quiet motor. There was enough room on the flatbed, so I also hauled home a fairly new Bobcat tractor with a front-end loader. I had the foresight to also get the backhoe attachment, the operator manuals and a supply of "consumable" spare parts such as spark plugs, fan belts and spare tubes and tires for both the Gator and the Bobcat. I'll probably be the only mechanic these rigs ever know, so I wanted to be prepared.

Next day I made another trip to Redding in the flatbed truck, north on Market Street to Caterpillar Road, and found a distributor of metal building kits. I located the plans and materials list for a low roofed open-front equipment shed. I figured out how to use their battery powered electric forklift, then hunted down and loaded everything from the parts list onto the flatbed, plus enough extra pipe framing and sheet metal to construct a front doorway over the cold cellar I planned to dig into a hillside. I tied everything down and headed home.

My mind was racing as I drove up the mountain. I now planned to make my homestead a lot nicer than I had originally intended-- more permanent, and ultimately self-sustaining. If I had to live out my life up there all alone, I wanted to have the best setup of tools and equipment so that I could "survive and thrive" as my beloved uncle would have said. I wanted my home to be nice enough so I wouldn't ever want to leave, and durable enough to last my whole life.

That reminded me that I wanted chickens and goats. On impulse I drove through the city to the county animal shelter to see what might be there. Turned out it had been shut down for some time, apparently. A sign said all the animals were now being handled at Haven Humane on Highway 273, so I drove on down there.

Several generic brown horses and two homely gray donkeys were in an outside paddock. They had water in a trough fed from an automatic pump, but they had no feed and were very gaunt. They probably hadn't been fed in the several weeks since the plague had taken away their human caretakers.

I opened the gate so they could get out and forage, and also opened the gate into the fenced-off and roofed over haystack. Maybe by the time they finished off the haystack they would have learned how to subsist.

I opened the door to the dog and cat kennels but a horrible eye-watering stench gushed out so I slammed it shut again. I would not find a dog at the pound. I was sure it would be the same at any pet store I might find. I would need to visit a few small farms around Redding and see if any farm animals and farm pets had survived.

I headed back north on Highway 273 toward Redding and turned left up Buenaventura toward Highway 299 to go home. Up on the flats near the weed-grown runway of the old Redding airport I spotted a huge pack of dogs chasing a small deer. I stopped the truck to watch.

There were about thirty dogs. They were some distance away but even so I was glad I was in a closed vehicle. The leaders looked healthy, but some of the stragglers were very thin. They were all fast. While still within my sight they overtook their prey. The deer was dragged down and killed quickly under a vicious pile of hungry dogs. In what seemed like just a few minutes the prey was totally consumed, nothing left. Some of the scrawny pack stragglers didn't get any. Part of me acknowledged that it was a natural process, the food chain in action, but still I shuddered.

On impulse I turned right onto Placer Street and drove down the hill to Market Street, turned left and crossed the Sacramento River bridge onto the Miracle Mile. Near the base of the hill leading up to Caterpillar Drive I pulled into the Old West Pawn Shop and Gun Store parking lot. Surprisingly, the door was not locked. I had read up a lot on guns before I left home, but at that time I couldn't afford what I wanted. Now, because of the plague, I could!

I browsed until I found a nine-shot sixteen-gauge pump shotgun. I loaded it fully, alternating buckshot with slugs, and took every box of sixteen-gauge ammo they had. That gun would ride next to my driver's seat. Then I found a double action Dan Wesson 357 Magnum revolver with a six-inch barrel and a deep holster made to fit. I grabbed all the .357 Magnum ammo they had. Finally, emotionally and physically spent, but wearing my new revolver and carrying my new shotgun, I headed back out to the truck.

I cried again as I drove up the mountain to my haven. I guess I was still grieving. It caught me by surprise. I didn't cry hard enough to have to stop this time. I guess the idea was sinking into my brain a little.

I didn't see the dog pack again, but I got home too late to unload. I did my evening routine, feeling the unaccustomed but reassuring weight of the revolver in the holster on my right hip. It was heavier than I thought it would be, but I was determined to wear it until I got used to it. After enjoying a hot meal I went to bed.

In the morning I carried the pistol with me to the outhouse. It felt kind of silly, but I did it anyway. After I finished my business I strapped the holster around my waist for the day. I did my chores, did my devotions, had breakfast, unloaded the truck, then took an extra box of shells for each gun and did some plinking. I wanted to shoot them regularly so that I wouldn't be too startled whenever the moment came that I had to use a gun seriously. In the books I had read it was called 'preparedness planning'.

After I shot up a box of shells in each gun, and thoroughly cleaned them, I started building my equipment shed, still wearing my revolver. I laid out all the shed parts and the tools I would need, then thought about what I would need to do to get the ground ready. If I wanted to do this right, and I did want to, then I had to start with my vertical posts exactly plumb and set into concrete.

It occurred to me that I would need a whole bunch of bags of ready mix and a portable (gas-powered) mixer. That meant I would need to make another trip to town before proceeding. Okay. Tomorrow. And there were no doubt other things I needed that I hadn't thought of yet. So I spent the rest of the morning working on another shopping list, trying to be as comprehensive as possible. I sure didn't want to make daily trips to Redding. Once a week should be enough.

After lunch I fired up the Bobcat, with the operator's manual in one hand. I took my time, figuring out how it all worked. Soon I was industriously excavating the steep slope behind my cabin tent, which would be the site for my future underground cold cellar.

I planned to make the cold cellar twenty feet deep into the hillside and twelve feet wide across the front. I needed to make the "dig out" a couple feet wider to allow for strong concrete walls on both sides and the rear, with a gravel French drain wherever the walls were up against dirt. I planned to build forms and pour a reinforced concrete roof, then cover the whole thing with several feet of dirt. I would plant shrubs and grass in the fresh soil so that, when it was all finished, it would look like a doorway set into the hillside.

As I worked my way into the hillside, making a nice pile of loose dirt off to the side for later use, I suddenly noticed some moisture under the spot where the Bobcat had strained for its last bucket load of dirt. Alarmed, I backed away, shut it off and jumped off to see what was leaking. Nothing was! It turned out that I had apparently tapped into a hidden underground spring! Great! If I did this right I might end up with the perfect cold cellar setup--a small stream of cold water flowing out of the hillside through my cold cellar and feeding a water trough near the entrance to it. I couldn't have planned it any better. Thank you, God!

Just before dark I practiced shooting the 16 gauge and the .357 again. My revolver aim was off because my hands were still tingling from gripping the vibrating controls of the Bobcat all afternoon. My upper body was also a little sore from the unaccustomed muscle usage.

After tuning up my gun handling skills I quit for the day. Later, by the time I finished the chores and dinner and wrote in my journal, I was glad to be able to fall into bed about an hour earlier than usual. This homesteading sure was a lot of hard work, even WITH the convenience of modern equipment, it seemed!

CHAPTER TEN

FRIENDS

I just reread everything I've written in this journal so far and I'm sorta embarrassed that I didn't put dates on any of my entries. For whatever it's worth I've decided I'm not even going to use dates. It doesn't seem to matter much anyway whether it was September or October, or whether it was the year 2045 or 2060. If this journal is ever read, by anyone, the things that I'm writing will already be "ancient history" as we used to say. So…

Reader, at this point the journal does jump forward. I wrote that last paragraph (about the dates) several months ago and put it down on the log next to me, then I got distracted by something. Before long I got up off my butt and got busy. Later I remembered to set it aside so it wouldn't get more beat up than it already was, then I kept forgetting to write in it until now.

I've lived at the homestead for more than six months now and it's almost springtime. I accomplished a lot through the cold months of winter. I now have a real tent cabin, which is basically a sturdy log cabin up to the eaves with tent canvas for a roof. I have an improved fire pit with an excellent smooth sitting log, a good bathing hole in the creek and a proper outhouse near the cabin, plus the old latrine.

My cold cellar is finished, enclosed behind a steel panel with a strong door. A spring of cold water comes out of the back wall of the cold cellar, chills the room as it flows through a ditch built into the cement slab floor, then empties into a livestock water trough just *outside the door. The trickle of overflow from the stock trough drains down a gravel course to the creek. All tidy and convenient.*

I've almost finished my new equipment shed. Like everything else so far it turned out to be way more complicated than I thought it would be. After it's finished I plan to put cement floors in both my cabin tent and the equipment shed.

During the lapse in my journal writing I brought in a gas powered cement mixer and several pallets of bags of Redi-Mix cement. I have mixed and poured many batches of cement, but now I have to wait for warmer days before I can continue. I'm getting it done though!

I also hauled in a bunch of dump truck loads of quarter inch gravel and resurfaced most of my road. I left it "au natural" out at the far end where it can be seen from the gate which, out of paranoia, I still keep locked. Driving the dump truck was quite fun. Loading the gravel into the dump truck was difficult--I never got past "awkward and slow" with the front-end loader at the gravel yard along Clear Creek Road south of Redding.

This all sounds like a lot of work, even to me, but I just tackle things one day at a time. I've actually done pretty good on my "to do" list so far. I'll get the cement floors done too, as time goes by. Not having a social life helps me get lots done. My only recreation is plinking with my guns or exploring the mountains around me in the Gator. As for my projects, since the days are so cold now it's basically a matter of waiting for a day warm enough to work the cement.

On days when it's too cold or wet to do concrete I'm building a feed barn for hay and grain. I plan to build a chicken coop and pen next, then a goat shed and pen. I don't know how long it will take, but I'll keep at it until it's done. I'll add the livestock as I complete their pens.

I still don't have a dog. Hopefully I'll find one soon. The only dogs I've seen are running in packs down around Redding. Hopefully someday I'll come across a canine survivor that's hungry for human companionship, as I am longing for a canine companion.

I suppose that's pretty much everything so far. My story has been told. My life has settled into a fairly predictable routine of chores, devotions, meals, hard work on projects, learning to garden and ranch, and the occasional scavenging.

I will end this journal now. May it bless any who read it.

Closing comments: I am amazed at the goodness and complexity of God. It seems that God has done a wondrous thing in cleansing the world of the wickedness of humanity, just as He did in the days of Noah. Back then God saved Noah by the ark. Now God has saved me by the homestead. Back then it was a flood. This time it was the Cremation Virus. Back then it was a mature man with three grown sons, and the mature man had been found righteous in the eyes of God. This time it was a confused and slightly broken young adult woman who wanted to be righteous in the eyes of God but who had failed miserably so far.

It has been less than a year since humanity was wiped out, but when I drive off my homestead I already see blades of grass growing up through tiny cracks in the vast network of pavement and concrete surfaces left by humankind. I can already see that the world is going to bounce back, all on its own, and begin to flourish again without the continuing damaging presence of mankind.

The food chain is in full operation around me but it no longer seems brutal or tragic, just natural. My senses are sharper--my awareness intensified--because I have come to realize that I am a prey animal to some of the larger carnivores. I am also a predator. With my human knowledge, my weapons, my fences and my vehicles, I'm probably a greater threat to the animals than they are to me.

My life philosophy now, based on all my experiences so far, is expressed in the words of Pre-Virus theologian A. W. Tozer (I think. It might have been Matthew Henry):

"All is wrong until God makes it right."

I engraved that saying onto a Manzanita burl and posted it at a fork in the dirt road that leads up to the summit of Browns

Mountain where my seldom used back exit road drops over toward Rush Creek Road.

God seems to be in the process of making it right.

Barbara set the worn journal down with a sigh of relief. She had thought she was finished with the journal a month ago but tonight she had picked it up and added the last part about her philosophy. She might pick it up again from time to time when there was more stuff that seemed important enough to add, but for now she was done with it once again.

It was only mid-afternoon, by her reckoning, but already starting to get dark. She was pretty sure it was now near the end of March. The shortest days of winter were past, but the long days of summer still seemed far in the future. The days were so short during the winter she had very little time for projects between sunup and sundown, so chores were often done after dark.

There had been three minor snowfalls, each lasting only a few days, and the lingering white coating on the meadow helped her vision after sundown. Even so, she liked longer days so she could do her evening chores before dark to preserve her flashlights and minimize her "footprint" by not shining lights.

Her animals were calm right now, so she was assured that all was well. She wrapped the journal in waxed paper and buried it under the extra sheets in the bottom of the trunk at the foot of her cot.

Her cold storage was packed full of food supplies scavenged from Redding and Weaverville. She now had two nanny goats and a billy goat sleeping in her new goat shed every night. She was pretty sure one nanny was bred. She also now had a small paddock and stall with a sturdy Kiger mustang stallion and a graceful, pregnant, Kiger mare living in it. She had a well-filled feed shed, and a large coop and covered pen for her small flock of Black Orpington chickens. Black Orpingtons were known to be hardy enough to endure cold weather.

Her animals were all from a neatly kept ranch she had found on the edge of Lewiston that hadn't been hit by predators. It had all kinds of livestock, and all the animals were so gentle they had obviously been well cared for. There was also a huge barn almost full of good quality hay.

The ranch was tucked up in a gully behind the school, so she had driven past it several times on her way to and from Redding without noticing it. Then one day she noticed the sleek and beautiful horses in the field and thought, *Having a good mountain horse to ride would help sometimes.*

The animals she didn't bring home with her from the ranch she released, so their chances of survival would be better. She had carefully closed the barn when she finished loading what she took, in order to preserve what was left of the hay and grain for her own use. It was only about a thirty-minute drive from her place, so she could almost have left it all there and made a daily trip. But she had already built her hay and feed barn, so she hauled about sixty bales home.

After she had put the journal away she walked over to the equipment shed and checked the fluids and tires on the Bobcat. There was a dust-blackened grease stain near one of the hydraulic connections, so she grabbed her wrench and tightened it. In the morning she would begin site preparation for a milking parlor. When she finished the milking parlor she would bring home a small Angus bull and a doe-eyed Jersey cow she had found on a small farm outside Weaverville. She liked goat milk for drinking, and her three Kiko goats were hardy little survivors. But the cattle would be a good self-sustaining source of beef if she could protect them from predators.

By the middle of the next morning she was churning up dust with the Bobcat. She enjoyed the acrid evergreen smell that wafted up as the Bobcat disturbed the deep bed of dried pine needles that covered the dirt and decomposed granite. *Even the dust is pleasant here in my homestead. Thank you, God.*

Before long she was scraping the top of a huge granite boulder just beneath the topsoil, right where she wanted to build the milking shed. The boulder's rectangular mostly flat top was about twenty feet long and some ten feet wide--way too big to be at all disturbed, or even impressed, by her little Bobcat tractor. She scraped around it until she had exposed the outer edge all the way around. An idea began to form in her head.

Okay, I'll build the milking parlor on the rock. It'll save me the work of pouring a slab. Solid granite will be better for their hooves and just as easy to clean.

Since all she had to do was arrange drainage, she had the site ready by noon. The underground boulder was a great blessing. She felt good about her accomplishment and decided to call it a day. Tomorrow morning she would start construction. This building, unlike the metal equipment shed, would be all post and beam. She had already hauled in a bunch of timbers and planks. She would need to drill down into the granite to anchor the corner posts. Her mind was alive with planning as she wrapped up her day's work.

That evening after dusk she built up her fire against the stubbornly lingering winter chill and enjoyed some pondering time over a cup of hot Echinacea tea. Crickets were chirruping in the darkness outside the glow of her fire, while a cold late winter breeze rudely jostled the tree branches over her homestead. She was thankful for the nearly constant breeze because it kept the mosquitos at bay in the meadow. Finally it was time to turn in.

She leaned forward to rise to her feet when she suddenly saw a pair of eyes glowing back at her, reflecting the light of her campfire! She could only see the eyes, but not the rest of the animal. What animal was that height? A tall wolf? A short bear?

Dang, my guns are all inside! I should always have one nearby. I gotta start remembering to always wear that holster!

The eyes moved a step closer. Her breath caught in her throat. She sat very still. She suddenly recognized the shape of a huge black dog as it quietly stepped forward into the circle of campfire light. Its eyes stopped glowing as it looked away from her and lay down near the fire, as if doing so was the most normal thing in the world. It was the biggest dog she had ever seen. Its head was huge! Standing, its shoulders had been as high as her own hips! And she was long legged! It was even taller than the large Great Dane her folks' neighbors had owned. And heavier. Its feet were huge and its legs were thick and strong looking. It's dark coat, more sable than black in the light of the fire, was short and coarse like an Airedale.

It seemed unafraid, and Barbara could understand why. There probably wasn't much to fear for a magnificent creature like this. She looked closer as it quietly lay there and noticed several things. It had already fallen asleep, it's flanks were hollow with hunger, it wore no collar, and she was a female.

"Friend," Barbara announced softly, her voice croaking from lack of use. "Your name is Friend."

When she spoke the name, the dog roused enough to raise her head as if to say, "Okay," then flopped back down as if exhausted.

"I bet you're hungry. Are you hungry?"

The dog raised her head again and stared at Barbara. The dog's tail swished gently back and forth across the dirt. The animal was obviously waiting.

"Uh huh, I thought so. Just a minute, I'll get you something."

Barbara had not yet stocked up on dog food *(No faith that I'd find a dog, I guess.)*, but she had the remains of a warm pot of baked beans with chunks of pork fat. She took off the lid and set the half full saucepan on the ground. Friend promptly stood up, stepped closer and hunched down over the warm food. As she gobbled down the first bite she lay down again with her paws on either side of the pan and continued eating from a prone position. Within a minute she had polished off every drop and licked the pot clean. She promptly got up and moved back over to her former spot near the fire, then flopped back down and closed her eyes to sleep.

"Okay! I have a dog. I hope she keeps guard as well as she looks like she could!"

Barbara slept better that night than she had in a long time. In the morning Friend was in the exact same spot, next to the cold fire pit, as if she hadn't moved all night. But huge paw prints in the dew-dampened dirt around the fire pit told Barbara the dog had gotten up and moved around at least a couple of times.

Good! I'm glad you're keeping an eye on things at night.

"Good girl, Friend," Barbara praised her.

At the sound of her name Friend got up and followed Barbara to the outhouse. *I really need to put a heater in here for the cold winter months! A vent fan and window would be nice too.* In good weather she still liked her old open-air latrine, but in winter she preferred the outhouse. Even though the seat was cold!

Friend did her business out in the brush while Barbara was in the outhouse. She followed Barbara to the creek and waded in, just downstream, to get a drink while Barbara rinsed the sleep from her eyes in the cold water.

"Friend, let's do the chores and have breakfast, then go get you some dog food."

Friend waited expectantly, following Barbara with her eyes while Barbara checked her pistol and strapped on the holster and gun. She "dogged" Barbara while she did her morning chores, curiously observing the various tame animals in their respective pens. After they had checked the perimeter, fed and watered the livestock and secured the generator for the day, Barbara fixed a big stack of pancakes for them both. Then she hooked up the trailer, called Friend into the Jeep and drove out Trinity House Road.

She would go into Weaverville for supplies today, instead of Redding. The empty Tops Supermarket, which had been Trinity County's only large grocery store, would surely have dog food and other dog stuff supplies.

As she drove around the last curve of "her road" before the steep straight slope down to the metal gate bar, Friend's head suddenly jerked up. She stared toward Browns Mountain Road and growled. Deciding instantly to trust the dog, Barbara skidded the Jeep to a stop. She visually swept left to right in short arcs. Nothing unusual. She held her breath and listened. Nothing over the sound of the Jeep motor. Even so, she reversed the Jeep and backed the trailer around the curve out of sight of the main road, shut off the Jeep motor and listened.

There was the sound of a motor! They both scrambled out of the Jeep and clambered up the bank above her road. Twenty yards up slope Barbara turned right and crept forward to a large decayed log that overlooked the gate and the short portion of Browns Mountain Road as far as the next curve in each direction. By the time she crouched down behind the log and pulled Friend down beside her she could hear a motor more clearly. Within seconds it grew much louder and then some sort of large vehicle came into view. It was driving slowly, and at the entrance to her road it veered toward her gate, which she had long since repaired and faithfully kept locked.

The strange vehicle looked like a huge cabover truck with an RV trailer, axles removed, mounted on the flatbed. From her vantage point above the road Barbara could see that the roof of the cab and sleeper berth was cut away like an open convertible. Openings were cut into the back wall of the sleeper and the front wall of the camp trailer so the driver could pass back and forth without having to climb down to the ground.

Whoever made it sure cared more about utility than aesthetics, she thought as she crouched behind the log. She absent-mindedly brushed at some large red ants crawling across the top of the log near her face. She jerked her gloved hand back out of sight behind the log and remembered to pull up her camo slouch hat from its usual place hanging between her shoulder blades on the chin string. It would be less visible than her blond hair. She kept her head low so just the hat and her eyes showed over the log. She held Friend down in a sitting position. Friend's head was as high as Barbara's. They both watched intently.

Barbara hoped the rig would back away from the gate and continue along Browns Mountain Road, but it stayed idling at her gate. Then the motor shut down. A man got out. Barbara was too far away to see his face clearly, but she could tell by his posture and stride that he was male. She watched as he studied the ground near the gate bar, then looked up the steep grade of Trinity House Road. Barbara and Friend were twenty yards above the road at a point about fifty yards from the gate, so they remained unseen, but Barbara groaned and whispered to Friend.

"He sees my tire tracks, Friend. I should have wiped the road with a branch after I drove through!"

Barbara's mind was now in hyper drive.

If so much of the world's population died, and so few are left on earth, how likely is it that another survivor would knock on my door way out here? Why IS he here, of all places, instead of passing through on Highway 299? He must be up to no good. If he gives me any reason to think he's dangerous I'll shoot him. I can't let him get the advantage. The odds would all be in his favor, except for my big pistol. Of course there's Friend, too. But I don't know what she'd do. She might decide she likes him better and leave me for him! Maybe he'll think the tracks are old and just drive away. He's rattling the padlock! Will it hold? It's holding! Oh no! He ducked under it! He's walking in! How far will he walk up this steep road? Will he go far enough to come around the curve and see my Jeep?

Barbara silently drew her pistol and waited. He strolled very slowly up the steep straight stretch of her road, his hands spread at his hips. His posture reminded her of an old west gunfighter walking toward a gun battle, of all things. And, not surprising, he was actually wearing two revolvers in low slung holsters. I guess he likes the persona.

He finally arrived at the top of the short grade, paused and looked around, then slowly made his way on around the curve.

Barbara and Friend were crouched behind the log, safely out of sight, but her Jeep was right there in plain sight in the middle of her road! He walked up to the Jeep, paused a moment, and then laid one hand on the hood.

It's warm. He knows it was just shut off. Now he's looking around!

He was close enough now for Barbara to see that he was only a kid, probably about fifteen, or even younger--not a grown man at all! Good! But he wore matching pearl handled revolvers in low slung holsters like an old west gunslinger. Barbara was pretty sure they were real--not cap pistols. He wore denims, cowboy boots and a cowboy hat. It suddenly occurred to Barbara that he really was just a kid, like Bobs, and he was playing cowboy! Only with real guns. Why not, since there was no one else around to make him feel embarrassed.

But, she thought, *even though he's just a kid, with those pistols he could still be very dangerous.*

Slowly Barbara stood up, her pistol at her waist but aimed toward the boy. She waited silently while he reconnoitered a circle, beginning downhill, back toward the gate from his position. Barbara was directly uphill, so he was passing the one eighty-degree point when his gaze swept across Friend and Barbara standing like statues.

Barbara's adrenaline was pumping, and time seemed to slow down. She was just close enough to see his pale blue eyes widen slightly, drop momentarily to her pistol, then return to her face. She did not see his hands move, but suddenly he had a pistol in each hand and blossoms of flame burst from both barrels!

Her thoughts raced! *How did he get those guns in his hands? His hands were empty, now they hold guns! He shot at me! I must shoot him! Why can't I? My gun is gone! Oh! Why is my gun flying through the air? Did I fling it? Why would I fling my gun? My hand hasn't moved! Why is my gun flying through the air if my hand didn't move? How is that possible? My hand hurts! He shouted at me! What did he say?*

"Hands up! I won't say it again!"

Why does he want me to put my hands up? She stood frozen, her right hand still reaching toward him as if she were still holding her revolver.

"Why," she asked? She couldn't completely suppress a tiny whimper as she suddenly clutched her aching right hand in her good left hand.

He hesitated, then answered in a tone of disgust.

"Cause you pointed a gun at me! Du-uh!"

Barbara was coming down from her sudden adrenaline rush.

"What?" she demanded incredulously, her voice hitting an embarrassing falsetto. "I pointed my gun at you because you are on my road! And you have guns! What the heck do you think I should have done?" She sounded shrill even to herself.

He looked down at his drawn guns, as if surprised to see that he was holding them. He quickly spun them back into the holsters. Like a Hollywood gunslinger. Then he grinned at her, very smugly.

"I'm a gunslinger! Why wouldn't I have guns?" He laughed. "You can put your hands down, lady!"

"I have to find my pistol. I dropped it, I guess."

"No, you didn't. I shot it out of your hand!"

"I dropped it," she insisted.

"Hah! Look! It's off to your right, where it landed when I shot it out of your hand. It probably won't work now, anyway, but I can fix it for you. I'm a gunsmith AND a gun slick!" He was still grinning, obviously not at all ashamed that he had hurt her hand and possibly ruined her nice pistol. She found it where he said it was, and it was broken.

"You did this," she asked, incredulously?

"I told you, I'm a gun slick! I practice a lot, and I never miss!"

Barbara picked up her broken pistol in her left hand, which didn't hurt, and awkwardly dropped it into the holster on her right hip. She took a quick look at her hand and there was no blood. But it felt like she had smashed it in a door.

She slowly made her way down the slope, pressing her right hand against her side and trying not to slip on the loose carpet of dry pine needles. It was so steep that if she slipped she would probably slide all the way down to the road on her butt! The kid had already made a fool of her. She sure didn't want to fall on her rear in front of him.

He waited near her Jeep until she stood on the road facing him. Friend had stayed pressed against Barbara's thigh as she carefully made her way down to the road. They came to a standstill near the boy and Friend let out a low menacing growl. It sounded so threatening even Barbara got a chill.

"Hey, I am a quick draw, ya know! If that monster comes at me it'll be the last thing he does!"

The boy backed up a little and Friend stepped forward, her hackles up.

Barbara laid her hand between Friend's shoulders, "It's okay, Friend."

"Whaddya mean 'okay'," the boy asked anxiously? "And I ain't your friend, at least not yet. It ain't okay for him to come at me! I ain't never shot no dog before, but I will!"

"She's a girl, and her name is Friend! I wasn't telling YOU it was okay! If I was talking to YOU I would have said Dummy," Barbara snarled!

Anger was starting to replace her feelings of panic and confusion.

How dare he charge up my road and shoot at me! "How dare you come up my road and shoot at me," she yelled at him!

"It was self-defense!"

"It was trespassing and armed entry," she shouted back!

This is just like arguing with Bobs! That thought softened her anger a little.

"So, what IS your name," she asked? I still sound churlish!

"It's Luke," he straightened his shoulders as he replied. "Luke Short."

"Luke Short is a western novelist, wise guy," she declared. "Are you really named after him or did you take the name after the plague?"

"I took the name," he admitted, then added, "Why not?"

"I don't care," she assured him. "I'll call you Luke if that's what you want."

"Okay. Uh, what's your name," he asked in return?

"It doesn't matter. You'll never see me again anyway. Just be on your way."

"Ha! At least you could invite me to lunch. Or I can take you to lunch back in that little town just north of here. Weaverburg, I think?"

"It's WeaverVILLE. And why should we have lunch? It's only nine o'clock in the morning."

"Ha! I've been up since before daylight. I'm hungry, that's why! Tell you what," he added, "my treat. Okay?"

"Ha ha," she sneered, though she was starting to find his spunkiness sort of appealing. "Everything's free now!"

"Yeah, I know. Neat, huh? C'mon. I won't ask to see your place. But I'd sure like to talk to someone who doesn't look dangerous." He grinned at her aching hand, but sounded a little wistful.

"Well, that's the first good reason you've mentioned. I haven't spoken to anyone besides Friend since the Cremation Virus struck," she agreed. She calculated for a moment. "Okay, Luke. I'll follow you in the Jeep. I need some things anyway. But you will NOT come back here. I live alone, and I like it that way. Capisce?"

"Ka-what," he asked, tilting his head to the side.

She felt a pang of loneliness for her dead brother, Bobs. He used to tilt his head to the side that same way.

"Capisce! It means 'do you understand?'," she explained.

"Oh. Okay. I do capisce," he avowed.

"No, you don't say it that way. You just say 'Yes, capisce'," she lectured.

"Were you a schoolteacher in your past life," he asked with an impudent grin?

"No," she grinned back. "But words are important, aren't they?"

"I guess so. Well, I'll see you in Weaverville!"

Luke led her to Johnson's Steak House at the Trinity Alps Golf Course clubhouse across the highway from Tops Super Market. He went into the kitchen like he owned it and fixed an early lunch, of sorts, from the food supplies left in their pantry and freezer, which against all odds was still running. After the meal they went into Tops so Barbara could load up a dozen large bags of dry dog food and grab a set of large dog dishes. While they were there she also grabbed a bale of pine shavings and a packet of water dish vitamins for the chicken coop. Luke was much shorter than Barbara, and slender, but he was stronger than he looked. He tossed the forty-pound bags into her Jeep with seeming ease. She was impressed.

"So, Luke, how old are you? Honestly."

"Aw, only fourteen. But I'm strong for my age," he bragged.

"I know. You tossed those bags easy. I was impressed."

His shoulders went back and he stood straighter.

"Well, babe, you impress me too," he leered at her.

She was instantly put off, but then burst out laughing. "Oh! You had me going there for a second," she told him, still chuckling.

"Hey, just because I'm younger doesn't mean you can make fun of me!"

"I'm not. Honest. But I'm almost twice your age and I'm a foot taller than you. There isn't a chance in the world we would ever get together, even though I like you. The thought just strikes me really funny. Okay?"

"Well. Okay."

He seemed disappointed but resigned. She was glad he got over his momentary delusion. That would have been a deal breaker, for sure.

"So, do you want to see where I live," she asked, after reconsidering?

"I thought it was some kinda big secret or something."

"Well, I reconsidered," she admitted. "We've gotten acquainted now, so it's okay. Do you want to follow me home?"

"Hey Toots, I'll follow you anywhere," he said, leering at her again.

"Okay, hold it! Before we go any further I want you to get something straight. My name is not Toots or Babe. It's Barbara. I'll call you Luke and you call me Barbara. Is that clear?"

"Okay, don't get your panties in a bunch," he wisecracked!

"Look, Luke. If we're going to be friends I need you to know a few things. First, I like my name and I don't like being called nicknames. Second, I don't like you to make references to my underwear. In fact, I would appreciate you being just a little more careful about how you speak to me in general, AND how you look at me. Those are ALL deal breakers. No second chance. Capisce?"

"Okay! Sheesh! I capisce," he hastily replied. "Sor-ry!"

"Good enough," she said. "Now, let's go. You follow me and I'll see you at my homestead."

PART TWO

CHAPTER ONE

ROOSTAFER

It was Rudy Christofer's best job ever--better than he ever thought he would have. His high school diploma and eight years of experience as a U.S. Navy radioman had not prepared him for an upward career path in civilian life. After his honorable discharge he took inventory of his skills and found he had very few to work with!

He felt that he was smart enough for most jobs, but after nearly a year of fruitless job search he had resigned himself to simple factory work. He faithfully showed up for work every day and worked hard at "the Aircraft," in East Hartford, Connecticut. For three and a half years he excelled as a Material Handler and survived three layoffs. He had kept his job through the first two layoffs but got demoted in the reshuffle during the third layoff. He found himself barely getting by on reduced wages as a night janitor, running a huge floor buffer in empty offices.

When the likelihood of another layoff loomed, he felt desperate enough to tackle the disgusting chore of job hunting once again. On impulse, driven by a sense of desperation, he applied for "an office job," as his wife put it, through a temp agency. He was surprised when they immediately hired him for a temp assignment at a prestigious "Fortune 100" insurance company that occupied a four-block-long nine story building.

It turned out that the one skill his navy radioman training had given him was the ability to type fast and accurately. He had never timed his typing, but the temp agency administered a typing test on an old IBM Selectric, exactly like the one he had used in the Navy, and he managed ninety-four words a minute with no mistakes! They said it was a new record for their office and sent him to a job in the typing pool of the huge insurance corporation. The typing pool wasn't a job to brag about, but it sure beat factory work and he hoped it might lead to something better. It soon did.

After only a month in the typing pool he was offered a very significant promotion to a permanent assignment as Administrative Assistant for one of the Vice Presidents, who apparently felt that having a male secretary was some kind of a status symbol. After all, the CEO had one, as did also the Chairman of the Board.

So now, after only four years of civilian life, he had his own office. It was actually the anteroom of his boss' office, but even so, he didn't have to share it with the tight-bloused, short-skirted gossips in the typing pool.

Rudy admired beautiful women, but his own wife, Willie (short for Wilhelmina), happened to be drop-dead gorgeous. His married love life was torrid, so Rudy didn't appreciate the blatant displays of physical charms presented by the pretty twits in the secretarial pool.

The only coworker he sort of liked was a married woman named Lynette. She was pretty, but dressed more modestly and didn't natter, natter all day. She worked fast and was articulate. Best of all, Rudy was sure that she didn't fool around at work.

Rudy had met Lynette's husband, Joe, one afternoon when he came and had lunch with her in the company cafeteria. Rudy and Joe might have become good friends if Lynette wasn't so good looking. Rudy and Lynette might have enjoyed a good friendship at work, but it probably would have been misunderstood by the other employees. It simply wasn't safe to become close friends with an attractive member of the opposite sex at work. Any misunderstanding among their coworkers could sully her reputation and negatively impact both their jobs.

And, of course, there was Willie. Men always noticed her even though she seemed unaware of her effect on them. Rudy had plenty of opportunities to feel jealous at the endless string of men who came on to Willie, but he chose to trust her explicitly and implicitly.

Willie, on the other hand, didn't seem to trust Rudy much. It wasn't because of anything Rudy had done, but because Willie's dad had kept a girlfriend for many years while staying married to Willie's mom. Everyone seemed to have known about it except Willie's mom.

One day Willie came to pick Rudy up after work and saw him joking around with Lynette outside the building. Willie was visibly agitated and interrogated him all the way home.

Rudy felt that he and Willie were an unusual couple. His own dominant characteristic was being average. He was average height, average weight, average income, average looks. He had always resonated with the term "mediocrity" in the old Simon and Garfunkel song Homeward Bound. Mediocrity was familiar and safe--people had low expectations of mediocre people. But down deep he secretly envied people who were exceptional at something.

The one exception in Rudy's otherwise mediocre life was his wife's extreme beauty. She was in the top five percent in beauty, charm and sensuality. She had style. He was amazed that a woman like her had married a man like him.

Rudy was crazy about Willie. Before their wedding he had been turned on by her shapely body and beautiful face. He felt incredibly lucky to have somehow won her affection. Their honeymoon had been the start of a wild sequence of amazing sexual encounters that kept him sated and grateful. Married life was incredible--at first--when it was mostly the sex.

But as time went by he discovered that being married to a real hottie had it's real drawbacks. Other men were always checking her out, which got old real fast. Some of the guys who fawned over her were handsome and successful. When she would notice some testosterone junkie's fancy car, Rudy would wonder, "I'm so average—is she tempted?"

This plus the fact that she always seemed to doubt his faithfulness eventually caused him to begin to wonder about her faithfulness! He noticed that lots of guys seemed to assume she would be willing to cheat on her husband, or at least fool around a little! Were they right? Was Rudy possibly missing some clues? Rudy started to feel insecure about his marriage. He was so careful to be completely faithful, but she still seemed to suspect him of cheating on her.

To make matters worse, Willie thought it was funny if Rudy acted jealous toward the men who sniffed after her like dogs. What did that imply, if anything? Could she be covering up?

Lately their marriage had begun to be characterized by a growing mistrust and wounded feelings on both their parts. She seemed to have begun to think less of him in subtle ways, including in their lovemaking. Since Rudy already saw himself as mediocre, her seeming agreement with that perception really made him doubt himself.

At the office, in sharp contrast, Rudy was highly respected and greatly appreciated by his boss, his coworkers and his subordinates. His boss had even started sending Rudy to specialized corporate training sessions. Everyone knew that Rudy was being groomed for advancement.

At home his marriage seemed a mess, but at work his career seemed great with everything going his way. He was friends with the beautiful Lynette, and some thought they were more than friends which didn't hurt his status, even though it was not true.

Rudy's boss started bringing Rudy with him to the corporate Board meetings and Rudy became friends with Alfred, the Administrative Assistant to the Chairman of the Board. The two of them were soon the "golden boys" of the Board of Directors. Rudy and Alfred were both expected to someday ascend to prominence in the company, since they were both on the fast track at the will of upper management.

Alfred, who had been with the company for several years, said that the current Chairman of the Board had once been the Personal Assistant to the Chairman. Their friendship grew as the weeks passed. One day Alfred confided to Rudy that he was gay, but no one else in the company knew. Rudy, in turn, confided his marriage problems to Alfred.

Both their jobs required absolute discretion to safeguard sensitive corporate information, and each of them was completely trusted by his boss, so they found it easy to trust each other. Rudy was the only one at work who knew Alfred's secret fears, and Alfred was the only one who knew Rudy's secret fears.

Rudy's home life continued to deteriorate. Despite all the positive affirmation at work he was often depressed. How had his marriage ever gotten into such a mess? How could he have been so shallow and distracted by her body that he never noticed her jealous nature and her magnetism to other men? Lately Rudy had become aware that all of his relationship stress had begun to diminish his sexual performance with Willie.

Now he wondered, *'All these other guys want her, why don't I want her like I used to?'*

Deep inside he felt Willie was partly right in her constant criticism--he was only mediocre, after all. Why should she have to be satisfied with his average-ness, in bed or anywhere else? She was exceptional; didn't she deserve an exceptional husband?

And why wouldn't she be jealous? Didn't he secretly enjoy seeing the bare thighs and cleavage in the typing pool at work? Didn't he secretly enjoy the huge billboard pictures of women in lingerie along the freeway? Rudy had been scrupulously faithful to Willie in his actions, but in his thoughts he sometimes enjoyed wild flights of imagination.

After all, wasn't it true that half the men at work were divorced, remarried and already cheating on their second or third wife? And wasn't the secretarial pool almost a bimbo pool for some of the corporate executives and mid-level managers to shop for their next score?

No wonder Willie was jealous. She should be! But Rudy knew deep inside that none of those things excused the strain in his marriage. And now her increasingly frequent innuendos of disrespect made him resent her even more.

He began to avoid her by working late. Hoping it wouldn't be too obvious, he enrolled in an evening course three nights a week at the university. Willie was innately suspicious, however, and figured out that he was avoiding her. It became yet another matter for her to criticize.

Her increased complaining made Rudy even more pessimistic about their future. It was a vicious downward spiral that could not continue indefinitely. Something eventually had to give.

At the annual company Christmas party it all fell apart. Someone had spiked the punch and Willie liked the taste. She was already tipsy when several men urged her to drink more.

Willie gave herself to the booze and the loud music and the circle of admirers. She soon became the life of the party. Some of the other wives dragged their husbands away and left early.

The men who remained, mostly single guys or unaccompanied married men, gravitated toward the life of the party. Willie was totally wound up and Rudy couldn't get her to leave. It was almost like a kind of sexual hysteria.

She was wearing a low cut, clingy dress for the formal occasion, and it was completely normal for her to look sexy. But because it was all coworkers and their spouses Rudy hadn't expected any more than the usual male flirting. The spiked punch was unexpected.

Willie was buzzed, now, and feeling 'in the mood.' She danced with one man, then another, then another. She put her arms around their shoulders and danced slow, regardless of the tempo of the music. She pressed against them and squirmed and let them take whatever liberties they were brave enough to try.

Rudy fretted on the sidelines as he saw his coworkers surreptitiously grope his wife. He didn't know what to do. Should he start punching guys out? The men were drunk, too, and later they probably wouldn't even remember why he punched them in the face!

Should he physically drag her away? She would probably resist, making a scene. It would be even more embarrassing than it already was. There just didn't seem to be any good option.

Finally, Rudy sidled over to where Albert was sipping a glass of punch in casual conversation with the only other man in the corporation that Rudy knew for sure was also gay. He caught Albert's attention and discreetly gestured with his head. Albert followed him over to a quiet spot off to the side.

"Albert, I guess you've noticed what Willie is doing. I just don't know what to do, but I can't stand to just watch her be humiliated like this. I'm heading home."

Albert nodded in sympathy, "Sorry dude, but I have no advice to offer you. I understand, though. Want me to call you when she's ready to leave?"

"Yeah, I guess. It's probably more like IF she's ready to leave. At this point it seems like she may be the last to leave the party."

"Well, Rudy, it could be worse—she might leave with someone else. Like I said, sorry."

Rudy nodded and headed for the door, knowing that things would probably get worse and not wanting to witness it. Things did get worse, and right away.

Just before he reached the exit he turned for a last look. He couldn't help himself. Willie was sandwiched between two men, dancing slow and sensuously with her arms upraised. They both had their hands on her torso. Several other men crowded in close until all Rudy could see was the top of her head. It was a one-woman party, with Willie giving the men whatever they wanted.

Sick at heart, Rudy turned and left for home.

He had been home about thirty minutes when Albert called to tell him she had just left with several guys, two from Rudy's department. Nonplussed, and wondering how he would face his coworkers on Monday, Rudy got the shower ready for her, ready to help her into it to start sobering her up when she got home. But she didn't come home at all that night.

He spent the long night on the couch, wide awake, watching the door, and thinking about his situation. By morning he had reached a conclusion: there was just no way he could face his coworkers after so many of them had seen his wife compromised and humiliated. Rudy would be the laughingstock of the company—the cuckhold! IF he stayed, that is. He had to leave.

Rudy didn't even know who all, or how many, might have actually participated in her humiliating sexual debauchery. Obviously they had no respect for him, to treat his wife like that even while he was present at the party. Rudy felt that he too had been humiliated. And he had failed to protect her virtue or her reputation. What kind of man was he? Surely there must have been something he could have done to stop it. The whole thing was just too much to deal with.

Bottom line, he absolutely could not work there anymore. His promising career had crashed and burned. His marriage, too. There wasn't enough positivity in his marriage to offset the enormity of this disaster. This whole marriage mess was simply too wrecked to salvage.

Suddenly, in the midst of his doldrums, as he wallowed at the bottom of the dark pit of despair, Rudy finally rebelled against his feelings of helpless mediocrity.

Desperately, he cried aloud, "NO! I reject this! I have options! This is not IT for me!"

He physically shook himself like a dog, mentally shaking off his despair and disgust. He made himself physically turn around and face the other way, mentally doing a full turn and facing a new and different direction.

He spent the rest of the morning forming and rejecting plans until he figured out what he would do. By the time Willie came dragging in, late in the afternoon, Rudy's plan was finalized. She went straight to bed without saying a word. He didn't speak either. All that evening he studiously avoided her. He slept on the couch again.

CHAPTER TWO

THE ROAD

Rudy got up early, before Willie awoke. The apartment was quiet except for her snoring. He didn't look in on her. Instead, he silently showered, dressed in his suit as if for work, poured a travel mug of fresh coffee to take with him, and left the apartment for the last time. He hoped he would never see her again.

It was earlier than usual, still dark outside. A few small piles of a recent late snowfall remained along the sidewalk where plows had left deep mounds that had melted down. The air was brisk but clear. The sky was slate gray with high clouds. A taxi slowly trolled past, looking for early passengers. He hailed it.

He didn't go to work. Instead, he went to breakfast. At eight o'clock when his bank opened he was at the door, briefcase in hand. He was their first customer. The sophisticated Assistant Manager raised a questioning eyebrow but didn't ask any questions as Rudy withdrew every penny of cash from the nest egg he had diligently accumulated. He only withdrew the cash.

Before he left the bank Rudy signed a power of attorney authorizing Willie to access and control the small portfolio of stocks he had acquired, which already had a considerable value. He didn't want her to suffer after he left. She probably couldn't help the way things were.

When he walked out of the bank he was financially totally divested and unencumbered. In his briefcase he carried slightly over a hundred thousand dollars in one-hundred-dollar bills. His diligent saving and reinvesting had paid off enough to generously fund the decision he had made during the night.

He had decided that he would simply disappear. He would abandon his marriage, his career, his home, his car, his fashionable office wear, his friends, everything. He would burn all his bridges and make a new start somewhere else. He was young enough to change his identity and have a different life. Maybe someday he would have a good marriage with someone else.

He would leave no trail for Willie or anyone else to follow. He would break all ties to the heartbreak of his past. He would start fresh. He knew that he was running away, and he didn't care.

He would go west, far from the stodgy New England world of traditions, social pressures and relationship disasters. His only concession to courtesy or protocol was to call his good friend and former coworker, Alfred.

"Hey, buddy, this is Rudy," he spoke quietly into Alfred's voice mailbox when Alfred didn't pick up.

"I'm leaving. Forever. I'm serious. I can't deal with Willie or the job after that party. I don't want to be followed or traced, but I want someone to know I haven't been killed or kidnapped, so I'm telling you. But only you. I signed over my investment portfolio to Willie so she won't be left high and dry. You can tell her if she doesn't think of it. I don't want her to suffer. Sorry to dump this on you, but you're my only good friend. I trust your judgement to handle this information however seems best to you. I really won't be back. Ever. Thanks, buddy, for being here for me."

He'd been plagued his whole life by being average, ordinary. But this course he had now chosen was definitely not ordinary. This would be the first of many extraordinary choices he had determined he would make from now on. He would, first of all, disappear thoroughly and well.

After he had called Alfred he erased all data from his cell phone and left it in the grass under the park bench where he'd been sitting. Then he walked away--both physically and symbolically.

As of now he was a new man with a new life. He would stay below the radar from now on. He had thought it out very carefully in the last several hours and he believed that he knew how to do it. Every purchase would always be cash--no plastic, ever again. He would camp out. He would make his own meals. He would not depend on anyone, or let anyone depend on him.

A Gypsy--that's what he'd be, a solo vagabond. His future was a blank page to write on, and he had figured out lots of things he never wanted written on it.

From the bank he went straight to the nearest sporting goods store and browsed thoughtfully for nearly an hour, making the clerk nervous. He brightened up when Rudy began picking out purchases. By the time he finished there was a large pile of goods at the register for the increasingly excited clerk to ring up.

He began with a titanium framed backpack, which Rudy packed right there at the cash register, item by item as the clerk rang them up. He also purchased two slim but sturdy canvas fanny packs. After all his other purchases had been rung up he transferred his remaining cash into them in the men's room. He left his briefcase in a stall with his monogram torn off.

Before he exited the men's room he changed into a new long sleeved chambray shirt, new khaki trousers, and his new (expensive) hiking boots. His newly purchased clothing was all in neutral earth tones and included seven pairs of socks and underwear.

He packed everything else into the backpack, which was olive drab. In his pack he had a surprisingly expensive ultra lightweight sleeping bag, a thin foam sleeping pad, an inflatable pillow that folded and stowed nicely, a small mess kit with a tin coffee cup and a pot for heating water, a jar of instant coffee and a dozen MRE's (Meals Ready to Eat).

He had also purchased a .38 Special in a shoulder holster, which he had put on, fully loaded, under his outer shirt. A box of ammo was in the backpack. He had also bought a hunting knife with a compass and waterproof matches hidden inside the handle. The sheath had straps to fit around his ankle under his pants leg. He put it on. Last, he had purchased a sturdy walking stick. He hadn't been able to think of anything else he would need, but he was sure more would occur to him during his first few days of travel.

Out the door he went. He walked west on Park Road until it became Tunxis Road, then continued on after it became Middle Road. After awhile he cut over to Farmington Avenue. The day was cool, but he worked up a sweat. It took the rest of the afternoon just to reach the suburb of Farmington, west of Hartford, and he was already in unfamiliar territory, so his first additional purchase was a map. While paying for the map he realized the "convenience store" he was in was essentially a travel store, so he looked around. He bought and added to his pack two bottles of drinking water, a bar of soap in a travel case, a washcloth, a small bottle of Ibuprofen and a latrine kit (roll of toilet paper and box of Ziploc bags).

From his new map he discovered that, at least on paper, the nation's infrastructure did not seem very hiker friendly. The law prohibited pedestrians on Interstates, which would have been the most logical hiking route but would have been the first place a private investigator would look for him. The surface streets and roads would be best, but it took some planning to determine a good route to go on foot. Eventually he figured out a workable route along Farmington Avenue to Route 10 which would get him the fifteen miles to Plainville. By the time he worked out a suitable route it was almost dark. He was only a few miles from the sporting goods store he started from, he was already sore and tired, it was still winter, for Pete's sake, and there was no place here to camp!

Just this once I'll have dinner at a burger joint and take a room in a motel.

Early the next morning he ate a fast-food breakfast and resumed walking west. It took him all morning to walk the fifteen miles to Plainville. By the time he got there his back and hips and knees all hurt. His feet were chafed in his expensive boots and his back was developing several raw spots under his expensive backpack. He was tired and hungry, and it seemed he had drawn curious stares all day long. If Willie hired a detective to track him down there were plenty of people who could say they had seen him heading west. He spent the afternoon sitting on a park bench nursing his aches and pains near the shoreline at Hamlin Pond Park in Plainville. Just before dark he crawled into some thick brush and made a cold camp.

A cold camp, he had learned while chatting with the clerk at the sporting goods store, meant no fire. No fire meant no hot food. And no coffee in the morning. He discovered that a cold MRE was actually worse than going hungry. But he forced himself to gag it down anyway, for the nourishment. He had a nightcap of two Ibuprofen pills and crawled into his new sleeping bag on his new sleeping pad on the very lumpy ground that had looked so smooth when he had arrived just before dark. Surprising himself, he slept the deep sleep of physical exhaustion.

In the morning he awoke cold and stiff and sore all over. There was no option but to get up and get started. He carefully hid his stuff in the bushes and limped to the convenience store across from the park. He savored a breakfast burrito and large cup of black coffee, then took care of his morning business in the restroom. He went back to his camp, reloaded his backpack and hoisted it into place with a groan. He readjusted the weight to ride next to his sore spots rather than on them, and again started walking.

He hurt, but he kept going. That day he followed Route 10 through Southington to Milldale, then veered westerly on Route 322, crossing under Interstate 84 which would be his landmark to follow west. He couldn't legally walk on the interstate, but he could follow it's direct course along the surface roads that ran parallel.

On the eastern outskirts of Waterbury he looked for a place to surreptitiously camp in Hamilton Park. Surprisingly, which Rudy would discover was often the case on his journey west, the most likely camping spot he could find was in the adjacent Old St. Joseph's Cemetery. Unlike city parks, cemeteries seldom had any evening or nighttime visitors, so they were not lit up at night. They also typically had nice green lawns, lots of trees and shrubbery, and often had water faucets that were not shut off.

It took him all the next day to hike to Southbury.

Three days of hard hiking to cover what I used to drive in an hour, he thought. I'm really in pitiful shape. Oh well. I'm not on a schedule. And if I want to stay below the radar, this will probably work. Things can always be worse, someone once said! I could possibly even be more sore than I am. Nah! No way! But I coulda been mugged or robbed sleeping out like this and no one would ever know. I have money, my health, and lots of reasons to keep on. I..can..do..this!

And so Rudy continued putting one foot in front of the other along byways that more or less paralleled Interstate 84, speaking to no one and finding hidden places to camp. Day after day, ever westward he hiked in silence. He made it through Danbury and into New York State, onward through Brewster, Newburgh and Middletown. He crossed into Pennsylvania without knowing when. Each day he planned his route for the day, then started walking, morning to evening, until he reached his planned destination for the day. There he stopped and set up camp for the night.

In an undefined rural Pennsylvania community named Quicktown he veered left and headed southwest on Madisonville Road to bypass the Scranton area, camping for the night at Nesbitt Reservoir, The next day he followed Highway 11 southwest along the Susquehanna River through Pittston and Kingston. Near a small community called Lime Ridge he walked under Interstate

80, which would be his new route guide all the way to Salt Lake City.

In Danville he shifted over to Highway 45 until he reached State College, Pennsylvania. There he veered northwest on Highway 322 into Shippenville, where he had to veer southwest on Highway 208. That took him almost all the way to Youngstown, Ohio. He had made it almost a third of the way across the country in only seven weeks.

Somewhere along the way the soreness had gradually left his legs and feet as he toughened to the rigors of non-stop walking. He got better at quickly recognizing likely camping spots. His whiskers grew into a full beard that he discovered was slightly gray. His longish brown hair grew long enough to tie back into a ponytail.

His expensive boots had given out after only two weeks, so he had replaced them with a pair of cheap sneakers from a K-Mart store. The cheap sneakers were more comfortable and lasted longer than the expensive boots, probably helped by the fact that he had slimmed down a lot. Less weight on his feet.

His ultimate destination, carefully selected after mulling it over while he walked, would be Portland, Oregon. Interstate 80 would lead him as far as Salt Lake City where he would veer northwest, following Interstate 84 once again, on into Portland. The days and weeks passed as he walked. As problems arose he solved them or walked away. His old life was in the past. This was his new life--walking! He was into the cadence of walking. He could stride out, arms swinging, and make the miles roll beneath his feet.

He reveled in the knowledge that he was free to make of his life whatever he chose to make of it. In fact, he decided one day, he would choose a new name. Rudy Christopher, the person he used to be, had a background and a personal history. He wanted to forget all that; totally disconnect from it. So, he would no longer be Rudy Christopher.

Maybe a combination name, like Rufer. No, people will think I mean Roofer. I'd have to explain it, which would draw attention. It needs to be sort of forgettable. Something odd enough, but not too odd, so people will say 'Oh, okay' and then forget it. Roostafer! That's it. Short enough, different enough, no need to spell it for anyone. From now on, Roostafer is my name.

Near Joliet, Illinois he veered south on Highway 6, which he followed for more than a week. He had been on the road for a total of about fifteen weeks when he reached the little crossroads town of Shannahon, which had a sprawling state park he could camp in. Highway 6 crossed a bridge over a sluggish stream called DuPage River and just north of the west end of the bridge a small inlet led into the dense trees. He found a secluded sandy beach hidden by foliage at the mouth of the small inlet.

He had not spoken to anyone for nearly three months except brief conversations in convenience stores where he often stopped to buy bottled water, or, on the one occasion, more Ibuprofen. That evening he had his first opportunity to try out his new name.

"Roostafer" had just set up his little campsite when he heard rustling in the nearby bushes. He quickly went on full alert ("panic"), his hand fumbling for the pistol he'd been leaving in his backpack! Two teenage boys clambered out of the thick growth and stopped in startlement at sight of him. Both boys were taller than Rudy, and the larger of the two remained silent while the other took the lead.

"Hey, sorry man! Didn't know anyone was here."

Roostafer's seldom used voice cracked at first.

"No (squawk)......Ahem, no problem. But I'm camping here and I don't want company, so….." There was a pregnant silence.

"Oh, well, we uh…. Ya know. Not too many places we can do our thing, ya know," the smaller one sort of whined.

Surprised at how dense they seemed, Roostafer pushed a little harder.

"Beat it," he snarled, putting on a fierce scowl.

Surprisingly, they didn't leave. They didn't even seem scared.

"Ah, come on, man. We ain't hurtin' anybody. We'll get in trouble if we smoke our weed anyplace else," the little guy argued. "Hey," he continued, "We'll share it with you if you let us hang out here awhile!"

With that, Rudy (Roostafer! he thought to himself) paused to think. *Is there a downside? If they're smoking pot they sure won't want to tell anyone. I haven't smoked any weed in a long time. Would I dare get high and lower my guard with these two punks?* After thinking it over he gave in and nodded at the two of them to have a seat on the small log across his tiny fire from the rock he had been sitting on. After they were seated he tried to strike up a conversation.

"So, what are your names?"

"Uh, well, uh…..." the smaller guy stammered.

"Hey, I don't really care. I'm just passing through. Just being polite, okay?"

"Well, uh, okay I guess. I'm Willie. My friend here doesn't say much, but he's Mikey. What's yours?"

Rudy had been waiting for that moment, though he hadn't realized it. But he savored it.

"Willie, huh," he growled? "I knew a woman by that name." Oops, I better not blab about my past! "Mine's Roostafer," he added, wondering how they would respond.

Neither of them seemed to take notice in any unusual way. Roostafer was pleased. The name will work.

He politely declined to take a hit when they lit and passed their first joint, then spent the next hour hypocritically lecturing them on the evils of drugs and alcohol. They meekly took it from him, which surprised Roostafer. Before this he had never seemed to have any credibility with young people. Now these two were hanging on his every word. Apparently being a bushy bearded transient traveling through town was some kind of glamorous to the two teenagers. The ponytail probably helped.

This whole thing is working, Rudy mused.

After a couple hours the boys left and Rudy immediately moved his camp deeper into the brush, back from the stream. He didn't want to give up the nice access to water, but his location at the water's edge was compromised. The sandy riverbed soil stretched back into the bushes, so he still had a soft bed that night. No one disturbed him and he left early in the morning, relieved. He had a fleeting thought that maybe he ought to get a dog but decided against it. Two days later he broke out in a poison oak rash and had to find a pharmacy to buy some Caladryl! It seemed there was always a downside to everything!

Roostafer walked west all through the spring and summer months. Every morning he awoke rested and ready for whatever adventure the day might hold. He hadn't felt so good since he was a kid. His body was lean, his legs strong, his lungs clear. Life was good.

The hot days of summer eventually passed, fall's cooler days were almost gone, and winter was banging on the door by the time Roostafer arrived in Oregon after a little more than eight months of walking. He thoroughly enjoyed the Columbia River gorge as he followed side roads westward across the top of the state. He spent a very comfortable night in Biggs Junction, on the bank of the river in a campground with heated restrooms with running water--both cold AND hot!

The steep rocky bluffs of the Columbia Gorge hemmed in the highway so there was no room for an access road, but a railroad ran parallel and was good for hiking. When he walked into Troutdale three days past Biggs he was tempted to set up a semi-permanent camp in Delta Park at the mouth of the Sandy River. It was so beautiful.

But the thought of cold winter nights along the river was daunting, so after a week of fair weather camping *(Probably Indian Summer, he thought)* he packed up and resumed his hike toward Portland, following Highway 30 through the suburbs. Guided by his now ragged map he veered onto N.E. Sandy Boulevard, and then onto Burnside, which seemed to be the central route, since the horizontal streets north of it were N.E. or N.W., while the ones south of it were S.E. or S.W. His hunch played out and he entered Old Town Portland almost exactly ten months after he left Hartford, Connecticut. His actual arrival in the City of Portland was uneventful, anticlimactic after the expectations he'd built up during his long journey. He checked into a cheap hotel near Old Town and sacked out.

CHAPTER THREE

THE RESIDENCE

His first day in Old Town Portland was gray, cold and wet. A capricious wind whipped around the buildings and sidewalks, erratically tossing leaves and ruining the cute little umbrellas of several female pedestrians. Roostafer was surprised to see so many people on foot--from businessmen in suits and waterproof dusters to office girls in nylons, high heels and opaque raincoats over their sweaters. Sprinkled among the workers hurrying to their jobs there were occasional indigents--homeless, street people, down-and-outers like himself. Many of the homeless were panhandling. They didn't hold a sign; they just spoke to total strangers who happened to be walking by on the sidewalk.

"Hey, buddy, got any spare change?" Or, "Ma'am, could you spare a quarter?"

In a few short minutes he saw a dozen or so pedestrian and pedestrienne passers-by pause, dig out money and hand it to a homeless person before hurrying on. A few even smiled and said, "Good luck!" This was a city that seemed to care about the "have-nots." But he didn't want to make a hasty assumption and then find out the hard way that he had been wrong. So he bought a fresh set of clothes at a nearby Good Will store, rented a room for a week at a side street hotel. After a nice shower and a good night's sleep he spent a whole day walking the streets--thinking of it as "street life orientation." He occasionally bought a few odds and ends so he could carry purchases and seem legitimate. By evening he had a pretty good idea of what-all was where-all in Old Town Portland.

The next morning, hair tied back and beard combed, and wearing his new clothes, he entered a small bank and opened a new account. He deposited all that remained of his stake--still over ninety-nine thousand dollars and change. When the bank clerk pressed him for a full name he divided it up as Roos Tafer and invented a Social Security number, hoping they wouldn't check it out. Apparently they didn't, since the process was successful. He now had a bank account that he could draw on any time for ready cash.

He wasn't sure what he might want to do yet, but for now living on the street looked like a good option. By the end of the week he had made friends with a couple of homeless people and had set himself up with a slightly damaged and disreputable looking shopping cart to carry his growing bunch of "stuff." He then checked out of the cheap hotel and joined the surprisingly populous ranks of the city's homeless.

On the west bank of the Willamette River under the Burnside Bridge there was a small homeless camp in the bushes adjacent to a nicely landscaped Japanese War Memorial. The regulars numbered around a dozen, with the total sometimes swelling to as many as fifteen or dipping to as few as six or seven.

After several weeks passed and he had successfully withdrawn funds several times at obscure Automated Teller Machines, he decided his bank account and secret identity were safe. As he had hoped, he was free to appear penniless, but he had money to fall back on if necessary. He then began to fully immerse himself in the homeless culture, panhandling for a couple of hours each day for lunch money and one beer, which he drank in the evening. At night he sacked out, on the ground, on a small mattress of stacked flattened cardboard, in the homeless camp under Burnside Bridge.

He had figured out a routine he could follow in order to get by without a job. A hole-in-the-wall greasy spoon cafe two blocks from the train station served a free breakfast and coffee to a few, pre-selected (polite and friendly), homeless persons each weekday morning. Roostafer got himself included by secretly slipping the cook a hundred dollar bill and whispering, "Let me know when it's used up." A week later he paid another hundred.

Saturdays and Sundays did not involve breakfast and morning coffee, unless he spent some of his panhandled money. But seven evenings a week he enjoyed a free supper at the rescue mission near the train station. The only cost was sitting through a preaching service presented by various local churches who took turns. The food was typically bland and simple, but nutritious and plentiful. They also provided basics such as aspirin, soap and toothpaste, and a book lending library.

Roostafer was surprised and pleased to realize that healthwise, after nearly a year on the road he felt pretty good. He had leveled out at a healthy one hundred fifty pounds--less than he had weighed since about age fifteen. He was leaner and healthier than he had ever been as an adult. Walking all the way across the country and walking the streets of Portland all day was darn good exercise. His bushy beard and long hair concealed all of his face except cheekbones, eyes and forehead. His head hair was dark brown, but his beard and mustache were salt and pepper. He had begun to feel a little vain about his bushy beard and long hair, but otherwise he carefully maintained a nondescript appearance to blend in with the other un-noticeable street people.

On the coldest nights Roostafer would go back and rent a room in the cheap hotel, but otherwise he had "his spot" under the Burnside Bridge. He had no idea that in a few weeks his life would suddenly and drastically change, late one night, under that historic old bridge.

But even before that, something even more drastic, and wonderful, happened. He was at the mission one evening, patiently listening to the obligatory sermon in order to get the free meal, when the speaker's words suddenly penetrated his wandering mind. The guy was talking about getting a new identity!

At first Roostafer panicked, thinking he had been somehow found out! But then he realized the man was speaking about religion, not about Rudy Christopher's secret past. But the man said it wasn't religion, it was a relationship.

What?

The preacher went on to say that when a person established a relationship with Jesus that person became new; old things passed away, everything became new. The idea suddenly seemed to begin to take root in Roostafer's heart. It sounded like what he wanted, so he began to listen. For the first time he heard the real Gospel--the good news that even though every person was a lost, dirty rotten sinner (*I know. That's so true,* Rudy thought.), Jesus, who never sinned, took the punishment of death for every sinner. If anyone called on the name of Jesus for salvation from the punishment of his own sins, Jesus' death on the cross would be applied to that sinner who would receive the eternal life that Jesus deserved. A new life. A new start. A new identity as a child of God. It was amazing! Incredible!

Roostafer took it personally, and heard, really heard, for the very first time in his life, that God loved him so much that He gave His only son, Jesus, to pay for Roostafer's sins so Roostafer could be forgiven and have eternal life. At the end of the sermon Rudy Christofer walked down the aisle with a couple of other men, knelt to pray with the preacher, and was gloriously saved! When he rose to his feet he felt a thousand pounds lighter! His guilt had been removed! The preacher was right--he was a new creature! He could feel the change!

The preacher talked to Roostafer and the others for a while after the meeting dismissed. He gave each of them a New Testament of their own and wrote their name inside the front cover. The preacher, whose name Roostafer never learned, urged him to read a chapter every morning, asking "what does this mean?" and then "what does this mean to me?" and then "what does this tell me about God?" and finally "what does this tell me about myself?". He made the men quickly memorize those four questions. Then he urged them to make it a habit to talk to God in prayer--just pretend like God was an invisible person standing there and simply talk to Him. Roostafer, along with the other men, promised that he would.

The very next day, a rare sunny winter day in Portland, Roostafer started his morning by reading the first chapter of the Gospel of John. Then he read the chapter in Proverbs that corresponded to the day's date, a practice the preacher had told him he ought to keep all the rest of his life. After breakfast, during his morning stroll around Portland, he talked to God out loud in prayer and asked God to direct his steps, exactly as the preacher had told him he should. Of course, he prayed with his eyes open, since he was walking, and he noticed that people gave him a wider path than usual. Apparently walking and praying aloud seemed a little crazy. Just after he had said "amen" he noticed a very curious thing.

He hadn't been paying very close attention to where he was walking, and he happened to find himself standing in front of the main entrance to a nine story office building on S.W. 4th Avenue. Directly across the street was a twelve-foot-high stone retaining wall that extended the entire block between St. Michael's Church and Portland Plaza. The whole square block atop the wall was a paved parking lot, and scrub willows had grown up along the sidewalk almost dead center in the wall. Just showing, peeking out from behind the small willow thicket, was the arched brick top of a plank doorway set into the wall. The streets on either side of the parking lot sloped uphill away from the Willamette River. The parking lot itself was level with the next street up the hill and had two driveways facing S.W. 5th Avenue. The east side of the parking lot, facing the river, was elevated atop the thick concrete wall. The door's existence in the wall didn't make sense.

Why would anyone put a door in a retaining wall under a parking lot? And such a door! It looks like it's made of oak planks like in the old days. The top is arched instead of square, so it was more decorative than utile. The hinges look like they were handmade by a blacksmith long ago--so ornate. It looks like it could be very old. Lord, is this You directing my steps?

A well-dressed elderly man "just happened" to come walking by and saw Roostafer staring at the door.

"Do you know anything about that door, young man," the stranger asked?

Startled that the man had spoken to him, Roostafer stammered his halting reply.

"Uh, no, sir. But it seems kinda weird."

"Oh yes. It is strange indeed. You see, that whole parking lot was once the site of a convent in the early 1900's. The convent was part of St. Michael's Church, right there across Mill Street. It faced away from the river with the front door where the driveways are. That old door at the rear of the building led into the nun's quarters down in the basement.

"You can see, just above the door," the elderly gentleman pointed out as he continued, "the old wrought iron fixture where a small bell used to hang. During the Great Depression desperate people would sometimes ring the bell during night and flee into the darkness, leaving behind an infant in a basket--an orphan for the nuns to feed and raise. The current mayor of Portland started life, many years ago, as an orphan at St. Michael's convent. After the old structure was condemned and razed, he rejected every effort to build on the seldom used parking lot. It was eventually forgotten, hence the willows growing in front of the door."

As the old man turned to leave, Roostafer asked, "How do you know all this?"

"I'm the current mayor," the old man smiled over his shoulder with a twinkle in his eye as he walked away.

Roostafer was astounded and thanked the Lord for bringing the mayor to give him that information. He thanked Jesus for watching over him and guiding his steps.

I don't know why you wanted me to know about this old doorway, but thank you.

Roostafer thought about it all afternoon as he panhandled the streets of Portland. By nightfall he had managed to garner more than twenty dollars and had decided to take a closer look at the door. He came back just after dark and parked his cart against the shrubbery. He waited for a late-evening pedestrian to get farther away, then dropped to his hands and knees and squeezed between the willow branches and concrete wall and crawled until he reached the doorway. So far, so good.

He felt around in the darkness and found what he thought he had seen in the daylight. The bottom rivets on the wide middle plank of the door had rotted through the wood. Roostafer got his fingertips under the end of the plank and pulled. It swung out about a foot but no farther, the top rivets were loose but still holding strong.

On a sudden hunch he reached through and groped around in the pitch-dark space but couldn't feel anything. There was an open space behind the door! This would be a perfect hideout, if only there happened to be enough room to stretch out behind the door!

Roostafer had no flashlight or matches, so he knew it would be pointless to try to explore it at night. He retreated, crawling backwards on his hands and knees until he could stand up next to his cart. No one was around to see him. He was unseen. Apparently this part of the city rolled up the sidewalks at the end of the corporate workday.

He brushed willow stems and leaves off his clothing as he wheeled his cart around and headed back to his campsite under the bridge, thinking about what he would do the next day.

In the morning he did his "devotions" as usual, training himself to be faithful in this new habit of daily Bible reading. After breakfast at the greasy spoon he visited the isolated little ATM he had been using and withdrew twenty dollars. He bought a small flashlight, extra batteries, and three large black carriage bolts. His plan was to contrive newer, solid looking bolt heads for the bottom of the door so it would look like it was repaired.

He arrived back at the door in the wall just after dark, wedged his cart into the bushes, dropped to his hands and knees and crawled into the doorway. First he pulled out the rusted bolts and installed the new bolts. Then he pulled the bottom of the plank out as far as it would go and squeezed his body through. Inside he paused and thanked God for making him so thin. He carefully pulled the plank back into place and turned on his new flashlight.

He had hoped to find a good hideout--a safe place he could retreat to that no one else knew about. He had psyched himself up to be content even if it was tiny, just as long as it was at least safe and dry. But what he found in the small glare of his tiny flashlight was far better!

He found himself standing in a narrow hallway that led off into the darkness beyond the range of his little flashlight. The ceiling was only six feet high, which meant the dirt over it up to the level of the parking lot pavement had to be at least four feet deep. The walls were only three feet apart. By modern building standards it was more like a tunnel than a hallway.

He found a narrow open doorway on the left, the wood frame intact but no door, and shuffled inside, sliding his shoes on the dusty stone floor in case of unseen obstacles. It was a long room, about twenty feet across and stretching off to his right a good fifty feet. It contained several ancient iron bed frames. Some of them still had metal bedsprings, but no mattresses or bed linens, no other furnishings, and no closets, he noticed.

Musta been a dormitory for the nuns. Primitive, though.

To his right, in the gloom at the far end of the room, another doorway led back out into the hall. He came out facing another doorway across the hall. The hall itself dead-ended in a pile of rubble to his left on the bottom step of a stone stairway that went up only a dozen steps and ended at the low ceiling. He crossed the hallway into the next room and found that it was an old kitchen with a double deep sink made of cement and a rusted old porcelain wood burning cook stove.

No chimney any more, of course, but a good surface for hot things if I can figure out how to heat up food or coffee in here without a smoky fire.

There was a huge old plank table in the middle of the room with a plank bench along one side. A small pile of boards off to the other side looked like it had once been the other bench, plus maybe a sideboard or hutch. A row of shallow shelves was carved into the stone wall at about chest height.

Impulsively, Roostafer twisted one of the old ivory faucet handles in the concrete sink. He was startled when it turned, a little stiffly, with a creak, and water dribbled out! The flow was so dark with rust it looked black in the weak glow of his flashlight. Still, it was water. He was amazed the water still worked after so many years.

He watched momentarily to see if the drain leaked. The water didn't pool up in the bottom of the sink or under it. *Good! No leaks.*

He left the faucet running to see if the water would clear up. Why not?

He couldn't hear a pump running, so it must have been put in after city water became available. If so, it just might clear up, even after all these years.

The last of the three rooms was a lavatory, also with a working sink and an actual flushing toilet, porcelain, with no seat. The commode was larger than modern ones. A short piece of pull chain hung from a tank mounted four feet above the porcelain throne seat. There were more stone shelves built into the wall opposite the toilet. Above the old pedestal sink there was a cracked and spotted mirror.

After he had shined his little flashlight into every corner, Roostafer went back to check the sink. The drain was still working, the flow had increased just a little and the water had cleared up some. Figuring it wouldn't hurt anything, after all this time, and that he would be back the next night anyway, Roostafer left it trickling. *Maybe it will eventually clear up enough to use for washing, even if it isn't good enough to drink.*

There were no actual doors in any of the interior doorways, but for Roostafer by himself it was everything he could have hoped for in a secret hideout. It was mildly chilly. Probably around fifty-eight degrees all the time, like in caves and cold cellars, he thought. If he covered the doorways with blankets he could probably figure out a way to heat one room.

Thank you, Lord, for giving me this secret hiding place. Help me to use it carefully, as a good steward of this gift from You.

To keep his newly discovered hideout a secret, Roostafer went back to his spot under the bridge that night and continued to sleep there for the next several nights while he surreptitiously set things up in his hideout a little at a time. The nights were getting colder, but his spot in the homeless camp was close to the fire barrel. There were things he wanted to do before he moved into the hideout, but he had lots of time. No hurry, he thought. Little did he know!

In the next few days he managed to obtain and install blankets across the kitchen doorways and moved the two best beds into that room. He put a double layer of cardboard and his sleeping pad on one of the bed's rusty but intact springs, spread a stack of a full dozen blankets on it, and added two real pillows with pillowcases. The other bed he simply covered with cardboard to use as a couch.

He purchased and hauled in a good supply of canned and other nonperishable food. He hadn't intended to stock up on so much food, but the Cash and Carry was running a special by the case. So…. *Okay, maybe I'm getting a little carried away. Whatever!*

The water had finally cleared up and the flow had increased slightly to what he thought of as a fast trickle. It tasted about as good as any other Portland city water, which was better than the tap water he'd been accustomed to back east. He put a new seat on the toilet and added more length to the short pull chain. He bought a long-handled scrub brush, rolls of paper towels and a big bottle of Formula 409 and scrubbed the kitchen sink and counter, the toilet and shower, and even the shelves on the walls.

He swept and mopped a path through the kitchen and into the bathroom so he could walk around in his socks without ruining them. Everything else he swept thoroughly, knocked down the cobwebs, and piled all the debris in the farthest corner of the long, empty dormitory room across the hall. The former kitchen was now a proper one-room living area.

The crawl-through entrance concealed behind the willow branches was not really secure. The city could decide to clean up those willows at any time. And it wasn't very convenient crawling through the narrow gap every time, especially if he was bringing in something bulky, like a rolled up sleeping pad. So, all things considered, he didn't really feel that he could depend too much on "the hideout." But it was there if he needed it. It was ready to move into at a moment's notice. Just knowing that he had a backup plan was a great comfort. Roostafer felt a renewed sense of confidence that he would be able to make this street life continue to work out satisfactorily.

He had, apparently, successfully disappeared from his former life. He had successfully walked all the way across America. He had survived on the streets of Portland as a homeless man for months. Now he had established a secret hideout all his own where he could get away any time he might need to and be safe and dry. All things considered, Rudy was quite pleased with himself.

Maybe he wasn't such a mediocre person after all.

CHAPTER FOUR

THE RESCUE

At the homeless camp under Burnside Bridge a commotion occurred late one night after most of the tenants had retired into whatever personal shelter they had created for themselves. It was caused by a new guy who called himself Bear. He was big and hairy like one. He looked to be about forty years old, with a little gray beginning to show in the raven black shagginess of his bushy beard and hair. He had a barrel chest, long muscular arms and short bowed legs. Roostafer thought 'Gorilla' would have been a better name for him. Bear had showed up several days earlier and was obnoxious to everyone from the start. No one liked him.

There was an old lady named Maggie who was liked by everyone. She was small, stooped and gray, toothless and arthritic, and one of the nicest people Roostafer had ever met. As the nights got colder the others had helped set up a sleeping shelter for Maggie. It was an intact wooden refrigerator crate lying on its side with one end open--just the right size to serve as a crawl-in shelter from the cold. They positioned it facing the burn barrel and threw a tarp over it as a windbreak so Maggie would be less cold at night. With several layers of cardboard on its floor Maggie was as comfortable as possible living under a bridge.

When Bear showed up he moved into the crate with Maggie, uninvited and against her will. Nobody was big enough to stop him. Since the worst of the winter weather seemed to be past by then, she simply surrendered her crate and went back to sleeping on the cold ground under her blankets. Bear had been calling the crate his own for several nights.

Now, on the night of the commotion, Bear arrived late, obnoxiously drunk. He gripped in his ham sized hand the thin arm of a frightened and whimpering young girl he dragged into camp. She was little and petite, looked about fifteen, had tangled blond hair, and wore a smudged white dress and low heels. Roostafer thought she was probably one of the many young runaways living on the streets of Portland.

Without acknowledging anyone in the camp, Bear continued to curse and revile the girl as he dragged her down into the crate behind the green plastic tarp draped over the open end. It seemed that Bear figured that he had found an unwilling replacement to warm his crate in place of old Maggie. Maggie and Roostafer shared a look as the girl's voice rose to a wail inside the crate. The sound of a loud slap could be heard, and the girl cried out, then was silent. Soon her low sobbing could be heard.

Other sounds began to eminate from the crate. Roostafer fleetingly thought how much it probably sounded like a gorilla pulling apart a helpless rabbit. He hated the thought of Bear bullying and molesting the young girl and hated himself for feeling so helpless to prevent it. Maggie was of the same mind, he could tell.

Lord, what can I do? Roostafer prayed.

"I hate this," he murmured to Maggie, who nodded in agreement, sourly pursing her lips in repulsion. The tarp covering the crate had been carelessly shoved to the side when Bear dragged the girl in. It gaped like a half-opened curtain. Roostafer couldn't quite see around the edge of the crate, but the horrifying noises gradually died down. Was it over?

All of a sudden Bear's head and shoulders flopped outside onto the dirt, face up. His mouth was open and he let out a loud snore. The girl's soft whimpers continued as Bear's head rocked slightly from the girl disentangling herself. Bear snored on, passed out drunk.

Roostafer had seen some hard things during his life, but this was the absolute worst.

Lord, what shall I do?

"I gotta do something," Roostafer whispered to Maggie. She nodded again, her lips pursed, and her eyes squinted with anger.

"I'll help if I can," she hissed back. Roostafer felt shame for his fear.

Roostafer had already secreted his boot knife and revolver, which he still had from his walk across the U.S., back in his new hideout, so he had no weapon. He quietly got up from his sleeping bag--the expensive one he had purchased in Connecticut and still used--and stepped over to his cart. He rummaged around in the cart as quietly as he could. There was nothing. Then he saw the old claw hammer he had "borrowed" from an empty jobsite that morning to use at his new hideout.

For a moment he hesitated.

If I do this, Jesus, there's no turning back. The girl's already been raped, and this won't turn back the clock. But dang, Lord! This can't be allowed!

With fresh resolve he quickly tiptoed to where Bear's head stuck out of the crate, face up, mouth agape and drooling as he snored. As he drew close, Roostafer could hear the soft weeping of the broken young girl.

God, I can't undo her violation, but with your help I can avenge it!

Before he could second guess himself, Roostafer raised the hammer and smashed it down against Bear's forehead! He had intended to just render Bear unconscious, but the tension and terror of the moment took over and his adrenaline kicked in so that he swung with all his strength! As if in slow motion he heard the dull crunch and saw the hammerhead smash through skin and bone. Blood splashed to both sides and the hammer stuck deep in the hole it had made. Bear never knew what killed him. Roostafer tugged on the handle but the hammer wouldn't come free. *Oh no! Now what?*

For a full thirty seconds no one moved. Roostafer found himself holding his breath. He wondered what would happen next. Suddenly he knew he had to get away, as fast as possible.

He wheeled away without a word, leaving the hammer stuck in Bear's forehead. He threw his bedroll onto his wobbly-wheeled old shopping cart and awkwardly shoved it up the embankment to the brightly lit sidewalk above. At the sidewalk he got a grip on his panic and slowed down to a typical homeless person's trudge so as not to draw attention.

Behind him he didn't notice Maggie get up and rush over to Bear's body. She used her long shirt tail to carefully wipe off the hammer handle, then scurried back into her sleep spot and burrowed out of sight inside her bedding. Roostafer did not know that in the morning all the homeless camp residents quietly got up, collected every piece of property and litter, swept the area clean of footprints, and vacated the site, never to return. Bear's corpse was left to be discovered by whoever happened to pass by.

What Roostafer did know was that he had to go somewhere else, as quickly as possible, and disappear for a while. And he had just the place--his hideout!

A few minutes later, as he patiently trudged along the sidewalk under bright streetlamps, he thought he sensed someone following him. He glanced back but saw no one. Maybe it was just his guilty conscience. Just to be safe he took a side street and made his way roundabout, going to the left a block, then to the right a block, wheeling his cart through the unlit tree covered lawns of the downtown park blocks. When he was finally sure no one was behind him he headed straight to his hideout.

He had just tucked his cart into the scrub willows and dropped to his hands and knees to begin crawling along between the stalks and the wall when he heard running footsteps coming closer. He turned in a panic and scrambled to his feet, ready to grab a weapon out of his cart (forgetting that his hammer was no longer there)! It was the girl—Bear's victim!

"What are you doing here," Roostafer whispered angrily?

She looked up at him, her eyes big with unimaginable grief, tears making tracks down her dirty cheeks, and sobbed.

"I got nowhere to go," she whisper-wailed in the darkness!

"Sshhhhhh," Roostafer urged! He thought quickly.

Maybe I can trust her, but probably not. On the other hand, she might have seen me kill Bear, and if I turn her away she might blab. Dang! I wish she hadn't seen me start to go behind the willows!

He had previously adjusted the bushes a little, and draped some 'camo' cloth he found at a hardware store, so the doorway was nearly invisible, even in the daylight.

But she knows where I was headed. It might be better to have her where I can keep an eye on her. I have enough food stashed inside for both of us til things cool off. Plenty of water, and the toilet even works now.

He had even put a lamp in his living area after he discovered there was still juice to the one old receptacle in each of the rooms.

"Okay," he finally whispered back to her, "but this is my place and you are only a guest. You gotta do what I say so I can be sure we'll be safe here. Otherwise, I'm arrested and you're sent away to juvenile hall or foster care. So, what I say goes! Got it?"

Her lower lip trembled as she held back her sobs. He imagined the whirl of thoughts that must be racing through her mind. 'Can this man be trusted? What kinds of things will he say I have to do?' He saw her make a decision, and then she tremulously nodded without speaking. He was sure by this point that she must be a runaway, as he had thought earlier.

He put a finger to his lips to remind her to be quiet, then gently took her hand, pausing to be sure she was okay with him doing so, after the way Bear had brutally dragged her. He crouched as he motioned her down to her hands and knees, then led her slowly along the wall behind the screen of shrubbery. At the door, after peering out through the strategic holes he had left in the shrubbery to make sure no one was watching, he pulled out the plank and squeezed through. The girl followed him bravely into the darkened hole.

She must be wondering what in the world she's getting into.

After she was through he pulled the plank shut, stood up and flipped the ancient switch on the wall so the one pale ceiling light midway down the hall came on. She peered around, amazed, her curiosity overcoming her sniffles. Roostafer quietly closed the hasp he had installed on the inside of the door just the day before, and locked it.

"I'm only locking this so no one can get in. You are not locked in. You can see where I hang the key. But I think we both need to lay low for a while, capisce?"

She nodded.

He had only one wash cloth and towel, but he let her use them first while he busied himself at the other end of the room. She washed her face and neck, her hands and arms, and her legs below the knees.

Out of the corner of his eye he saw her peer toward him in the dim light. He kept his face turned away while she wrapped herself in the towel and washed up under her skirt. When she was finished she dried herself with the towel and wrapped herself in it while she put on the shabby but clean men's clothes Rudy had laid out for her. She looked tiny in the baggy shirt and trousers. Rudy's heart ached for her abject misery.

Now that they were safe inside he could speak to her in a more normal voice, but he instinctively kept his voice low.

"Tomorrow you can take a proper shower while I fix breakfast. No hot water, but the cold water's almost room temp. And don't worry, you're safe here. I ain't no peeping tom, and besides I'm old enough to be your dad, or maybe even your grandpa. We're both safe here, and we can stay as long as we need to until things quiet down outside."

"Where are we," she asked in confusion?

"This was a convent before either of us was born. Now it's a parking lot, but they never filled in the basement. It's my secret place no one knows about, and I don't want anyone else to find out about it or it won't be safe anymore. Gotta keep it secret. capisce?"

"You mean no one else knows about this place?"

"Well," he chuckled softly, "The mayor knows but he's keeping it secret."

"Okay. I won't tell anyone," she declared firmly, though her voice trembled.

She doesn't need to know right now that she can't leave for a while. It might upset her again. There'll be time to talk about it tomorrow.

Roostafer gave her the bed with the clean bedding on it. He dragged the other bed frame with bedsprings on it from across the hall and cobbled together a second mattress of layers of cardboard. He had stocked a couple of extra blankets in case it got really cold at night, so he took the two spares to use as a bottom sheet. He would use his old sleeping bag for a cover. He took one pillow and left the other for the girl.

After they were both settled under their respective covers, Roostafer's mind continued to race, trying to plan out how best to make this work. He suddenly realized he didn't even know her name.

"You still awake," he spoke softly into the darkness?

"Yeah. I'm still too wired to sleep yet."

"Me too," Roostafer agreed. "What's your name?"

"Real or street?"

"I'll call you by your street name if you want."

"It's Lizard, short for Elizabeth."

"Okay. I'm Roostafer."

That settled, he asked her if she would mind if he prayed out loud before going to sleep. He explained that he was trying to form the habit of praying and if she didn't mind, it was easier to pray out loud.

"No, I don't mind. I think I'd like to listen."

After gathering his thoughts for a moment, Roostafer prayed aloud.

"Father in heaven, thank you for watching over us today. You kept us alive, even though things got really crazy. Thanks for this safe hideout. Help us to sleep good and wake up rested. And help us be careful tomorrow not to give away our hideout. And help us become true friends so we can really trust each other. Thank you for saving me from my sins and giving me forgiveness and eternal life. In Jesus' name I pray, amen."

As he drifted off, he heard Lizard whisper in the darkness, "Thank you."

When he awoke in the morning he felt rested and refreshed. The hideout was pitch black. It was probably daylight outside, but no light had found a way into the hideout. He'd have to see about finding a clock with a lit-up face whenever the time came that they could safely go outside. Meanwhile, he turned on the flashlight he had kept under his pillow and checked his watch. Seven fifteen. Had to be morning, not evening.

He got up, slipped on his shoes and turned on the overhead light. He suddenly felt the need for more light, so he went around and turned on every light and lamp in every room. That was much better. *If it's daytime, it should look like daytime.*

He resolved, and immediately told Lizard, that they would leave all the lights on, all day, from now on. Nighttime was okay for it to be dark, but not daytime.

He silently thanked the Lord for helping him think to sneak so many things into the hideout already. He fixed a simple breakfast by heating a breakfast MRE for each of them on his little Sterno stove, and brewing a pot of coffee. There was a long list of additional things he had planned to stock in the hideout, but hadn't gotten around to yet. But he had enough essentials for them to get by for a while.

After their crude breakfast, Lizard went back to sleep, so Roostafer took his cold shower, put on clean clothes and began heating some water for her to wash with in her shower whenever she got up.

Lizard woke up about an hour later and seemed much better than the night before. Roostafer surreptitiously watched her for any signs of psychological trauma, but she seemed cheerful and pleasant, as if yesterday didn't happen.

Maybe that's best--just go on as if yesterday never happened. Thank you, Lord.

After her morning ablutions, while Roostafer waited patiently with his back turned, there was nothing for them to do. So they talked. As they chatted amiably about non-essential things, she gradually got quieter, until she was only answering in monosyllables, if at all. Roostafer sensed she was approaching a crisis of some sort and wished he knew more about psychology.

He had just asked her how old she was, and was waiting for a reply that never came, when he heard her begin to cry--hard. Her deep anguish was heart breaking, as she finally let out her pain in great wracking sobs. Roostafer found himself shedding tears of sympathy as he sat silently, letting her cry it out.

He was seated on her bunk and she was on the one folding chair he had managed to drag in so far. As she wailed out her grief and sorrow, she got up and stumbled over to Roostafer and fell onto her knees at his feet. He put his hand on her head and gently caressed her hair as a mother would a child. She let herself go.

Her face reddened and contorted in inner agony while deep sobs wracked her torso. For several long minutes he simply petted her hair and waited. Finally her loud sobs, punctuated by hickups, began to quiet down a little. Then she quieted to just sniffles, and then, finally, she was still. Roostafer heard her snore softly against the side of his knee.

For the next two hours he didn't move, so as not to wake her. When she finally stirred, his back was aching fiercely, but he felt that it was worth it, for her to be able to cry it out.

It can't hurt anything, and it might help, Roostafer thought to himself.

That good cry did seem to clear the air a lot. After that she seemed to let down her guard some and be less wary and defensive. Roostafer felt that she even acted almost normal.

Over the next few days they established a basic, minimal housekeeping routine, and talked a lot. They did the laundry together, by hand, in the shower, taking turns soaping and rinsing their own clothing and hanging it on a makeshift clothesline to dry.

He scrubbed out the toilet and sink, because she said they weren't clean yet. She rewashed all the dishes and rubbed most of the spots off the mirror. They agreed that Roostafer would fix the meals and Lizard would do the dishes. They learned more about each other--their favorite colors, favorite sports, what they liked to do for fun, favorite comedians and music, and so forth.

As the hours and days passed, they steadily became friends--real friends, just as Roostafer had prayed. Roostafer thought to himself that if he had a daughter he would want her to be like Lizard. Lizard secretly wished her dad had been like Roostafer.

The days turned into weeks and the weeks into a month. Roostafer noticed that they only had MRE's for a few more days. He mentioned it to Lizard and they were both silent for a while, thinking of the implications.

"We could sneak out after dark tomorrow night," Roostafer thought aloud. "There's a market over on Burnside that's open late. We could buy some regular food. No one will suspect anything, not if we act all normal."

"Okay, whatever you say," Lizard quickly replied. "You decide. You know best."

"Whoa there, girl," Roostafer protested! "I definitely don't know best! You wouldn't believe all the stuff I don't know! I make mistakes all the time! My 'decisions' are just guesses, really. I'm just stumbling along trying to not mess up too bad, that's all."

"Okay. Whatever you say," Lizard repeated, with a mischievous dimpled grin.

I love this little girl. Lord, please help me keep her safe. Even if something happens to me, please keep her safe. In Jesus' name, Amen.

CHAPTER FIVE

THE RELIEF

They waited until after dark the next evening, then turned out all the lights and sneaked out through the willows to the sidewalk. While they'd been hiding out all those weeks someone had taken Roostafer's old shopping cart, so they walked along the empty sidewalk, beside the empty street, empty handed and self-conscious about it. Everything was strangely quiet. They went several blocks without seeing any cars or pedestrians. The streetlights were on, but no stores were open, and no one was about.

"Must be some holiday I forgot about," Roostafer muttered, breaking the silence.

"Maybe there's a big event going on somewhere," Lizard suggested. "You know, like a homecoming game at the college or something."

"I suppose so. Must be some reason no one's around this time of the evening. I'm pretty sure this is Thursday night, though. Wouldn't be a homecoming game on a Thursday night."

They walked several more blocks and finally came to a store that was open. A bicycle shop, of all things. The shop's hours were stenciled on the front window and it said that they closed at 5:00 p.m. Monday through Friday. But the front door was propped wide open and all the lights were on. They both looked in the door as they walked past, and then stopped and peered in the display windows.

"I didn't see anyone. Did you, Lizard?"

"Nope. Wanta steal a bike?" She dimpled at him.

"Don't be naughty, girl," he laughed. "If you really want a bike, we'll get some money at the ATM. I have a little in the bank we can use. But where would you keep it?" She looked at him appraisingly.

"Well, one learns something every day!" She dimpled again. "You have money in the bank? Wow! I was only joking about the bike, but, if we're going to live together and buy food and stuff, we will need another shopping cart or wagon or something. Right?"

"Hmm. I guess you're right. But I like to keep things simple. Let's be careful not to let things get complicated, okay? We'll just get us another old shopping cart."

She pretended to pout, thrusting her bottom lip out.

"But I want a Mercedes Benz," Then she laughed, skipped a few steps and turned to walk backwards in front of him. "And a jet plane, and a helicopter, and a mansion on a hill! Capisce?"

She's really just a child. Being silly seems natural for her. She needs time to finish growing up, so I gotta remember to be patient with her.

"Okay," he grinned back at her. "We'll get all that stuff for you first thing in the morning. But for now, let's walk on up to the market and get a cart full of groceries. Capisce?"

She laughed aloud again and swung back alongside Roostafer, placing her hand on the inside of his elbow. He liked the feel of her little hand hanging on his arm.

This must be what being a dad feels like. He felt a flash of regret about losing Willie and, thus, a chance of having kids.

They arrived at the market and stopped in front of the entrance, looking in through the plate glass. Lights were on inside, but they couldn't see anyone moving around. The door was locked, even though the sign said they were open until midnight. They turned, together, and noticed that the parking lot was empty. The market was close enough to the sports complex that they would have heard the cheering if a game was going on.

Roostafer hunched his shoulders with a sudden chill, and leaned close to Lizard, instinctively lowering his voice.

"Something's wrong. This isn't right."

Her gaze lit on the newspaper box next to the door. She whispered back.

"Hey, look at the headline!"

They both leaned close and she read aloud from the front page of The Oregonian.

"CREMATION VIRUS HAS NO CURE"

"I think maybe we better buy a paper and read that article," Roostafer averred.

But neither of them had any coins.

"Hey," Lizard said excitedly, "Didn't we walk past the Oregonian building?"

"Oh, yeah, we did," Roostafer replied, sounding relieved. "Let's go back and see what we can find out. But let me do the talking, okay? We're risking a lot."

"Okay, Roostafer. Whatever you say." She gave him a dimpled smile again.

Must be nice to have such faith. Oh...I guess I should have that same kind of faith in You, Lord. Sorry for forgetting, God. Help me keep my eyes on you, no matter what's going on down here on earth. Thanks for your watch care over us.

At the Portland Oregonian building the front door was unlocked and they walked into the brightly lit reception lobby. No one was at the desk but there was a copy of a very thin newspaper on the coffee table. They sat and read the full front-page article together. It told everything about the Cremation Virus plague and declared that this was the final issue of the newspaper. It urged any survivors to help themselves to anything in the building. Everything but the front page was blank paper.

Roostafer finished reading first and leaned back, speechless. When Lizard finished a moment later she flopped back alongside him, also speechless. She was first to gather her thoughts enough, after more than a full sixty seconds, to be able to speak.

"Roostafer?"

"Yeah?"

"I remember seeing little clothing outfits on the ground on the way down here. There were slacks and a shirt on the driver's seat of that red Mercedes we walked past. There was a housecoat and slippers on the front porch of that old house."

"Yep. I noticed. And there's a skirt and blouse and pantyhose and high heels right here behind the reception desk," Roostafer added. "I guess this lady stayed as long as she could."

They stood there in silence, processing the enormity of what they had just read, and some of the drastic implications of what had happened. Finally Lizard spoke again, thoughtfully.

"If we're all alone, Roostafer, does that mean we still need money to buy stuff? Couldn't we just, like, you know, take what we need? Would it matter, if there isn't anyone else?"

"I suppose so. Somehow, in this case, it doesn't really seem wrong to do so."

"Okay. So, let's figure out what we need most, for now, and just get it and go home. I want to think about all this, but not out here in this big empty city. I'm scared."

"I know just how you feel." *That's nice that she thinks of the hideout as home.*

Back at the market, without any hesitation, Rudy smashed in the front door.

"Oh, darn! Wish I hadn't done that," he immediately said.

"Why not? There's no cops around."

"Yeah, I know. But we might not be the only people left alive here in Portland, and now it's obvious someone has broken in. We should have broken in a back or side door so the front would still look intact."

"Why?"

"Well, just in case, you know? Just in case there's other survivors, and they aren't nice. I know you're nice, and you know I'm okay, but we really don't know about any other survivors we may meet."

"Oh. I see what you mean. You think that maybe a brutal serial killer survived? Ha ha." Her laughter seemed forced. "But we're in here now, so let's just get what we need and get home fast, okay? Next time we can be more careful!"

They took two grocery carts and looked around. There was a small non-grocery section and they grabbed extension cords, a new coffee pot, paper plates and plastic ware, napkins, paper towels, lots of toilet paper, and a small microwave oven. They added a face-lit battery powered clock and a couple of pocket-sized LED flashlights, with spare batteries for everything. Then they went to the grocery section.

In the second cart they loaded ten jars of instant coffee, non-dairy creamer, a bag of raw cane sugar (Lizard said it was more healthy than white sugar), and a bunch of boxes of pop tarts. They layered the bottom of a third cart with six dozen cans of green beans, a dozen each of sliced carrots, pickled beets, creamed corn, halved peaches, and halved pears. On top of all that they added several dozen cans each of spam, sardines and tuna fish. They dragged the loaded carts outside, then went back and got a third cart and loaded it with pillows, blankets, slippers, sneakers, pajamas, windbreakers and gloves, which they promptly put on (it was a chilly night), and picked out extra socks and underwear, and pullover knit caps.

When they finally headed out the door it was full dark. They had three full carts to push up the street--the one with the canned food was very heavy, so Roostafer pulled it behind him while pushing the next heaviest cart. Lizard pushed the third cart in front of her.

No one was around. *Of course!* Roostafer thought to himself.

The street was silent but for the sounds of their shopping carts clattering along the cracks in the sidewalk. Without speaking, they moved out into the smoother pavement of the street so the carts would be less noisy. When they came to the bicycle shop, Roostafer stopped the carts in the street.

"I want to come back after we get this stuff home and get a couple of bicycles. We could take a car to use, if we wanted to, but they make noise. Bikes are quiet. With bikes we can travel without being heard."

They left the carts in the street and moved through the doorway into the bike shop. He added another thought.

"Let's pick out the most practical bikes we can. It doesn't matter what they look like or how much they might have cost. It only matters that they work good for us. We can put them just inside the door and hope that if any other survivors come by in the next hour they'll overlook them."

"Okay, Roostafer."

Lord, help me not to fail Lizard. I don't want to let her down. She seems to trust me so much, but she's been betrayed, abused and exploited. I don't want to be someone who adds to her bad experiences. Let me always be a blessing to her. In Jesus' name, Amen.

After thinking about it, they decided to balance their two new mountain bikes atop the two lightest carts, and not take a chance on losing them. After loading them up they carefully continued on to the hideout.

When they got there Roostafer went in first, quickly modifying the door so it would open inward normally. After many trips they had the carts unloaded, then took them around the corner and left them up in the empty parking lot over the hideout. Near the shopping carts they chained and padlocked the bikes to a steel signpost set into concrete. Then they went back inside the hideout to put away all their new stuff.

The next day they went back out again and brought home a small flat screen TV with a built-in DVD player and a large selection of DVD movies. Then, for several weeks, they played it safe and stayed inside most of the time, watching movies, snacking, and talking about what they should do, and when to do it.

They agreed that the first thing they needed to do was try to somehow confirm that the newspaper article was true. What if it had been a hoax? Or a gag? Or what if some of the details were inaccurate? Maybe only Portland was hit with the plague and the rest of America had simply quarantined this one city!

They thought about possible ways to find out. Roostafer suggested they could find a ham radio and try the airwaves and Lizard agreed. Lizard suggested they begin exploring the Portland area on their bicycles and Roostafer agreed.

They decided to start with Old Town which was in north central Portland, on the west bank of the north-flowing Willamette River where it entered the mighty west-flowing Columbia River. They planned to work their way clockwise around the Greater Portland area, going next into northeast Portland, then down to the southeast part of the city, then the southwest area, and finishing up with the northwest quadrant of the city. It would take some time to make the full sweep, returning to their hideout each night, but they had the time.

They would look for ham radio equipment during their travels around the metropolitan area, and if it turned out that Portland really was their very own huge ghost town, as the newspaper said, then the sweep would give them an opportunity to search out a better living situation amongst all the now empty homes around the sprawling city.

It would be risky, Roostafer stated firmly. They would have to be on full alert at all times. If they met anyone at any point along the way Lizard was to hide and remain unseen while Roostafer "reconnoitered" to make sure the person was not a threat. If things went badly Lizard was to return to the hideout and stay out of sight for at least a week before venturing out again. Longer, if she could stand the solitude.

They had been hiding below ground for almost two months by the time they finally came out and began their recon sweep of Portland. They cruised around Old Town for a whole day, peddling as far as twenty blocks in every direction. The next day they rode across Burnside Bridge and cruised the streets of northeast Portland as far north as the airport. The third day they rode eastwrd all the way out to check the city of Gresham. It was a long hard day. The next day they went south through the downtown area and crossed the Ross Island Bridge, riding way out S.E. Powell Boulevard and then turning right on S.E. Foster to the Gun Room store on S.E. 56th.

They stopped there while Roostafer picked out a handgun for each of them. For himself he chose "the Judge," a .45 caliber Taurus revolver that would also handle .410 caliber shotgun shells. For Lizard, he selected a Ruger double action .357 Magnum. They went downstairs to the basement firing range and spent an hour plinking at targets to get used to the pistols.

Back upstairs they selected holsters for the handguns, plus a 30.06 Winchester rifle for her and a Browning 12 gauge pump shotgun for him. They spent another hour back downstairs firing the long guns. Both the rifle and shotgun were set up with slings, so they "wore" the guns home that day, hauling several boxes of ammo for each weapon in their backpacks. The extra weight made for another long hard day, but they agreed it would be well worth it.

All told they spent almost two whole weeks riding around greater Portland and the outlying suburbs. Everything went like clockwork, but even so they dragged themselves into the hideout every night exhausted from the unaccustomed labor of pedaling. Neither of them had been aware of just how hilly the Portland environs really were, and how out of shape they really were. But at least they now knew for certain there was no one else in the area.

They were also able to locate a powerful voice transceiver system. Roostafer dug deep in his memory of his old navy days to figure out how to set it up to continuously transmit a looping voice message. He recorded the message himself, explaining to Lizard that it would be safer to send it in a male voice, just in case some sexual predator bad guys were around to hear it.

His recorded message said, *"I am broadcasting from Portland, Oregon. There are survivors here. We would like to contact other survivors. Please come to Portland International Airport, set up camp and send up a smoke signal at mid-day. We will see it and come to you. We do not mean to harm you, but we will be armed."*

Now that they knew they were alone in Portland, they decided to move to a better place to live. After considering their situation, as much as they knew for sure, anyway, they decided to look for a house--one that was hidden among trees on a hillside overlooking the airport would be best. It had to be inconvenient to get to, and have a good escape route too, just in case they someday encountered other survivors who were not friendly. Lizard fully agreed with Roostafer's self-admitted paranoia.

There was an upscale residential area situated on the ridge slope above the Portland Reservoir and the once-famous Rose Garden and Japanese Gardens. On the city map they were looking at it was called Sylvan. They both liked the suburb name, and after checking out several possibilities they found a house that they both liked. It was on a steep, narrow lane that seemed unimpressive on either end where it exited and re-entered a broad avenue, making it both hard to find and easy to defend. The house was spacious, with a picture window with sliding doors out to a large second floor deck overlooking the now empty city and the distant Portland International Airport. And they didn't mind at all that it had a beautiful unfenced in-ground pool below the deck. The pantry was so well stocked that she joked that they must have been preppers.

"We might not have electricity much longer," Roostafer commented to Lizard with a worried frown. "But let's enjoy it while we can. I wanta set up the ham radio here at the house where the antenna is clear of the big buildings downtown."

"Roostafer," Lizard queried tentatively?

"Yeah, girl."

"Ya think I could get a car?" She had a wistful look on her face.

"Whaddya want a car for?"

"Oh, just cause I've never had one, or even driven one. And now I wouldn't even need a license. Would you teach me to drive!"

She gave Roostafer a little dimple smile and his heart melted.

"Well, that's two questions for me to figure out how to answer," he retorted with his own grin. "I don't know if I can take this kinda pressure!"

She waited while he thought about it. After what seemed to her like a long moment, he finally replied. "But, seriously, that's a great idea! I'll get me one too! But let's wait a few days, okay? We need to get our routine established here--you know, figure out who's gonna do what, and do some escape drills; stuff like that. And I think we both ought to start working out. You know, exercises, in the basement weight room. To get in better shape. We need to make sure we don't get soft and fat. Okay? I don't know about you but all this bicycling has reminded me that I sure have gotten soft!"

"Okay. You're right, of course. I can wait a few days more for my first car," she dimpled.

They could have easily picked out cars that people had parked in their garages before they died, but somehow it felt creepy. So, a week later, after they had established a good daily routine that included two whole hours of working out each day, they went car shopping. Out toward the east near Gresham there were several sprawling car dealerships where they each found just what they thought they wanted.

Roostafer chose a huge Ford F-350 'dually' four-door diesel pickup. Lizard picked a low-slung Mercedes convertible, which was also diesel. Roostafer spent part of the afternoon rigging both vehicles with high quality CB radios so they could stay in contact with each other.

Feeling daring, they topped off the fuel tanks and drove out to Portland International Speedway to put the vehicles through their paces. They each raced their own vehicle as fast as a hundred miles per hour, just to see how it felt. Then they practiced emergency stops, emergency acceleration, and Roostafer showed Lizard how to do a controlled skid. When they both felt confident in their new vehicles, they traded and did it all again.

"I don't like your big pickup! I'm too high off the ground!"

"Ha! I don't like your convertible cause I'm sitting ON the ground! Feels like I need to wear asbestos underwear!" They laughed together, and it felt very good.

The day had been fun and exhilarating but they were both exhausted by the time they got back to their new home on the hill. They only made one wrong turn before they remembered how to get there--way up near the top of N.W. Fairhaven. For some reason finding it in a car was a little more complicated on bikes. They unloaded the bikes from the pickup and parked both vehicles at the curb, hoping they would be inconspicuous among all the other parked cars.

Roostafer made sure the looped radio transmission was still functioning, they had a pensive supper, then went to their rooms and slept all night.

The days seemed to pass quickly. The spring warmth was a welcome relief after the cold winter months. Several days of sunshine in a row convinced them to clean and fill the pool. They added an hour of swimming laps to their daily workout routine and began to tan up over their winter palor.

Every day Roostafer checked to make sure that the message loop was running. Every morning, afternoon and evening one of them would scan down the hill to the airport with the big binoculars they kept on the deck. Day after day of the "on watch" routine came and went, with no other human life showing up. They didn't really mind. Life seemed good.

In mid-summer the 'food chain in action' showed up, and it was at their back door! They strolled out on the deck with cups of coffee that morning, bleary eyed, and found a half-eaten deer carcass down in their unfenced back yard near the pool. The pool water was slightly pink.

"Hm. Looks like the work of a dog pack. And it looks like the pack took a swim in the pool after they gorged," Roostafer hypothesized, as he leaned over the railing. Then he heard Lizard gasp!

He followed her gaze down into the bottom of the deep end and saw the second half-eaten carcass--a mountain lion!

"Well," Roostafer thought quickly how to allay Lizard's shock without lying to her. "Musta been some drama playing out here while we slept. I think the cougar musta taken down the deer, then the dog pack took down the cougar. I'm not sure, but that's how I figure it. Guess we ought to be really careful not to come outside unarmed."

They both heard the sounds of underbrush rustling beneath the deck at the same time. The sound was moving toward the steps at the far end.

"Hurry, Lizzie," Roostafer hissed. "Get inside!"

They bolted for the sliding door and just got it closed behind them when more than a dozen Mastiff-type hounds slid to a halt outside the thick safety glass, letting loose with loud snarls and snapping fangs as strings of drool flung from their jowls! Lizard went into a full instant panic, whimpering in fear and clutching at Roostafer as she hid behind him.

"Well, there-there," he soothed, as he held her in his arms. "They can't get through that heavy safety glass. We're safe in here."

He led her out of the room where the hounds could no longer see them, and the pack quieted down. Apparently the pack had been sleeping against the wall of the house under the deck and woke up at the sound of their voices.

"Lizzie," Roostafer spoke softly. "I don't think I like this house anymore. I think we should abandon it, and even leave the city. Those look like domestic dogs that have gone feral. They'll stay around the city cause they're used to this area, and now that they know we're here they may keep coming back until they get us."

He thought for a moment, then continued, "If we go out into the country we'd only have the normal food chain to deal with--you know, bears, bobcats, and stuff. Not a huge pack of hungry city dogs like this. We'll get things ready today and head out in the morning. I'll bring the pickup inside the garage after the dogs leave, so we can load up our stuff safely. We'll pull out in the morning."

Their idyllic relaxation time in the lovely house on the hill had been short lived. But their plan to leave was a good plan, Roostafer was sure.

CHAPTER SIX

THE RETREAT

By morning the feral dog pack was gone. Roostafer backed the pickup into the garage and closed the big door. They loaded all their clothing and toiletries, their guns and ammo, and enough food to last at least a week. They hoped to scavenge along the way, but the food stowed in the truck was a backup they both liked.

Roostafer also loaded bolt cutters he had found in the small workshop in the garage, and a few other things that might be useful, such as a large tarp, two folding camp chairs, a folding camp table and two sleeping bags. He also filled and loaded several five-gallon Igloo thermos water jugs in case they had trouble finding safe drinking water. The pickup bed was full when they pulled out after lunch.

Lizard felt momentarily sad that she had to leave her Mercedes convertible, the nice big house, the view and everything. But she was confident that Roostafer knew best.

They headed south, both of them looking forward to a little warmer climate. It had been a mild winter, and the days were getting warmer now, but Portland could turn nasty very quickly. Two and a half hours later they cruised through Salem on I-5. The Interstate had been clear of vehicles except for one place near the exit marked "Donald."

"I'm amazed the world wasn't left in chaos, Lizzie."

"Yeah. Everything seems almost tidy. It's like everyone just coincidentally decided to stay home on the same day. Sorta spooky!"

"Yeah," Roostafer agreed.

They saw two different packs of feral dogs roaming the empty city streets near the freeway. In the southern end of Salem, near the Kuebler Avenue off ramp, they were saddened to see a pack of what looked like timber wolves in hot pursuit of a beautiful Gypsy Vanner stallion. Roostafer was sure the wolves would win. Lizard, it turned out, was an avid equestrienne, and told Roostafer a lot about that particular horse breed as they continued south.

They passed through the smaller town of Albany without seeing any feral dog packs. But as they traversed the sprawling university city of Eugene they saw several more packs. It seemed the packs were segregating more or less by breed. The first pack, back in Portland, had been mastiffs. In Salem they had seen a huge pack of pit bulls and a small pack of fleet-footed Dobermans, plus the wolves that were chasing the horse.

Here in Eugene they saw a pack of large shaggy black haired dogs with a few large shaggy white dogs mixed in. Lizard identified them as Newfoundlands and Great Pyrenees. Then there was a pack of mixed boxers and pit bulls, and a third pack of German Shepherd type dogs.

At Cottage Grove they exited I-5 and followed old Highway 99 through town. They didn't see any feral dog packs there, so in the rural foothills just south of town they looked for a place to stop for the night. At the onramp where Highway 99 dumped back onto I-5 they veered right onto Longview Lane, then just before it crossed the railroad tracks they turned right into a steep driveway. At the top of the quarter mile driveway was a large farmhouse with a gravel driveway that looped around a house perched on the top of the grassy hill with shade trees all around it.

Roostafer parked behind the house so the pickup was hidden from view of any possible passersby. The house had been left locked, but they were able to break in through the rear door. There was a slight gap between the door and the doorjam, so Roostafer used a knife to press the locking pin back and open the door without damaging it.

There were a couple of dusty clothing piles that used to be living people, but otherwise the house seemed fairly clean and secure. The electricity was off, but Roostafer found an emergency generator in a storage shed. He fueled and fired it up and the lights worked again.

They didn't trust the spoiled food supplies left in the freezer and refrigerator, but the generator gave them hot water and lights. They noticed that the owners had been about the same size as they were, so after they each took a shower they exchanged their dirty clothes for clean ones from the closets in the large master bedroom. They enjoyed a hot supper together, then watched a DVD movie.

It was almost 10:00 pm when they each chose one of the two smaller bedrooms and turned in. Neither of them wanted to use the master bedroom where the previous owners had slept. They both still felt tired in the morning, so after breakfast they lingered over cups of fresh coffee before heading south again. As they pulled out onto I-5, Roostafer made a comment he soon regretted.

"Well, no bad guys so far."

That morning they drove through Sutherlin, then Roseburg, then the casino community of Canyonville and then a little crossroads village called Azalea.

Just after they passed the exit to Wolf Creek, the highway climbed a long grade before dropping down into a scenic place called Sunny Valley. As they drove over the summit Roostafer suddenly slammed on the brakes and brought the rig to a full stop. Neither of them was buckled in, and Lizard had been dozing against the passenger door. She banged hard against the dashboard, bounced back into the seat and swatted Roostafer's arm with the back of her hand.

"Why'd ya slam on the brakes for," she protested?

"Smoke," was all Roostafer said in reply, as he reversed and backed around the curve of the summit to be out of sight of the valley.

"Oh! So, that means people, right? Maybe they're safe! Are we gonna go meet 'em?"

"Maybe, but maybe not. We need to be careful," Roostafer cautioned, then suggested, "Let's find someplace nearby where we can wait safely, and come back after dark. At night we can see exactly where the lights are on. Then we can check it out tomorrow in the daytime with the binoculars."

"Okay. There were buildings back at Wolf Creek. Is that far enough back?"

"Well, let's go see how it looks," he agreed.

Wolf Creek turned out to be a little community just west of the freeway. They stopped at the country grocery story and saw evidence that someone had plundered it, so they continued on out of town along Lower Wolf Creek Road. A couple of miles out into the hills they cautiously checked out a steep paved driveway that led uphill past a three car garage. Up the hill, hidden behind trees, they found a large country mansion. It had obviously been the home of wealthy people. They watched the house for awhile with the binoculars but saw no signs of people, so they went on up the driveway and parked behind the house to explore on foot. They discovered that the house had been built for off grid living, with extensive solar panels, functional wind turbines and a large propane tank. It was perfect for a temporary hideout.

Best of all, it was completely out of sight of the road. But just to make sure, Roostafer found the keys to a massive H1 Hummer parked next to the house and took it down the driveway, parking it so that it completely blocked the steepest part. If anyone tried to drive in they would have to stop at the steepest part of the driveway, revving their engine, and hopefully it would give Roostafer and Lizard time to exit down the rear service road, which he hoped led to a good escape route. Even if it only lead to the rear of the property, it would at least relieve the immediate threat.

It was all sort of iffy, but they were, after all, well armed and well rested, and at least it was a plan. They didn't feel totally safe, just knowing there were other survivors nearby who might be dangerous, but despite their feeling of restlessness they appreciated the comfortable amenities of the well-situated manse.

They only found two remains—empty clothing laid out on the big bed in the master bedroom, with undisturbed ashy dust settled in the cloth. They had seen quite a few by this time, but it still inspired grief, knowing that it represented living persons who had died. They carefully collected and folded the clothing and put it in a small box, then swept the dust into the box on top of the clothes. They placed the box of remains out in the enclosed back porch.

Roostafer removed the bulbs from the Hummer's tail lights, and after dark they took up their firearms and vision gear, loaded into the Hummer and drove out with the lights off. Roostafer drove slowly, on full alert, back to the summit overlooking Sunny Valley. He parked before the crest and they both got out. Without a word they stepped away from the Hummer, facing down the mile-long grade, their ears straining in the darkness.

The occupied house was immediately obvious. Every light was on, forming a yellow glow around the house in the misty night air. The building was at the bottom of the grade, just off the exit. According to the traffic sign next to the Hummer it was exactly a mile away.

They stepped forward, pistols holstered and long guns slung over their shoulders. For this recon mission Roostafer carried a night-vision spotting scope and Lizard carried regular binoculars. They wore dark clothing and pullover caps. Their faces were smudged with soot from the mansion's fireplace. Neither of them had ever done anything like this, but they had seen it in movies. They hoped they had thought of everything.

They sneaked down the hill, keeping to the pavement where their boots were quiet. About fifty yards from the off ramp they paused to use the night scope. Roostafer slowly panned back and forth, then passed the scope to Lizard without saying anything. She took a long look and passed the scope back to him.

"Lizzie," he whispered, "I see one guard posted outside. There are others inside."

She softly agreed, then whispered, "Roostafer, did you see the girl?"

"Girl? No. Where?"

"Inside--I saw her through the window. She's pretty, and she's in her underwear."

Lizard sounded scared. Roostafer's mind raced.

"How many guys did you see inside," Roostafer asked?

He had avoided aiming the night vision scope at the brightly lit windows, in order to avoid the glare, but obviously Lizard hadn't thought of it.

"Two, but there could have been others," she answered, grimly.

They stood silently in the darkness for a few moments, thinking.

Then Lizard whispered. "She's in trouble. I'm sure of it. She's the only female, so why would she be undressed, unless she was forced to?"

"Are you sure, Lizzie? Is it possible she wants to get pregnant so she's trying to inspire the guys? She might think she's the last woman on earth or something."

"No. If she wanted a baby she would pick one man, not advertise to the whole group. No woman would do that."

Harumph! My wife did! He suddenly felt melancholy at the memory.

"Okay, Lizard." His face was grim. "Let's study the layout and figure out if we can do anything."

"How, not if, Roostafer. This isn't optional, okay?"

"Okay," he quietly reassured her. *Wow. She sounds sure of herself, like a grown woman. My little Lizard girl is growing up right in front of my eyes.*

She shivered in the chilly darkness and snuggled up under Roostafer's arm while he studied the place with the scope.

"Well, it'll be risky, and scary, but I think there's a way we can do this," he whispered in the darkness.

"The guard is near the woodpile," he explained. "which is near the house lights, so he probably can't see out into the dark very well. If I neutralize the guard without making noise, then I'll be clear to get the drop on the ones inside."

"Lizzie," he paused to gather his thoughts, then continued softly. "I think we have to kill these guys. If we tie them up and drive away they'll come after us. They'll ambush us and take back that woman and you too. In other words, if we fight fair they'll win, we'll lose. So, Lizzie girl, if we do this, we can't fight fair."

She was silent for several moments before responding to his unspoken question.

"I'm okay with that. If she's being forced," Lizard whispered through gritted teeth, "they deserve to die!"

"Okay. I agree. Let's go," Roostafer whispered. They moved forward silently.

CHAPTER SEVEN

ANOTHER RESCUE

Roostafer didn't tell Lizard what he figured was happening inside the house, but she saw that the guard had moved closer and was watching through the wide open front door. She guessed what must be happening.

"Kill them," she hissed at Roostafer! "Hurry!"

Roostafer and Lizard had reached the driveway gate. The house was less than twenty yards away. The guard was near the house, his back to them as he watched through the doorway, mouth hanging open.

Roostafer took Lizard's rifle and quickly affixed the noise suppressor he had been sure they would never need. In one smooth motion, before he could second guess himself, he raised the rifle, jacked in a shell with a soft 'snick', and shot the gate guard in the back of the head. The gun's hushed 'phhhht' sound seemed loud in the darkness. The man silently tumbled forward as Roostafer levered in another round.

Roostafer quickly walked forward. Lizard strode beside him, her handgun gripped tightly in both hands, cocked and ready. Roostafer glanced at her, then paused long enough to quietly lay her rifle on the ground and draw his own pistol. He clicked back the hammer as they approached the open front door of the house. They had practiced for this possibility.

This is evil, what these men are doing. God, please help us do this well!

Roostafer put out his other hand and held Lizard in place as he stepped into the doorway. Three men had the naked woman spread out and tied down on the kitchen table across from the entry door. They were all roughly abusing her at the same time. Roostafer stepped through the door, glanced right and left to make sure there were no others, and grimly commenced firing. Two rounds into each man! It was over in five seconds. The men were so focused on their brutal rut that they never noticed. Not even the third target had time to react.

Roostafer had killed four men in about forty seconds and he felt nothing. They were mere varmints that needed killing. It meant no more than shooting rabid skunks. He clung to that thought as Lizard rushed past him to untie the woman and help her climb down off the table. In the glare of the kitchen lights Roostafer caught a brief glimpse of abrasions and bruises distributed over her body. He saw swollen bruises on her face just before he looked away.

He mentally catalogued what he had seen--two black eyes, her jaw swollen, her lips puffy and bleeding. He had glimpsed raw blisters on her body from torture burns, and her thick brown hair was dirty and tangled.

She limped as Lizard helped her toward the back room. She was almost a head taller than Lizard. Roostafer grieved for both her physical and emotional pain, and he knew that Lizard grieved for her even more.

While the women were in the back room Roostafer dragged the men's bodies outside. He piled all five of them behind the wood pile, then found a leafy branch to brush out their tracks in the dirt and cover the blood trails. He couldn't get the blood off the floor inside the house, but at least the outside was tidied up. If there were other men in the gang who were away at the moment, they wouldn't see any obvious signs when they returned.

He heard the shower running. Lizard knew how to help the woman begin to put the ugly situation behind her. When

Roostafer had finished cleaning up the killing floor as much as he could, he sat down on a kitchen chair and tried to mentally debrief himself, reviewing every action he had taken.

It went well. We had to do it. There was no other way. This woman deserved to be rescued. This makes five men I've killed. I'm so glad Lizard knows what to do for the poor woman. Dear Lord, I can't help them get through this, but You can. Give them both the resources to help each other heal in their hearts. Let them not be damaged or twisted because of this. Bring them to wholeness again. I pray this in the name of Jesus. Amen.

When the two women came out of the back room Roostafer was relieved to see the woman was now cleaned up and fully dressed. Neither of them looked at Roostafer as Liz led her straight through the kitchen and out the front door. He silently stood and followed. The two women looked straight ahead, their eyes to the ground, as they walked down the driveway and onto the highway. The woman limped, but Lizard motioned Roostafer back when she saw him start to move closer to help.

When they arrived at the Hummer no one had said a word yet. He feared the woman might be in shock. She had groaned softly a couple of times, while they hiked the long mile up to the vehicle. They got in, Lizard and the woman taking the back seat. Roostafer started the engine and headed back toward their hidden mansion.

The woman surprised them both when she suddenly spoke into the continuing silence. She spoke at length. Her voice was quavery at first, but became calm and steady. She was articulate, her speech almost refined. Once she started, the words came in a steady stream, as if under powerful pressure that was rigidly controlled.

"Thank you for rescuing me. My name is Roseanne, spelled with an 'e' at the end. My friends call me Rose. You are my friends, so please call me Rose. I was a nurse, a Trauma RN certified as a Paramedic, before the Cremation Virus. I don't know why I survived. I was alone and getting by all right until those men found me two weeks ago. They took away my clothes and tortured me. They raped me--many times and as many ways as they could think of. They made me cook for them and do their laundry. They took turns beating me. None of them showed me any mercy or compassion. As a trained nurse I can tell you that I have at least one broken rib, a sprained ankle, two broken teeth, and numerous cigarette burns on my body. I have one punctured eardrum, many abrasions, and my wrists and ankles are raw from being tied up at night. My breasts, my vagina and my rectum will be very sore for a while. But, as a nurse, I can also tell you that all these things will gradually heal. I will probably eventually fully recover. As a person, I want you to know that I am glad those men are dead. It doesn't bother me. During my last beating I was knocked down and one of them kicked me when I was on the floor. That was how my ankle got hurt. But I will put all this behind me and not look back. You don't have to act like it never happened. It's simply a part of my personal history now. I only hope I'm not pregnant. But if I am, I will have the baby and love it and raise it as normally as possible. If any of this bothers either of you I will be happy to be dropped off somewhere by myself to get by."

Just as the words "get by" came out of her lips, her head dropped forward and she began to snore softly. She had fallen asleep during her own sober soliloquy.

That's good, Roostafer thought to himself. *Sleep is probably good medicine right now.* Lizard pressed Rose back until her head rested against the headrest.

When they got to the little isolated mansion, Roostafer quietly and gently carried her in. She wasn't heavy. Lizard opened the doors for him as they took her upstairs to the plush master bedroom suite. She slept while they tucked her, fully clothed, under the luxurious down comforter on the big soft bed. They left a nightlight on, near the doorway, in case she woke up before morning. Exhausted, they sought their own smaller bedrooms.

Roostafer and Lizard slept soundly until midday. Lizzie checked on Rose at noon and found her still asleep. At suppertime

Rose was still asleep. At that point Lizzie talked about it with Roostafer and they agreed to wake Rose up to eat. Lizard went in alone and gently nudged Rose's foot to wake her. Rose gasped and sat up with a cry of alarm, clutching the blankets in front of her.

Lizard quietly waited with an encouraging smile on her face. Rose looked around the room in a panic for a brief moment, then her eyes focused on Liz and she remembered where she was. She fell back down onto the soft bed with a groan of pain.

Lizzie spoke softly, "Rose, it's evening. You've been asleep fifteen hours. You can go back to bed after supper, but we think you should eat something cause you're so very thin, so we decided to wake you up. All right?"

"Yes," Rose answered after collecting her thoughts for a moment. "I am hungry, that's for sure. I'll get up." She startled. "Oh, I'm still dressed." Her eyes moistened momentarily. "Thank you for not undressing me."

"You're welcome. I know what it's like. Roostafer rescued me from a rapist too."

"Roostafer? She paused. "Is that his name?"

"Uh huh. It's made up. I call myself Lizard, short for Elizabeth. Roostafer is short for the name he had before the plague."

"Oh. All right. I think I understand. Thank you for explaining. But I think I'll stick with the name Rose. And thank you for reassuring me about Mr. Roostafer."

"Oh sure. Whatever," Lizard gave Rose one of her dimple smiles. "You don't hafta keep thanking us. We just did the right thing. Roostafer says we shouldn't expect thanks for doing what's right. Thanks are only for going above and beyond the call of duty. I think he was in the navy or something," Liz added with a shrug.

Rose smiled back, slightly, as they arrived at the sprawling eat-in kitchen. Roostafer had put a third place setting at the kitchen table. The three of them sat down to a hot supper of steaks, baked potatoes, green beans, with an apple pie for dessert.

"I hope you like your steak a bit rare," Roostafer said to the two women. "I didn't have time to ask before I broiled them, and I'm not that good at it anyway."

"I'm sure they're perfect, Mr. Roostafer," Rose replied. "However, I haven't eaten lately, so I doubt I'll be able to eat much. But I feel famished, and this looks wonderful!"

"It's just Roostafer, Rose. Not mister. Okay?" Roostafer smiled at her.

With her education and training, she most likely does have her wits about her, like it sounds. Thank you, Lord, for bringing us together with such an amazing woman. Bless her with a quick physical recovery, Father, as it seems You are blessing her with a quick psychological recovery. And thank you, Lord, for the level headed wisdom she adds to Liz and me.

"Oh, yes, okay. Just Roostafer it is. I will remember. And, happy Labor Day to both of you." She said it in all seriousness, without cracking even the merest hint of a smile, as she picked up a small bite of meat on her fork. Roostafer wasn't sure if Rose was normally so taciturn, but he and Lizard were cheered to hear her say those words. Neither of them had been aware that it was Labor Day.

CHAPTER EIGHT

THE REVIVAL

The three of them agreed it would be best to take some time for Rose to rest and recuperate. The isolated mansion was a perfect place for it. Roostafer and Lizzie unloaded the rest of their stuff from the pickup and they settled in to stay awhile.

Rose didn't want to use the luxurious master bedroom, but Roostafer and Lizzie stood firm and made her accept it as her quarters. The three of them easily sorted out all the other arrangements. Rose soon proved herself to be highly competent in all things domestic. Under her influence, and occasional direct orders, Lizzie learned to keep a cleaner house and practice better personal hygiene.

Until she came under Rose's influence Lizzie had been enjoying the convenience of simply putting on new clothes when her old ones got dirty, but Rose insisted they do laundry to conserve their wardrobes. Rose also gave Lizzie cooking lessons. Rose was naturally tactful, despite her terse way of speaking, and felt protective toward the younger and poorly raised Lizard, so Roostafer saw little of Rose's mentoring work with Lizzie. But he saw and appreciated the results. Lizzie had begun to keep herself cleaner and pick up after herself, and Roostafer noticed.

He often found himself with little to do inside the house, so he frequently retreated to the outdoors. He made it his job to investigate their resources and supplies. He was able to determine that they only had enough propane to last about a month. The water tower tank was kept full by a small wind turbine and the house water was gravity fed from the tank. He found a pH test kit in the shed and added a little chlorine to the tank, following the instructions on the bottle. The place was so well organized that it was easy to figure things out.

The Hummer they had found at the place was low on diesel, but they didn't really need the vehicle. In the equipment shed they found a fairly new flatbed ATV trailer and two full sized ATVs. One was a two-passenger with a steering wheel and a canvas roof. He decided they would take them whenever they left the place. There were no feral dog packs in the area so far, and all in all it was peaceful and restorative staying in the grand house. They all enjoyed the respite.

By the end of four weeks Rose had gained a little weight, the abrasions had healed and the bruises had faded. She looked much healthier. A sadness lingered in her eyes, but she would smile once in awhile. Roostafer was surprised to learn she was a only a few months his senior. He had guessed her to be several years older. It saddened him to think how rough her life must have been until now.

But as she regained her strength and conviviality, she began to look more her age. Lizzie and Roostafer and Rose enjoyed the evenings around the propane fireplace getting acquainted while they played cards and table games. They all knew and liked the dominoes game Mexican Train. They played many rounds and Lizzie had excellent short-term memory. She kept track of what had and hadn't been played, and she often won. But when it came to the card game Hand and Foot, Rose was by far the most frequent winner.

Roostafer complained that, between the two women, he never got to win. Rose and Lizzie called him a sore loser, making the letter "L" with their hands against their foreheads, and laughing at him. As the weeks went by they bonded together like a family.

As was his habit, Roostafer took a little time each morning to read his Bible and pray. One day Rose asked him why he did it; why it was such a big deal to him. Lizard and Rose both listened intently as he answered.

"Well, Rose, you see," he gathered his thoughts, "I ran away from my former life. I had a great job with prestige and respect, a gorgeous wife, and a great luxury apartment. I was involved at the Board Room level and being groomed for promotion in a Fortune 100 company. In some ways I really thought I had it all. But then, just like that," he snapped his fingers, "I lost it all. Wife, status and job, all gone. My answer was to run away. I planned my flight to be able to give up everything, even my name, which was Rudy Christofer. I left it all behind and started over."

"Then, out in Portland, living as a homeless man on the streets and trying to be socially invisible, I went to the local Mission for supper one night and the preacher talked about being a new person. It caught my attention, and I listened. He read from the Bible that if any one is in Christ he is a new creation; old things pass away and all things become new. It's exactly what I was trying to do, unsuccessfully. I could only do it with my external surroundings--my circumstances. I needed it for my life!"

"So I went forward at the end of the sermon and he read more bible verses to me. He showed me that every one of us, including me, is a dirty rotten sinner. I knew I was. He showed me that every sinner deserves to die. I knew for sure that I did. Then he showed me that Jesus died in my place so I could have eternal life, instead of having to die for my sins. It really says that in the Bible. I wasn't at all sure I could believe that, but right then I decided to choose to try to believe it. Yeah, I was really that tentative!" He grinned sardonically at the memory.

"So he told me the words to pray and I prayed them. I can honestly say with all my heart that it really did all come true!

God forgave me, for everything! He took the heaviness off my heart. He filled me with peace and joy. He gave me hope! I am convinced that He knows everything I'm going through, and that I'll get to spend eternity with Him, wherever He is, after I die. I knew for certain at that exact moment that I had been born again, spiritually, and I really did become a new person. I had tried to run away from my old self and it had never worked. But Jesus set me free from my old self instantly, and made me a new person on the inside."

"It's amazing, I know, but Jesus really did all that for me, so I love Him. Because of Him, God is now my Father in heaven and I can talk to God in prayer. He wants me to, and I want to. He wants to speak to me and teach me things and guide me, and He does that when I read His word. I try to read it every day, just 'cause I've found that there's always more to discover."

"I like to talk to Him every day to thank Him for things, and ask Him to bless and protect us. And I like to tell Him how much I love him, and ask Him to help me be strong and protect both of you. God is preparing me to be the kind of person who will be comfortable in His presence for all eternity."

"I don't want you to think I'm preaching at you. I'm just answering your question as best I can. But I do want to add one more thing that isn't really about me. The neatest thing about all this is that you can pray that prayer too, either one of you. God will hear you like He heard me, and respond to you like He responded to me. He'll forgive whatever sins you've committed, and take away all your guilt, and give you true inner peace. God is almighty, so He has the power to give you a whole new life too. I killed a man in Portland to protect Lizzie. I killed four more when we met you, Rose. I don't think it was wrong for me to do that, but if it was, I know that I'm already forgiven. So, no matter what either of you might have ever done, or for whatever reason, I know that God will forgive you, too, if you ask Him."

Rose and Lizzie both sat with stunned expressions on their faces.

"Mr. Roostafer," Rose finally responded, "I think that's exactly what I want to do. I need God to forgive me. Will you tell me the words to pray?"

"Me too, Roostafer," Lizard softly added.

All three had tears in their eyes as they bowed their heads and Roostafer led them in the same simple salvation prayer he had once prayed and still remembered so well. All three raised their heads afterward with shining faces. They sat there together, in silence, smiling hugely at each other. It was a moment they would all remember for the rest of their lives, and always treasure. They sat in comfortable silence for several minutes, just smiling at each other.

"Now I feel free to tell you both that I love you," Roostafer declared. "You are my sisters in Christ, since we all in common have God as our Father in heaven. I love you more than if you were my real sisters by physical birth. And I will try to always treat you with respect, and always try to protect you, even with my life if necessary."

Their conversation ended with an emotional group hug that lasted several minutes. They stood and closed their eyes and swayed softly in each others' embrace, basking in the richness of the moment. It was if their souls had melted together, and in a spiritual sense, they truly had.

From that day on the two women joined in with Roostafer's morning Bible reading and prayer time. Rose and Lizard began feeling a little more comfortable praying out loud as they practiced it together with Roostafer. They began to give encouraging words back to Roostafer, as they realized he had been giving to them all along.

As the days went by and they grew closer together they would occasionally squabble like siblings, too, especially over their frequent card and domino games, but they learned to always make up right away. They really and truly became the loving family they had each longed for. Roostafer felt even more powerfully the primeval urge to protect them from any harm. He didn't know it, but the day would come when he would have to lay his life on the line for them.

PART THREE

MALE VOLENT

"Mr. Volent, sir," whined the fearful underling. "Shall I bring your tea now, sir?"

This underling was as stupid as the others. None of them was intelligent enough to be considered worthy of his regard. "Mr. Volent" didn't answer, but remained motionless where he stood with his back to the underling, gazing out through his tinted glass east wall across the rooftops of the city below. Why should he deign to answer such a moron? Why should such a great personage as himself allow any such lowly person to interrupt his private reverie?

On impulse he drew his concealed revolver, spun smoothly around and pressed the barrel against the underling's temple. The underling was in such a stupor of ignorance he didn't even react, other than his eyes opening wider in even greater terror than before.

"Why should I let a moron like you interrupt my very important meditation," he hissed at the terrified underling. "You are so stupid you can't remember that I have my tea at four, not at three fifty. Always at four! But is it four yet? No it isn't!"

Now angry because he had let himself slip and actually used his valuable time to explain himself to an underling, he suddenly jerked the trigger. The fool's head exploded into the room, making a terrible mess of blood and brains on the polished floor. The loud pop of the small caliber pistol brought one of his bodyguards on the run.

"Guido, remove this underling and call another one to clean up the mess. Tell the kitchen to replace this one with someone who knows when to serve my tea," he ordered the bodyguard.

"Uh, yes sir, Mr. Volent, sir. But, uh, sir, my name is Jeff," the bodyguard stammered fearfully.

"Oh, I know it was," Mr. Volent smiled as he explained patiently. "I've changed it. I like the name Guido, so you are Guido now. Understand?"

"Oh, of course, Mr. Volent. My name is Guido. I'll get right down to the kitchen."

Guido quickly grabbed the corpse under it's arms and dragged it from the room.

It was unbelievable how stupid the survivors of the plague were. He had once been an underling himself, before the plague. But he had been an ambitious one, thwarted by lack of opportunity. There had also been the problem of a lengthy sequence of jobs where he just so happened to work for unreasonable fools who failed to see his true potential. It wasn't his fault that they were all so blind to his inate greatness.

The plague had been his golden opportunity to begin being the man in charge that he had always known he was destined to be. After the plague, of course, every person he met fell under the charisma of his natural leadership ability. It was, he felt, almost like having a supernatural power over others. He spoke and they obeyed. They feared his displeasure because he never rewarded loyalty, but he always punished failure.

The survivors he had collected after the plague were only just bright enough to know that it was deadly to fail him, but too stupid to figure out the subtle humor of the name he had chosen for himself after the plague. Before the plague he had been a commoner named Herman Masters.

He had hated his childhood nickname, Herman Munster. He grew up wishing his parents had given him the first name "Slave."

Down deep inside he felt exactly like a very frustrated slave master who had no slaves, and no respect.

After the plague he chose the powerful sounding name, Male Volent. The word "malevolent" was an apt description for his attitude toward what little was left of mankind. No one had ever tried to make things nice for him, so why should he care if they suffer? His sole responsibility in life was to make things nice for himself. No one else would, so it had to be himself. And it didn't matter if it cost others, or what price they had to pay for him to enjoy all the nice things he had always missed out on.

He had established his new, royal residence in one of the tallest buildings in the ghost town of downtown Los Angeles. His building was surrounded by skyscrapers that were not as tall. It allowed him to enjoy looking down on everything else within view.

In the lobby of "his" skyscraper there was a memorial plaque that said it was the tallest building between Chicago and Malaysia. It was also the tallest building in the world that had a helipad on the roof. The building had been completed in 1990, so he was certain it had been exceeded in both of those categories since then, but he liked that it was also designed to withstand an earthquake up to 11.3 on the Richter Scale.

Like anything else not directly related to his own comfort, Mr. Volent found the building's pedigree only mildly interesting. He did hope, however, to recruit a qualified helicopter pilot soon, and enjoy being the only man left in the world to be flown places by his own pilot in his own private helicopter from his own helipad on his own building.

What did matter to him about the building was that it was big enough and configured adequately to serve as a sort of micro city. It's seventy-seven floors provided enough space to adequately house hundreds of subjects, er, uh, residents. It had an executive restaurant on the twelfth floor and an executive gym on the twenty-third floor.

He had designated the top seven floors as his private office and quarters. The next ten floors down, sixty-one through seventy, were sealed off for security purposes, with every access door welded shut. The elevators would stop there if he pushed the button for any of those floors, but the steel inner doors would not open. He generously allowed his two staffers and eight bodyguards to live as sumptuously as they cared to on the sixtieth floor, the highest floor under the seventeen restricted top floors. His underlings were all housed in the open fifty-eighth floor barracks and his slatterns were all billeted in the open fifty-ninth floor barracks.

His small cadre of armed bodyguards worked six hour shifts, two guards at a time. One guarded his private quarters and served as his personal assistant when necessary. The other patrolled constantly from the ground floor entrance up to the sixtieth floor. The building's ground floor access was locked and alarmed during the 9:00 pm to 7:00 am curfew he had imposed. The roving guard carried with him the underlings' current work schedules from staffer Bob so that he could make sure everyone was always where they were supposed to be.

Staffer Bob was the facility manager and accountant. Staffer Dale was the security chief, whose only duty was to ensure that Mr. Volent's private floors were always secure and the guards were always properly on duty as scheduled. His underlings, supervised by staffer Bob, had formerly numbered eleven. Now only ten, he remembered, since he had just shot one of them. The underlings were nothing more than lowly servants at the beck and call of his staffers, his guards and, most importantly, himself.

"I have two staffers, eight guards, and ten underlings. And a partridge in a pear tree," he sang the last phrase. "Heh, heh, heh, heh!" Then he frowned, "Only twenty men to serve me. I need more." He paused, thoughtfully, "Yes, I do need more."

He had begun talking aloud to himself when in private. After all, he certainly couldn't discuss his lofty ideas with his staffers, bodyguards or underlings. No one else was intelligent enough to comprehend his thoughts and plans. But it helped him keep his thoughts straight if he said things out loud.

"Oh, yes, there are also the five slatterns. So, twenty-five people," he mused.

He had chosen the women's label himself, just as he had chosen the term "underlings." He only liked to use names with his staffers and bodyguards, and he chose the names he used for them. It was simply too tedious to remember all the names of the eleven (now ten) underlings and five slatterns.

The status of the slatterns was, of course, lowest—even lower than the underlings. The slatterns did the laundry, the cooking, the cleaning and any other drudge work that needed doing. At the end of their workday they were required to take a thorough shower and be available, under his personally supervised scheduling, to service his staffers and bodyguards.

He would not double book any of the slatterns, so the staffers and bodyguards only had alternate night privileges. It was a good system, of course, because he had conceived and implemented it himself. Being kind to his people was the only minor unproductive indulgence he allowed himself.

"So, only twenty-five people to serve me. Hm. There must be other survivors who need my leadership. If I had a small, well equipped military unit I could bring in more survivors from farther away, like northern California, or Nevada or Arizona. I need a pilot, more slatterns of course, and someday my own private chef. More supervision for the slatterns and underlings wouldn't hurt either."

Up in his own private top seven floors, his office occupied the huge lobby of the seventy-sixth floor and his bedroom suite sprawled throughout the entire seventy-seventh. The roof of his bedroom suite was directly under the helicopter landing pad.

The building's auxiliary power supply had kicked in when the city utilities had finally failed, and was still running. Everything in the building still worked. He had named the building Volent

City. Soon he hoped to find a survivor who would have the skills to make a sign for the main entrance.

"I want a fancy sign that says The City of Volent. Yes. That will do nicely."

There was a discreet knock at the door.

"Enter!"

"Your tea, sir," the underling said as he shuffled quietly into the room.

Mr. Volent waited silently, without turning to look at the underling, until he heard the door close as he left. He waited a few moments more, then turned and sat down to enjoy his afternoon raspberry flavored green tea, alone, as he preferred. As always there was a vanilla pudding cup, a spoon for the pudding, and two snicker doodle cookies on the tea tray.

There was another knock on the door.

"I'm having tea," he shouted angrily!

"Sorry, sir," he heard a muffled reply.

After he finished his pudding and cookies, and sipped the last of his tea, he gazed out the window for a few minutes, then decided the interruption had been delayed long enough.

"Enter!"

An underling stepped in, eyes to the floor, and waited for permission to speak.

"What is it?"

"Mr. Volent, sir, Security Chief Dale sent me to tell you that some more subjects have arrived at Volent City, sir."

"Very well. Ask Security Chief Dale to make sure they are cleaned up, then bring them to me in one hour. I will personally conduct their citizenship orientation."

"Yes sir, Mr. Volent, sir," the underling scurried from the room.

Shortly there was another knock on his door.

"Enter!" His feeling of impatience was mollified when he saw it was his security chief.

"Mr. Volent, sir," the man said earnestly, "you have always had me give new arrivals a citizenship orientation, sir, and I've always done my very best, sir. You've always said I did a good job, sir."

"Oh yes, uh, Dale. You've done okay, but I will interview these myself. I'm looking for a certain kind of citizen right now. I may brief you about it soon, but not yet."

"Er, uh, well, Mr. Volent sir, if you want to brief me now I'll be happy to do this interview for you sir. No need for you to bother with such routine stuff, sir, when you have lots of important stuff you gotta deal with, sir."

"Why thank you, staffer Dale, but that won't be necessary. However, I will allow you to do part of the orientation while I simply observe them. If I find what I'm interested in, then I'll address them myself. Don't worry about your level of performance--it has been satisfactory. And now, that WILL be all!"

Having been reminded of his subservient position by Mr. Volent calling him staffer Dale, and by Mr. Volent's stern tone, the security chief quickly excused himself, head down, and exited the room. Mr. Volent made himself comfortable once again in the plush leather chair behind his oversized mahogany desk. He leaned back with his hands behind his head and thought about how their conversation had gone.

He's getting a little pushy. Questioning my decisions. Almost arguing! He wants to know more about what I'm doing. I'll have to keep an eye on him. If he does it again I'll have to decide what to do. Should I be lenient and hope he improves? Or should I just shoot him now before he gets worse? If I don't shoot him, WILL he get worse, so that I've only put off the inevitable? Maybe he's teachable. Maybe I could train him to serve as my future chief of staff. Perhaps I ought not to shoot him, and see if he improves.

If people only knew how much thought and effort I routinely put into leading them well, I'm sure they would be much more sympathetic! No one understands my pain, my disappointments, my frustrations, my rage. No one really cares about me. When the chips are down, I am all I've got. Everyone else is, by dire necessity, last place after me.

He was still lost in his private reverie when Security Chief Dale returned with the group of new inductees for Volent City. Mr. Volent remained seated, staring over their heads as if lost in thought, while Security Chief Dale lined them up against the wall just inside the door. The seven men were dressed in loose cotton draw-string trousers and long sleeved pullover cotton shirts--all a dingy off-white. The five adult women were wearing loose cotton shifts that were low cut in the bodice and ended mid-thigh. The twelve adults all looked like they were were wearing homespun pajamas. The two adolescent girls at the end of the row had been dressed in frilly teddy bear pajamas. As ordered, Chief Dale had instructed the new arrivals to remain silent unless asked a direct question.

He handed Mr. Volent a stack of personal data sheets which the new arrivals had been required to fill out. Each data sheet had a photo to match with the face, the person's name, age, place of birth, education level, special skills, former political affiliations if any, former income level, and any training they had ever received, particularly in weapons, combat or martial arts.

Mr. Volent reviewed the data sheets while Security Chief Dale addressed the group.

"This here is Mr. Male Volent. He's the founder and Supreme King of this here Volent City, which is the name of this here whole building. If he speaks to you, you will address him as Mr. Volent Sir."

While Mr. Volent pondered their data sheets and studied each new person, Dale went on to explain the hierarchy in Volent City and other pertinent information. When he described the typical duties and the assigned lodgings of underlings and slatterns the whole group began to hang their heads. Sullen expressions came over their faces.

When Dale finished, Mr. Volent thanked him and asked him to stand by while he addressed the inductees. Mr. Volent scanned the data sheets for several more long minutes before he finally spoke from the comfort of his leather high-backed executive chair.

"These data sheets reveal that none of you is exceptional in any way, or even at all special in your own right. Do not expect to be given special treatment that you do not deserve. I will now ask questions and you must answer truthfully. When I have filled in a few blanks I will assign you to your positions in Volent City. At the end of my interview I will allow one question from you all, as a group. There will be no individual, personal questions. I will allow you sixty seconds of my valuable time to decide what one question you all want to ask me. After I answer your one group question you will be dismissed to begin your productive assignments as new citizens of Volent City."

He paused for a moment, then continued, "My first question is for, uh, Julie."

The younger teenager looked up. She was bone thin, diminutive in size, with straight black hair--probably dyed, since her freckled face was otherwise fair skinned over her pale neck and shoulders. She looked fragile in the skimpy pajamas.

"Julie. You are thirteen. Are you a virgin?"

She blushed and hesitated, then stammered, "N-n-no."

"Are you pregnant, Julie?"

"Of course not," she replied indignantly! "I'm only thirteen!"

Security Chief Dale suddenly loomed over her and cuffed the side of her head, nearly knocking her down. He growled, "You will address Mr. Volent as 'Mr. Volent sir.' Understand?"

She cowered away from him and quickly murmured, "Yes sir."

"Okay. Now answer Mr. Volent again, the proper way!"

"Uh, No sir, Mr. Volent. I ain't pregnant Mr. Volent sir." She still sounded sarcastic.

Mr. Volent continued as if there had been no interruption, "Are you using birth control?"

"Well, duh, of course," she assured him with a little sneer.

Security Chief Dale casually cuffed the side of her head again, harder this time. Her head slammed back against the wall and she collapsed to the floor. After she groggily climbed back to her feet rubbing her head he growled at her again, "Be polite with Mr. Volent! Ya hear?"

The side of her face was red where Dale's palm had struck. Her eyes widened with fear as no one came to her defense. Her shoulders slumped and she dropped her gaze to the floor. "Yes sir. Sorry, Mr. Volent, sir," she murmured humbly.

"My next question is for Cindy."

The other adolescent lifted her gaze from the floor and calmly made eye contact with him. She had carefully noted the brief interview with Julie and was resolved to avoid being hit by that big security guard. She was auburn haired, lightly freckled across her nose and cheeks but otherwise fair skinned, and slender, but not as thin as Julie. She was a little more filled out, being a little further past puberty than the other teenager.

"You are fourteen. Are you a virgin?"

"Yes sir, Mr. Volent."

"Do you use birth control yet?"

"No sir, Mr. Volent."

He ignored her then and asked a few of the others about specific personal vocational experiences and training, and then directed his last question to the only man whose data sheet had a blank line on it.

CHAPTER TWO

GENERAL BEAR

"This last question is for Albert Bayer." He fixed his gaze on the tallest of the seven men. Albert Bayer was a little over average height and a little beefy in the chest and shoulders. His longish dishwater brown hair was unkempt and he sported a week old growth of whiskers. He had arrived wearing army fatigues with no rank insignia, but with his last name stenciled over the breast pocket.

Mr. Volent continued, "You are the youngest adult male in the group, at age twenty-five, and you left blank the line where you were supposed to list former political affiliations and income level. Why? And do consider your answer very carefully. I want the truth."

"Yes sir, Mr. Volent," the young man instantly replied. "I went into the army before I finished high school, ended up with a court martial and was in Leavenworth when the plague hit. I never had no political whatever-you-called-it, and I ain't never had no income to speak of."

"Why were you court-martialed? What did you do?"

"They said I killed my platoon sergeant, sir."

"Did you?"

"Uh. Well, I guess I pretty much did, sir."

"And what did your platoon sergeant do to make you kill him?"

"I see you understand, Mr. Volent sir," Albert Bayer replied with a half sneer, half grin. "Sometimes people just make you kill 'em, don't they? Well, this here platoon sergeant went and insulted my manhood. He called me a fairy! I'm a red blooded American male, so what else could I do but protect my honor, sir?"

"I understand indeed, Al. Exactly how did you kill him?"

"Uh, well, I pretty much just beat him to death cause they wouldn't let us have real weapons at that time. Turned out he wasn't half the man I was. He pretty much died knowing he was dead wrong about me, for dang sure."

"Very well, young man. From now you will take charge of military training for a few men I'll assign to you. Your new name and title is General Bear. Train the men with the strictest discipline, so they will always instantly obey your commands. Do you know how to do that?"

"Well, I guess I pretty much do, sir!"

"Very well. You will report directly to me, and no one else. Is that clear?"

"I guess so, pretty much clear, sir."

"A simple 'yes sir' will do, General Bear."

"Yes sir."

"Security Chief Dale, after the group has asked their one question, please escort the other six men to the underling quarters and make sure they report to Staffer Bob for assignments. Then escort the females to the slattern quarters and be sure they are received by Senior Slattern Martha for assignments. I will keep General Bear here with me for further instruction."

He turned back to the group of new citizens and addressed them again.

"Now then, you have sixty seconds to decide what you want to ask me. Security Chief Dale will see that you do not go over your limit and waste my precious time."

With that he spun his chair toward the window, clasped his hands behind his head and leaned back to gaze out over the empty city as the group whispered and murmured softly behind him. Shortly, the recently renamed "General Bear" spoke up.

"Mr. Volent, sir, we have our question, if you don't mind, sir."

He kept his back to them as he said, "Very well, you may ask."

"Well, sir," the former Albert Bayer asked on behalf of the group, "these two girls are so young, sir, we wondered if they could be excused from serving as slatterns until they're at least sixteen years old. That's our only question."

"Well asked, General Bear. Here is your answer. Yes, they will both be excused from serving in the general population of slatterns. Julie, age thirteen and no longer a virgin, is assigned exclusively to Security Chief Dale and to you, General Bear. She'll serve only the two of you, and her sleeping schedule will be equally divided between the two of you alone."

Dale and Bear glanced at each other, grinning, as Mr. Volent continued.

"Cindy, age fourteen and still a virgin, is assigned to me. She will live in my personal quarters and it is no one else's business what duties I may assign to her. That is the answer to your one question. Furthermore, regarding living arrangements in general, General Bear will have private quarters on the sixtieth floor, which is currently occupied only by Security Chief Dale, staffer Bob and the security guards. Julie will have her own room on that floor. The only keys to her room will be held by General Bear and Security Chief Dale. Cindy will have her own room in my suite and I will hold the key."

He turned to Dale.

"Security Chief Dale, you will see to all these arrangements immediately. When I finish with General Bear he will come and find you. Show him around, and see that his accommodations are suitably furnished for his high rank. Tomorrow morning after breakfast General Bear will report to me here in my office for his first daily briefing. Have Senior Slattern Martha report to me right away. I will instruct her in how to train both Julie and Cindy so that they will know what is expected of them. Senior Slattern Martha's performance will be evaluated based on Julie's and Cindy's success or failure in their duties. You and General Bear will evaluate Julie, and I will evaluate Cindy. After they have been trained by the senior slattern, which should only take an hour or two, then you will keep Julie on your floor and bring Cindy to me. General Bear, please stay here for the moment. The rest of you are dismissed. Take charge, Security Chief Dale. That is all."

He turned his chair toward the window, smiling with satisfaction as he listened to the sound of their feet shuffling on the plush carpet as they made their way out of his office.

This is good. Cindy is prettiest of the lot. By the time she's ready to warm my bed she'll understand her role very well, and she'll also understand her advantage as my personal slattern. She ought to be grateful. The arrangement with Julie will keep Dale and the General happy too. Yes, this is very good.

He turned his swivel chair around to face General Bear who was now standing alone against the wall just inside the door.

"Please come and sit down in front of my desk, General Bear."

"Oh, why thank you sir!" He managed to duck his head in subservience as he stepped forward with alacrity and took a seat in the padded folding chair. He found himself looking upward at Mr. Volent who sat in a taller chair behind the massive desk.

"Now, General Bear. I will allow you to be privy to my most secret plans for adding more citizens to those already under my care. You are to discuss this with no one, and that includes pillow talk. I do not want you to form any kind of attachment to young Julie, anyway. You may very well only have her for a short while until I'm able to assign you a better looking and more experienced girl of your own. When that time comes, you can tell that one anything you like, because if she compromises any of my confidential plans you will receive the same discipline I give her. Is that clear?"

"Yes sir, Mr. Volent sir. In other words, not a word to anyone."

"Are my words not clear enough, General Bear?"

"Oh, yes sir, Mr. Volent. Your words are crystal clear!"

"Very well. Every morning as soon as you finish breakfast you are to report to me here in my office. If you knock on my door and I do not invite you to enter, you will wait until I call you in. That is my policy with everyone. Each morning I will receive your very thorough report of your work during the previous twenty-four hours, and then I will assign your duties for the next twenty-four hours. Do you understand?"

"Yes sir, Mr. Volente."

"Very well. When you leave here you will proceed to the sixtieth floor so Dale can assign your quarters. You and Dale will agree on a schedule of sleeping arrangements for Julie. Defer to Security Chief Dale as the senior staffer in this one matter, but in all other matters you are under my direct oversight. Until you report to me tomorrow morning you will observe all the male underlings and select one who will be your second-in-command. Try to choose someone who is physically fit, trainable, and able to remember and accurately relay your orders to others. After you have had some time to train him, you will use him to help you select a small cadre of recruits which you and your Second will train to serve as armed combat troops. I will give you further details as time goes by, but I want you to teach them how to fight the way you fought when you killed your platoon sergeant, as well as become proficient in the firearms I will assign to all of you. That is all for now, unless you have a question."

"Yes, Mr. Volent, I pretty much do have a question if you don't mind sir."

"Very well. What is your question?"

"Well, uh, Mr. Volent sir, just exactly what kind of authority do I have over my Second, over my troops, and over all of the others here in Volent City, sir?"

"Good question, General Bear. It seems that you and I have similar priorities. In answer to your question, you have all authority over all the others here in Volent City when you are obeying my direct orders. You may require whatever is needed from any of the others in order to carry out any orders you have received directly from me. To keep discipline, you may punish any underling or slattern as you so please. If you're into torture, do it privately and try not to leave any evidence. Also, try to avoid killing anyone. We need more underlings and slatterns, not less. Understood? As long as I am satisfied with your performance you are functionally my Second. Any problem you may have with either Security Chief Dale or Facility Chief Bob, who are organizationally next in line after you, must be brought directly to me for resolution--do not exercise your own authority over those who do not report directly to you. Always pass the buck up to me when it comes to my other middle managers. Everyone else is under your direct authority. I hope you understand. You can always ask clarifying questions in our morning debriefings. Now you are dismissed."

As General Bear left the room Herman Masters turned to his massive picture window once again, waiting for the senior slattern to arrive.

I'm a little tired. I'll be glad when this day is over. I wish I already had my helicopter. Maybe I can get the underling cook to fix me a special dessert this evening. That would make me feel better. These people are so utterly pitiful. They are just helpless without me to run their lives. They have it so good here, thanks to all my hard work. But do they show their appreciation? NO! My job as King of Volent City is really a thankless one. I put up with so much. And I carry the load alone. I must make sure that the senior slattern trains young Cindy properly.

Just then there was a gentle tap on his door.

"Enter," he shouted!

The senior slattern opened the door and timidly slipped around it, then closed it silently behind herself. Herman Masters turned from the window, after making her wait several minutes, and sat in his raised chair behind his huge desk.

"Please stand before my desk so I won't have to shout to be heard."

She quickly moved closer, seeming oddly graceful in her drab off-white shift over sturdy work shoes. When she presented herself in front of his desk he inspected her carefully. She looked about fifty, and healthy for her age—even robust, in a way. She was clear faced, with a wide forehead and high cheekbones. Her hair, just beginning to gray, was pulled back tightly into a large, well-pinned bun on the nape of her neck.

Hmm. On the whole she's quite plain, but piece by piece she isn't too shabby for an old woman. Other than her face, her skin is quite smooth. Fills out her dress quite nicely too, except for a thick waist. Not bad. Poor posture though.

"Stand up straight. You're old and ugly, but you don't have to slouch."

She quickly stood straighter, her arms at her sides, her palms cupped against her thighs. She stared straight ahead. He decided it was a reasonable facsimile of 'at attention' and was pleased. At least I get a good response sometimes! She's well built when she stands tall!

"I forget your name. What is it?"

Of course I remember her name, but she needs to be reminded how unimportant she is.

"It's Martha, Mr. Volent sir."

"Very well, Senior Slattern Martha. I just sent two young girls to you for training as personal attendants. This is top priority for you right now. By 'training' I mean in everything--valet, housekeeper, cook and dishwasher, secretary, and sex slave. Julie is thirteen, but not a virgin. She is assigned to be shared exclusively between Security Chief Dale and my new staffer, General Bear. She will have her own room with them on the sixtieth floor. I myself will personally keep the older one, Cindy, who is fourteen and still a virgin. She will share my quarters, which you are not allowed to enter except by my order. Cindy will clean my suite from now on, so be sure she is properly and thoroughly trained. When you've finished with her, ask Security Chief Dale to bring her to me.

"Teach them how to do laundry the way I like it, how to keep their quarters and any other assigned areas tidy and clean, and how to prepare and serve meals and refreshments. You've done well training the other slatterns, and I trust you will do well with these two. They must be trained to serve, but will be excused from working in the general population of slatterns so that they can exclusively serve their assigned masters.

"You are to teach them the proper attitude of submission toward their master. You know the drill: Always answer 'yes' and never 'no.' Always stare at their master's junk and smile at all times during sex. Same as you've taught the other slatterns. These two are very young, so be sure they know that their master has absolute authority over them. Their body belongs to him, to do as he pleases.

"Martha, I remind you of these specifics because these two girls will be evaluated more strictly than the other slatterns. I will evaluate Cindy myself. Chief Dale and General Bear will evaluate Julie. If the girls fall short in any regard they will be disciplined, and you along with them. So make sure they "get" all of your instructions. Be sure you understand and remember the gravity of these important instructions."

Have I covered everything? Oh, one more thing...

"Oh, and uh....Martha. I recommend that you begin your training of these two with a proper whipping, to ensure they pay attention. The whipping is to be severe enough so they are grateful when you stop, just as I, myself, have done with you and the other slatterns. When you whip them, make it clear that those are my exact orders. And please try not to leave permanent scars. That is all."

He turned his chair back toward his window again, listening for the whisper of Martha's sturdy work shoes across the deep carpet. When the door clicked shut behind her he breathed a sigh of relief.

If that woman wasn't so good at training the slatterns I'd have her put down. Ugh! I hate having to look at her plain face. Ugliness so wears me out. I need a diversion. Let's see, how many subjects do I have now, with the addition of this new batch? Three staffers, eight bodyguards, sixteen underlings now, and ten slatterns plus the two specially assigned girls. Forty-nine people to serve me! Or, is it thirty-nine? Oh well, in either case things are getting better. Now, if General Bear can manage to move forward in the recruitment campaign I will assign, I will soon have a true city here, with everyone under my authority, subject to my every whim!Then maybe I will finally be happy!

CHAPTER THREE

THE REAL GENERAL BEAR

Albert Bayer caught up with the group of new inductees following Security Chief Dale. His thoughts raced. He couldn't believe his luck! General Bear? That old weirdo running this place had made him a flippin' general! From juvenile delinquent to college dropout to GI in just four years, then onward and upward to felon, to plague survivor. And now, a general? Not too shabby! A general at age twenty-five!

How, he wondered, could he work this to his own advantage? What could he actually get away with? He was sure there had to be strings attached. The old weirdo wouldn't really give him so much authority, would he? There was a lot of truth to the old saying, 'if it's too good to be true it's too good to be true.'

The real ultimate question was, what could he NOT do? What limits would that old crazy guy set for him? What would happen if he went too far? The old guy didn't seem upset that he had killed someone, and he made it sound like almost anything would be okay now.

And what was the story on the chick? How would that work, one chick for two guys? He's ask that Dale guy about the chick. Carefully. No sense making him mad.

That Dale guy looks sorta tough, but he's the only guy in this place who does. The others are uniformly wimpy, and that's being kind. They were probably all salesmen and teachers, or politicians and accountants. Albert couldn't know for sure, because Mr.

Volent was the only one privy to everyone's rap sheet, which he called a profile. These guys all probably never had a fist fight in their lives, let alone beat somebody up, or killed anyone. Might be tricky finding a Second, in a group of weaklings like these.

So, okay. First things first. He didn't need much time to get moved in to his quarters, since he didn't own anything. He hoped this outfit had plenty of stuff he could plunder. Now that he was a general he was glad he had at least finished high school. You couldn't be a dummy and be a general, that much he knew.

When they reached the fifty-ninth floor, Dale asked Albert to watch the men at the stairwell landing for a couple of minutes. He unlocked the metal door and led the five women and two girls inside. Soon he returned with a middle aged school teacher type whom he said was Senior Slattern Martha. He relocked the door and ordered her to report to Mr. Volent.

Dale led the men and Albert down the stairs to the fifty-eighth floor. He unlocked that door and ushered the six men and Albert through the doorway. The whole floor was almost entirely open, with a dozen structural support columns scattered throughout, and over in a far corner a walled off area with toilets and showers.

"General, please stand by while I orientate these here underlings," Dale said.

He turned to the others, "You are underlings. Lowest on the totem pole of all the men in Volent City. You do whatever any staffer tells ya. Got it? It ain't hard work, but ya always gotta be really polite--specially to Mr. Volent. After Mr. Volent you're under the authority of me and General Bear here, then after us Facility Chief Bob, and then any of Mr. Volent's guards. You'll get your daily assignments from Facility Chief Bob. You'll recognize him by the green plastic visor he always wears--Mr. Volent's sense of humor. The guards are the ones carryin' rifles and pistols. All the men who are not underlings--they're all your bosses. None of you is a boss over each other, cause all underlings are equally at the bottom."

He thought for a second, then added, "Oh, you can 'relay' orders to the slatterns, but you can't give 'em orders from your own self. Got it?"

Then he added one more thing, "Oh, and if you break any of these rules we staffers have complete discretion to punish you any way we see fit. Remember that. Now that you know all this, if you have to be punished, it's your own fault for being stupid!"

The new men were all scowling by then, but they nodded. Dale laughed wickedly.

"Now don't forget any of this crap! We got no judicial system here. Mr. Volent is judge and jury, and sometimes executioner. Be sure you respect him at all times. His unhappiness is likely to be your death penalty, and really quick! Got it?"

They nodded again, less sulky and more fearful now.

"The right answer is 'Yes sir Security Chief Dale.' Now try it again."

"Yes sir, Security Chief Dale," they all answered in unison.

"Okay then. Remember the way you're supposed to answer a staffer. It goes double for Mr. Volent. Now, you can sleep wherever you want to on this floor. If you get in a fight with another underling you'll both be disciplined. So don't. Always work things out peacefully. You'll be brought to the cafeteria morning and evening for meals. Morning muster is right here before breakfast. You will be present, standing in line freshly showered and fully dressed at exactly seven in the morning, unless you're dead. At muster you'll be given individual work assignments for the day. As soon as you finish eating you start work. Stay on this floor at all times except for work and meals, except once a week you'll be assigned to work out in the gym after supper. Got it?"

They all nodded, except one who muttered, "Yes sir, Security Chief Dale."

Dale nodded at the one who replied and said, "You're dismissed. Go stand over there. The rest of you, give me twenty pushups! Right now! Hit the deck!"

His sudden loud shout startled them into immediate obedience. He yelled at them some more while they did pushups, leaning close and shouting obscenities in their ears while they strained to obey. A couple of them were so out of shape they were barely able to do the twenty.

Security Chief Dale leaned down over the last two and yelled some more. "If you think you can't do twenty pushups, you stinking maggot, think again! If you stop, I swear you're dead meat! General Bear is helping me count, so DON'T STOP 'TIL YOU'RE DONE you disgusting pieces of camel crap!"

Albert thought Dale did a pretty good imitation of a drill sergeant in army basic training. The men were all red faced and panting by the time they got to their feet and fell into formation once again.

"Okay," Security Chief Dale continued in a calmer voice. "Next time it may be thirty pushups, or fifty, if I'm in a bad mood. I suggest you take good advantage of your gym workouts. Now go pick out your bed and get situated. You're on call as of right now. Oh, by the way, you can call each other whatever you want, but from now on you're simply 'underling' to Mr. Volent, me, staffer Bob, the guards and General Bear. Got it?"

"Yes sir, Security Chief Dale," they replied in unison.

With that he turned and led General Bear from the room. Once they were outside the door and it was relocked, he turned to Albert and explained.

"We keep the underlings and slatterns locked in at all times except meals, except for a few individuals who are let out for specific jobs. Staffer Bob supervises the underlings and slatterns while they work during the day and gives them any new orders. Mr. Volent didn't tell me exactly what he's got planned for you, but I guess he's gonna come up with some troops from somewhere for you to be in charge of, or something like that.

"Meanwhile, here's a master key to the building. It'll open any door, and any lock, anywhere in the building, except the ten floors from the sixty-first to the seventieth--those are sealed. Everyone has a master key except underlings and slatterns. You can go into the slattern dorm any time you want and do any thing you want. But most of them ain't worth your time--they're either old or ugly or both. Those two new chicks, Julie and Cindy, are the only good meat in the city. But the others do what they're told and they work hard, or they're either punished or terminated. Same with the underlings."

"General Bear" had been thinking about all he was hearing and he came up with a question. "So, why don't they poison Mr. Volent when they fix his meal? Man, I wouldn't put up with this crap if I was an underling. I'd do something about it!"

"Ah, General Bear. Now I see why Mr. Volent singled you out. You've got guts! Well, you'll need 'em, my friend. Mr. Volent gives us staffers all kinda perks, but requires absolute and instant obedience. If he tells ya to kill someone ya don't ask why or how, ya just do it as quick as ya can. Same with anything else he says. Ya just do it. Got it?"

"Oh yeah, I got it," Albert sneered. "He's king and I ain't! Clear as a bell!"

"Good. Don't forget it, even for a second, or it'll cost ya big time. Come on, I'll show ya the slatterns' quarters. It's sorta interesting cause they can't wear nothin' there. Course they ain't much to look at. For work they can only wear a smock or a shirt and skirt."

Albert (General Bear, he reminded himself) enjoyed the first few minutes in the slatterns' quarters. He'd never seen so many naked women all at once. In fact he had never seen even one woman totally naked before. It was overwhelming at first. Then he began to notice the details. Upon closer observation he noted that, aside from the two new teens, most of the slatterns were probably at least forty years old, and showed plenty of personal wear and tear.

Oh well. He would have that pretty brunette teenager almost all to himself. He wondered when that would start. Probably Dale would get first turn.

"General, this is how it works," Dale explained, while they stood in the middle of the floor and scanned the naked women going about their lives--some reading, some napping, some sewing or doing Yoga-like floor exercise--all very studiously ignoring the two voyeurs.

"Mr. Volent sets up the schedule of which slatterns will service the staffers and guards and when. He has it all worked out. I never figured out how it works. But I been getting' a bed warmer about twice a week. Never know which it'll be."

"So how's about the new chick we're gonna share? How will we work that?"

Albert Bayer noticed that the nearby slatterns were listening, though they pretended to be engrossed in their various tasks. He didn't really care, since they had no power.

"Hey, I got seniority cause I been here a long time. You're new, so you get seconds. Sorry, friend," Dale said with a grin that said he wasn't really sorry.

"Okay, whatever. I can settle for getting her every other night. Specially since I ain't had any chick in a real long time. I'll probably be rough on her the first night. What about that?"

"No problem. As long as she's ready for me the next night. If we wear her out, there'll eventually be others. But hey, if she's really hot, then be careful, eh? No sense tossing out a good one. Now come on and let me show ya our quarters so ya can get on with whatever Mr. Volent told ya!"

The women watched silently as the two men turned and left, carefully relocking the door.

CHAPTER FOUR

MANIFEST DESTINY

"General Bear, how nice to see you again this morning," the self proclaimed king said in his oily nasal whine, pretending that his lackey general had come in voluntarily. "Let's see, it's been three weeks since you arrived, and you've already learned to give good reports each morning, just the way I like them. So, tell me, what do you have for me this morning?"

"Well, Mr. Volent sir, first of all here's the cup of hot tea you like me to bring you each morning to enjoy during my report. Second of all, things are pretty much going forward on schedule, just exactly as you said they would."

Mr. Volent smiled, pleased that he had been right, as General Bear continued.

"Our military unit currently numbers seven commandos, plus my second-in-command and myself, for a total of nine hardened soldiers," he exagerrated. "We've pretty much trained on all the weaponry you gave us, and we've completed all the 'assault and subdue' exercises you assigned. So I'd say we're ready to handle any unwilling inductees, sir.

"Thirdly, uh, pretty much just so you'll know, which I guess you most likely already know anyway, sir, is that Volent City's total population as of right now is up to fifty-six people. Among the new underlings there are two more likely additions to my commando force. I'm not quite through vetting them, but they're looking good so far, sir. That's pretty much the end of my report, Mr. Volent sir."

"One question, General Bear. Whose commando force?"

"Oh, sorry sir," Bear grovelled. "I just get so excited about being your General. Please forgive me, Mr. Volent sir. It's absolutely YOUR commando force, no ifs, ands, or buts about it. My mistake, sir. I SURE don't think it's MY force sir! Never!"

"Very well, General Bear," Volent smiled, his ego adequately stroked. "Your report is adequate, once again. Now, I have a mission for you, but first I'd like to hear about any disciplinary actions you've taken during the past week. I haven't asked you to include this in your daily report before today, and I will not ask very often, but please do catch me up for now."

Alfred Bayer, now General Bear, sat at attention in his usual chair facing Mr. Volent's desk and replied obseqiously in his usual laconic drawl.

"Well sir, uh, pretty much just a few minor incidents to report, sir. I gave senior slattern Martha nine lashes with the bamboo rod which you assigned because Cindy spoke to you disrespectfully yesterday, sir. She promised to make Cindy understand the gravity of her mistake by passing along the exact same number of lashes. I reminded her that neither Cindy nor Julie were to be marked in any way by bruises or welts. And for what it's worth, sir, I had to include Julie, cause we had a similar incident with her. On the off chance they had put their heads together and it wasn't just a coincidence, we've restricted them from seeing each other for a month. You might find Cindy a little more lonely for a while, and maybe a little more clingy. If it becomes a problem, you just let me know sir, and I'll pretty much make sure that senior slattern Martha handles it PDQ!

"Other than that, Mr. Volent sir, I only had to discipline one underling this week. One of the older guys spilled some food in the cafeteria and started to just walk away without cleaning it up. I had two of the others bend him over a table in front of everyone, including the slatterns, and I hauled down his britches and gave his bare butt a good walloping with my heavy leather belt. He was welted up bright and shiny when I finished. He elected to eat his next couple of meals standing up. It was quite funny, sir."

"Very well, General Bear. Your assignment, then, which I've prepared in writing to give to you as you leave my office, is to prepare the unit for departure on a recon mission which I expect will take you approximately three weeks. You will leave in the morning. While you are away, check in with me each morning by short-wave radio at the same time you would normally make your daily report, just as we have practiced.

"I'm sending you north on Highway 101 through California as far as Arcata, where you will turn east on Highway 299. You will follow 299 to Redding where you will turn north on Interstate 5. Go all the way to the top of the Ashland summit and exit I-5 onto old Highway 99. You will follow 99 down the hill to Highway 66 and head east along Highway 66. In Klamath Falls you will take Highway 140 to Highway 39 and go south back into California. When you reach Highway 299 I want you to go east into Alturas, then south along Highway 395. Follow 395 through Reno and on south until you connect with Interstate 15. Take I-15 south to Interstate 5, then head south back here to Volent City. The whole route is marked on this map, for you to carry with you, along with the print out of my official orders. These orders authorize you to take any military action you may deem necessary to complete your mission.

"Your mission is to reconnoiter for lights by night and smoke by day, or any other signs of any human inhabitants. Note on this map the location of any people you find. Make an entry in your mission logbook each evening. Log all intelligence such as locations of people, how many, how well fortified and so forth. Upon your return you will turn in your mission logbook to me to confirm in writing all the information you have reported to me on the radio. Any questions?"

"Well, Mr. Volent sir. I pretty much only have one question. Do you want me to bring those people back with me or leave them where they are?"

"This is a recon mission, General Bear, not a recruitment campaign. Be patient, your time will come. Do not bring anyone back at this time. In fact, stay concealed as much as you can. If you see any lights at night or smoke during the day, keep out of sight. Approach carefully, so you can check them with your night scope or binoculars. Write down the intelligence and report it to me on the radio the following morning. Bring me the hard data in your logbook and I will make the plans after I have the hard data. Is that clear?"

"Oh yes sir, Mr. Volent. You make the plans and give the orders, and I'll see that it gets done. Absolutely clear, sir!"

"Very well. Make your preparations today and deploy immediately after breakfast in the morning. Be sure you plan your travel to include time for scavenging supplies and booty. If you come back loaded down with loot, er, uh, supplies for Volent City, I won't mind at all. Just stay below the radar, for now, with any people you may find. Dismissed."

I will finally find out what's going on in the rest of California. Then, when we have acquired more people, I'll survey Oregon, Washington, Idaho, Nevada and Arizona. My city's population will grow even more, and the six western states will all be subdued. Volent City will become Volent Nation! Then I will need more middle managers, of course, but there are plenty around. Hell, half my underlings could probably succeed as a middle manager if I let them. I just have to choose and train them until there are as many as I decide to use. Volent Nation will become a magnificent reality! This is my destiny! My manifest destiny! And then, who knows? After Volent Nation, perhaps Volent World? We shall see.

In the morning Herman watched through his binoculars from his picture window, seventy-seven stories up, as General Bear drove away from the city leading the troops. The commandos were paired up in two man teams--a driver and a gunner. Each 'team' had its own armored vehicle with a tripod-mounted assault rifle mounted on top, a grenade launcher and a dozen RPGs, a dozen hand grenades and a thousand rounds for the assault rifle. General Bear drove a hard top Jeep Wrangler and his Second Lieutenant brought up the rear in a big diesel dually pickup loaded with bivouac supplies under a canopy. Every member of the team also wore a Glock in a side holster and full body armor and had at least rudimentary training in hand to hand combat and tactical warfare.

Go, my deadly pets. Go and find subjects to fill up Volent City for me. Go and bring back intelligence about my next human conquests. Go and find me a helicopter pilot, a doctor and a dentist. And find me suitable mates--uncommon slatterns who will give me uncommon sons to carry on my name, and my manifest destiny!

CHAPTER FIVE

THE RECON MISSION

General Bear checked his map once more in the glow of his flashlight. The trip was not going the way Mr. Volent had laid it out at all. They were supposed to make their first overnight stop in Ventura, but there were so many abandoned vehicles blocking Highway 101, called variously El Camino Real or Ventura Freeway, that they only made it to Thousand Oaks by nightfall. It was ridiculous. They were supposed to have refueled in Ventura, according to the plan, but they needed to refuel now. He had led the convoy off the highway at Westlake Village, but he couldn't find a gas station and the fuel gauges were almost to the E for empty.

He switched off his flashlight and led them back onto the highway toward the next exit. It was full dark and no lights were on anywhere--no street lights, no building lights, no traffic lights, and no moonlight. This part of the L.A. basin was literally a ghost town. The arc of his Jeep's headlights did not seem very bright at all.

He led the unit off the highway at the Hampshire Road exit and veered right. At the first big intersection they found a 76 gas station and convenience store, but it had apparently emptied it's tanks during the last days of the Cremation Virus. They didn't even find anything useful in the convenience store, except a couple cases of Bud Light. Instead of returning to the freeway they headed back the other way on Hampshire Road.

On the other side of Highway 101, which along this stretch was called Screaming Eagles Highway, they found a large Chevron gas station and convenience store. This one had gasoline for General Bear's Jeep, but no diesel for the other five vehicles. By this time General Bear was taking notes in the logbook so he could remember the details for his morning short-wave check call to Mr. Volent. He'd have to report all this fruitless running around, a thought which did not make him happy. He made a quick logbook entry and led his team back to the highway. It was very late when they finally found a Mobil station with diesel pumps. After they fueled the other vehicles it was almost midnight.

General Bear agonized, privately, in his thoughts. Should they go on into Ventura and get back on schedule, or call it a day here in Thousand Oaks and get much some needed sleep before tomorrow's (probably) equally difficult day? He made the decision to continue to Ventura. Maybe he could sort of forget to report these problems in the morning and figure out a way to keep Mr. Volent from ever finding out. At 2:39 a.m. they finally pulled into the Ventura Vagabond Inn, as per Mr. Volent's itinerary for them, and quickly sacked out in a block of rooms on the ground floor.

His seven commandos stayed up just long enough to polish off the two cases of beer they had liberated, and in the morning his entire highly trained force was a little hung over. He had trouble getting them up and going, but he was glad none of them had been awake early enough to witness the chewing out he received from Mr. Volent over the radio. Unless he could make himself look very good for the rest of the trip, he would be in desperate danger when they got back to Volent City.

They got underway again at 9:00 a.m., an hour later than planned. The fuel supply Mr. Volent had marked on the map in Ventura turned out to be a total dud. It was good that they had fueled up in Thousand Oaks, but he knew he wouldn't dare mention that in his report. He logged in a fueling operation in Ventura just as Mr. Volent had laid it out.

He rarely ever felt thankful for anything, but when they finally got back onto the highway he was thankful to see that the lanes were almost entirely clear now that they were getting away from the L.A. basin. Traveling at the slow speed of twenty-five miles per hour (in order to be able to carefully observe as they traveled, just as Mr. Volent had ordered) they only made it as far as Pismo Beach by nightfall. This was their next overnight stop, according to Mr. Volent's schedule.

They bivouacked at the Quality Inn, each in his own private room, just as Mr. Volent had directed. During the night two of the men sneaked out and broke into the Pismo Beach Winery that was located just across the street.

The commandos were all able to get up in the morning, despite their hangovers, but only because General Bear and his Second drew their side-arms and forced the issue. Another little detail about the mission that wouldn't make it into the logbook. The Pismo Beach Five Cities Chevron still had fuel, so they were able to top off and get underway by 9:00 a.m., not quite as early as the 8:00 a.m. on Mr. Volent's schedule, but early enough.

Several of the men grumbled to each other over the CB, so General Bear halted the column. He made them all wait while he walked back along the column and chewed out each commando who had complained, one at a time, and made each one do a hundred pushups. They could normally do the pushups easily, but being hung over added a whole new aspect of discomfort to the physical exertion. After each one finished his pushups he had to listen to General Bear yell in his face about maintaining radio silence except for necessary transmissions because of the possibility of local base stations monitoring the airwaves.

He doubted there actually were any, because they hadn't seen any lights at night or smoke during the day. But he didn't want any more incidents to have to cover up from Mr. Volent. He was already probably in trouble, but at least it was only for his own decisions. He sure didn't want to take a rap for someone else's screw up. After they resumed travel they only made about half a mile and had to stop again. A dozen smashed vehicles were piled up across the road.

It might have seemed like the aftermath of a huge multi-vehicle smashup, except it was the same on the southbound lanes, as well as both lanes on the access road to their left between the highway and shoreline cliff, and both lanes of the surface road on their right that ran between the highway and inland mountains. Eight lanes in a narrow bottleneck between mountains and ocean, all blocked with a total of about 85 wrecked vehicles. It obviously had to be intentional.

General Bear figured there was probably an identical blockade a few miles north, which meant there were probably some survivors living near the highway between the two blockades. He was proud of himself for his cunning ability to figure that out.

He unfolded his map and studied it for several minutes, then called his Second to walk up to the Jeep. It took a few minutes for the Second to walk the length of the convoy and General Bear wished he had told him to drive up. But he finally arrived and General Bear explained the situation. Saying it out loud helped to clarify it in his mind, so by the time he finished explaining it, pointing out their location and route on the map, he had decided what they would do.

"We'll backtrack a ways and take this here Price Canyon Road east, then follow Thousand Hills Road back down to the highway near Palisades Park. There'll most likely be a road block on Thousand Hills Road, and it may be manned, so we'll go very slow. We'll bivouac on the ridgetop above the highway and look for lights down along Highway 101 during the night. If there's no lights, we'll proceed back to the highway and on north and we'll be back on our route.

"But if we see lights down there then we'll send a recon team of two commandos to check them out before morning, using night scopes. In the morning we'll still pull out and head north without letting them know we were there. Pass the orders back down the line and give me a double click on the radio when you're back in your vehicle and ready to go. Understand?" He was proud of himself for sounding so much like Mr. Volent.

"Yes sir! I understand," his Second answered, obviously as impressed with General Bear as General Bear was, and spun away.

There was another unmanned blockade on Thousand Hills Road. They used their biggest rig to push one of the vehicles out of the way and opened a lane, then proceeded to the ridge top overlooking Highway 101. Palisades Park beach and recreation area lay directly below their vantage point. That night the flickering light of a campfire on the beach could be easily seen from their position.

He ordered his Second to send two armed commandos down in the dark with night vision goggles to find out how many, their approximate ages and genders, and their fortifications. He ordered them to report back to camp as soon as possible without being detected. Two hours latter they returned to report that it was only an old woman and a young boy living in the manager's cottage of the trailer park, but there were several new unmarked grave mounds in the grassy area near the entrance. General Bear figured there must have been some male survivors who had set up the road barriers and then had for some reason died. He was disappointed that he wouldn't have something juicier to report to Mr. Volent on the radio. But at least it was something.

In the morning they went back to Price Canyon Road, then north to Highway 227, which took them on up to San Louis Obispo. He led his team south on Highway 101 until they found a road block just north of Palisades Park, just as he had predicted. It felt good to be able to write in the logbook that his assessment had been correct. He turned the convoy around and continued their northward journey on Highway 101, which was called Cabrillo Highway in this section.

Some time during that afternoon General Bear decided to just abandon Mr. Volent's detailed itinerary for their trip. He couldn't count on the fuel stops having fuel, the hotels were poorly chosen as far as keeping his men out of liquor stores and other deviltry, and their one discovery of people had thrown them a whole day late on their schedule, anyway. If they found any other survivors or had to stop for any other reason it would put them even further off the schedule. It wasn't worth the hassle to keep worrying over the useless made up itinerary.

It seemed obvious that the schedule had been set up on the short sighted assumption that there would be no survivors for them to find. That was a flaw, he could argue to Mr. Volent, if absolutely necessary. So, he arbitrarily decided to simply not worry about following the schedule. He would scout for fuel stops on his own.

And, since he now planned to ignore the schedule, he decided he would also ignore some of the route plan. Since he was the only one in the unit who had full access to the itinerary, no one would ever know until they got back. By then he would have thought up a good explanation for whatever he had done differently. His life always went that way.

They headed north again and in San Louis Obispo he turned off Highway 101 and headed north on Highway 1. Before the Cremation Virus he had heard many times about "scenic Highway 1," so this was his chance to finally see it. He hoped they didn't find survivors. The trip was very pleasant, other than having to be on the alert at all times, and the only part of the trip that was stressful was having to think fast when they found survivors. There would likely be no survivors along this lonely stretch of highway. So.......

The next stop on their itinerary was supposed to be King City, along Highway 101. But since they were now proceeding north on Highway 1 instead, which along this stretch was called Cabrillo Highway, General Bear decided he would make his own itinerary.

His commandos didn't need to know that he was no longer following Mr. Volent's itinerary. It might undermine their confidence in his leadership, and then he'd really have problems. He didn't think he would keep calling Mr. Volent any more with a morning report. either. After all, what could Mr. Volent do to him from hundreds of miles away.

Yes sir, from now on General Bear was personally in charge!

The map Mr. Volent had provided was a regular road map that included points of interest. He wanted the men to appreciate his leadership, so that day he stopped the convoy in San Simeon and let the men swim in the ocean at Hearst Memorial State Beach. They lined their vehicles up facing the ocean like tourists in the empty beachside parking lot and enjoyed a couple of hours of recreational swimming. Then they loaded back up and drove up the steep grade to Hearst Castle. They spent the night there, drinking beer and wine and swimming in Neptune's Pool until after midnight. The place had it's own generator, which still worked, so they were able to turn on the lights and have a hot meal and heat up the castle rooms for sleeping. The antique beds in the sleeping rooms of the museum were uncomfortable, but it was still memorable. In the morning they drove back down and got back onto northbound Highway 1.

They had been on the road an hour when they came to a well developed tourist spot called Ragged Point. General Bear stopped the convoy there and they spent a fun hour scavenging among the leftovers of the upscale vendors. There was a convenience store, an inn and trailer park, a wine shop and a very nice resort. He wished he had known about it before, because it would have been much more comfortable than sleeping up in Hearst Castle.

He spent some time poring over the map while his commandos pillaged. He noticed there was a place called Tusi Army Heliport not far inland. If he ever changed his mind about kowtowing to Mr. Volent, it would help considerably if he could bring back a report of a nearby helicopter for whenever they might find a pilot. So, after they got underway again, he watched for the turnoff onto Nacimiento Fergusson Road and led the convoy up into the mountains. In his rearview mirror he saw the commando driving the vehicle behind him craning his neck to look, wondering why they had gotten off the highway.

An hour of slow driving on a narrow paved road brought them through the low hills and up into the army base. He slowed the team down even slower than their customary twenty to twenty-five miles per hour, and crept quietly into the isolated military base. Sure enough, there were a dozen or more choppers of various sizes and types, all tied down out on the airfield. Better yet, there was a whole yard full of heavy duty army vehicles.

He stopped the convoy at the base admin office after they had forced their way through the locked gate. He ordered the men to spread out and recon the whole base, looking for any hidden survivors, or anything that might be of value, such as weapons or supplies. He reminded them that any survivors hiding on the base would most likely be well armed, so they were to be on high alert at all times. Their orders were to rendezvous back to him in one hour.

The commandos checked their weapons, click-checked their communication devices, studied the base layout as it was shown on the wall display in the lobby of the main office building, and then headed out on foot in pairs. He ordered his Second to man the radio and coordinate the recon communications.

He himself went looking for the head honcho's office. There had to be one. He roamed the hallways of the main office building checking the signs on the doors. It seemed the commanding officer had been a Brigadier General--only one star. Albert went into the general's office feeling a sense of awe, but quickly noticed that the office was surprisingly Spartan. It had the same thin carpeting as the rest of the building and a plain wooden army-issue desk like the one in the Colonel's office down the hall. He had expected it to be fancy, with maybe a side bar, a private bathroom, and even a secretary's desk outside the door. Since he himself was now a General, he felt disappointed.

He appeased himself by snatching up the General's collar insignia and shoulder boards that he found in the top drawer of the desk. The coat rack near the door had a fatigue jacket hanging on it. He checked and it had the insignia, and it was almost a perfect fit. He took the time to carefully remove the sewn-on name tag above the right breast pocket. The shirt had belonged to General Brown. He came out of the office wearing the jacket and the hat that went with it. He browsed through the files in the Aide's office but there was nothing interesting. There was no electricity, so he couldn't turn on the heat or make coffee or do anything else to make himself more comfortable. He found more uniform jackets hanging in a coat closet off the lobby and impulsively decided to put his entire team into actual army uniforms before they departed the base. So far they'd been wearing "similar" camo style civilian stuff.

At the end of the hour he was waiting for the Second and the commandos when they arrived back at the entrance to the main office building. No one had seen any survivors, but everyone had reports of stuff they had seen that they thought would be useful, such as new 'civvy' clothing and shoes in the Post Exchange, pharmaceuticals in the Base Med Center, army vehicles and auxiliary equipment such as trailers and tankers, and even a few AR-15s and M-15s. General Bear assured them that he would report it all to Mr. Volent by radio in the morning, and that Mr. Volent would send a salvage team.

He startled them all by ordering them to go back and find proper army uniforms that fit, including ranking insignia. He arbitrarily designated his Second as a Colonel and each commando as a Sergeant. He directed them not to worry about dress uniforms, but be sure they came back in proper fatigues with correct rank insignias. They were also to look for additional fatigue shirts and jackets with no insignia, to take back for any additional commandos they would acquire in the future. He assured them that they would retain their rank of Sergeant over any new recruits.

They were to load the extra uniforms into the cargo box of the Second's truck.

When they pulled out in mid-afternoon they were several hundred pounds heavier with dozens of new uniforms which were now the property of Volent City, as far as the men knew. All their fuel tanks were topped off, and General Bear, wearing his new uniform, had made the appropriate log entries about the supplies.

General Bear led his uniformed commando unit south on Mission, then north on Jolon until they hit Highway 101 again, then followed it north. Even at their frustratingly slow twenty-five miles per hour it was only a few minutes before they turned left onto Central Avenue on the outskirts of Greenfield. They could see the buildings of Greenfield on their right when he led them to the left on Elm, which became Arroyo Seco Road almost immediately and climbed up a narrow valley alongside a small river into the low peaks of a range of mountains.

Oak studded rolling hills sloped down to the river bottom lands as they traversed picturesque agricultural fields with the hills behind them. It seemed like each of the scattered farm houses had a swimming pool. Just as they approached the curve where his map said they should veer right onto Carmel Valley Road, General Bear diverted them off the road down a driveway to the left. The driveway sloped down to a beautifully landscaped farm house near the river. It had the biggest private swimming pool General Bear had ever seen. They took a nooner from their journey to swim, drink some beer and enjoy a long lunch.

After the break he ordered them back into their uniforms and led them back onto the pavement. The convoy veered onto Carmel Valley Road and followed it's winding course about thirty-five miles to the former tourist mecca of Carmel by the Sea, passing through the very upscale village of Carmel Valley, where it seemed like every other block had a wine tasting room. In Carmel by the Sea they eased through the touristy looking town very slowly, watching for any sign of survivors. They topped off their fuel tanks and kept going on through Monterrey.

As they drove past exit signs for Light Fighter Drive on their right, General Bear strained to see what was up the broad thoroughfare that would inspire such a name. He caught just a glimpse, in his peripheral vision, of a sign that said Deca Commissary and U.S. Army Exchange. He knew what that meant, so he led the convoy off the exit and into the parking lot of the biggest military exchange store he had ever seen.

After they raided the PX, restocking clean socks and skivvies, he led them next door to the Commissary where they stocked up on all kinds of boxed and canned foods in warehouse quantities. When they pulled back onto the highway the Second's (Colonel's) truck was full with all the food they had added to the bundles of uniforms they'd already collected. They promptly exited the highway at Exit 410 onto Reservation Road and pulled into a WalMart Supercenter there.

"Recon, this is Bear, chow break. Over."

He listened to see if anyone would be stupid enough to say anything on the radio in reply other than a double click as he had ordered. He received a series of double clicks that added up to the right total. Good!

He led them up to the main entrance of the store and they parked in a row across from the front doors. The electricity was still on here, somehow, even after more than a year had passed. They glutted themselves, General Bear along with them, and several of the men griped about having to stuff their bloated bodies into their vehicles and drive again. Apparently they had figured this was the final stop for the night.

General Bear nodded to his Second. "Colonel, have the men give you fifty pushups and then get them back into their vehicles. Next time anyone complains, increase the number of pushups to seventy-five!"

General Bear heard the grunting and low voiced curses behind him as he casually walked to his Jeep and climbed in to wait, his engine idling. Soon he heard the engines fire up behind him and pulled out, watching in his side view mirror to make sure they all followed. Of course they followed. They knew, deep in their little Sergeant brains, that they had it pretty good, traveling along like this, touring the abandoned state, all expenses paid, with an important mission to give them a sense of purpose. Why would they want to slip away? Even so, he watched his mirror and made sure that all the vehicles moved into place before he felt good about their obedience.

Late in the evening they pulled into the south end of Half Moon Bay and he led them into the parking lot of The Ritz Carlton Spa overlooking the ocean at Miramonte Pointe. Their grumbling had long since faded into silence. When they saw where they would spend the night this time, there was grudging respect on their faces as they climbed out of their parked vehicles. There was a Mullins Bar and Grill at the end of the huge parking lot, so they all fell into their luxurious rooms that night with their bellies stuffed afresh and their wits addled with the best booze they could scavenge from the fully stocked bar.

The next day they got a very late start and slowly traversed through Pedro Point and Pacifica, working their way through the suburb cities toward Daly City on the once densely populated south Peninsula of the San Francisco Bay area. They exited the highway and followed Skyline Boulevard and The Great Highway north along the shoreline. At Point Lobos they stopped briefly to look at Seal Rock, then continued around the tight curve toward the city.

He led the line of vehicles a block to the left onto Clement, then followed it past a golf course into crowded city streets and back onto northbound Highway 1. All this way it had been called Cabrillo Highway, but now the signs said Park Presidio Boulevard.

When they got close to the entrance to the Golden Gate Bridge he turned right onto Highway 101 into San Francisco, then on up into the Pacific Heights area. He looked for the tallest skyscraper so they could use it as a bivouac site. The tallest building he could find was adjacent to Lafayette Park. He ordered his team to occupy the skyscraper.

He set up a shift rotation and assigned two men at a time on four hour watches through the night. One would guard the only unlocked ground floor door, while the other would station himself on the roof and perform a three hundred sixty degree slow scan every ten minutes. The guard on the roof would note and describe the location of any lights they saw either come on or go off during that time. Each hour the rooftop scanner would walk down the long stairway and relieve the guard at the door, who would then climb the long stairway and continue the scanning for the next hour.

In the morning he continued the high elevation recon, looking for smoke or movement in the daylight, rather than lights. He had been certain they would find a few survivors in a big city such as this, but there were no indications of survivors, in any direction.

The next morning, after he had locked himself in his quarters for thirty minutes, telling the Colonel he was making his daily radio report to Mr. Volent, they pulled out and headed across the Golden Gate Bridge. The Colonel was the only one of the group who had ever seen it before. The sergeants ooohed and aaaahed as they drove slowly across. General Bear felt nothing but scorn for their stupidity.

When they left the north end of the bridge, the highway seemed to have three names: Redwood Highway, El Camino Real, and William T. Bagley Freeway. He knew it wasn't a good example to the Sergeants, but General Bear broke radio silence just to make a wise crack about those dumb Californians not knowing what they wanted to call a strip of pavement.

He got some polite chuckles and wished he'd kept his mouth shut. The last thing he needed was to lose the little bit of respect he was getting from his team thus far. He sensed that they were all on the brink of total rebellion and chaos all the time, and he was just hanging on to his arbitrary authority over them by the skin of his teeth.

Problem was, they all knew that they weren't a real army. They all knew that Volent City had no 'rights' anywhere outside the building it lived in, and Mr. Volent wasn't really a king. They all knew they were simply on a scavenging and "casing the country" mission, and the whole thing was really just a silly but serious adult game.

And they all knew they were better off if they played along, even though they were basically nothing more than organized thugs. In the new order it was better to be a well armed thug with well armed backup than to be out there alone trying to survive.

It was even official policy that they were to sneak. Clandestine equals fear. You can't sneak boldly and confidently. And, even though General Bear had given the men lots of latitude so far, they all knew that their well being now depended entirely on his benevolence. They were much more highly motivated to give him respect than he thought they were, but much less motivated to practice military discipline than he thought.

General Bear secretly hoped they didn't find anyone for a few more days. The commandos needed time to get more settled into the routine of the mission. If they were all hyped up when they spotted the next survivor there was no telling what they might do. He worried about the kinds of savagery that might emerge from some of the men as they discovered that they held power over the lives of others who were helpless to resist. What would happen?

He didn't have to wait long to find out. In Marin City he impulsively led his convoy to exit Highway 101 back onto Highway 1. He had studied both routes the night before they pulled out of San Francisco and hadn't been able to decide which one to take. Highway 1 was more scenic, but passed through no large towns. Highway 101 passed through a few coastal towns of northern California, but was mostly a plain freeway out of sight of the ocean. All of a sudden he had impulsively decided to go up Highway 1. He liked seeing the ocean on his left.

About an hour up the road they came upon some survivors at an Audubon Society preserve beside the road. By the time General Bear realized that there were people there, the commando convoy was already close enough to be heard by the survivors!

Luckily for the commandos, and unluckily for the small group of survivors, the bird watchers, who had gravitated to the preserve because of their love of birds, were not armed with anything stronger than binoculars. The 'clandestine' aspect of their mission temporarily set aside, General Bear ordered the commandos to sweep in and overwhelm the two elderly men and half dozen women of various ages. The survivors had taken up residence at the sanctuary to continue the program of caring for rescued wild fowl. They offered no resistance.

General Bear ordered the two old men handcuffed, then ordered the women to be lined up for closer inspection. Of the six female captives, five were at least in their fifties. The sixth one was probably about thirty years old, somewhat attractive and reasonably well built. All the women were modestly dressed, but General Bear noticed that his men took lots of liberties with their hands as they lined them up for his evaluation.

He posted two of his men to guard the women with instruction that they were not to be injured or molested yet, and sent two of them to guard the entrance gate. He sent the Colonel and the remaining commandos to search the facility for any other survivors or weapons or anything of special value they might want to take with them.

Then he went back to the line of frightened women. He ordered one of the guards to bring the young one into the back office where he would personally interview her. After the guard was dismissed back to his post, General Bear seated himself behind the desk and leaned back in the comfortable executive's chair. He ordered the woman, wide eyed with fear, to sit on the edge of the desk with one foot on the pulled out bottom drawer. She was dressed conservatively, like the other women, in a knee length skirt and a long sleeved sweater. When she reluctantly sat as he had instructed, frowning her dislike, her skirt pulled up and he laid his hand on her bare thigh.

He left his hand there while he asked her for her name, her age, and a few other general questions. She squirmed in obvious discomfort at his touch, but gradually calmed down a little. He began to slowly slide his hand back and forth, going a little higher each time, until he had her skirt pushed up almost to her hip. She continued to squirm the whole time, and finally reached to push his hand away. He froze her with a glare.

"Do you want to be handcuffed?"

She shook her head 'no' as her eyes flooded with tears.

"Then relax. Pretend that you're handcuffed and keep your hands behind your back. Sit up straight and put your shoulders back as if you're proud to be a woman. I must examine you to make sure you have no signs of the plague before we proceed. If you're clean enough, I may use you myself before I let you go to my men."

The guards and the old women in the outer room heard her cry out several times over the next half hour. When she finally came out of the toom she was weeping silently, obviously braless under her sweater, and no longer wearing a skirt. Her long bare legs were alabaster white and gracefully slender over her pink bikini panties. The old ladies gasped, while the guards leered appreciatively.

General Bear spoke to the nearest guard. "Sergeant, see that this slightly used slattern is cleaned up properly, as well as the old slatterns, and then find a room where they can all service you and the other commandos. Rotate two men to relieve the gate guards so they can also enjoy a turn with the sluts. In exactly two hours we'll get underway. This young one shall be loaded in the Colonel's vehicle, handcuffed, and dressed appropriately for her duties as a road slattern. The old slatterns and underlings will be locked in a back room before we leave. Leave a way for them to escape in a few hours. When we leave in two hours every commando shall be back in proper uniform and locked and loaded. Dismissed."

As he turned away he thought to himself, *Well, that didn't go too bad. She's pitifully ignorant about how to please a man, but presumably she'll learn a few things in the next two hours. I think I earned a little more respect from the men. I sounded just like Mr. Volent. That can't hurt my standing with them. So far, so good. I think I'm going to enjoy being a General!*

PART FOUR

THE HOMESTEAD

"Yeeeee-hhaaaaaaaaa!" Barbara screamed, exulting, as she galloped Bruno full tilt across the finish line ahead of young Luke Short who was on the mare, Bonnie.

"No fair!" Luke shouted back, unable to keep from laughing. "I had to holster my pistol after firing the starting shot!"

"Ha," she retorted gleefully! "You're a gunslinger, remember? You don't even have to look to holster your pistol! Admit it, you were beat by a girl! Ha ha!"

"Nuh-uh!" He argued with overdramatic passion. "I let you win cause you're only a girl!"

They were both grinning as they swung to the ground and walked the sweaty horses back toward the paddock to cool them off. She was teaching him Karate, he was teaching her the fine art of the fast draw, and together they were learning to ride and care for their newly acquired Kiger Mustangs. They had quickly come to mutually respect each other's specialized self defense skills, and they had discovered a mutual love of horses.

Barbara knew that young Luke also enjoyed the freedom to banter back and forth, as she did. A friendly ridiculous insult once in awhile seemed in some strange way to assure them that their friendship was safe and secure. Barbara usually tired of the banter first, and this was no exception.

"Seriously, Luke, you're a good rider. If we traded horses you'd beat me easy. I can see that by the way you kept up with me on

Bonnie. I think you got even more out of her than she knew she had. Good riding!"

"Aw, she's just a great horse, that's all. I almost fell off when we came around that big old red cedar at the end of the ridge."

"Yeah, right. Now you're really sayin' you just let me win because I'm a girl."

"No," he paused reflectively, getting serious in return. "I've been doing a lot of thinking, and to me you'll never really be just a girl. You know what I mean? You're a grownup and I'm a kid. You're a woman, not a girl, and I'm a boy, not a man." He paused, then continued.

"But, I'm okay with that. I don't mind. It's just the way it is. Someday we'll meet other people and I'll find a girl my age and we'll probably hit it off. I'll be older by then, and I'll want to get married and settle down. But you and me? That wouldn't work. You're more like my big sister--not really like a girl, if you know what I mean."

"Yeah, Luke, I do know what you mean. The feeling's mutual. I've said before you remind me of my little brother Bobs. That's how I like you, as a brother."

Barbara was deeply relieved to hear these words from her co-inhabitant at the homestead. Luke had showed up about eight months after the Cremation Virus had decimated earth's population. The few survivors of the plague were scattered across the entire depopulated earth. Somehow Luke had happened upon her at her new homestead in northern California.

She had quickly overcome her initial wariness and invited him to live at her homestead in the Trinity Alps outside Lewiston, California. He was fourteen when he had arrived, and he had acted like he had a crush on her at first. But now they had just celebrated his fifteenth birthday by taking a weekday off. It had been a year since the plague and Barbara couldn't remember the last time she'd taken a whole day off. The day of rest, and the relief of settling this awkwardness with Luke, felt really great.

Young Luke's willing and able-bodied help had contributed much to the quality of life at the homestead. Between her ingenuity and determination and his young man's strength and enthusiasm, the homestead now also included a sturdy thousand gallon water tower fed by a solar powered pump from the fresh spring inside the cold cellar. The house, the barn and the one outside faucet all now had gravity fed fresh water.

Even with Luke's help the plumbing had been hard work, but it wasn't overwhelming. Whenever the tank got full the pump would shut off. The cold spring water flowed constantly out of the cold cellar into a stone and mortar water trough for the livestock, and the overflow drifted down a gravel bed into the creek near their swimming hole.

With Luke's help, working hard eight to ten hours a day, six days a week, she had built a 20' by 20' milking barn and a 20' by 20' three room cabin--both sturdy pole and beam. The milking barn had a concrete floor, with a 10' by 10' section walled off for the milking stanchion and a 10' by 10' section for a livestock nursery. The half intended as a nursery had become storage, and was filled with a small supply of hay bales, sacks of grain and dry dog food.

The cabin's full width front room was their combination living room and kitchen. The back half had a four foot wide hallway down the middle to a back door and each of them had an eight by ten bedroom off the hallway. At the end of the wall was a door out to the add-on privy.

Behind the cabin, between the cabin and the base of the hillside, where the cold cellar was, they had installed an array of solar panels to power a freezer, a hot water heater, ceiling lights and wall outlets in the cabin, and red security lights over both the front and back porches.

They had added another solar panel and had run a power line for lights in the milking parlor, the chicken coop and the goat shelter. They had dug trenches so all their outside plumbing and electric lines were underground. The solar panels provided a cover over the door to the cold cellar set into the side of the hill behind the cabin.

The cold cellar, which Barbara had just finished when Luke showed up, now had shelves on one side up to head high which were well stocked with all sorts of canned and boxed foods, and on the other side drying lines stretched across the ceiling loaded with fruit and vegetables hanging to dry, along with bear and deer jerky. It also held a generous supply of dried herbs, heritage fruit and vegetable seeds scavenged from plant nurseries in Redding, and a bin full of raw and slowly drying potatoes. A pull-chain ceiling light made up for the lack of a window.

Their cabin had a full attic with a tongue and groove floor and drop down ladder, and that space was filled with surplus blankets and linen and other household supplies, as well as thousands of rounds of ammunition for each of their various guns. They had built the cabin over a cellar made of steel reinforced concrete. It had an outside covered access, which they normally kept closed to keep the yard animals out of the cabin.

Just for fun, because Luke was still a kid and wanted a secret tunnel, when they dug the cellar they had spent several extra weeks digging a trench six feet deep and three feet wide and lining it with reinforced concrete walls and floor. Then they built forms and poured a six-inch thick steel-reinforced cover for the trench, roughly six inches below the surface level of the ground and covered with dirt.

Luke's secret tunnel from the cellar under the house started behind an innocent looking floor-to-ceiling book case craftily mounted on tiny wheels and hinged at one edge so it would swing out like a door. The tunnel led across the back yard to the underground cold storage vault, where it came up through a trap door hidden under a throw rug.

Then, to complete the project, which seemed to have taken on a life of its own, they had spent several more weeks extending the tunnel from the cold storage vault on around the base of the ridge where it emptied into some dense brush in the gulley that led up to the peak of Browns Mountain. The whole project was under at least six inches of dirt, with grass and wild flower seed liberally scattered over it.

They added one more small solar panel and ran a strand of small red LED lights in both tunnels. Within a few weeks the fresh dirt on top had grown in with plant life and the secret escape tunnel was well hidden.

Barbara was surprised to find that it was exciting to compete with Luke, racing against the clock, to see who could make the quickest transit through the tunnel and all the way to the peak. At the word "GO" the racer would open the "secret" rug-covered trap door in the hallway of the cabin, drop into the cellar, exit through the portal concealed behind the hinged book case, carefully closing it behind him or her, then run full speed through the tunnel past the cold cellar to the foliage-covered exit, and on up the gully to the peak. Luke was slightly faster than Barbara and could do the whole distance in a minute and thirty-five seconds, but Barbara was almost as fast at a minute and fifty seconds.

All in all, Barbara was very pleased with their situation at the homestead. If they ever became unable to leave the homestead for any reason, they could probably survive for as long as a year before their supplies would be depleted. And if they were ever trapped inside the cabin for any reason, they had a secret emergency exit.

The Kiger stallion was named Bruno and the pretty little mare was Bonnie. They now also had a beef cow named Bossy who was due to calve in about a month, and their own small Angus bull named, not surprisingly, Angus. Their livestock also included a huge billy goat (named Billy, of course) and a nanny goat named Nanny. Nanny had young twin kids who were as yet un-named, and a large enough bag to produce enough milk for her kids and the humans. Their flock of chickens had grown to more than twenty. A growing flock of half-wild Guinea Hens lived in the trees around the homestead and came down in the evening to eat with the chickens, which were always fed just before dark so they could be closed into the coop at night..

The Guinea Hens were by far the best watch animals, even better than Friend as far as alertness, but Friend was the true guardian. Friend was the tallest dog either of them had ever seen. She was completely black, lean bodied, with a dense wiry coat. Her head was huge and her jaws enormous enough that they found it surprising she didn't drool like many large-jawed dogs.

Late in the summer Barbara and Luke moved the last of the hay out of the big barn in Lewiston into their own smaller hay barn. Back in Lewiston they used the ranch equipment to mow the large hayfield that had grown waist high, rake it into windrows to dry for a few days, and then bale it. They had nearly refilled the big barn in Lewiston, and the supply at the homestead was enough for their own animals for a full winter.

The livestock they had released down at the ranch in Lewiston had mostly stayed in their familiar fields and seemed to be surviving well. Several calves and foals had been born since Luke's arrival. When they ran low on beef they would be able to spare their own stock at the homestead and take a yearling from down in Lewiston.

Their most recent major project had been to construct defensive barriers on the access roads into the homestead. They had engineered natural looking jumbled barricades of a fallen tree with small boulders and shrubs on Barbara's road and the one that came up from Browns Creek Road out of Weaverville. The barricades were at narrow spots between the steep sides of the road. On the lengthy third road that came over the ridge from Rush Creek Road they built a barricade but, believing that no one would invest the time and work needed to get past the iron gates and the other barricades further down the hill, Barbara left her little sign on the top of the ridge that said "All is wrong until God makes it right." For some reason she just couldn't bear to remove it.

At the beginning of Barbara's Road, where Luke had walked in through the gate when they first met, they placed a barrier at the top of the steep grade just inside the gate. They set up a circuitous ATV route around that entrance that could only be found if one knew where to look. The route around the barricade had a false barrier of dead brush where it exited from Browns Mountain Road and they made it a practice to always brush out their tracks after driving through. Even to their own eyes it was invisible, so they felt confident it would fool anyone driving around looking for isolated survivors.

They also repaired and reinforced the iron gate bars where each of the three entry roads ended at a larger road. Basically, if anyone managed to somehow get past any of the iron gates, they would soon encounter a natural looking barrier and hopefully give up. Since the old maps all showed nothing up in Trinity House Gulch on Browns Mountain, Barbara hoped no passing stranger would ever feel motivated to make the effort to get past the barricades. If they did they would be reduced to proceeding on foot, and hopefully Friend or the Guinea Hens would sound the alarm in time.

Friend had proven herself to be an uncanny guard dog. She had alerted them one afternoon when a huge bull elk wandered into the valley, and once at night when a small pack of coyotes came through. Sometimes Friend would take off after dark and be gone all night, but the Guinea Hens always stayed nearby, roosting at night in trees near the cabin. Friend would always return in the morning, usually with some sort of small game such as a raccoon or rabbit.

Once she brought in a bear cub she had killed in the night. That made Barbara a little nervous, but she didn't want to stifle the wildness in the huge dog. If anything happened to both Luke and her, Friend would need to know how to survive on her own.

Barbara and Luke talked about lots of things while they worked side by side on projects during the day and rested in the evenings after dark. Their main topic was usually related to their survival. They had agreed to try to always think "what if…" Luke explained to Barbara that it was called contingency planning.

He rarely spoke of his childhood, but had said that his dad had been a survivalist prepper and an expert in contingency planning. By asking each other "what if….." around the fire pit in the evening they kept thinking up more projects they wanted to get done. Usually it felt urgent once they thought of it.

But after finishing the work on the three roads coming into the homestead they had taken it easy for several days, doing nothing more than the morning and evening chores. It had been nice, like a vacation.

They had learned to always saddle the horses in the morning, leaving the cinches loose, and use the horses to go anyplace on the homestead that seemed too far to walk. The last few days, with the road project done, they went on a long ride each day, exploring further along the ridge top into the Trinity Alps toward Weaverville and over the peak toward Lewiston.

They found and explored a couple of isolated cabins several miles away, almost to Weaverville, but didn't find anything of immediate value to their survival. One cabin contained a wooden crate half full of gold bars, of all things. It was just like any other dumpy old historic cabin in the Trinity Alps, but at the back of the tiny living room was the stash of gold. It defied conjecture, and had no real value any more--at least not for Luke and Barbara. They left it there.

They practiced Karate and fast draw daily, and worked out with a very strenuous aerobic exercise regime. But their only real accomplishment for the past few days had been improving their general familiarity with the surrounding wilderness and giving the horses good exercise.

THE MEETING

Barbara could see that Luke was starting to feel a little bored after several days of leisure. He had "felt a little bored" (his words) a few weeks earlier and had dug himself an underground firing range so he could practice his fast draw without being heard all over the alps. It only took him four days to complete it, working like a madman from dawn to dark. He spent the next day concealing the entrance with strategically placed artificial bushes and greenery. He had been okay since then.

It was a side of him she hadn't noticed before. When Barbara asked him about it, he admitted that last time he had "felt a little bored" he had built the big rig flatbed camp trailer he was driving when he had stumbled upon the entrance to the homestead. He sheepishly admitted that, looking back, he had been this way since he was a kid.

She wondered, grinning to herself, if he thought he wasn't a kid any more. She also wondered what he would think of to do this time, now that he was "feeling a little bored" again. They were both surprised at the way his growing feeling of boredom was resolved.

The next afternoon he decided to try to beat his own time racing through the emergency tunnel. As he raced up the brush choked gully he mentally noted certain spots where he needed to clear a better path for a faster climb. With the stopwatch in one hand he scrambled up the steep narrowing slope, furiously striving to reach the summit so quickly that Barbara would not be able to beat his time.

As he topped out he punched the stopwatch button and checked the time, his oxygen starved lungs gasping for deep rapid breaths. Then he looked up and his gaze automatically swept the horizon, a survival habit he and Barbara had been cultivating.

He froze. Due east he saw a thin column of light grey smoke.

Light grey meant wood, as in a campfire. He had just talked about this with Barbara. They had agreed that if a building or petroleum product happened to combust for any reason, the smoke would be dark. But this smoke was almost white. It had to be from freshly cut wood.

A smoke signal? Yes!

It seemed to be originating from down toward Redding near the east end of Whiskeytown Lake, probably at or near the rest area on Highway 299. From there going eastward the road dropped down steeply into the village of Old Shasta, then dropped less steeply four more miles into Redding. From that spot where the smoke was rising, at the top of the grade coming up out of Redding, a person would be able to see the whole upper Sacramento Valley. It would be a perfect place from which to look for signs of survivors and from which to send up a smoke signal that would be visible for many miles in almost every direction.

Luke's thoughts were racing. Did someone want to be found by a particular person or group of people, or was the signal intended for anyone who might see it? Or, could it simply be some naive survivor being careless about making their presence known? He needed to get back down to Barbara to figure out what to do. But he also needed to stay up here and watch for any answering signal that might appear.

He glanced over his shoulder down toward the homestead. Oh no! Barbara had just started burning a small brush pile and white smoke was beginning to rise lazily into the sky! It looked exactly like an answer to the signal!

He spun away down the steep slope as fast as he could, sort of a controlled fall, taking giant strides down the exposed ridge top that rose steeply behind the cabin. He had to get Barbara's burn pile extinguished as quickly as possible!

She gave him a startled look of alarm when he charged in and started kicking dirt onto the smoldering pile of leaves and pine needles. To her credit she quickly figured out what he was doing and helped him finish stomping out the last scattered embers.

"I'm so sorry, Luke! I wasn't thinking!"

He was winded from the run up and down the mountain and his stomping spree over the fire and spoke between gasps for breath.

"Problem! (gasp) On the mountain, (gasp) Saw a smoke signal (gasp) from the rest area at Whiskeytown!" He finished in a rush, aware that his voice was shrill in between his gasps for breath, but he didn't care. He leaned forward with his hands on his knees to breathe deeply.

Barbara saw that he was near panic and spoke soothingly.

"It'll be okay. Thanks to you we got this smoke stopped. It's gone already. I doubt they noticed it. But even if they did, they'll never find the homestead. Remember, we've barricaded the roads, right? So it'll be okay."

His brow furrowed as he thought for a moment. His gasps decreasing to mere huffing and puffing.

"We should go see who it is! Could be people like us! Or, it could be bad guys!"

Barbara understood the contingency dynamics right away.

If whoever was sending up that smoke signal saw the smoke from the homestead, they would think it was a response and come looking. If they were bad guys, it would be better to encounter them away from the homestead, by ambush, with Luke and Barbara at the advantage. The alternative was to sit passively waiting here to see if the homestead would be discovered.

If it turned out that they were people like themselves, survivors with good intentions, they should try to make contact with them anyway for mutual encouragement and assistance. If they were bad guys, with evil intentions, they should get proactive and go meet them with an ambush to improve their odds of victory.

Barbara and Luke were as ready as they knew how to be, for either contingency, but they both suddenly felt very vulnerable right then. In either case, whether these were good guys or bad guys, they needed to go meet them away from the homestead. And, since there was a chance they might fail, they needed to set up the homestead so the animals would be able to survive if they didn't make it back. It was a detail they hadn't considered yet, despite all their planning and discussions.

They got to work, thankful that together they made a great team. By nightfall they had set up the animal pens so the gates were fastened shut but would fall open when the water source inside the pen got low enough. Luke came up with the ingenious idea to set up a float system that would release each gate. It helped that the water troughs were just inside the gates to the pens. The horses drank the most, so their tank level would get low enough to open the gate by evening of the second day. The goats, probably the third day. The chickens, probably within five days. All this was assuming, of course, that neither Barbara nor Luke made it back to reset the triggers and resume doing the chores.

Whiskeytown Lake was too far to travel by horseback, so after dark they loaded their two well-muffled ATVs onto the tilt flatbed and headed down Trinity House road as quietly as possible. Once on the pavement they kept their speed down, with the motor idling in a medium gear. Though they were more than twenty miles away, in the still of night the sounds might carry across Whiskeytown Lake more than they realized.

When they got down Highway 299 as far as the old historic Tower House near Whiskeytown Lake, they turned off into the visitor's parking lot hidden behind trees between the highway and

Clear Creek. The truck would be out of sight while they proceeded the last couple of miles on the ATVs. They were careful to not rev the motors on the ATVs as they quietly followed the highway back a thousand feet until they could turn off onto South Shore Drive.

They figured the people up at the rest area would be watching Highway 299, and probably wouldn't pay much attention to the side road going around the lake from their position. Luke and Barbara might be able to sneak closer if they followed the dirt track that wound through the deep forest on the south lakeshore. It was further, but their motor sounds would be shielded by the deep woods, and they would be able to approach the strangers from the rear.

After what seemed like an hour they finally dropped out of the forest onto the paved road, then drove past the turn off to Brandy Creek. All too soon they were crossing the earthen dam which had been dedicated by President John F. Kennedy before he was assassinated, way back in the 1960's. At the dam the road sign indicated that the rest of the road was called the J. F. Kennedy Memorial Road.

Luke didn't agree, in vehement shispers, but Barbara was sure and insisted that they had about another full mile to go before the junction with Highway 299, where they believed the smoke signal had originated. Luke continued with her, sulking privately to himself in the dark as they drove at little more than a walking pace, their headlights off. Soon they passed the entrance to the park headquarters and Barbara motioned them to a stop. After a whispered conversation they pulled into the headquarters entrance and drove their ATVs around to the side of the main building to hide them while they proceeded the last little way on foot.

There were abandoned service vehicles parked all over the place, as well as several civilian vehicles. One civilian rig, a huge Ford F-350 pickup, looked like someone had been on a camping trip and got caught here by the Cremation Virus. The back was loaded with camping gear and supplies and had a small empty flatbed ATV trailer hooked to it.

Feeling quite clever, they drove their ATVs up onto the trailer and shut them down. It looked so natural no one would ever notice the ATVs. They stepped down, pulled their long guns out of the scabbards on the ATVs, and put on the night vision goggles they had acquired for just such a moment as this.

They had practiced moving quietly, and they were both heavily armed. Luke wore his two fast draw holsters and carried a 12 gauge pump shotgun on a sling over one shoulder. Barbara wore her new pistol (that replaced the one Luke had shot out of her hand) in a belt holster, and carried her little .410 shotgun loaded with slugs.

They turned to go and suddenly heard a soft woman's voice.

"We're peaceful. Please don't shoot at us."

The soft spoken words did not trigger their adrenalin, so Luke didn't turn and shoot like he had with Barbara. Instead, in perfect unison with Barbara, he stopped in his tracks. Like a well trained marionette team they both spun back around. Standing near the hood of the pickup that was attached to the trailer where they'd just parked their ATVs were two women and a man, all of whom were also wearing night vision goggles.

When Barbara and Luke didn't shoot, the three slowly stepped into view from behind the hood. On closer inspection it was a young man, a woman slightly older than him, and a teenage girl. Barbara and Luke stared, transfixed, at the first people they had seen in almost a year, other than each other.

The man was just under six feet tall, physically fit, with a pleasant face--at least the little bit they could see between his longish hair and very bushy beard. He wore camo pants and jacket, with a checkered flannel shirt under the jacket. His outfit was topped off with a canvas slouch hat and Barbara almost laughed when she noticed that he wore camo sneakers. He had a Browning 12 gauge pump shotgun, just like Luke's, hanging from a sling over his shoulder and he held it with one hand, casually pointed at the ground in their general direction.

The older woman was slender but straight shouldered and broad hipped, almost as tall as the man, and her auburn hair was just starting to turn grey at her temples. She was pretty, in a maternal sort of way, but there were worry lines around her eyes. She was the one who had spoken and she smiled shyly. She wore a corduroy jacket over floral nurse scrubs that didn't conceal her shapely curves, and her empty hands were spread out to her sides in plain view.

The young girl was petite, almost fragile looking, with wispy long blond hair and delicate wrists and ankles. She was obviously past puberty but seemed very young and vulnerable. On second look, though, she seemed a little less fragile and slightly seasoned, but still had an aura of feminine youth and innocence. She appeared to be unarmed and wore a lined bolero jacked over a low cut body shirt with matching leotard leggings under a knee length plaid skirt--all of which enhanced her schoolgirl image.

Two little black children who looked about eight years old stood peeking out from behind the trio of adults. The little boy was slightly taller than the little girl, but they looked like twins. They hung back, fearfully, their eyes large, clinging to the teenage girl's hands.

While Barbara and Luke assessed the strange looking trio with the two ebony children, they were being thoroughly examined in return. Roostafer was stunned speechless. He had never seen such a beautiful woman in his life. She was perfect in every way. She stood inches taller than himself. Her eyes, even in the dim greenish light of the goggles, blazed brightly under silky white lashes and brows. Her long tresses were a gleaming halo around her Mona Lisa face with its broad forehead, graceful cheekbones, and gently curved cheeks united at a perfect chin. Her neck was a graceful alabaster column sweeping gently out to delightful square shoulders. Her bulky denim jacket over a checkered flannel shirt (like his own) disguised her shape somewhat, but he got an impression of athleticism and energy. The waistband of her trousers, loose like Rose's, was as high off the ground as Rose's bosom. The word statuesque came to his mind.

He knew, with the tiny part of his brain that wasn't almost hysterical with fear, that he was already genuinely and helplessly smitten. He suddenly feared that she might be already married. He longed to sit down with this woman and learn everything about her. Without her having said a single word, she was already absolutely fascinating. Having only just met her, and not yet even spoken with her, he already felt that his life would never be complete without her. He felt giddy, silly, recklessly ready to surrender or grovel or whatever would be necessary to make sure that she never went away.

And then, suddenly, everyone was talking at once. The night went from awkward total silence to chaotic verbal bedlam. After about twenty seconds of the noise, young Luke raised both arms straight over his head and shouted at the top of his voice.

"STOP!"

Everyone immediately fell silent. Luke continued.

"It's the middle of the night, we're all tired, we can get to know each other in the morning, okay? Let's all get some sleep first! "

"Right," Roostafer immediately agreed, speaking for his group.

Barbara spoke up. "We have a small homestead about an hour's drive from here. You're welcome to follow us and we'll put you up for the night. In the morning we can get acquainted and figure out where we go from here. Does everyone agree?"

"These people have agreed for me to be the leader of our group," Roostafer explained, secretly proud of himself for sounding so calm and confident, while inside his heart was hammering in his chest as he looked at her and listened to her fascinating voice. He replied to her invitation, "We accept your gorgeous….. Uh, I mean, your kind invitation."

Now he was embarrassed. There was just so much to say. So many questions. He felt an overwhelming need to look into her eyes, hear her voice, hold her hand, touch her hair.

Wait! What was I saying? Oh yes!

"We'll just need a minute to love our, … I mean, load our ATVs, then we're ready to go."

The amazing young woman answered him. "We left our flatbed truck down the road a ways. And we loaded our ATVs on your trailer to hide them, so we'll need to unload them to ride back to our truck."

"Oh sure! We'll just follow you then, okay ladies?" He tilted his head toward Rose and Lizzie, but couldn't tear his gaze away from the tall goddess. Rose and Lizard shared an amused glance, then agreed.

Barbara and Luke glanced at each other and then she answered for them both.

"Okay then," Barbara answered in an animated voice. "I take it you, sir, are driving."

She couldn't believe how flirty that sounded. What was wrong with her?

"We'll just head west on Highway 299 and turn in to where our park is trucked."

Neither she nor he seemed to notice her solipsism. But everyone else did. Luke shared an amused glance with the other two women.

On the short, quiet, drive back to the Tower House parking lot everyone was obviously doing a lot of thinking. Back at the flatbed, Barbara invited Rose to ride with her to the homestead. The man called Roostafer claimed to be the leader, and Barbara was powerfully attracted to him. But her bad history with men demanded that she use caution. Rose was obviously older, and Barbara instinctively felt she could trust her. She wanted a chance to speak with her privately and make sure the man wasn't just a charismatic fake who was snowballing Rose and the teenager against their better judgment.

By the time they drove into Trinity House homestead it was almost midnight. Rose had talked the whole way, in answer to Barbara's carefully worded questions. She had told Barbara about how Roostafer and Lizard had rescued her, and had summarized their trip from that incident until they reached Whiskeytown Lake. But she ran out of time before she could explain the presence of the twins.

Her initial wariness resolved, Barbara was once again anxious to get to know the startling man whose calm confidence so intrigued her. She liked hearing his voice. She liked the way his gaze swept up her body, acknowledging his vibrant awareness, but came to rest on her eyes, as if her eyes were the destination he desired. When he looked into her eyes she felt a little gawky and self-conscious, but was somehow simultaneously very aware that he also saw her as beautiful.

She was also curious about the kids. What was their story? She'd heard how Rose had joined the group, but how did the twins fall in with them? And the teenager, Lizzie--how did she join up with Roostafer to start forming this strange group? She looked forward to hearing the rest of the story. But first, she had company to take care of. Little kids first!

Barbara sent Luke to the cold cellar to get a late night snack for everyone while she climbed up into the loft to make up beds for the twins and Lizzie and Rose. Roostafer could sleep in Luke's room.

It wasn't until she fell into bed and her thoughts whirled around with memories of the evening that Barbara realized no one, not even herself, had considered the possibility of anyone sleeping in her room with her. Did that mean something? If so, what?

In the morning it seemed that everyone was exhausted except Barbara and Roostafer. The two of them were up early--alone with each other for the first time. Barbara brewed a pot of coffee and invited him to join her, each of them carrying their fresh cup of coffee, as she did her morning chores.

He listened, fascinated, as Barbara described how she had started with the latrine, then put up the tent cabin, and so forth. While she talked she worked, showing him how each of her chores was accomplished.

First she milked the nanny goat, then fed hay to the goats and cattle and horses, then gathered the eggs and fed the chickens and Guinea Hens. Roostafer followed her around, not helping but very impressed by the scope and quality of the layout of the homestead.

"Barra-burra," he began, intending to say how impressed he was. But he saw her startled reaction at the way he had mispronounced her name and interrupted himself. "I'm sorry. Did I offend you, calling you that?"

She hesitated a moment, trying to frame her thoughts into words, then said, "Oh, I'll be okay. Just caught me off guard, that's all. My Uncle Cliff used to call me that in his Irish brogue. He was my best friend growing up, and he died a few months before the plague. I guess I'm still grieving for him."

"Well, if you don't want me to call you that, I won't," he assured her. "But with your whole name being so obviously Irish, it sorta rolls naturally out of my mouth, if you know what I mean." He smiled as he explained himself.

"I understand. Really. I don't think I mind if you call me that, but it may take me a few times to get used to it. Okay? No one has called me that since Uncle Cliff."

"Okay, sure. I'll just call you Barbara 'til you say it's okay for me to take it to the next level."

She gave him another odd look, then continued with her chores, showing him how and where she always did security checks at the three entrances. Friend loped along with them as she led the way on her ATV, Roostafer putt-putting along behind her on his.

When they got back to the homestead the others were beginning to stir. Barbara showed Roostafer the cold cellar as she refilled the pancake mix canister from the kitchen, and brought in butter and syrup for the pancake and eggs breakfast she planned to fix for everyone. She was pleased when Roostafer pitched in and helped, cracking the eggs into the frying pan with a familiarity that told her he was no stranger to cooking.

When everyone was up and had gathered around the table, their mouths watering at the sight and smells of a huge stack of fresh pancakes and fried eggs, Roostafer pleased her again by offering to give thanks while everyone joined hands. It was the first time their hands had touched and Roostafer and Barbara both felt a tingly jolt at the contact.

They bowed their heads together and he prayed, "Father in Heaven, you continue to amaze us with your generosity and kindness. You protect and preserve our lives. You provide us with all we need. You brought all of us together in this big empty world, and you gave us this moment to share this meal together. Thank you, in the blessed name of our Savior Jesus Christ, for this wonderful food and all the other blessings we enjoy. We receive all of it from your hand, with humble hearts. Amen"

Barbara thought it was the most beautiful prayer she had ever heard. Her eyes were moist with tears of gratitude toward God. As she sat down she noticed that Rose and Lizzie were also very moved. Luke, however, seemed a little embarrassed by the emotion of the moment. It wasn't the first time Barbara worried about his soul. She noticed that Luke's lack of empathy to the moment was also noticed by Roostafer, who cast a quick glance at her. She discreetly shook her head and Roostafer acknowledged with a solemn wink. She was secretly pleased that they seemed to be so spiritually like-minded.

"Barbara showed me around while she did the morning chores," Roostafer addressed himself to Lizzie, Rose and the twins. "She said we're welcome to stay here at the homestead and I'd like us to accept the invitation. We will need to build an addition onto this cabin for additional sleeping rooms, or build a second cabin, but all of us can share the work so I think it'll go quickly. Lizard and Rose, I know it's amazing, but much of this homestead was built by Barbara, by herself, during the first year after the plague. Luke's only been here a few months. Luke, I can see you're a good worker by all you've helped Barbara get done since you got here."

"Roostafer," Barbara cut in, "and all the rest of you, Luke and I will be glad to have your company and your help with all the work. There's still much to do. And you're all welcome to add your own ideas. We sort of play it by ear. Our latest project was to put barricades on the three roads coming in, with the secret bypass we all came in on last night. We still have access to just about anything we need in either Redding or Weaverville, but we're working on getting ourselves set up to be self sufficient before the preserved consumables run out. So yes, there's plenty of work for everyone. Even the little ones can learn to help with the chores and housework. When they're older they can help with everything, as adults."

"Oh," Rose declared with a smile. "Al and Meg are two hard working kids! Aren't you," she pulled them into her lap. The children glowed with her praise but didn't speak.

"So, when are you going to tell us their story, Rose," Barbara asked?

"I don't know if I should. They are pretty good talkers themselves, when we give them a chance. Aren't you, Al and Meg?" Rose chuckled.

Though the twins had been remarkably silent since last night when the two groups met, it now seemed as if their vocal floodgates had suddenly been flung wide open.

"Oh, yes, Miss Barbara!" Al spoke with a decided city accent. "My real name is Alfa, and she's Omega, cause I was born first!" His face lit with a smile as he chattered on. "Daddy and Mommy lost their job after the plague. They were pastors, but the church people was all gone. We stayed in the Parsage and kept cleaning the church, but nobody came back. Then one day some bad men came. They was commanders. They took all of us in their big truck with lots of canned food and bottles of booze."

"It wasn't booze," his twin sister interjected smugly. "It was wine and beer!" She obviously wanted to talk too, but couldn't get the chance.

"That's booze, too," he argued, then swept on. "Some of the men started messin' with Mommy, like, you know, huggin' her and stuff. Grownup stuff. Daddy got really mad and told those men off. Then those men took Daddy and Mommy away and made us stay in the truck. But Mommy told us before she went away, 'If these men leave you alone, you sneak away and don't let 'em see you. You go back to the house and wait for us to get back.' So that's what we did."

"Lemme tell it now!" Omega interrupted and took up the story. "So we was in our house, cause we found the way back. We walked all night and didn't get home 'til lunch. And we had to fix our own lunch. And we fixed our own supper too. And we took our baths. And then after a long time Miss Rose and Miss Lizard and Mr. Roostafer came and got us and now they take care of us and Miss Rose is sorta like our Mommy now, but not really. And Miss Lizard is like our Auntie and Mr. Roostafer is like our Uncle. But he reminds us mostly of our Papa. Nana went to be with Jesus, and Papa lives alone far away and only comes to visit once in awhile cause it gets harder all the time."

"So," Alfa finished, "here we are. All together in one place. We like it here. Can we get our own horses?"

All the grownups (including Luke and Lizard) chuckled at his closing question. In his mind, obviously, there were other matters far more pressing than sharing histories.

"Thank you very much, Alfa and Omega," Barbara said softly. "I'm sure we can find a nice pony for each of you down at the ranch where we found Bruno and Bonnie."

"Luke," Barbara turned to the boy who had been staring at Lizzie the whole time. "Would you mind taking the twins out and showing them the animals while we talk some more?"

"Sure," Luke replied, his adolescent voice breaking. He caught a little smile from Barbara, and hoped no one else had noticed. Specially Lizzie.

"Come on, kids!" He looked at Lizard, "You can come too, if you want."

She smiled, but shook her head. She wanted to stay with the adults and be in on the discussion.

"Yes," Roostafer startled Lizard, "You go with them, Lizard. That'll give us a few rare moments to talk about stuff you and Luke wouldn't care about. Capisce?"

Lizard obviously wanted to stay and listen in, but she obviously wanted to go with Luke too, but she was even more obviously startled by Roostafer's assertion. Without a word she nodded at Roostafer, gave him the very tiniest dimple she could, and left the room to follow Luke and the twins.

CHAPTER THREE

CROSS TRAINING

The adults waited until the kids were gone, then Roostafer spoke--softly, the way Barbara had spoken.

"I'm afraid that sooner or later we'll have to deal with those commandos. We caught a glimpse of them over on the coast and hid as they went past. They didn't seem very well organized, but they're very well armed. It looked like they were searching for survivors to take as slaves or something. From the tracks and indications left in Weed, they apparently raped the twins' mom and beat up their dad. They already had other women as prisoners, and they took both the twins' parents along with them. We haven't told Al and Meg those details.

"None of the commandos looked smart enough to have organized the group, so I think they were sent out from somewhere else. My guess would be down in or around L.A., where a wannabe despot would be more likely to find enough survivors to form a community. I think that if or when their community grows enough they'll be back through here again, looking for more supplies and more slaves."

He continued, "This is only what I think. I don't really know. But I do know that we need to be ready to defend ourselves in case a well armed band of outlaws does manage to find the homestead."

"Barbara," Rose spoke, "I don't want to embarrass Roostafer, but he's a really good leader. He's brave, and he's daring, and he knows ….."

"Okay, she gets the point, Rose," Roostafer interrupted, embarrassed.

"That's fine, you guys," Barbara answered. "I doubt I would be a good leader, anyway, and I don't even want to lead. I know nothing about strategy or tactical stuff. But Luke and I do have something to offer besides the homestead. I have a brown belt in karate, and I'll be happy to teach it to all of you. Luke's doing really well since I started training him a couple months ago. And he is a really amazing fast draw expert with those cowboy pistols of his, and a crack shot. He's been teaching me how to handle a pistol. I imagine we can all help each other cross train and improve our survival skills. When Luke shows you our emergency escape tunnel I think you'll be impressed. And, for the record, Roostafer, while I feel very possessive about homestead stuff, you are hereby officially in charge of organizing our defenses. I know that Luke agrees."

"Well, okay. I think my first official order will be for all of us to start teaching each other everything we know that will be helpful in general. Rose is a nurse, so she can teach us all emergency first aid and be our Medic. Lizzie is a better shot than I am, and she's a knowledgeable equestrienne. All things considered, we have lots of potential here to work with. But I want us to keep moving forward on whatever projects are needed for the homestead, too. The supplies in Redding and Weaverville won't last forever. Sustainability should always be our underlying buzz word!"

Barbara was deeply pleased by Roostafer's words and tone. She felt grateful that he wanted to keep developing the homestead, and that he was forward thinking about everything.

Later that same day she started Roostafer, Rose and Lizzie on their karate training. Luke also started them on quick draw training. He showed everyone how to trim the extra leather off their holsters, add tie-down thongs, and file the front sight off their pistols.

That evening after the twins went to bed the rest of them sat around the table talking strategy and tactics. Roostafer admitted he didn't know that much about it, but he had picked up a few ideas from his experiences in the navy and after the plague. He proposed two mottos, to start with. The first was, *"If you can't avoid a fight, hit first and get the advantage."* The second was, *"If you're in a fight, hit as hard as you can and end it as soon as possible."* "These should guide all of our preparations. We should all memorize the two mottos, including the twins.

In order to be able to 'hit first and get the advantage' and 'hit as hard as we can and end it as soon as possible', we should see if we can set up a big gun, like a cannon, at a strategic spot. We need it to be simple enough for any of us to use and big enough and placed well enough to cover all or most of the homestead. We all need to learn how to use it and be prepared to do whatever is necessary to protect the gun from capture, including blow it up.

"We need a clear field of fire to cover the three roads coming in, plus the homestead itself. If we have to damage the homestead to survive, we can always rebuild, but we can't rise from the dead. Capisce?"

He noticed Barbara give him another quick puzzled look and wondered why she kept doing that. Was he offending her? He sure hoped not.

"I'd like us," Roostafer continued his first warfare lecture, "to meet together at the start of each training day, let's say eight o'clock, after chores and breakfast and morning devotions, and coordinate our training schedule for the day. I'd like us to meet again at the end of the training day, let's say four o'clock, and debrief before we scatter to all our evening chores. I see by your expressions some of you aren't familiar with the term, "debrief". It means discuss it, looking for ways to improve it. We'll call these meetings morning and evening muster. This will help us organize our training.

"So, tomorrow morning at our eight o'clock morning muster we'll strategize our training for the day. That means by eight o'clock we need to be done with breakfast, chores, devotions, everything. From eight o'clock on, we focus on combat training. We won't use live bullets for training. The sound would carry for miles. We'll practice by dry firing. We'll break for lunch at Noon. Light snacks only. No heavy eating while we're in training.

"After the first round of training, er, actually, cross training each other, then we'll get into some tactics. I plan to go down to Redding tomorrow afternoon and see what sort of big guns they might have at the armory, if any. I assume there's an armory.

"Barbara will teach karate from 9:00 to 10:00, and Luke will teach fast draw from 10:00 to 11:00. Barbara and Luke, I can't begin to express how grateful I am that you welcomed us to the homestead. And I think your combat skills will go a long way to help us prepare to defend ourselves."

Barbara could see that Luke was vastly pleased to be honored for his quick draw skills. He stood a little straighter and held his head a little higher. She caught him sneaking glances at Lizzie. She also noticed that Roostafer noticed the glances. When he caught her eye he casually winked at Barbara. She felt herself blush and mentally kicked herself. *Settle down, girl. He's just being personable. Don't read more into it than it deserves!*

She was amazed how much she already liked him. He used some of the same phrases that Uncle Cliff had often used—the exact same words. He had the right priorities. He was charming, mature, confident, and most important of all--he looked her in the eye when he talked to her. *Could he be the man for me?*

By evening muster everyone was tired and irritable. Learning new things was never easy. They each felt the pressure to learn quickly, so they all worked hard at it. When they sat down around the cold fire pit for evening muster Roostafer asked Barbara how the karate training went.

"Well," she began with a smile, "everyone seemed to pick it up naturally. It was as if you all had prior training, except Roostafer. He's slow. I think even Alfa or Omega could take him!"

They all burst out laughing. Suddenly the strain was released and drained away.

"Seriously though, everyone did fine. We don't have the right outfits for proper karate training, but everyone seems to be in good shape and willing to work hard. Those are the two most important factors. I think by the end of the week each of you will have advanced at least one belt color. Good job, everybody!"

Everyone joined in a moment of applause, then Roostafer turned to Luke.

"How did the hand gun training go, Luke?"

"Aw, great, of course. After all, you got a great teacher!"

They all laughed with Luke, then he continued.

"None of you have the right kind of pistol for a fast draw, but with the front sights filed off and the holsters adjusted it's working okay. Just a reminder, I practice an hour or more almost every single day. You should too, no matter how good you get or how tired you might be. It might save your life some day. You'll be glad you did."

The group was subdued the rest of the evening as they pitched in with the cleanup and evening chores. Then everyone scattered out to do their hour of fast draw practice. By lights out, everyone was glad to hit the sack.

The days passed. Each morning Roostafer led a short devotional time for the group. He would read a paragraph out of the chapter in Proverbs that corresponded with the day of the month, asking a couple of questions to stimulate discussion. They all participated except for Luke, and the discussions were often rich with personal perspectives. Even young Al or Meg chimed in sometimes. During a discussion of Proverbs chapter three, verses five and six, where the text said *"Trust in the Lord with all your heart and lean not on your own understanding. In all your ways acknowledge Him and He shall direct your paths."*, as soon as Roostafer finished reading it aloud, Al piped up.

"We trusted the Lord didn't we, Mr. Roostafer? And God brung us right to the homestead!"

"That's right, Alfa. And before that God directed my path to find you and your sister. And I'm sure glad that He did!"

"Me too, Al," Barbara interjected. She happened to be holding Al on her lap at the moment and she gave him an extra hug. "I'm especially glad you and Omega came to live here. I love you both very much."

"Aw, mush!" Luke said with a grin. He dropped his gaze in embarrassment for speaking.

"I sorta like mush, Luke," Lizzie said, as she turned toward him and smiled. "I thought you did too."

Luke blushed furiously and clamped his lips together, not willing to answer.

"Well!" Barbara observed. "I think there's a double meaning for the word 'mush,' eh guys?" She burst out laughing as both Luke and Lizzie blushed and looked everywhere except toward each other.

Rose rarely offered her thoughts about things, but whenever she did her statements were always carefully thought out and thoroughly communicated.

Now she commented, "Hey guys, I, for one, am glad of all the love we can generate for each other here at the homestead. And I hope we feel really secure in our love for each other, enough for it to survive and thrive when times are tough, or if more people arrive. Ya'all know I don't usually say much, but I think we have a chance here to build a life that's wonderful. We all have stuff we need to put behind us. This is a perfect place to do life right, even if we never have before. I believe God will, indeed, direct our steps if we listen to Him and follow what He says. So, anyway, we can tease Luke and Lizzie, and even Roostafer and young Barra-burra," she smiled briefly toward Barbara, "but I for one am thankful to God that we love each other the way we do."

"So, gang," Roostafer guided them back to the Scripture text, "what does it mean when it says 'with all your heart'?"

"That one bugs me a little," Barbara commented. "It tells me God wants me to not hold back. That's hard to do because I can't see Him, and I wonder sometimes if He's even listening. Why would he care about me? I understand God caring about the world in general, but why me?"

Little Omega raised her hand. "I know," she cried triumphantly! "Cause God loves you! I 'member John three sixteen…" She hesitated a moment to remember the exact words, then recited. "God so loved the world that he gave his only gotten son that whoever believe in Him will not perish but have lasting life." She finished with a flourish, knowing she got it right.

"That's exactly right, Meg," Roostafer agreed. "God cares about everything in my life, and yours, and Barra-burra's, and Luke's, and Rose's, and Al's and everyone else who trusts in the Lord with all their heart. And it's because He loves all of us so much."

Morning discussions like that were becoming more the 'norm' than the exception by the end of their first month together. In order to figure out what day of the month it was, so they could read the corresponding chapter in Proverbs, they got an old fashioned windup wrist watch with the date on it from the Walmart Super Center jewelry counter in Anderson, a few miles south of Redding.

With Rose's coaching and encouragement, Alfa and Omega had volunteered to hand print a new calendar page every month. They collected a stack of white twelve inch square card stock and each month they drew the lines, labeled the days of the week and filled in the numbers of the days of the month.

They had all agreed to consider the current year 'year one AV' (After Virus). In Barbara's new "Trinity House Journal" she entered the date as August 14, 0001AV.

They all liked it because, as Roostafer put it, "It helps me remember to look forward, not back. This is our first year, and only the Lord knows what is to come."

By the end of their second month together they had finished adding on to the cabin so it now had four bedrooms and a second bathroom. The twins were too old to share a room any more, so Barbara had her own bedroom, Roostafer had his own bedroom, Rose, Lizard and Omega shared a bedroom, and Luke shared a bedroom with Alfa. It seemed to work okay, and they still had the loft in case they needed more sleeping room on short notice. And very soon they did, very abruptly.

The date, according to their new calendar, was October 23, 0001ATV, when the Buell family showed up. Jim and Daria Buell were in their late thirties and their seven children ranged from age seven to fifteen. Their eighth and youngest child had succumbed to the Cremation Virus but the others had, surprisingly, all survived.

They arrived much the same way Roostafer's group had arrived, only from the other direction. Roostafer's group had come up out of Redding to a high elevation and sent up a smoke signal from the east end of Whiskeytown Lake. The Buell's, however, came across Highway 299 from the coast and camped on top of Oregon Mountain summit, just west of Weaverville, to send up their smoke signal. They sent up smoke for two days before it was noticed at the homestead, and Trinity House didn't respond until the third day.

Roostafer and Luke were pouring concrete up near the top of Browns Mountain, finishing the bunker emplacement around the rapid fire semi-automatic fifty caliber gun they had found at the armory in Redding. They were just ending their workday and had climbed atop the bunker for a last look around before heading down the hill for evening muster and supper.

Luke was first to see the smoke. They had a powerful spotting scope mounted on a sturdy tripod behind the bunker up at the peak of Browns Mountain, so it was easy to determine the location of the signal fire. A few minutes later at evening muster they told the others. Roostafer asked everyone to give their daily progress reports first, then they discussed the signal.

After the contingencies had been thoroughly hashed out, Roostafer offered a plan.

"I think that Luke and I should go to Weaverville early tomorrow morning and send up an answering smoke signal from the north end of town, near the old airport. We could leave the signal fire going as a distraction while we circle around and approach from the south. If it turns out the person or group sending up the signal seems okay, we could send up a double signal and bring the person or group to the homestead. If they don't seem okay, we wouldn't send up another signal, but simply sneak away and come back the long way around to avoid being followed."

"So," Barra-burra frowned, "How long do you think you would be gone?"

"Depends. There's an old saying, 'No battle plan survives the first gunshot.' If there's a problem we could be delayed. But if everything goes as planned, we'd be back sooner. If they're friendlies, we'll probably be back by about noon. If they're bad guys, probably not till about sundown."

Roostafer nodded at Luke, grimly, "If we aren't back by day after tomorrow, you should assumed we've been either taken or killed. No one is to come after us. Everyone is to remain at the homestead and continue the good thing we've started here at Trinity House."

"I don't like it," Barra-burra pushed back. "From a practical standpoint, we can't afford to lose both of you. The contact party should be a man and a woman, which means you and me."

"It'll be safer if it's Luke and me, two men. If they are slavers, we'll be less appealing to them than a woman."

"Don't forget, Barra-burra, that I'm a gunslinger," Luke tried to reassure her.

"But you're the only gunslinger we have," Lizzie fired back, her brow furrowed.

"Luke and I solemnly promise to be extremely cautious."

The matter was thoroughly and volubly argued for many minutes, until finally Roostafer raised his hand. Everyone fell silent.

"You asked me to lead us. I've listened to all the arguments and I agree with both views. Weighing all the contingencies, my decision is that Barbara and I will go. Luke and Rose will be in charge until we return--Luke substituting for me and Rose substituting for Barbara. That way we know that the homestead is protected." He nodded to Luke and Rose.

"Barbara and I need to leave early tomorrow, properly outfitted, and with everyone's blessing. While we're gone, the rest of you should prepare for the possible arrival of new people. If, for any reason, we are unable to return, you substitute leaders will be permanently in charge. Any questions?"

He paused, slowly turned and made eye contact with each one around the circle."Let's pray and commit this to God.."

Everyone bowed their heads and joined hands as Roostafer prayed.

"Father in heaven, may your holy name be exalted and glorified by our lives, and when the time comes, by our deaths. Guide our steps. Direct our decisions. Protect Barbara and me as we check out this signal smoke in the morning. Protect our loved ones while we're gone. And, Father, may we find a group of good people tomorrow who will be blessed, and a blessing, here at Trinity House Homestead. Father God, we love you. Thank you, in the name of Jesus, for hearing and answering our prayers. Amen"

Murmurs of 'Amen' accompanied Roostafer as he turned with a sigh and headed to his room. He planned to leave at sunrise, so he went to bed. When he awoke before sunrise, he was surprised that he had fallen right to sleep.

CHAPTER FOUR

THE SMOKE SIGNAL

The sun crested the distant eastern horizon around Mount Lassen, bathing the homestead in weak morning daylight as Roostafer and Barbara rode their ATVs down Browns Mountain Road to Little Browns Creek Road, then on down to the highway a mile east of Weaverville. The signal had come from Oregon Mountain, where Highway 299 crested the summit west of town. They stayed on back streets for concealment and it took almost an hour to reach the little airport north of town.

They set up a smokey answering signal fire with damp foliage on the runway pavement. Once the fire was going good, they hurried back through town on their quiet running all terrain vehicles and drove up out of Weaverville along Oregon Street so they could approach the summit along the small unpaved Jennings Road.

They approached the summit by mid morning. Just before cresting the last hump in the dirt road they were on, they shut off their muffled ATVs and crept foreward on foot. When their eyes were just high enough to see over the hump, they were about a hundred and fifty yards from the edge of the highway pavement.

A large luxury motor home was parked in the eastbound lane overlooking the city. The coach was up on its levelers, with the awning and slide-outs fully extended as if it were set up in a campground. Beneath the awning a middle-aged couple sat in folding camp chairs sipping coffee, casually watching them approach. The man waved cheerfully, as if they were in a campground waving to their neighbor campers. To Roostafer and Barra-burra, the moment seemed surreal.

"Well, Barbara, I guess we didn't do a very good job of sneaking," Roostafer murmured to her. "I don't see any weapons, though I assume they have some," he continued, "but we might as well go on in, since they already know we're here. Agreed?"

"Sure," she replied softly, not taking her eyes off the couple. "We are armed, after all, in case it turns out that we do need weapons."

"Okay. Lets go slow and easy."

They waved back, with Roostafer holding up one finger in a 'wait a minute' gesture, then turned and got back on their rigs, started them up and drove slowly down to the pavement. When they were about fifteen yards away from the big motor home they stopped and shut off their motors. The couple set down their coffee mugs and rose to meet them with genial smiles on their faces. They were dressed like tourists in matching aloha shirts and baggy cargo shorts over flip flops. The man even wore a floppy straw hat. Both wore sunglasses.

The man greeted them cheerfully.

"Hi there! We've been expecting you!"

"Hello," Roostafer answered, reservedly. "Is it just the two of you or do you have others hiding out of sight to cover us?"

The man hesitated, apparently puzzled.

"Cover you? Why would we do that?"

"Yeah. You know, for safety? Like with guns?"

Roostafer caught Barbara's look of amazement. He too was startled that these people seemed so unconcerned about their safety. Don't they realize some bad guys survived the plague?

"Do you know that some bad guys survived the plague? We ourselves happen to be fully armed, just in case you two turned out to be bad guys!" Roostafer heard his own anger buried deeply, he hoped, in his voice.

"Uh, no. We uh, well…. I mean, no. We haven't had any problems with anyone. We're from British Columbia, eh? The sprawling metropolis of Kamloops, northeast a ways from Vancouver. We've actually had quite a marrvelous journey coming down the coast. Let's introduce ourselves, eh? Then we could have some refreshments and tell each other of our adventures, eh?"

Roostafer couldn't sustain his inner annoyance in the face of their cheerful demeanor.

"Well, I think that's a great idea," Roostafer replied, smiling back at them. He cast a meaningful look at Barbara as the man turned to pull two more folding chairs out of the storage compartment in the belly of the motor home. Roostafer noticed that he seemed to have quite a few more chairs stored there.

"But my lady friend here," Roostafer quickly interjected, "will just stand around for a bit and sorta keep an eye out. Never know when a predator might show up around here, ya know. I mean, there's just no telling who else might have seen your smoke signal."

Roostafer didn't want to be too relaxed just yet. He and Barbara exchanged a quick but meaningful glance and she followed his subtle lead, casually moving over toward the corner of the motor home to stand at the ready. Roostafer nodded his approval. The RV couple seemed as unconcerned as if they were in a comfortable RV park two years before the plague.

The woman spoke for the first time. "Would you like coffee, young lady?"

Barbara nodded toward Roostafer as she answered politely, "No thanks."

Roostafer sat down with the apparently friendly couple as Barbara moved on out past the end of the motor home where she could see both directions along the empty highway.

Roostafer introduced himself and Barbara, but said nothing about the others or the homestead. The couple introduced themselves as Jim and Daria Buell.

"Dar and I lost a daughter to the Cremation Virus. In fact, we lost all our kinfolk and, as far as we know, everyone else in Kamloops besides us. Amazingly, we survived, but we don't know why."

"Just the two of you, Jim," queried Roostafer, thinking about all those other folding lawn chairs stowed in the belly of the coach?

Jim hesitated a moment. "Oh, well, as to that, I guess I can admit that, uh, well, yes." He paused, then added, "I mean, in answer to your question, yes, we actually do, in fact, have you 'covered,' as you said so descriptively a little bit ago."

He went on after a pregnant pause. "I'll call them in now if you don't mind."

Roostafer quickly assured him he didn't mind, as long as they didn't point weapons at him and Barbara. Jim gave some kind of signal that Roostafer didn't see and suddenly seven children stepped out from various places of concealment around the motor home. Without speaking they came and lined up near Jim and Dar, ranging from large to small.

"These are our kiddies, eh? The oldest, at fifteen, is that boy there, named Able. We call him Abe most of the time. Next oldest, at fourteen, is that boy, Baker. Third oldest, at thirteen, is that boy, Charlie. Fourth, at twelve, is this girl, Delta. Fifth, at age eleven, is this girl, Echo. Sixth, at age ten, is this boy, Frank, and seventh, age nine, is this girl, Georgette."

He turned to his wife with a smile, "Did I get all of them right, dear?"

Abe was holding a handgun that looked to Roostafer like an old Colt 1911 semiautomatic. Baker held a small caliber lever action rifle, probably a .22. Charlie held a single shot .410 shotgun. The four younger children were unarmed. Eleven year old Echo and ten year old Frank were the same height and kept surreptitiously poking each other when they thought the grownups weren't looking. Otherwise the seven squirming siblings stood at what they probably thought was a reasonable facsimile of 'attention.'

Roostafer couldn't quite hold back a smile. "Well, Jim and Dar, you have a fine looking bunch of youngsters there, and I'm relieved that you're wise enough to be armed. I noticed all the camp chairs under the coach, so I thought there might be more of you. Oh, and by the way, Jim, did you happen to be a Canadian navy radioman?"

"Uh, why no. Never served, actually. Why do you ask?"

"Just wondered about your kids being named alphabetically, using the terms used in the nautical phonetic alphabet followed by radiomen in most of the world's navies. I was a U. S. Navy radioman, so it caught my attention. Must be some kinda story there, I imagine?"

Jim chuckled with good natured pleasure. "Yep, sure is. I'll be glad to tell it to ya, if we have the time. Maybe after we've gotten a little better acquainted, eh?"

"Okay. So how about if we start with a few questions, okay? Like, what have you been doing after the plague, Jim?"

As the adults began 'interviewing' each other, the kids pulled out lawn chairs for themselves and sat down around them to listen. Barbara stayed near the rear of the coach where she could hear the conversation and still see both ways along the highway.

"Oh, at first we pretty much hunkered down, ya know. We were out of sorts for awhile, eh? Of course we heard all about the plague, and all the people dying. Our youngest daughter, Hillary, died from it, too. But after a few months we figured out that we were apparently gonna survive. Then we got kinda bored, ya see. No jobs to go to any more, eh? So we figured we'd just mosey on down the highway and see who else survived. We also hope to get ourselves a little better situated than we were up their with no others anywhere around."

"Have you found many other survivors?"

"Oh yeah. Some, but only a few. There was a small community living in houseboats and yachts in a marina way up on the Fraser River in Vancouver. Then, down in Bellingham, in Washington state ya know, there was a half dozen people living in luxury in a huge mansion on the shore of Whatcom Lake. Further south, near Olympia, we met a small group of survivors who had banded together and were livin' in a ritzy motel with a pool and all, eh? Each of those groups seemed a little 'off' in some way, so we didn't linger."

Roostafer interrupted Jim, "Did you follow Interstate 5 most of the way?"

"Why, no, as a matter of fact," Jim sipped his coffee and then continued. "From Olympia we took Highway 8 to the coast and came down Highway 101, all the way though Oregon till we got to Arcata, here in California. I saw that route on Google Earth years ago and always wanted to make that drive, so why not? We got tired of Arcata, which is a ghost town like most others. After a few weeks we headed inland on Highway 299 and stopped here above Weaverville to make a fire. That's how we been finding people. We just make a smokey fire and wait a couple days. If anyone's around, they show up, eh?"

"Did you find any survivors down along the coast in Oregon? Or here in California?"

"Yes, actually. There was an odd group in Gold Beach in Oregon--one old man and four young women. He tried to get our little girl, Delta, to stay there with him. Something hinky strange there, I think. We were glad to move along, eh?"

Barbara had moved a bit closer so she could hear better.

"No one you met along the way wanted to travel with you?"

"No sir, nary a one. But we don't mind, eh? We have a touch of the wanderlust. Always wanted to travel, ya know. But after spending a bunch of years in Kamloops, never goin' anywhere 'cept on good old Google Earth, eh, we don't really hanker to be around a bunch of strangers, ya know? But now seems like the time to be makin' new beginnings, planning a new life for themselves, eh? That's really why we're doing this trip. Ya see, we're looking for a special sort of place, where we can be content and settle back down again. Then maybe we'll never travel again, ya know, since things has changed. I suspect in a few years the surplus supplies will mostly either spoil or be used up. We hope to find a place by then. For now, the highway seems to beckon."

"What kind of place are you looking for? You mean like a homestead for just your family, or a certain kind of community, or what?"

"Well, ya see, Roostafer and Barbara," Jim glanced behind him toward Barbara, then looked back at Roostafer. "Dar here is a school teacher, eh? It's in her heart, and she's a really good one. The Lord blessed us with a passle of our own kids, ya see? It seems like the Lord is sayin, 'Yep, Dar, I want ya ta teach.' Me? I'm nothing more than a darn good grease monkey. I aced auto shop in high school and never wanted to do nothing else besides make motors run smooth. So, we figure we need to find a place that sorta specializes in kids and motors, ya know? Not likely, but something to look for, eh?"

"Dar, you haven't said much of anything. Do you agree with Jim?"

"Oh yes sir, Mr. Roostafer. We talked about this a lot after everybody disappeared. We came to agree on this plan. Both of us, eh? It's our plan together, not just Jim's, or just mine. And I appreciate you asking. After seeing that man in Gold Beach! Why, that man gave me the creeps!"

Before continuing, Roostafer exchanged a long glance with Barbara.

"I'd like the two of you to stay here a couple more days. If we don't come back in two days, then you won't see us again. But give us two days, okay?"

Jim hesitated a moment, exchanged a glance with his wife, and then replied with characteristic heartiness, "Well, sure! Ya see, we're on vacation in a way. We'll just camp here and enjoy the view a couple more days. We'll go down the grade and do a little shopping in town, of course. But we'll camp here until the third morning, since ya asked us to. Then, if we don't see you again, we plan to go on into Redding and follow Highway 44 past Mount Lassen and maybe head for the Reno area for awhile. We're just not sure where we want to go next."

"Then it's agreed. Barbara and I may be back with a proposition for you. But if we don't come back, then we wish you good luck in your travels."

Barbara, who had been listening to the conversation as she slowly drifted closer, spoke loud enough for Jim and Dar to hear. "Roostafer, I think it'll be all right to bring them home with us. The Lord knows we can use a good mechanic and a school teacher at the homestead. After they meet our group, if they choose not to join us, I think if we ask them to keep our location secret during their travels, they will."

She turned to Jim and Daria and added, "We can trust you, can't we?"

"Oh sure, eh? If you wanta keep yer whereabouts secret, why that's nothing to us, eh? We wouldn't violate yer trust, would we Daria Darlin?" Jim put his arm around his wife's shoulders and gazed happily into her eyes.

She returned his look with equal ardor, "Why, no sir! Miss, if you want it kept secret, of course we wouldn't blab." Then Dar turned toward Barbara, "But just what sort of homestead do you have that you want it kept secret?"

Barbara looked to Roostafer to respond. He looked at the Buell family in silence for a moment, thinking of the many possible answers to her simple question.

Finally he replied, "It's incredibly special. It's in an isolated spot, very beautiful and very well guarded, but most important, every one of us living there has been threatened or hurt by bad guys since the plague. So we're all very security conscious. Lately we heard of a gang of outlaws who call themselves commandos. They go around beating up the men, molesting the women and girls, and taking people south into slavery. We have two young children at the homestead who escaped when their parents were taken. We are prepared to defend ourselves to the death against them if they ever find us, but we'd really rather that they don't find us. Does that make sense to you?"

Jim spoke quickly, "Oh sure. We certainly understand. We won't betray anyone. And it sounds like it might be the sort of place we're looking for, if everything you say is true. But if you wouldn't mind, of course we'd like to see for ourselves before we commit to anything, eh? Would ya mind if we came along on sort of a trial basis?"

Roostafer and Barbara glanced at each other and then Barbara spoke for both of them. "Wouldn't mind at all, Mr. Buell. If you have any misgivings we sure wouldn't want you to feel that you were trapped and couldn't leave any time you want to."

"Well then, I think we got ourselves an agreement, eh? We'll be ready to roll in about two minutes."

It turned out that their seeming nonchalance was just a show. Each of them folded his or her lawn chairs and slid it into the luggage bin under the coach, Daria and young Abe rolled the awning back in and fastened it in place, then it took about a minute to retract the slide-outs and they were ready to go.

"We need to send up a signal smoke so the others at the homestead will know that we're bringing guests. Give us a few minutes, okay?" Roostafer had suddenly remembered their agreement with the others back at the homestead. Jim and Daria exchanged a bemused glance, but waited by the door of their motor home, watching with interest to see what these American survivors were planning to do.

Within a few minutes two small fires were blazing a hundred feet apart. They placed an evergreen branch on each one so that two columns of white smoke rose up briefly in the still air, like twin chimneys, from the summit of Oregon Mountain. They doused the fires after a couple of minutes and mounted their ATVs. As they started down the long grade toward Weaverville, Roostafer shouted over his shoulder to the Buells, "Okay, follow us!"

Riding the ATVs on pavement, at much higher speeds than off-road, was a bit nerve wracking for both of them. Before they reached the edge of town at the bottom of the grade Roostafer had slowed down to a more sedate half throttle. It still seemed plenty fast to the ATV riders, but plenty slow to the Buells in their big motor home. After they got through town and made the turnoff onto the rough narrow lane of Little Browns Creek Road, the vehicles were more evenly matched. Then, when they veered onto Browns Mountain Road, which was steeper, rougher and had switchbacks, the ATVs had the advantage and had to hold back for the slower, cumbersome motor home.

All the way up the steep two mile climb to the ridge top the right shoulder rose steeply upward toward the summit and the left shoulder dropped just as steeply down to Browns Creek at the bottom of a narrow canyon, which got farther and farther away as the road climbed. Soon the creek was barely visible far below.

After they topped the crest it was the opposite, with the steep hillside on their left and the steep dropoff on their right. About a half mile past the crest they veered left into the unmarked beginning of Trinity House Road, which was even narrower, and even steeper. Here, on "Barbara's road" the motor home labored very slowly, squeezing through the narrow places and cautiously negotiating the tight curves.

At the top the road ran straight for almost two hundred yards through a sunny meadow surrounded by tall evergreens, then there was a fork in the road. The left fork followed the ridge as it continued to climb, but less steeply, toward the peak. Roostafer and Barbara veered right onto a narrower track that headed downhill.

The Buells followed in the motor home, but the road quickly came to a dead-end where a huge mound of boulders and dirt blocked the road. From their seats high up in the motor home they could see that on the other side of the apparent landslide the road continued far on down the escarpment. Roostafer and Barbara had pulled to a stop and dismounted from the ATVs.

Jim and Daria Buell wore identical looks of mixed concern and confusion, wondering why they were stopping in the middle of nowhere. Where was the so-called "homestead"?

"Barra-burra, my fair lass, methinks our visitors are wonderin' a bit right now whether we might be outlaws after all, eh?" Roostafer asked Barbara with a twinkle in his eye.

She answered in like manner. "Oh, me bucko, I be pr-r-r-retty sure of it."

Roostafer laughed aloud. "I can't roll my r's like that. That was great. But let's go reassure Jim and Dar that we aren't thugs, before they try to turn that big outfit around."

They walked over to the driver's side window and Roostafer addressed Jim.

"We placed this barricade here so if anyone happened up this dirt road they would be discouraged from driving down into our homestead valley. From here you can see the general layout," he gestured with a sweep of his arm behind him, "the alluvial fan sloping down the inside of the curve of this ridge we're on. Just about exactly between us and the peak across the way, just where the ridge gullies all converge and form Trinity House Creek, is the site of our homestead. The forest green metal roof of every building is camouflaged with Gilley netting, and we built under the mature trees as much as possible, so that nothing would show from the ridge top around the homestead."

He went on, "We have a hidden detour around this barrier, but I'm afraid it's engineered for ATVs and horses, so the motor home is too big to fit through. But after we get down to the homestead we can come back up with a Jeep and trailer, or even a flatbed truck, to haul your belongings down for you. I'm afraid your rig will have to remain up here."

"Okay, Yank," Jim replied, "But what about our coach, eh? Since you're all so bloody worried about security," he grinned sheepishly as he said it, "d'ya think we ought to leave it parked here pointing down yer little road, eh?"

"Good point," Barbara inserted herself into the conversation. "Let's back it onto the road in front of the fork and park it there pointed back the way we came in. We can brush out the tracks with branches so a casual observer won't know which way the people went. And, if you accept our invitation to join the homestead, we can decide then what to do with the motor home. That sound sensible? At least for now?"

Not to seem like a senseless wall flower, Daria chimed in, "Well, I think that's a wonderful idea. Don't you agree, Jim darling?"

Jim good naturedly shrugged his shoulders, "Well, close enough to unanimous for my sake, eh?" He spoke aside to Roostafer, but loudly enough to make sure the ladies heard him, "I've learned never to buck the tide, so to speak, when my Missus asserts her opinion, eh?"

They all chuckled as Jim climbed on behind Roostafer and Daria mounted behind Barbara. The seven kids trotted along behind the ATVs as they carefully bounced around the shrubbery at the top of a brush-choked gully mouth and found a well marked track that led down the slope parallel to, and slightly above, the overgrown dirt road. They arrived at the bottom in a couple of minutes and were met by all the other members of the homestead, who had heard the vehicles' motors ever since they entered the upper meadow.

Introductions were made all around, and Rose announced graciously that, since it was late afternoon already, dinner was nearly ready. She invited everyone to wash up and come to the table. There was a friendly rush to the creek where washcloths and hand towels hung on hooks set into two small pine trees. With the addition of the nine Buells, it suddenly seemed to Barbara like a big crowd filling her little homestead.

As they enjoyed the meal of fresh barbecued t-bone steaks, mashed potatoes and gravy and a tossed salad, it became obvious to Barbara that little Meg had immediately attached herself to matronly Mrs. Buell, and little Al had latched onto fatherly Mr. Buell. She wondered, chuckling inwarely, how the Buell kids would feel about having black twin younger siblings.

The conversation around the table was animated, and the topic soon came around to conjecturing about the future. There was a brief lull in the discussion and Little Meg suddenly turned to Mrs. Buell, gazed adoringly up into her kindly face, and asked point blank the very exact question that was on Barbara's mind.

"Will you stay with us?"

CHAPTER FIVE

THE VILLAGE

Daria looked at Jim, their eyes met and a "look" passed between them.

Daria looked back into Meg's eyes and said, earnestly, "Of course, dear Meg. I'm going to be your school teacher. And Jim is going to make all the motors around the homestead purr like loud kittens. Aren't you, Jim?"

Jim smiled broadly at everyone and nodded his head as he said, "Well, that's right! I noticed a little wheezing and hiccupping going on with those two ATVs and I just can't very well go off and leave 'em that way, eh?"

"That's good, Jim and Dar," Roostafer responded with a smile. "We've room enough here for more people, and none of us even thought about the need for a school teacher, or a good mechanic." He paused thoughtfully for a moment, then added, "In fact, I guess we probably need to be a little more forward thinking and consider the possibility that more people might join us at some point in the future."

His gaze swept around the table to include all the adults as he added, "We just might build the Buell cabin situated in such a way as to allow for another cabin or two, later on."

"I think that's a lovely idea," Rose uncharacteristically asserted her opinion. "And while we're at it I'd like to suggest a cabin for me to live in and use as a hospital." She continued in a rush, embarrassed at her own boldness, "I'd like a place to keep emergency medical supplies and have a couple of beds where I can tend to anyone who may suffer any kind of serious injury."

The conversation took off at that point, with each adult adding his or her own input until they were excitedly talking louder and louder to be heard over each other. Finally, Barbara laughed and raised both hands for attention. The room quickly quieted down and she smiled around the table as she spoke.

"Okay. Here's what I'm hearing. We need a martial arts studio, a bigger underground firing range, a bigger stable for more horses so each person will have their own plus a few spares, a small hospital, a school room, a store, another home and two spare cabins for the future. Did I cover it all?"

There were murmurs and nods of agreement around the table. She went on.

"Okay. It seems that we need a village. I just can't see us moving down into Lewiston or Douglas City where we would be more vulnerable. I propose that we build our own village right here at the headwaters of Trinity House Creek. And I don't mean that we simply add to the homestead. We all get along, sure. But this is still just a small homestead. We need a real village separate from the homestead."

"Oh, you charming girl," Daria Buell quickly responded, "I think you've really nailed it, eh? And the perfect place is that lovely meadow at the top of the ridge where the RV is parked, don't you think so, Jim dear?"

"Well of course, Dar darling," he agreed with a smile. "Might take a bit of engineering to get running water up there, but the septic systems will be darn easy!"

Everyone laughed at his remark, and every adult immediately got a thoughtful look on his or her face as they began to ponder the many implications of the idea.

After several moments of relative silence, young Luke spoke up. "Okay. Here's a deal. I'll make it my own personal project to enlarge the underground shooting range so there are three firing lanes instead of just the one, and I'll figure out how to put in an exhaust vent for the additional gunpowder smoke. I don't know what else will be decided on, but that one I will tackle. And if anyone needs a helping hand on whatever they're doing, be sure and ask and I'll stop whatever I'm doing and come along and help."

"Well, Miss Barbara," Jim spoke earnestly, "I see how you got so much done around here in just a year, with Luke's 'can-do' attitude, eh. I want alla you ta know that me and the Missus feel exactly the same. We Buells have only just arrived, eh? But we already know we believe in this place, and we wanna be a part of it. We want our kids to grow up here at Trinity House, and we'll do our share of the work and more, if you'll let us stay."

The conversation whirled around the table the rest of the evening as excitement grew over the idea of a new village named Trinity House. Preliminary plans were proposed for obtaining and hauling the construction materials. Jim suggested they put in a solar powered village well, and offered to run the lines for the plumbing and electricity. Luke suggested they lay out a "Main Street" and plan all the building placements around it.

"That's a great idea, Luke," young Lizard said, flashing a big smile at him.

"Yeh, Luke, good thinkin'," added Jim. "Ya got the makin's of a good city planner, young feller."

"Nah, I was just thinking if I had to have a gun fight with a bad guy, I need a street to do it in so all y'all can watch me win," he admitted with a grin. Lizard playfully slapped him on the arm and they all chuckled at his uncharacteristic humor.

For nearly an hour their words lifted into the air around the group as they shared their ideas and dreams. Finally Barbara stood up and excused herself to go do the evening chores. Al and Meg wanted to help, as usual, and Jim and Dar wanted to go along to start learning how things were done, so the five of them tromped out together. Rose, Lizard and Luke tackled the cleanup, which only took a few minutes with the help of all the Buell kids.

Roostafer found himself the odd man out, so he grabbed the stopwatch and timed himself on a mad dash through the emergency tunnel and all the way up to the gun mount and lookout at the peak of Browns Mountain. He remembered Luke's and Barbara's best times, and he was chagrined, upon his arrival gasping for breath, to discover that they both beat his time by a huge margin. Since he was up there, he set himself in the lookout station and spent the last few minutes of sunset scanning the distance for any signs of other people.

The horizon was clear. Life was good. The future held promise for all of them. Now, if only the commandos would go away and never be heard from again. There was lots of work to be done, so it was time to get some rest. After one more full three hundred sixty degree scan with the big spotting scope, Roostafer headed back down the hill.

The next few weeks seemed to fly by. Jim Buell and Roostafer left early the next day for Redding with the flatbed and came back late in the evening with a portable sawmill and all sorts of construction tools, including some the others had never heard of. The others, meanwhile, had measured and staked out a forty foot wide "main street" and had already staked out and prepared several quarter acre lots with forty foot by forty foot building sites.

The second day they all helped set up the sawmill, with the littlest children getting underfoot but the adults putting up with it good naturedly. The older children helped as best they could. It was ready by lunch time, so, as soon as they finished eating, the two men, Luke, Able and Baker started making lumber. Roostafer and Jim fed the logs into the saw while Luke tailed off and stacked the cut lumber. Able and Baker kept the branches and sawdust debris cleaned up whenever they could dart in without interfering with the work. The first couple of days they managed to stockpil a good supply of eight by eight beams, keeping all the larger trimmings to run back through the mill to make smaller boards.

It was hard work, but all the adults helped. Rose and Daria helped Able and Baker carefully clean the mill site at the end of each day, bagging up all the sawdust to use as mulch in the flower and vegetable gardens they intended to plant. The growing attraction between Roostafer and Barbara provided some amusement for the other adults, and the growing infatuation between Luke and Lizard delighted everyone.

When they were satisfied that they had plenty of beams for the time being, they started making two by sixes and two by fours. By the end of a week they figured there was enough green lumber to begin construction. Following the precedent set by Barbara with her homestead buildings, they dug holes and poured concrete for the basement and foundation of each of the several buildings they intended to erect simultaneously.

They also dug the trenches for a network of underground escape tunnels which would interconnect each building, with a main tunnel leading to the head of a deep brush-choked gully that would allow emergency egress down toward the homestead. That particular gully had been selected because it ended across the creek from the hay barn at the upper edge of the homestead. They all agreed that a little paranoia was far better than much regret, so they wanted a clandestine path between the village and homestead.

With all of them working together they were able to complete the tunnels, basements, foundations, framing and roofing for the Buell's cabin, the schoolroom, and Rose's hospital by the end of four weeks of very hard and long work days. They celebrated with a toast around the campfire that evening, then took turns rubbing liniment on each others' sore muscles and ointment on the fresh blisters. Everyone had older blisters which had healed already.

The next morning they began the utilities work. Under Jim Buell's eagle-eyed supervision, they installed the plumbing and wiring. They placed solar panels on the roof of each building and wired them in. Jim Buell was a wealth of information and spent much of his time showing the others how to do stuff, then they would work at it until they were finished. His passion was internal combustion engines and other machines, but he had worked in residential construction for many years and seemed to know everything.

Quietly, not discussing it with anyone else, Jim started another building at the intersection at the very end of the street where they had originally left the motor home parked. For several evenings he worked on it after everyone had knocked off work. Luke hung around and helped, but Jim just smiled and went back to his task whenever Luke tried to get him to say what the building was going to be. The concrete floor was divided in two large halves with a very narrow basement in the middle of each half. Though everyone was wondering what Jim had in mind, Luke was first to guess what the building was intended to be. One evening while he and Lizard were grooming the horses and she asked him again for the millionth time if Mr. Buell had said what the building was going to be, he finally revealed the mystery. "Oh, that," he said with a self-satisfied grin, enjoying the moment. "An auto shop, obviously!"

Once the secret was out Jim had lots of help with his special building project. Barbara and Daria even made a clandestine trip down to Redding to pick out the perfect set of tools for what Jim had begun to call his "car parlor." He said, with a grin, if the dairy barn was a milking parlor, the auto shop was rightfully a car parlor. By the time the two women left the vacant, but far from empty, Sears store, after drawing from the inventory of several other 'man' stores, and headed for home they had just about filled the back of the flatbed truck. Jim was warmly surprised at the thoughtful gift from the two women.

It was, all things considered, a happy and productive time for all the residents of the new village. As the days grew a little shorter and the hot summer temperatures cooled off to chilly nights they continued to work hard all day every day. Everyone fell into bed exhausted each night, and some of the kids really struggled to get up and ready in time for breakfast and group devotions each morning, but by the time of the first early morning frost a few weeks later the village had become an actual reality. The "crunch" construction experience had drawn all of them close together into a tightly knit group--more like a family than a village.

Jim and Daria Buell and their seven children, with Alfa and Omega added for a household total of eleven, now had their own four bedroom post and beam log cabin with a matching one-room schoolhouse next door. Nurse Rose had her own medical clinic with her private residence in the back half of the ground floor. Extra beds enough for a half dozen patients had been placed in the finished attic, with a solar powered small elevator between the floors.

Jim had also installed a concealed button in the elevator that would take it to the basement, which had a secret entrance to the emergency escape tunnel. And Jim's car parlor was completed to his satisfaction, where he could tinker with any likely motor when he wasn't already involved in helping someone else with any of their various projects.

Barbara and Luke found themselves once again living alone down the hill at the homestead, except that now they had good friends close by. They enjoyed daily visits and occasional sleepovers by the young twins and, oftentimes nine year old Georgette Buell, who seemed to have taken on the twins as her own personal "parenting practice" project--even though she was only a year older.

Ten year old Frank Buell came down for a sleepover once, but didn't want to any more after that. He seemed to prefer hanging out with Luke in his spare time, which was okay with everyone, except that young Frank didn't seem to have much spare time. Mr. Buell had assigned chores to each of his seven children and Frank's daily job was to sweep the front porch of every house in the village and homestead. He also had to 'police' any litter that didn't make it into a trash can. Slow was his normal speed. Not having to hurry was more important to him than having time to play with the others, so he spent most of his time working at a plodding pace.

The village residents liked to spend time down at the homestead, working with the horses and other livestock, 'plinking' in the enlarged firing range which Luke had finished, or honing their martial arts skills in the ad hoc gymnasium Barbara had set up under an awning in her back yard.. Every morning Alfa and Omega would come down the hill to help Barbara with the animal chores, and every evening Jim and Dar came down the hill for the same purpose. With the regular extra help, Barbara had the time to start milking both the nanny goat and the cow, now that both had weaned their offspring. Everyone appreciated having fresh milk for their meals.

Lizard coached the others until they were each able to catch and saddle their own horse, as well as do their own hoof and tack maintenance. Even little Al and Meg did their share, learning how to milk the nanny goat, how to groom their ponies. and how to clean the stalls.

Luke was satisfied that the others were competent with their handguns and knew how to clean them properly, handle them safely and shoot with increasing accuracy. Barbara had taught everyone martial arts to the point that they were able to pass at least one belt. She had obtained the proper gear from a martial arts store in Redding and required that each person keep a record of the moves they learned so she could test them and promote them when they were ready to advance. Young Luke and young Lizard excelled. They almost seemed to compete with each other, and often chose each other as sparring partners if Barbara allowed it.

One evening they all sat around the campfire at Barbara's homestead after a marshmallow roast and several scary stories. Roostafer made a casual comment, "Tthings are sure going well. I hope it lasts." Little did they know how timely his concern would turn out to be.

CHAPTER SIX

FRESH GRIEF

Charlie, age thirteen, the most introspective of the Buell children, had recently come to the conclusion that he was adopted. He didn't believe that his older siblings, Able and Baker, and his younger siblings, Delta, Echo, Frank and Georgette, were really his brothers and sisters. He had begun to suspect it when he realized one day that, after him, three of the four younger ones were girls. It was as if something had changed. In fact, he could actually feel some weird sort of change in his body, which he didn't realize was the impact of raging hormones as his body experienced puberty.

As he cast about to understand the changes he was sensing, this was what he had discovered. Specifically, both of the kids older than Charlie were boys, and after him both of the next two were girls. Then little Frank and little Georgette came along. Charlie had obviously been a sort of turning point. Not only that, but Charlie was the only one with dark hair. He'd heard it said all his life. All the others were "tow headed," but Charlie had thick dark hair. What else could it all mean but that he was adopted?

Young Charlie had never heard of Middle Child Syndrome, but he was smack dab in the fullest throes of it. He didn't feel any connection with any of his siblings. Able and Baker were both rough and tumble, big boned boys who loved to shoot guns and do dangerous things, while Charlie liked playing alone and always seemed more likely to catch whatever illness or infection might be going around. Delta and Echo were natural tomboys who took after Able and Baker in almost everything. Then, of course, Frank and Georgette were the babies of the family--the youngest boy and the youngest girl. That was definitely a special category in this family. So, all things considered, Charlie had come to feel that he was just "out there, in the middle," all alone. He felt absolutely certain, after lots of careful consideration one sleepless night, that he was not really a blood relative of these so-different kids that he was stuck living with. He felt a deep sense of loss at the thought that Dad and Mom were not his real parents, whom he didn't know.

On top of everything else, the others all got to do fun chores, like feeding the animals, cleaning out and maintaining the spring, or helping in the garden. But not Charlie. No sir. Charlie had to go around and empty trash barrels. At first he had been required to help his dad wrestle all the heavy garbage barrels into place--one in front of the front porch of each building. Then, every day he had to lift out the heavy bag of trash from any full barrel and load it onto the trailer behind the ATV. Then he had to haul all the full bags to the landfill and offload them. Once a month he had to use the Bobcat to bury the full bags under a layer of dirt and scrape out a new spot for the next bunch of bags.

His chores, by necessity, had to be done alone. He actually preferred being alone, but in this case it added to his feeling of isolation. To his young mind, doing his work alone was no longer an indication of his parents' trust in him. Instead it was an indication that no one wanted to spend time with him. He didn't remember how thrilled he had been to be allowed to drive the ATV, and operate the Bobcat, both without supervision. No, now he was in a grand funk. Nothing in his life was right, everything was wrong.

So, when he got to the landfill that morning, as had been the case a few times before, all these feelings of despair had welled up inside his heart and he was quietly crying. He just felt that no one understood him. He felt all alone, and hopeless. On this particular morning it seemed worse than usual, so he stopped the ATV, unhooked the trailer filled with full garbage bags, and drove on past the dump site. Maybe he would run away. At least for a day or two. That would show everyone how important he was, when all the garbage started to stink. Then they would treat him with honor and respect.

The landfill was situated up near the top of a gully just below the ridge crest, so as he drove away from the dump site he soon came out onto the ridge road near where it forked about a half mile from the village. The left fork led down the north slope to eventually cross a small wooden bridge and empty out onto Rush Creek Road which was no longer in use. He'd been told about it, but had never been down there. The right fork continued along the ridge top until it ended up at the peak of Browns Mountain where the lookout station was. He'd driven the ATV that way several times hauling stuff up to the lookout.

This time, choked up with emotion, he turned left and started downhill.

Still crying, and guiding the ATV poorly through his tear-blurred vision, he twisted the hand throttle and caromed down the winding dirt road at increasing speed. It somehow seemed that if he went faster it would confirm his impulsive decision to take this unplanned route. He blundered his way around a couple of sweeping curves, then came into a tight hairpin. He braked just in time to avoid a wreck and got around the curve, then stopped the ATV to wipe his eyes.

He had just started again when the road led under a thick canopy of trees for a dozen yards. He was temporarily blinded after the bright glare of the morning sun and in the dark shade he never saw the black mama bear standing in the road with her two cubs.

Charlie drove full into the chest of the mama bear, who interpreted it as an attack. She was slammed backward by the impact but leaped back onto her feet. With a loud roar she fell upon young Charlie, fiercely crushing him to the ground. Her gaping jaws closed brutally on his head with crushing force and he was killed instantly. She pulled him off the ATV as it slowly continued on past, and continued to maul his dead body in her fear and rage. The ATV rolled over a small embankment and down a steep slope until it crashed to a stop against a large boulder, at which time the motor died.

In the sudden quiet, all that could be heard was the snuffling of the mama bear as she thrust herself between her cubs and the supposed danger. When she was satisfied that there was no life left in the strange creature she thought had attacked her and threatened her twins, she turned and, with a final angry roar, fled with her cubs into the dense brush. Silence fell over the site. All was once again still. Charlie's lifeless body lay in a tangle of mangled slack limbs covered in blood.

Later that morning young Frank noticed that his older brother Charlie hadn't come back from the landfill. Frank, who had begun to enjoy playing "Injun" and spying on the others, sneaked up to the landfill to spy on Charlie. He couldn't find him there, so he searched for him. Finally, unable to find his brother to spy on him, he went back to his dad and told on Charlie for not being at work.

Jim Buell scolded Frank for being a tattletale and sent him back to his own chores. He was a little worried about Charlie not being where he could be found, so he went and discussed it with Roostafer. Together the two men approached the women. It was decided that Barbara and Rose would go on horseback to look for him. Barbara would, of course, also be accompanied by her huge constant companion, the monstrous dog, Friend. They went fully armed, just in case, but they agreed that Charlie was probably just moping by himself somewhere, as he had often done lately.

When Barbara and Rose arrived at the landfill on their horses they could see the ATV tracks leading away from where the trash trailer had been dropped. The two women followed the ATV tracks on up the hill, and then along the dirt road. At the fork they could see that the tracks went down the north slope fork. In front of them, at the notch of the Y of the fork in the road, was the carved wooden sign Barbara had placed a year ago that said "All is wrong until God makes it right."

Barbara looked at Rose. "This doesn't look good. Why would he go down there? I'm pretty certain he knows he isn't supposed to go over the summit of the ridge. At least I'm pretty sure I said that when I showed all the kids around."

"You did, but maybe he didn't remember. He IS only a boy." Rose smiled.

"Yeah, he is. But still, I'm a little worried. Where would he go down there?"

"Maybe he just went exploring. He does like to be alone more than the others."

"Maybe that's it, Rose. But, boy or man, this is gonna earn him a chewing out."

"I thought it would," Rose smiled again.

She had grown very fond of Barbara. In fact she was very fond of every individual living at the village. Her life had been ho-hum until the Cremation Virus, then it had become a horrible nightmare. But now she finally found herself surrounded by good people she cared deeply for. They already had powerful memories in common. She knew she could trust them--the adults anyway. The kids, like this little Charlie kid, were still largely unproven. Hopefully, though, they would all survive to become adults and learn enough from their parents and the other grownups to be just as good and fine as the rest.

The two women turned their mounts down the hill and continued along the road, following the tracks.

"He sure swerved around a lot, Barbara," Rose commented.

"Yeah, I noticed. Wonder if he was going fast or something."

As they approached the deeply shaded canopy of trees their horses began to snort and act skittish. Then they discovered the scene of the tragedy. Friend went on the alert—the scruff of hair along her back standing erect as she sniffed the air and growled low in her throat. As their mounts nervously danced sideways and tried to turn and flee, the women noticed the scuff marks in the dirt road, along with the well defined tracks of a very large bear and two small bears. They saw the ATV wrecked down the slope, and the tracks where it had rolled through the deep dust along the edge of the road. Both of them at the same time looked where Friend was sniffing with her head to the ground and saw young Charlie's bloody corpse in the brush.

Barbara groaned, in stunned shock, while medically-trained Rose stared, stony-faced.

"Oh, Rose, poor Jim and Daria!"

Rose hesitated a brief moment, then replied, grimly, "Yes. We' have to tell them. I believe the truth is' always best, no matter how bad it hurts."

They stood there in silence, pondering the terrible implications of the boy's death.

"Come on, Barbara. We'll tie him across the back of my saddle."

They stooped to the task but found that rigor mortis had set in to the point that they couldn't bend him at the waist. Rose commented that it would be a few hours before the rigor mortis relaxed enough to reposition him. They decided to carry him to the edge of the road and come back with a vehicle to fetch his body home for burial. But they hated to leave him there like that, thinking that scavengers might violate the boy's body. Rose finally offered to stay while Barbara went back for help.

"Yes," Rose insisted. "You have the fastest horse! But please come back as soon as you can. I don't want to be out here alone any longer than necessary."

"Don't worry, Rose, I'll be right back with help."

"Please be sure and bring a blanket to wrap him in."

"I will."

Rose stood silent vigil over the body, her weapon at the ready just in case, while Barbara galloped away up the hill.

At the homestead Barbara went first to Roostafer and reported what they had found. Roostafer grabbed young Luke and headed off in the Jeep with a blanket. Both, as usual, wore their belt guns. Barbara slowly went on up to the village to find the Buells and tell them.

Two days later they buried young Charlie Buell. His body was the first to occupy the small plot of ground designated as the Village Cemetery. It was on a knoll behind the homestead, not far from where the emergency tunnel's upper entrance broached the gully that led to the peak of Browns Mountain. The knoll overlooked the pastoral beauty of the alpine meadow where the homestead seemed to blend with the flora and fauna.

They had allowed room for approximately twenty graves and enclosed the site with a picket fence, made of unpainted wood so it wouldn't glare in the sunlight. There was one huge spreading cedar tree in the middle of the cemetery.

Roostafer stood with his back to the tree as he led in a simple and brief burial service. After the last "amen" Jim and Daria were first to drop dirt onto the undersized coffin made with their own hands. Then each of the other children did the same. Then the twins, and Luke, and last of all the adults, all helped fill in the grave. A simple wooden cross was planted with the inscription, "Charles Evan Buell, age thirteen."

Everyone went back down the path to the homestead, where life somehow went on. In the evening the chores had to be done as usual, and one of the nanny goats seemed to be going into labor. During the night she gave birth to triplets--all three were pure white. Early in the morning, while everyone was admiring the kid goats, Friend charged across the meadow into the brush and killed a stalking bobcat. They decided to lock the nanny and her newborn kids inside the barn at night for their first few weeks.

And so, the days continued to pass at the homestead and the village. Things were different, but life went on. The Buell household now numbered only ten, counting the twins. Everyone felt yet another loss--yet another grief to bear.

PART FIVE

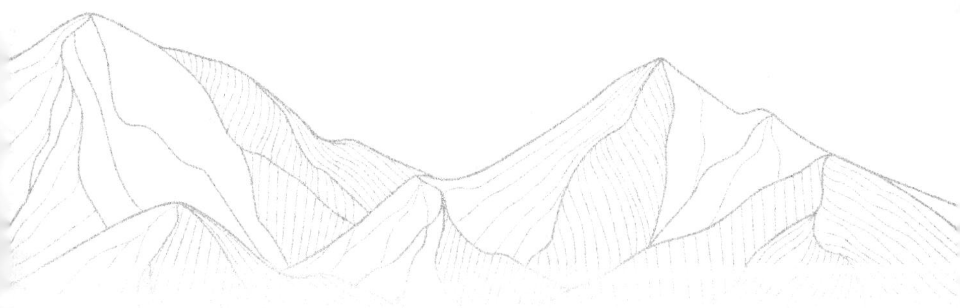

CHAPTER ONE

NEW BOSSES

General Bear and his troops had only been back in Volent City part of one day and a night. Now it was the morning after their arrival on August 20, almost a year from the Cremation Virus catastrophe. Volent City already seemed to be coming apart at the seams.

Mr. "Male Volent" (a sick pun on the word malevolent), formerly known as Herman Masters, forty-eight year old self declared King of Volent City and sole 'owner' of fourteen year old Cindy, seemed to be losing his power. And he blamed the encroaching corruption in his kingdom, rightfully, he felt, on General Bear who had just returned after being away for several months. The real problem, of course, was that his childishly bratty despotism simply didn't work on adults.

The 'commandos' who had just returned were completely transformed from the rag tag group he had sent out. They were now organized. They had learned, out of practical necessity, to observe a form of military-style chain of command which had been set and enforced by General Bear, with himself at the top. Their loyalty was now toward General Bear.

The General had not intended it as a power play, although he might have if he had thought of it—it had simply been necessary while they were away from Volent City on their reconnaissance mission. The commandos' fear of Mr. Volent had decreased as the miles increased. They had needed a substitute authority who was physically present to keep order. General Bear had found it necessary to take charge more and more as the weeks passed until their eventual return.

The commandos had come to know General Bear and more or less trust his leadership, and had become conditioned to following his orders. He was now their boss, not King Volent. So, when Volent called the commandos to stand at attention in his office, they only obeyed after General Bear repeated the order. Mr. Volent noticed that minor detail and things happened fast from that point forward.

The 'king' immediately tore into General Bear in his loudest voice, proclaiming him guilty of dereliction of duty, guilty of disobedience of direct orders and guilty of outright treason. During the several tense minutes that the verbal tirade lasted, General Bear and his commandos were initially stunned, and then increasingly alarmed into assuming a defensive posture.

As Mr. Volent continued to yell at General Bear, he got up from his desk, stomped around to stand face to face with him, and then began to actually pummel the general's chest with his fists! General Bear was not hurt by the weak blows, but Mr. Volent was wearing a pistol in a holster at his belt and General Bear remembered very clearly what he had previously seen of Mr. Volent's temper. The gun made him very nervous.

As Mr. Volent's outburst progressed he seemed to work himself up even more, rather than regain his composure. Soon it began to seem as if Mr. Volent might actually draw his weapon in his bizarre rage, so General Bear discreetly hand-signaled his men.

The commandos obeyed his order instantly, with military precision, and quietly and efficiently "arrested" Volent. Volent's two 'guards' and Security Chief Dale, who happened to be in the room at the time, were oblivious to the looming crisis and then, too late, clumsily attempted to intervene. They were no match for the trained commandos, but their impotent attempt triggered a more severe action. Not one of them survived the sudden roar of gunfire. When the unexpected altercation subsided and the blue smoke had cleared, Mr. Volent had lost his power, his life, and the lives of his closest minions.

Everything had suddenly and violently changed at Volent City. The king was dead. The head of security was dead. Two of the four security guards were dead. The proverbial dragon's head had been completely severed.

The population of Volent City had briefly swelled upon the arrival of General Bear and his team of eleven commandos, since they had brought back with them a dozen young women to add to the ranks of the slatterns. But the sudden disposal of Mr. Volent, Security Chief Dale, and the two security guards brought the total population back down by four souls. And now General Bear and his commandos seemed to be in charge. Seemed.

General Bear, whose real name was Albert Bayer, unlike the former Herman Masters who had renamed himself Mr. Male Volent, did not aspire to be the king of anywhere. He only aspired to live opulently and hedonistically on the richest of the spoils which he and his troops could liberate as they roamed the country. His troops shared his relatively modest vision for their own future. He had been a considerate and fair leader so far, granting them all the same spoils he himself enjoyed. Living proof was that the twelve healthy young women they had brought back with them had become experienced courtesans during their brief captivity on the road, submissively serving the degenerate desires of the commando squad.

General Bear was now the sole current 'owner' of thirteen year old Julie, with Security Chief Dale now dead. That would have left a girl for each commando and a few left over to throw in with the slatterns of Volent City, but it didn't happen. Instead, several opportunistic Volent City underlings immediately volunteered to join the commandos—making a total of fourteen commandos. So, as it turned out, none of the attractive and nubile young women was donated to the slattern pool.

Since General Bear had no despotic ambitions, he once again rallied his commandos and they left Volent City, never to return. He didn't know or care what might happen in the sad little nest of beaten down leaderless survivors at Volent City. He mildly hoped they would survive.

His plan was to continue to sweep the country, capturing and enjoying the choicest of the spoils from whatever pockets of survivors and material resources they would discover. They had seen no groups large enough or organized enough to resist them thus far, and it was reasonable to expect that would continue to be the case.

General Bear had it all worked out in his mind. They were now free to take the best of all they found for their own personal enjoyment and not to report to anyone. He wouldn't have to keep a log of their travels. He wouldn't have to worry about making things look proper for Volent.

Their chosen slatterns would serve as personal servants and bed warmers until they were someday replaced by fresher, younger ones. The used up slatterns would be released after they trained their replacement. The girls would, as before, do all the cooking and cleanup, keep the men's uniforms clean and mended, set up and take down the camp whenever they had to rough it, and always be ready to service the men's sexual desires on demand.

General Bear had told the commandos it was the same cultural system as the ancient Native American tribes before they were ruined by the influence of European immigrants. That supposed historical basis had impressed the uninformed commandos and even gave them a sense that their debauchery was somehow noble. But their thoughts were not at all lofty--what they liked most was that from now on, whenever they stopped to go skinny dipping, they were free to turn it into an all out drunken orgy. The men all agreed that it was a good plan.

Back in Volent City after they left there was now a new boss, formerly known as Facility Chief Bob. Having learned by observing Mr. Volent, he tried to follow much the same process. He changed his name to King Bob and selected two of the youngest and strongest underlings as his guards. It was nearly a seamless transition from the perspective of the slatterns and the rest of the underlings.

But, within a week, one of the new guards assassinated King Bob and, with the other guard's help unlocked every lock in the building and released everyone. The former slatterns and underlings all quickly dispersed to their personally chosen destinations and pursuits. The tall sky scraper which had been called, for a year, Volent City was once and for all vacated.

Meanwhile General Bear led his troops east this time, along Interstate 10. They drove through the ghost towns of Pomona and Ontario, then up the grade and through Beaumont and Banning. They were accustomed to traveling at twenty-five miles per hour and continued the tactic now. General Bear had come to realize that the slower speed enabled them to observe more details. And, after all, there was no appointment to keep or deadline to meet. On the other hand, failure to notice a detail could be fatal.

Hmm. I actually got something good from that dead old despot, General Bear thought to himself.

As they approached the small desert community of Cabazon, General Bear noted in his logbook that the altimeter in his "command vehicle" indicated they had climbed to nearly five thousand feet above sea level. He was no longer required to make log entries while they traveled, but he continued out of habit. It was easier now, though, since he had assigned a driver to his command vehicle. Keeping the log book was another good thing he had received from that old reprobate, Mr. Male Volent.

The convoy now consisted of fifteen commandos counting General Bear, plus fourteen slatterns and General Bear's girl, Julie, who he learned had just turned fourteen. They traveled in seven two-person units: the command vehicle, two tactical assault vehicles, a troop carrier hauling the slatterns, a supply truck, and two more tactical assault vehicles bringing up the rear.

His Second Officer, a former marine named Rudy who had been dishonorably discharged for dealing steroids in basic training, drove the supply truck. General Bear knew it was vital to control the supplies, personally, even though there was always plenty for everyone.

He had hoped to make it to Palm Springs by nightfall so his commandos could wallow in the luxurious remains of one of the richest places in America, but at their slow speed he decided at the last minute to stop at the Morongo Resort and Spa in Cabazon. He had discovered during their first recon mission that Indian casinos were some of the best places to bivouac. The ones that included a resort along with a casino always had the nicest accommodations.

The casinos often had independent backup generators that kept the water and electricity running so that the showers worked. The freezers worked too, so there was still good steak and caviar to go along with the high quality alcoholic beverages they always had stocked. Whenever there was a casino and resort available they used it for their overnight bivouac.

This was one of the most opulent casinos they had ever seen. Even after a year the pumps and filters in the huge swimming pool were still functional, so the water was pristine after they skimmed off a few leaves. Inside the restaurant everything was covered by a patina of fine dust, but it only took the slatterns an hour to tidy up the main dining room and enough sleeping rooms for everyone. Another hour passed before the women had a decent feast laid out for all of them to enjoy together.

The commandos would never clean up after themselves when they departed a bivouac. If they ever happened to come this way again they could always have the girls clean it up again. After dinner the commandos took their bottles of liquor to the pool and enjoyed the first of many sessions of skinny-dipping-turned-orgy.

General Bear reserved Julie for himself alone, but after the other men got drunk he allowed them to just grab the first girl they could reach. Last to grab got the last girl. After awhile round two began for several of the more lecherous men who wanted more than one turn with a slattern. One commando, who had consumed slightly less alcohol than his buddies, enjoyed a third girl, forcing her to perform until he was finally able to succeed.

By the time "taps" was sounded at 2200 hours (General Bear had learned how to do it himself), every commando was fully glutted, fully sated and loudly snoring, with the exception of the one man unlucky enough to be assigned the first shift of guard duty. But, at thirty minutes before midnight that commando woke up his relief and fetched his own bottle. By zero one hundred hours in commando parlance, he had finished the bottle and finished with the girl he had chosen and awakened. He had the presence of mind to make her take a quick swim before he used her, to wash off the residue from whoever had used her last. By one o'clock in the morning he too was sound asleep. The girl, too, had gone back to dreamland. Everyone was asleep except the slightly drunk guard assigned to stand the mid-watch. He fell asleep at his post, too, and failed to wake up his relief at 3:30am as he was supposed to.

Reveille, usually at zero six hundred, was two hours late, at which time the rudely awakened mid-watch and his intended relief wisely kept their mouths shut about the screw-up. General Bear was a little too hung over to notice, so…..

They got underway by zero nine hundred after everyone had consumed at least two cups of coffee and eaten a breakfast of scrambled eggs and toast hastily prepared by the slatterns, who were also hung over. Just beyond the second Cabazon exit General Bear saw the marker that said 5000 feet elevation. He smirked with self satisfaction.

He was so disgusted with the men's lack of discipline by that time that he routed them on past the Highway 111 exit that would have led to Palm Springs. He noted that the highway name changed at that exit from Christopher Columbus Transcontinental Highway to the Sunny Bono Memorial Freeway.

California is so weird, General Bear mused..

He took the next exit onto Highway 62 and followed it north, almost all the way to Twenty Nine Palms. He knew it was a Marine Corp base and town, and assumed it would be deserted like almost all the other places they drove through. But this time, on a hunch, he decided to act as if it might be occupied. One never knew. And it wouldn't hurt to keep the men alert.

As they approached the west end of town he slowed the convoy to a crawl to minimize the dust. He had recently observed that, as time passed, the highway surfaces were acquiring a thickening layer of dust. Here in the desert it was even worse than down in the Los Angeles basin and along the coast, so that even with their slow twenty five miles per hour they usually made a column of dust that was visible for miles.

After creeping the last few miles, he brought the convoy to a halt in the parking lot of a small motel a half mile before the edge of town. From the motel the highway sloped downhill into Twenty Nine Palms, so the site had a slight elevation advantage. It was early evening so he bivouacked the commandos for the night and posted a two-man watch—one to continuously scan the city with a night vision scope, and the other to walk the hotel perimeter every thirty minutes.

He explained to the men that this was a "high alert" situation because their target, the nearby marine base, would probably turn out to be a vital supply depot for military gear, so it was more likely to be inhabited by survivors. He allowed the men to use the pool, but there was no drinking, and no lights were allowed after dark. There was no electricity anyway, but he wanted to make sure nobody turned on a flashlight. They must 'see but not be seen'.

Sure enough, in the morning he received the report that there had been a vehicle driving around in the town during the night. The location of the vehicle when it shut off it's lights had been noted on the town map they'd found at the motel's front desk. The vehicle had parked for the night at a mobile home park on the north end of town across from a big Baptist church.

During the hottest part of the afternoon General Bear assigned one man to stay with the supply convoy vehicles and deployed the rest of his men around the one large unit in the park that was obviously occupied. He figured that in this desert climate the occupants would most likely be taking a siesta. When his men were in place he calmly walked up to the front door and knocked. There was no immediate response so he knocked again, more forcefully. He heard movement inside the house. Then the door opened.

Standing in the door was a man who looked, to General Bear, like a natural born underling. He was middle aged, pot-bellied and balding, unshaven but not bearded, narrow shouldered, and wearing a grubby looking once-white tee shirt and Bermuda shorts. He was bare footed, pale and soft looking. And his wide eyed, slack jawed facial expression was so stereotypical of confusion that General Bear laughed in his face.

"Uh, like, wow! I, uh, ya know, didn't know nobody else was around! Where'd you guys come from?" The man was almost inarticulate in his surprise.

"I'm General Bear and these are my commandos. Are you alone?"

"Oh yeah, I'm alone all right. I've been all alone here since the Virus hit. I didn't even know anyone else had survived!" He paused to take a breath then rushed on, "So, where you guys from? I bet L.A., right? There was so many millions of people there I figured that's where the survivors would be if there was some. How many of you are there? There must be a government if there's a military, I guess. Right?"

"No, there's no government and no military. We are 'free commandos'. We travel around and live off the land and do what we want. Do you know this area? We're gonna look for military gear out at the marine base. Can you guide us?"

"Oh, yeah," the man replied enthusiastically! "I worked there until I retired a couple years ago. I know that base like the back of my hand! I could show you where everything is! I know where the keys are, too. I was a supply clerk there, ya know!"

The man paused for a breath and then rushed on. "I'm Radar O'Rourke. They called me Radar because of Radar O'Reilly, on MASH, ya know! Remember that show? I was like Radar--I could find stuff; whatever you need I can find! Can I go with you guys? There's nothing for me here. I'll even put on a uniform again if ya want. Please? I know where to find just about anything you want!"

General Bear held up his hand to stop the guy's nonstop barrage of words.

"You have five minutes to grab whatever's most important out of your house. If you have any weapons turn them over to my Second in Command, Colonel Rudy." He turned to the men at his back. "Second! Secure any weapons and ammo he surrenders and have him load his garbage in the supply truck. He'll ride with me until we get to the main supply depot."

And so General Bear picked up one more new commando, number fifteen, making his squad a size that seemed just right. At least, for now. His men spent a couple of hours pillaging the military base. The supply truck was heavily loaded when they pulled out. The newest commando, Radar O'Rourke, was once again sitting in the passenger seat next to General Bear's driver. This time O'Rourke led them out of the base on Rainbow Canyon Road, instead of back toward town. He had promised General Bear that what he had to show them would be well worth the time.

They drove north into the desert for several miles, passing through two unmanned security gates. They finally arrived at a left turn onto Coyote Valley Road, which led them into another military base hidden at the edge of the desert against the low foothills. It was a veritable gold mine of military vehicles and supplies. There was a separate whole compound full of thirty camo painted army tanks, and another huge yard full of armored personnel carriers (APCs) and Hummers. General Bear didn't have any commandos qualified to operate a tank, but he started looking for a fuel truck. That would definitely be handy to have along with them. Several thousand gallons of diesel would keep them provisioned for a couple of weeks--certainly long enough to make it through long stretches where there were no tanks, or the fuel was used up.

When they pulled out the next day, after bivouacking in actual military barracks for the very first time, they had upgraded into more modern military vehicles. Now the convoy consisted of General Bear's Jeep, which he felt would encourage the men to hold him in higher, 'seperate' status, and then two Hummers weaponized with RPGs. Following the two Hummers were two Armored Personnel Carriers (APCs), the front one loaded with gear and grub, and the second one loaded with slatterns. Bringing up the rear was another weaponized Hummer and, following at a little distance (for safety, because General Bear was a little superstitious) was a fully loaded fuel truck, driven by the newest commando, Radar O'Rourke. General Bear considered the tanker a worthy prize, just as O'Rourke had promised.

Following O'Rourke's advice once again, General Bear led his commandos west along Coyote Valley Road and worked his way across the scorching desert until they connected with a road that brought them out onto Highway 247. They followed that highway northwest through Lucerne Valley and on into Barstow.

They found no survivors in Barstow, so when they pulled out General Bear led the convoy west on Highway 58 to Kramer Junction. They camped there overnight, using the showers in the truck stop, which had it's own backup generator, and sleeping around in the private and comfortable sleeper berths of the many abandoned big rigs. From the truck stop inventory they were able to upgrade their radio systems for better communication between vehicles. General Bear also allowed the men to pick up extra clothing for the slatterns--skimpy, clingy and see-through seemed to be the main theme of the men's "shopping." General Bear didn't care; it kept the men happy.

In the morning, after a generous breakfast prepared in the truck stop restaurant by the slatterns, they got underway by zero eight hundred, in accordance with the pattern General Bear had come to prefer, and headed north on Highway 395. They found no signs of survivors as they made their way past Ridgecrest and on through Lone Pine and Big Pine. Bishop was a fair sized village with several decent hotels but only one very small casino. They eased into town just at dusk, watching for any signs of people. The Holiday Inn and La Quinta motels were both two story buildings, and there didn't appear to be very many two story buildings in the whole village, so General Bear bivouacked his commandos in the Holiday Inn. He posted a two man night watch, as usual, one to guard the sleepers and one to scan for lights during the night.

At reveille General Bear was informed that there had been signs of survivors during the night, and they were surprisingly close--in fact they were just a few blocks up the highway at the Best Western. He sent three men on foot to reconnoiter and they were back in less than two hours. A small group of survivors were barricaded in the motel. The Best Western was a U-shaped complex. The driveway came in through a portico beneath the second floor at the bottom of the U into a large inner parking lot with a swimming pool along the rear side. The entire property had a high wrought iron fence around it, so that it appeared defendable.

The advantageous layout made it possible to barricade the entire facility with only a half dozen strategically placed vehicles. Within a stones throw from the front entrance there were several restaurants, a gas station and a convenience store. The motel's sleeping rooms and swimming pool made it a pretty good place to hole up, at least for the short term, or as long as food supplies might last.

General Bear was a little impressed, but he had a good idea how to breach their defenses. With all those precautions, he was doubly interested in seeing just what was being protected. He assumed it must be something valuable. He set up overt surveillance from the top of the Vagabond Inn diagonally across the street and instructed that commando to allow himself to be seen, but keep protected at all times.

That guy was merely the distraction, to hold their attention. The real surveillance was a second commando high up in an oak tree overlooking the pool and the central courtyard parking lot from the rear of the motel property. He had climbed the oak tree just before daylight wearing a Ghillie suit. He quickly hung a tree blind seat and made himself comfortable, then held himself nearly motionless all day. He was, for all practical purposes, invisible as long as he kept still. Which he did.

At nightfall General Bear received the report from both surveillance commandos. The decoy across the street had indeed been spotted early in the morning, as expected. At least the survivors holed up in the motel were somewhat alert. From the two commandos' observations General Bear was able to determine that there were probably five people barricaded in the Best Western compound. Three were grown men, one was an adult female, and one was a young female, probably elementary school age. The four adults were armed with side arms, but the spies were too far away to tell what caliber.

Since the Best Western group knew they were under surveillance, General Bear figured they would hunker down and maintain their guard. He decided to have his men sit tight, at least for a day or two. That would allow time for the defenders to grow weary and, likely, become less alert. Also, he had a disciplinary matter to attend to.

It had come to his attention that one of the slatterns had begun to refuse to service the men a certain popular way. She had gotten away with it twice before he heard one of the men grousing about it. General Bear hadn't been sure whether to confront the insubordination until a second slattern had recently joined the little rebellion. Since it was the men's favorite and most frequent sexual demand, General Bear considered the rebellion a serious matter that had to be dealt with immediately and decisively. His arbitrary control over his men was so tenuous that he felt it was imperative to keep them happy.

Early the following morning, back in their own bivouac, General Bear called a formal muster after breakfast and, in front of the commandos formed up and standing at attention, he interrogated the men about the two slatterns' disobedience. He wanted every commando (except the two on surveillance duty at the moment) and every slattern to hear every word of the testimony and see the immediate consequences.

First, General Bear cited the two men involved for "permitting a slattern to disobey." He ordered the two men stripped to the waist and he himself personally administered four lashes to each man with the riding quirt he'd been carrying in his vehicle since the beginning. The lashes were lightly administered, so the men realized that it was more or less a token punishment. The quirt didn't break the skin, but only stung. But the slatterns were suitably wide-eyed at what they thought was severe discipline.

When the two men were back in uniform and back in ranks, standing at attention with the other commandos, he then cited the two slatterns for "direct disobedience of a reasonable and lawful order." Then he ordered the men to strip the two women to the waist. Each of the men who had permitted the disobedience was required to administer four lashes to each of the two women, for a total of eight lashes each.

This time the punishment was administered harshly, at General Bear's orders and under his direct supervision. The women were forced to lean forward with their hands on the hood of General Bear's Jeep while they were whipped. The women screamed from the pain as the blows fell. Afterwards their backs and ribcages were bruised and striped by the quirt. They were shoved aside, then, and all the other slatterns were given two lashes each, including his very own Julie.

When the whippings were done with, General Bear explained to the men and the weeping slatterns that disobedience was such a serious hazard to their success that everyone had to be on guard against it. Those who knew, and didn't report it immediately, were guilty along with the ones who did it, and that was why they all received punishment.

After everyone was dismissed from muster to go clean up and administer ointment to their wounds, General Bear called his Second to join him in the back seat of the command vehicle. He explained his plan regarding how to attack the Best Western, and then discussed the details with the Second. When everything was clearly understood, the two of them exited the vehicle and called the two squads together. The two squads were briefed on the plan and they all began to clean their weapons.

At zero four hundred hours the next morning the commandos locked the slatterns inside their APC and left to take up their positions. The spies had observed that the barricaded survivors always came out of their rooms at zero six hundred hours, so, at fifteen minutes before six, the commandos began a full-on assault. General Bear had called it a 'blitzkrieg'. They had previously identified which rooms were occupied by the three men, and they took those first. None of the doors were even locked. Each man was incapacitated before he even finished shaving. After that it was almost an afterthought to capture the woman and the girl child.

They made the male captives kneel in front of the vehicle barricade and bound their wrists to the car bumpers. Once the three male captives were positioned to observe the fate of the woman and girl, General Bear let his men take both female captives down onto a mattress laid on the concrete and sexually abuse them for about an hour. He made sure his commandos understood that this was their reward for effective service, and they could do whatever they wanted with the females.

When the hour was finished General Bear ordered the men to release the two females. The battered victims stumbled away barefoot and naked. A block away they climbed into a parked vehicle and the woman drove it away. None of the commandos ever saw them again, or even thought of them again.

The slatterns were nursing the wounds of the lashes they had received the previous morning, but probably wouldn't have cared anyway. They were too young to notice the hurts of others—each of them still so self centered that she only cared about her own pain. And, in any case, they were locked up in the APC and couldn't see much of what went on outside the truck.

They had heard the gist of the morning's attack plan from one of the men who had used them during the night, despite their injuries, but it wasn't their business and now they knew better than to pry. Additional lashes were to be avoided at all costs.

General Bear interrogated the three males and deemed them to have no potential as commandos. He therefore used the opportunity to "blood" his men and had each of the captives executed by a firing squad of three commandos. His ten regular commandos had the unique experience of performing an execution under General Bear's orders, relayed through Colonel Rudy. Colonel Rudy and the new guy named Radar were excused from the exercise.

The corpses were left hanging from their bonds. General Bear dismissed his troops and gave them permission to clean up by taking a swim in the pool before lunch. At noon General Bear pointed the convoy north once again. They promptly forgot about the mountain village of Bishop. Whatever spoils might lay ahead of them were all that mattered.

CHAPTER TWO

NEW CHALLENGES

As his commandos left Bishop and headed north on Highway 6 into Nevada, General Bear thought it was pretty cool that the highway was called the Grand Army Highway. He still thought it was weird that the state of California had considered it so important to name their highways. They had even spent taxpayer money on putting up signs with the highway names.

When they turned north on Highway 95 an hour later he began to wonder if they might have been better off to stay on Highway 395. But he didn't want the men to think he was indecisive, so they continued on their course.

Highway 95 traversed some beautiful country, but none of the commandos was impressed and the slatterns couldn't see much through the high windows of the personnel carrier. By the time they got to Fallon, Nevada all of them were bored with the empty wilderness. They wanted towns and cities where they might find people and goods to capture and enjoy.

Instead of turning east on Interstate 80 to face another long empty stretch to Winnemucca, General Bear leaded them west again, through Fernley and into the bigger prizes of Reno and Sparks. He hoped to find survivors and luxuries to keep his men happy.

They spent almost two weeks in the urban sprawl of Reno and Sparks before they realized there was not a single survivor in the whole area. General Bear figured that the few who might have survived the Cremation Virus must have migrated out into the country. Each night the Commandos drank themselves into oblivion in a different casino, and then slept in and lazed around the swimming pool the first half of each day. But two weeks of paradise was a little too long for most of them, and certainly for General Bear. They were beginning to seem restless.

There had been no more disciplinary problems with the slatterns. Having them along was working out all right so far, except that none of them was much of a cook. However, the meals were plentiful, and free. That was good. And the men had all the action they wanted after dark. That was good, too.

Things could have been much worse, but even so everyone was bored and ready to leave by the time they finished searching the last quadrants of the twin cities for nonexistent survivors. After the emptiness of their two weeks in the Reno and Sparks area, General Bear impulsively decided to keep going west. The convoy dropped down through Tahoe and South Tahoe, then followed Highway 50 down into Sacramento.

It seemed like a good decision at first, but a week in Sacramento failed to turn up any more survivors. If there were any in the area, they were well hidden. Potentially deadly boredom once again began to set in. This time it led to a snarling fist fight between two of the commandos. They battered each other with their fists, and then were further injured by the seven disciplinary lashes they each received. General Bear had been enjoying the good life so long that his arm was sore after administering the discipline. After that he joined the men in their three-times-a-week calisthenics routine.

He took the men north from Sacramento for no other reason than that they were bored and the Bay Area had been reconnoitered the previous trip. The city of Sacramento had been rich with resources, but no survivors. The hedonistic lifestyle, day after day, with no action, was beginning to leave the men feeling jaded and numb. The fist fight and subsequent lashes had been their first excitement in over a month.

General Bear began to wonder if any of his commandos might think of deserting. And, if so, how could he deter that sort of thinking? Their first morning in Redding he was outwardly furious but inwardly not surprised to find the new guy, Radar, and one of the slatterns were absent from morning muster without permission. In the military it was called 'AWOL'.

He immediately dispatched the men in teams of two and searched the area, but the deserters were not found. Next morning, hoping to restore some sense of discipline among the ranks, he resumed drilling the men each day as he had done at the start. There was a lot of grumbling at first, as the men began the once familiar routine of strenuous daily calisthenics, weapons stripping and cleaning, and hand to hand combat practice. The change did, however, help relieve the boredom for the next few days.

They continued to move northward each day. By the time they reached Eugene a week later the men seemed just about ready for a full scale mutiny. General Bear felt a desperate need to find some survivors for his Commandos to attack and conquer and rape and pillage.

On a sudden impulse he turned the convoy around and headed back toward Redding. He would find that deserter, Radar, and the slattern with him, and make examples of them. That would help the morale of his marauders for at least a month!

Man, if these guys only knew the lengths I go to for their happiness! General Bear was not aware how much he was beginning to think like Mr. Volent, whom he had despised.

Meanwhile, Radar and his companion, whose name was Molly, had made their way west out of Redding along Highway 299 as far as Whiskeytown Lake. Radar was driving a small pickup he had taken as they had sneaked through Redding on foot. He still wore his uniform and carried his sidearm. Molly still wore her customary slattern outfit--a thin, clingy shift and high heels. Radar hadn't let her take time to change, although he had promised her she could as soon as it was safe. He wasn't intending to be mean to her, but it was really important that he get her to cooperate with his efforts to travel quickly and silently, so he didn't cut her any slack at first.

At Whiskeytown Lake they turned off of Highway 299 and went north a couple of miles to the remains of the little village of Whiskeytown. He and Molly settled there in a cozy, well appointed cottage. He figured it was close enough to Redding for ready access to supplies, but hidden away enough for safety. They found enough clothing left over in the several nearby abandoned homes so Molly could wear decent clothing again. She, in turn, urged Radar to brush up on his personal hygiene a bit. He didn't really mind. It was little enough to have to do to establish some rapport with the first pretty female who had given him any attention in more years than he cared to admit.

After several days Radar began to relax his vigilance. Molly seemed content to do all the cooking, cleaning and laundry. He spent his mornings fishing in the lake and kept them supplied with fresh fish to eat. Molly agreed to cook any fish he caught if he would clean them and start the grill each evening. They didn't have any briquettes, so Radar used scraps of wood and made it work. He carelessly included a couple of pieces of damp wood and ended up with quite a bit of smoke, but didn't worry about it. After all, the commandos were long gone by now, and no one else was around to notice. At least, that was what he wrongfully assumed.

But, up on the peak of Browns Mountain, fourteen year old Baker Buell was standing watch. As he had been trained to do, each hour he made a careful sweep of the horizon with the big binoculars kept in the watch tower. He was feeling a little bored and lethargic but knew it was important to keep up the surveillance. He had worked hard that morning helping to dig another tunnel before his watch started. During the afternoon up at the lookout he had practiced tomahawk throwing and quick draws with the seemingly heavy pistol.

Throwing the tomahawk and archery were two new disciplines the men and kids in the homestead and village had recently taken on. Each day was filled with practice, in between work projects. They were all improving their skill with the tomahawks and bows and arrows, fast draw with their handguns, and martial arts. But it took a lot of practice, every day, and lots of times it seemed more like work than fun.

Gun practice was restricted to the underground firing range to minimize noise. All the other disciplines were practiced outdoors, and could be done while standing watch at the tower. Baker Buell, like his brothers Able and Frank and his sisters Delta, Echo and Georgette, worked hard in hopes of being better than his siblings. The older teen, Luke Short, and all the adults, encouraged the friendly rivalry, and even practiced it themselves.

So far no one had been able to achieve a fast draw as speedy and accurate as young Luke. No one could best Barbara in martial arts. No one could strip and clean a weapon as quickly as Jim Buell. Each member of the group had a strength to contribute. Young Baker was unequalled at tying fishing flies and tending the huge mulch pile near the garden. He was often praised for his skills in those areas, but secretly he really wanted to be the best tomahawk thrower in the group. He practiced extra hours each week beyond the few required by common agreement among the group.,

This day he threw the tomahawk until his right arm began to ache and his aim began to deteriorate. As his additional hour of practice ended, he put his weapon in its holster on his belt and did the next scheduled turn with the binoculars. That was when he saw the thin column of grey smoke rising from down near the lake. He had been taught that grey smoke meant damp fuel, which meant a campfire or fire pit. If it was a building, or building materials, the smoke would have been dark. This whitish smoke had to mean people.

Baker turned and grabbed his slingshot. Each lookout kept a slingshot nearby with a small assortment of signal ammo. The signal ammo consisted of a thumb sized steel ball with a two foot streamer of thin aluminum foil attached to it. The shiny ball with it's shiny streamer was easy to spot flying through the air on a sunny day. All the members of the homestead and village were trained to be on the lookout in case a signal might be quietly fired some day.

Baker fired the signal shot in a high arc across the homestead's alpine meadow, aiming out into the open where no one was working. Far below he could see his relatives and friends at various outdoor tasks around the homestead and village. He saw several of them stop and turn toward the lookout. They had seen the signal. He knew that two or more of the others would soon arrive to check and verify whatever had been sighted, just as they had practiced many times. He quickly grabbed the Lookout Log and made an entry about the sighting.

Sure enough, he had just finished his log entry when Luke and Roostafer burst into sight from the mouth of the steep gully that came up from the homestead. While they caught their breath, young Baker made his oral report, then Luke and Roostafer both confirmed the sighting.

They praised Baker Buell for his vigilance and he swelled with pride. Luke added his confirmation entry in the log book. Baker had another hour of watch duty, so Roostafer solemnly assured him that he would be informed of whatever was planned by way of response. As Roostafer and Luke strode back down the hill, Baker picked up his tomahawk for a few more throws. He suddenly felt a fresh burst of energy.

It is said that timing is everything. Sometimes it really is. The next day a "contact party" went out from the homestead comprised of Jim Buell, Roostafer and Barbara. The only adults left in the village were Daria Buell and Nurse Rose. All the kids were working in the large garden area down at the homestead along side Barbara's Road where it came down the final slope into the homestead. The teenagers Luke Short and Lizard were in charge of the six surviving Buell kids and the twins, Alfa and Omega, who were being raised by the Buells.

The task assigned to all the kids that day was to thoroughly weed the potato patch, the melon patch, and the squash and pumpkin patches. They were to feed all the pulled weeds to the goats. It was a job none of them enjoyed, but they persevered for the sake of the watermelons they all looked forward to eating after harvest time, which was not far away.

At the same time that Mr. Buell, Roostafer and Barbara were sneaking over the ridge between Lewiston and French Gulch on their way to investigate the smoke which had so obviously come from a cooking fire, Radar and Molly were driving west up Buckhorn Summit on Highway 299 toward Weaverville. When they arrived at the summit, Radar stopped the truck to look back and spotted the slight haze of the diesel exhausts of the commando convoy as it motored past Whiskeytown Lake about ten miles behind them. He panicked and fled hastily onward down the west slope of Buckhorn Summit.

Near the bottom of the grade he impulsively turned off toward Lewiston. Satisfied that they would not be noticed, he stopped the pickup a half mile up the road where he could see down onto a short stretch of Highway 299. He wanted to make sure the convoy went on past before he came back onto the highway and returned to their cottage at Whiskeytown.

At that moment, Jim, Roostafer and Barbara were driving their ATVs up the old Lewiston Turnpike, a narrow gravel route that had started out as a stagecoach road in pioneer days and had been little used since the paved highway had been built. They expected to drop down off the eastern slope of Buckhorn Ridge in about an hour and make their way toward French Gulch to see if that was where the smoke had come from.

Radar and Molly waited about twenty before the low rumble of the convoy's heavy vehicles gradually became audible. Soon the first vehicle, General Bear's Hummer, came into sight through a break in the trees as the convoy moved at it's usual slow speed.

If Radar had stayed calm and not moved he might have remained unseen as the convoy passed by below. But he panicked again. As the second vehicle came into sight he quickly jumped behind the wheel of the little pickup and took off toward Lewiston. The armed lookout in the second vehicle saw the briefest hint of movement and grabbed his radio mic. Within a few seconds the convoy was turning off the highway toward Lewiston in hot pursuit.

General Bear ordered his driver to go as fast as safety permitted--the first time the driver had been allowed to exceed twenty five miles per hour in all the grueling weeks of disciplined driving. The driver happily floored the throttle on the huge Hummer and the convoy following him maintained as close a formation as they could on the winding mountain road. By the time they came down the hill on the last straight stretch into the village of Lewiston, General Bear could actually see the old pickup truck speeding away to the left on Lewiston Road.

He checked his map and saw that the road wound around and eventually led back to Highway 299. Breaking radio silence, he ordered the last two Hummers to reverse direction and return to Highway 299, make haste to the far end of Lewiston Road and come in from the other end. The little pickup truck would be trapped between the convoy vehicles, the deserter and the slattern would be captured and his commandos would be entertained by the suitable punishment he assigned to the two who had fled. This evening his troops' morale would be vastly improved. He felt sure that for at least the next month morale would not be an issue.

For just a moment the timing seemed to favor Radar and Molly. As they approached the turnoff to Browns Mountain Road, far up ahead they spotted the two Hummers coming toward them from in front, but were not seen by them. The vehicles coming from behind were out of sight past several tight curves.

Radar jammed on the brakes and cut the wheel to the right onto Browns Mountain Road. If he could just get around the first curve before the commandos appeared, it might seem as if he and Molly had mysteriously vanished. But before he could reach the end of the first short straight stretch and around the curve, the convoy appeared behind them and spotted the pickup.

Radar sped across the Bucktail Bridge and through the small, abandoned residential community near the banks of the Trinity River. He raced the little pickup on past the end of the pavement and up the bumpy dirt road, pushing the underpowered vehicle to its limit. The small pickup had a slight advantage over the heavier convoy vehicles maneuvering along the narrow dirt road. It was a very slight edge.

Radar and Molly had gained a little more distance ahead of the convoy, but even so, General Bear in the lead vehicle was only about two hundred yards behind them when Radar steered the minitruck into the curve with the turnoff onto Trinity House Road. For the very first time since the homestead had been founded, the steel gate had been left wide open.

Now, timing seemed to work for General Bear. The turnoff was so steep and sharp that the little pickup, very light in the rear, spun out when Radar tried to veer off on the loose gravel. While Radar backed up to get straightened out again, the heavier convoy vehicles were able to close the gap somewhat.

Seeing in his mirror that they had gained a little, Radar feathered the gas pedal to coax as much speed as possible out of the small pickup it's rear wheels scrambled for traction up the steep, narrow initial grade. He was going about twenty-five miles an hour, slewing dangerously near the dropoff on the left side that sloped all the way down to the rocky creek, when he came around the first curve on Trinity House Road and encountered the barrier erected by the Homestead residents. It was a cedar tree, laying across the road from the upper side. The right side of the road had about five feet of clearance. On the left side of the road, where it dropped off down toward the creek, the massive trunk rested on the ground.

Desperately, feeling certain it wouldn't work, Radar steered the little truck for the narrow gap on the right. He flung himself down on the seat, covering Molly who hit the seat just ahead of him, as the pickup slammed under the barrier. Only the driver's side hit. The passenger side just cleared. The passenger side wheels plowed a deep rut in the soft dirt at the base of the cutbank, and the truck just managed to power it's way through the small opening as Radar kept his foot mashed down on the accelerator.

The crunch of the impact was so loud that the kids heard the sound from where they worked in the garden more than a mile away at the homestead. They didn't know what had caused the loud crash, but they could tell it came from down Barbara's Road, as they had started to call it. The Buell kids and the twins looked to Luke and Lizard.

"Well, kids," Luke spoke while he gestured with his hands for them to settle down and pay attention, "I don't know what that was, but it probably isn't good. The adults are gone right now, except for Nurse Rose and Mrs. Buell up at the village, and neither of them is trained to fight anyway. So, it looks like it'll be up to us to keep ourselves and them safe until the grownups get back."

Able, oldest of the Buell kids and nearly Luke's age, spoke for all of them.

"You're in charge, Luke. What do ya want us to do?"

Taking a lesson from the gentle leadership provided by Roostafer, Luke answered quietly and calmly.

"What I want you to do is check your weapons and gather into a loose group, with the youngest in toward the middle. Us older kids will be on the ends and we'll line up so we're facing the road. But keep pulling weeds so it won't look like we're prepared. If anyone comes up the driveway who we don't know, we're just a bunch of kids working in the garden. But be ready to act fast. If they turn out to be enemies who pose a danger to the Homestead, it'll be a chance to practice our fast draw for real. Make sure your gun is fully loaded and ready to fire."

Luke and the younger kids were all wearing their belt weapons as they worked in the garden, just as they had been taught. Each wore a leather belt that held a holstered revolver and a reload pouch, a tomahawk, a slingshot and bag of steel ball bearings, and the older boys had also started carrying throwing knives.

Every one of them, including Luke, Lizard and Able, had complained at least a few times about the bother of the extra weight of the weapons getting in their way while they worked. Now they were suddenly glad they wore them. What if it was, in fact, a bunch of bad people coming in the road? They were fully prepared, in case that was what was going to happen.

When Radar and Molly came busting down the last slope into the homestead they saw just a group of kids working in a garden. *No help there,* Radar thought. He kept going as fast as he could past the group of kids, tearing around the sharp curve over the culvert and heading back up hill toward the village that he didn't know was ahead.

Just about the time he and Molly reached the village and encountered Rose and Mrs. Buell, General Bear and his commandos arrived at the garden. They were on foot, and very winded from running double time the length of the long uphill road from where they had to leave their vehicles at the barrier. They had also carried their assault rifles at port arms for the run. It was far more strenuous than their little daily calisthenics routine.

General Bear could see the remaining wisps of dust in the air from the little pickup as he and his men approached the raggedy looking little group of kids working in the garden. He noticed right away that one of them was a very pretty female teenager. On sudden impulse he ordered his thirteen men to halt and stand at full alert, weapons ready. First they would tie up the kids, take turns with the girl, then continue their pursuit. First things first, he always thought.

He made the mistake of giving his men that explanation loud enough for the kids to hear. He thought it would fill the kids with fear. Instead, General Bear saw the oldest boy murmur something to the other kids. They all dropped their rakes and hoes and sort of wandered a few steps forward. General Bear noted that they had accidentally scattered into what would have been an excellent tactical spread if they had been soldiers. His men formed a half circle facing the line of kids and came to a "present arms" position, which General Bear felt sure would intimidate the kids.

He noticed, and was puzzled by, the apparent lack of fear on the faces of the kids. *They must not know the implications of the way we're deployed against them.* He stepped forward from the side and found himself face to face with the youth who seemed to be in charge. He noticed that the boy wore tied down cowboy pistols and some other things hanging on his holster belt. Then he noticed that the younger boy next to the youth had a tomahawk in his left hand. His right hand hung down near a holstered pistol. Then General Bear noticed with some surprise that, actually, every one of the kids was wearing a holstered pistol and other kinds of assorted weapons.

Oh well, they're just kids. If they were men I'd be concerned.

"Men," General Bear ordered in a deep voice, "Take these children's weapons and place the female teenager in custody. If anyone resists, use as much force as necessary."

Things happened very fast, then, it seemed to General Bear. He suddenly seemed to be in sort of a daze, as if he had gone deaf and everything was occurring in slow motion. He suddenly realized he wasn't in a daze, he was merely deafened because of the loud sounds of gunfire very close by. He noticed a light haze of blue grey gunsmoke from discharged weapons. His thoughts then raced!

Smoke is from the kids, not my commandos! They have pistols in their hands! All of them! The kids are firing their pistols! My commandos are dropping! We must shoot back at these kids! Why can't I shoot back? What? I'm hit! I'm falling! Is that a tomahawk in Second's chest?

Within a few seconds, every commando was dead. Not one of them had even been able to fire his weapon. The kids had used their fast draw skills very effectively and had continued to fire their weapons at the invaders until there was no more threat. Just as they had been taught.

Luke and Lizard were the only two who were old enough to fully comprehend what had just happened. In the sudden silence, with their hearing muffled after the loud roar of gunfire, the kids stood staring at the devastation wrought with their pistols. They were speechless, in shock. Luke was first to regain his composure and quickly shouted an order!

"Everyone!" He got their attention. "To the village! One guy in the pickup got past us! Rose and Mrs. Buell need our help! Let's GO!"

Suddenly they were all running full speed up the dirt road toward the village. Luke ran fastest, then Able, Baker, Lizard, little Frank Buell, then the Buell girls, Delta, Echo and Georgette, and lastly the twins. That desperate run up the hill to the village turned out to be good medicine for the kids. They had to put the gunfight behind them and focus on their footing as they ran. They had to focus on getting there as quickly as possible to help rescue Nurse Rose and Mrs. Buell. Somehow it forced them all to get back in focus, mentally, and helped them begin to get over the psychological impact of the gunfight.

When Luke raced into the village ahead of the gang of kids he found Mrs. Buell and Nurse Rose standing on the street in the dissipating dust, looking toward where the little pickup had just disappeared on down toward Browns Mountain Road.

"Luke, what's going on?" Nurse Rose demanded. "We heard gunshots!"

"We were attacked!" Luke blurted between gasps for breath! "We shot the soldiers, but that pickup got away. I think they were running away from the ones we shot!"

"You shot some soldiers?" Mrs. Buell asked, immediately going into a full motherly panic.

"We need to catch that pickup! They know where we live!" Luke was near tears with frustration over the pickup getting away.

Nurse Rose hurriedly interjected, "No, Luke! You must NOT! Wait for the men to return. I'm sure they heard the gunfire. They will decide what must be done!"

Nurse Rose saw Luke's jaw clench and grabbed his arm as she went on.

"You must not go on your own! Wait for Roostafer and Jim! Just block the roads and keep us safe until the men get back! Mrs. Buell and I spoke with the man and woman in the pickup. They're running from the commandos so they can live the way we do. They're not with the commandos. When Roostafer and Jim get here we can decide what to do about them, if anything!"

Relieved that he had something he could do, even if it wasn't chasing the pickup, Luke nodded and spun away. He grabbed Lizard, Able and Baker and spoke in a rush.

"We'll take the quads! Liz and Able go back and relock the gate at the bottom of Trinity House Road. Make sure the blockade is intact. Baker and I will go the other way and do the same on that end after we make sure the pickup's gone! Meet back here ASAP. Let's go!"

Nurse Rose shouted after them, "When you're done we'll be in the cold cellar!"

The four oldest teens hurried away while the women gathered the younger kids together and headed down to the homestead. They herded the kids into the cold cellar and locked the solid steel door. The cold cellar had food and water and access to the emergency tunnel. They put on the sweaters and jackets which were kept hanging on hooks inside the door and settled down to wait. Mrs. Buell assigned Delta and Echo to take turns watching through the peephole and got the kids to start quietly singing some of the simple homestead songs she had been teaching them. They started with The Crooked Little Man and then sang The Little Old Lady Who Swallowed The Fly. They had just started The Farmer In The Dell when they heard someone knock on the door.

It was Luke and Baker, back already. Nurse Rose let them in.

"Did Lizzie make it back?" Luke's concern was evident in his voice. "And Able?"

"No, Luke," Nurse Rose replied. "But if they aren't back soon you can go look for them. Give them a chance to get here, first." She smiled at his anxiety.

Luke and Baker came inside, donned flannel shirts and sat down to wait, fidgeting impatiently. About two minutes passed and there was another knock on the door. They heard Lizzie's voice.

"Hey, it's Lizard and Able. Let us in!"

It was only a few more minutes before they heard the muffled growl of their own quads entering the homestead grounds. Luke carefully opened the heavy steel door a few inches and peered around it to be sure it was their own men before he flung it open for the others to come out with him. Roostafer, Barbara and Mr. Buell quickly assessed the situation, noting the dead commandos scattered on the road next to the garden.

They asked Luke to report and he gave them a full account of what had happened. The adults looked with amazement at the kids, and then with understanding concern as they noticed the semi-glassy eyed look on several of the younger ones. Nurse Rose, Mrs. Buell and Barbara immediately gathered the younger children together and headed up the hill toward the village to get them out of sight of the corpses.

The men and Luke and Lizard got busy disposing of the bodies. They used the Bobcat to dig a mass grave halfway up the mountain upslope from the garden where no one ever went. After the Commando carcases were covered with dirt and rocks, they headed back down Barbara's Road to dispose of the convoy's vehicles.

Mr. Buell suggested that one way they could dispose of them was to drive them off a high bank and let them crash down into the canyon. They would degrade as the years passed and gradually become part of the environment once again. They all agreed that no one wanted to keep any of them, so they started with the two vehicles at the back of the line to drive them away.

Mr. Buell slid behind the wheel of the truck, not knowing that the women were in the back, and started the motor. As he started to put it in gear to back up and get it turned around, he felt the truck move as the women inside the van box were jostled around. The countermotion caught his attention, reminding him of how the motor home used to jostle when all the holding tanks were half full. But he realized that this rig was a cargo carrier. He asked himself what kind of cargo would move around like that? It dawned on him that the movement could very likely mean people!

He quickly set the brake again and shut off the motor. He climbed out and gestured urgently to Roostafer with hand signs. When Roostafer trotted closer, Jim gestured him to be silent, and whispered to him.

"I do believe there's people inside the back of this rig, eh?"

The two of them quietly went around to the back door, weapons ready. Luke and Lizzard noticed what they were doing and quickly backed them up. There was a padlock on the latch, so Jim Buell went and got the bolt cutters from the toolbox on the Bobcat. When everyone was ready, Jim Buell crunched through the padlock with bolt cutters and let the pieces fall to the ground. He glanced at the others to make sure they were ready, then grasped the two trailer door handles and lifted them in tandem, jerking the double doors and flinging them wide open. As the doors gaped apart, everyone stood poised for whatever they might find.

The moment was anticlimactic when they were startled to find a cluster of young women huddled together at the front of the box, staring at them with wide fearful eyes!

"Ahem! ... Well!" Jim Buell was obviously flabbergasted.

"Roostafer, I don't believe we have anythin' to worry about here, eh?"

"I guess not, Jim," Roostafer replied sardonically. He turned to the cluster of terrified young women inside the truck box, noting that they were unkempt, gaunt and poorly dressed..

"Ladies, we don't plan to hurt you. In fact, let's consider this a rescue. My name is Roostafer, this here is Jim, this here is my young friend Lizzard, and this fella here is Luke. We live at a homestead not far away, with my wife, Jim's family and a few others. You're all invited to come on up to the homestead where you can take showers and have a good home cooked meal. I think we can find some better clothes for you, too. Are ya'all interested?"

There were timid nods of assent as the girls slowly started making their way toward the open rear of the truck. Jim and Roostafer helped each young woman climb down from the high truck bed to the ground, where they looked around them in amazement. It was a picturesque spot in the Trinity Alps, on the smooth gravel road with the narrow entrance to Barbara's Road climbing steeply along a steep ridge face and curving mysteriously out of sight around the shoulder. Old growth Douglas Firs and Digger Pines stretched toward the sky, shrouding the road in cool shade with patches of bright sunlight. The nearby Trinity House Creek gurgled softly over stones as it flowed toward the Trinity River a quarter mile downstream.

The only thing that marred the beauty of the spot was the rugged ugliness of the manmade vehicles parked in a row on the road. Preliminary explanations were exchanged and initial inclusive introductions were made. The former "slatterns" were more than willing to help dispose of the extra vehicles and accompany them back to the Homestead to have a supper meal that would include the homestead's women and kids.

"Ladies, we could use the APC to haul everyone up to the homestead together, if you don't mind riding in it once more. We can keep the back of it open so you won't feel like you're still confined. But if you prefer not to ride in it any more, you can all walk in. It's about a mile, uphill all the way, so you might want to ride instead of walk."

The women conferred for a moment and said they'd ride in it once more, since the back would be open. By the time they all arrived at the Homestead, the road bed near the garden had been cleaned up and the signs of battle cleared away. The homestead was pristinely picturesque.

Supper was almost ready, but Barbara and Mrs. Buell dropped everything to come out and meet and greet the confused young women. Nothing would do but for the recently released young women to all go take long hot showers and put on decent clothes.

"Hope they won't take too long," Roostafer groused with a grin. "We haven't eaten since breakfast, ya know."

Barbara turned back with a frown and snarled, "Finish fixing supper yourself if you can't wait another hour!"

Roostafer immediately backed up with his hands out in a posture of passive self defense, and the others all stood very still and silent as the ladies trouped away. After they had departed, they exchanged grins.

"Roostafer, me good friend, I don't think you shouldda said that, eh?"

When the refugees were cleaned up and ready, everyone gathered in the dining room and sat down wherever they could find a seat. The Buell kitchen was big, but not big enough for almost thirty people. After the meal the kids were sent to do the evening chores, with Barbara and Roostafer along to oversee. The refugees had said there were no more commandos, but the adults didn't want the kids to be left alone after they had just killed people.

Later that evening, when all the kids had gone to bed, the adults gathered around for a conference. Roostafer took the lead, addressing the people he knew, who were becoming more like family than friends, and including the former slaves who were welcome without reservation.

"We've seen no sign of any other soldiers besides the ones we killed here today. The one called 'Radar' who escaped with Molly is probably not dangerous on his own, but we will be on our guard in case we ever see him again. If we are able to make contact with him eventually, we will play it by ear."

Roostafer took a slow look around the room at the faces of the people gathered in the dining room. Some of them he had come to know and love. Some were fresh new faces--possibly one day they would also be individuals he knew and loved. He compassionately scanned their faces as he continued.

"Everything has changed as of today. Now, our littlest children have seen brutal battle and bloody corpses. Today we buried thirteen evil adults who were all killed by our children. We must be sure to praise them for their actions, and for their victory over evil. We must be ready to show love to them through the difficult reaction they will no doubt experience. It isn't easy to take a human life, even for a grownup. Only the Lord knows how it may affect our kids."

"Today all our training and preparation was validated. We were ready. This is the exact outcome we would want from such a crisis. But we must continue to remain ready. Today may not be the last time this sort of thing happens. There could be another group of people who have given in to the evil that can thrive in some human hearts."

Again he paused and took a slow look around the room.

"But we must not let this corrupt our faith, and erode our optimism. I believe it's still true that most people are like us--good people trying to figure out how to rebuild their lives in a good way after the Cremation Virus."

His voice rang with conviction as he continued.

"This new world will be whatever we choose to build. Today we got rid of some vermin. Now we must get on with our lives. We will milk the cows, raise our garden, and take care of our fruit trees and our fresh water supply. We'll maintain our roads and barricades. We'll choose to love each other no matter what. We'll seek what's best for each other, and listen to each others' opinions and concerns, and value each other."

Roostafer's face reddened as he continued, his voice charged with passion.

"This is a NEW world we're in. It's OUR world. Today we cleared a big hurdle. We took a giant step toward building a GOOD new world! Let's be sure that we continue to move forward from here! Let's rise UP from the ashes and dust of the Cremation Virus!"

He had tears in his eyes as he concluded and, emotionally spent, suddenly sat down.

The room sat in startled silence for a very long moment, then burst into spontaneous applause! Roostafer ducked his head, embarrassed, as young Luke and Mr. Buell came and slapped him on the back and congratulated him.

Barbara Sinead O'Dell looked at Roostafer, now, with new eyes.

There is much more to this amazing man than I suspected. I want to get to know him better. He may be worthy of my respect and my love, and worthy to lead all of us. "Lord", she silently prayed, "*is this the man You have for me? I wouldn't mind at all, if he is, Lord!*"

THE END